# About the author

Lawrence Bartlett was born and raised in Maine. Following attendance at Tulane University in New Orleans where he earned a Master of Architecture, and several later years of employment in Philadelphia, he and his wife moved back to Maine. Currently, he is retired following twenty-seven years as an electrical engineer and owner of a consulting engineering firm. Mr. Bartlett presently serves as a volunteer supporting youth through various community organizations and at the local high school.

LIVING IN MAINE WILL GROW ON YOU

# LAWRENCE BARTLETT

---

## LIVING IN MAINE WILL GROW ON YOU

Vanguard Press

VANGUARD PAPERBACK

© Copyright 2022
**Lawrence Bartlett**

A CIP catalogue record for this title is
available from the British Library.

ISBN 978 1 80016 370 6

Vanguard Press is an imprint of
Pegasus Elliot MacKenzie Publishers Ltd.
www.pegasuspublishers.com

First Published in 2022

**Vanguard Press**
**Sheraton House Castle Park**
**Cambridge England**

Printed & Bound in Great Britain

# Dedication

To my wife Virginia and our three daughters Molly, Jane and Sally

# Prologue

What a godforsaken place, he thought as he walked out through the front doors of his hotel onto the sidewalk. It was April, which ordinarily meant the return of warmth that ushered in a bloom of spring flowers and green lawns. But ever since he had arrived, the weather had been nothing but cold, damp and dreary. In fact, the entire city seemed gray. Hamburg, Germany had never presented itself as a fancy tourist destination. On the contrary, it had a long history of being a working-class city, a seaport that took pride in its docks which provided a maritime connection between Germany and the rest of the world.

James Macintyre thought to himself that he would be happy if he never came back. It had been a difficult week of negotiations with Hamburg Shipping, a global marine transport corporation. Although he had been successful representing the interests of his company, Billings Shipyard, Inc., the meetings had left him without any energy to enjoy this final day of freedom. He was scheduled to take the flight out first thing in the morning from Hamburg to New York, with a change of planes in Frankfurt. From New York he would be taking a commuter flight back home to Billings, Maine. Tomorrow would be a long day of travel and, since his business negotiations had ended last evening, this was his opportunity for a day of relaxation. But given his lack of energy and the grayness of the city, he didn't feel much like seeing local attractions.

What he surely didn't feel like was yet another meeting, but this was exactly where he was headed at eight a.m. in the morning. It was a meeting that was not on the business agenda. In fact, he wasn't exactly sure what this meeting might be about. He had concluded the final contract negotiation session last evening just after ten p.m., or as his German counterparts would have said, *twenty-two hundred hours*. As he left the building to get into a taxi, a man he did not recognize came out of the building hurrying after him.

"Herr Macintyre. I would have a word with you, *bitte?*"

James had nearly given an excuse just to get away. He was beyond tired and had reached his limit. Instead, he turned to the man and said, "Certainly."

The man looked up and down the sidewalk as if checking to see if he was being watched, and then simply put a folded piece of paper in Macintyre's hand. With that, the man turned and hurried around the corner of the building and disappeared.

Macintyre stood in surprised silence for a long moment and then looked at the paper. He unfolded it and read:

*Please attend an important meeting tomorrow morning at 8.30. Come to 157 Braunstrasse, Suite 7.*

He pondered the message all the way back to his hotel, and by midnight as he was retiring for the evening, he had decided that this was a meeting that he would not be attending. Although the man had come out of Hamburg Shipping's office building, there was nothing official about the note that would suggest that it was in fact a Hamburg Shipping request.

As he got up in the morning, however, the thought occurred that if this was indeed a meeting relating to his negotiations, and he did not attend, it might have consequences that would negatively affect the deal that he had just brokered.

He found a taxi at the adjacent street corner and gave the driver the address. He had been informed by the hotel concierge that Braunstrasse was only about ten minutes away by car. The taxi arrived after winding through streets crowded with morning traffic. James paid the driver and got out into yet another gray overcast day. In front of him stood an office building that was urgently in need of repair. This did not look like a facility from which a multimillion Euro company would operate, he thought, but there was no turning back now.

After climbing three flights of stairs, he reached a hallway with two office doors that were both closed. The first door had a glass panel with painted lettering that read *# 6 Werner Brandt, Anwalt*. The second door had a similar glass panel with only *# 7* painted on it. An uneasy feeling arose from the pit of his stomach as he walked up to the door. He reached to open the door but before he could put his hand on the knob the door opened. The man he had seen in the street the previous evening greeted him with, "Good morning, Herr Macintyre. Come in."

There was an outer room of the office and straight ahead there was a second inner room which could be seen through an interconnecting open door. The man led him into the inner room which had its shades drawn and was lighted by a single dim overhead light. In the middle of the room was a large wooden desk. There were no papers on the desk, no telephone, no filing cabinets in the room, or any other indication that the office was actually being occupied in a gainful business. As his eyes fully adjusted to the darkness, Macintyre was surprised to see seated at the desk Johann Steiner, the financial officer for Hamburg Shipping.

The accountant motioned for Macintyre to sit in the only other chair in the room and spoke to the man at the door. *"Danke. Warten sie an der saal, bitte."* The accountant then turned his attention back to Macintyre and said, "I believe we may have an opportunity to do additional business together, Mr Macintyre now that our two companies have agreed to form a partnership."

With a bit of confusion, James asked, "What kind of business?"

"Very profitable business," the accountant replied. "Very profitable business, indeed, for both of us I should think."

After an hour and one half of discussions, Macintyre left the office. When he had disappeared down the stairway, the man waiting in the hall returned to the inner office.

The accountant said, "We have come to an agreement. But Herr Macintyre will have to be watched very carefully. I have made arrangements for you to travel to the United States and take a position where you can keep an eye on our new partner. If all goes well, your services will not be needed. If, however, our Herr Macintyre creates problems, he will have to be removed."

# Part 1: New Beginnings

# Chapter 1

It was a typical late June summer day in Maine. Although the sky was clear blue and the sun shone brilliantly, the temperature had just enough of a touch of chill to make one aware that summer in Maine is mostly a fabrication created to attract tourists. Sally Brown sat down on the front step of what was to become her third house in four years. Packing boxes were piled on the sidewalk behind the rented moving van, each with hand lettering identifying their contents by room, *books/living room, dishes/kitchen, and linen/bathroom.* How very *organized,* thought Sally. But then, why shouldn't they be? She and her dad had this moving thing down to an exact science. This would be 'a keeper' her dad had promised in the car as they drove up to the vacant house. Sally couldn't help but think that if this was 'a keeper', she would certainly need warmer clothes.

Billings, Maine was a confusion of identity. Like many small communities along the coast of Maine, it included large sea captain houses built in the latter half of the nineteenth century. These stately homes suggested a stability that comes from families with great local history, and even greater bank accounts.

The main street in town largely consisted of quaint shops for summer tourists, along with a local restaurant, a barber shop and three banks. Just a block away from Main Street was the town library. The Paulsen Free Library was set within a landscaped park with a gazebo in which the municipal band played concerts on Friday evenings. Across from the park was an enormous, white wooden church that towered over the park, providing the center of town with an unmistakable picture postcard New England character.

But not far from the stately examples of Georgian and Classic revival architecture was housing for the less well-to-do. With its population of about nine thousand, Billings was not large enough to have slums, but it did include poor neighborhoods. And with these neighborhoods came the typical urban challenges, most notably alcohol and drug abuse. As a further contradiction to its picturesque image, on the south side of town existed one of Maine's largest blue-collar employers, Billings Shipyard, Incorporated. Better known by the locals as BSI, it remained as one of America's last working shipyards. As such, it became the every workday home, to over five thousand welders, pipe fitters, steel workers and tradesmen. The influx of workers who mostly commuted from surrounding cities made for an uneasy coexistence with the local residential population.

Sally picked up the box she had been carrying and trudged inside. Her dad met her in the hall.

"You're going to love Maine," he said enthusiastically. "I hear the high school here has a great debate team! Give it a chance. Living in Maine will grow on you!"

Without answering, Sally climbed the stairs to her room. Sally dropped the box she was carrying and sat on the floor. She understood that the job her dad had landed at BSI would be a good opportunity for him. Actually, he was lucky to get a job at all, having jumped from company to company so many times in the past few years. Steven Brown was an electrical engineer with a PhD who specialized in the design of high-tech electronics systems. Sally remembered how it had been an exciting afternoon for her dad last month when he had received the phone call informing him that Billings Shipyard would be hiring him. He would serve as the lead engineer for the program development of a new weapons guidance system for a prototype class of US Naval ships that was being constructed at the shipyard. The excitement had been largely her dad's however, since the news cemented the fact that another move was now inevitable.

Moving was her dad's way of dealing with adversity. Sally knew that her dad felt that she was having difficulties coping as a teenager and she also knew that he had no idea what to do. Her father rationalized Sally's 'hard times' in school as being a result of the death of her mother from cancer in the spring of her seventh-grade year. That day in April seemed like forever ago thought Sally. She wouldn't deny that her mother's death had been devastating. But deep down inside, Sally knew that her troubles that next fall at Kennedy Middle School in Philadelphia were simply her own fault. She was expelled from school in the eighth grade for 'behavior problems', which led to a move to Hartford, Connecticut. But nothing seemed to fit in Connecticut and, when Sally's grades continued their downward spiral, her dad thought a transfer in mid-year of her freshman class was needed. This resulted in a move to historic Boston. And then there was that incident last year at Boston Latin High. The result was, Welcome to Maine.

Well, thought Sally, there are no more states on the east coast that are north of Maine. This had better stick.

"Hey Sal," her dad yelled from the living room. "Should we put the couch by the door or over against the wall by the window?"

Sally couldn't help but think, does it really matter? We probably won't be here that long, anyway. But instead, she just said, "By the door, I think."

Life had taken an interesting turn when Sally was about eight years old. At first, Sally didn't understand that she was any different from all her other friends. The second grade at Germantown Elementary School, just outside Philadelphia, was like many other elementary schools. It had its share of problem children with learning and behavior issues, as well as its share of gifted and talented children that showed 'such great potential'. When Sally was first singled out for special attention as a G&T student, she thought it was great. She didn't really think of herself as any more gifted than her friends. It was just that for some reason, the answers came easier to her. By the time she was ten, she began to understand not only the truth of her abilities, but also the consequences.

It was early in the fifth grade that the school principal called a meeting for Sally, her mom and her dad. She could still remember that meeting like it was yesterday. The principal sat at his desk with a file folder that had the words SALLY E. BROWN typed on the top. It was as if everything that was important in the life of Sally Brown had been distilled into words and had been put down on the papers that were contained in that file. Sally wasn't really needed at the meeting and, in fact, during the entire conference, the principal had spoken to her parents without even once acknowledging her presence.

The principal reviewed Sally's standardized test scores and went over her performance records starting from the second grade.

"Mr and Mrs Brown, I don't need to tell you how special Sally is," the principal stated. "She has clearly demonstrated abilities that place her into a category by herself in this school. She has superior academic gifts."

Her parents were especially proud of Sally, as all parents are of their children. But they were not fully aware of Sally's 'gifts'. How she had come to hate that word 'gifts'! If these are gifts, she thought, why can't I just give them back?

"It is the school's recommendation," the principal pronounced, "that Sally be transferred to the Pennsylvania Middle School for Arts and Sciences. It is a facility that specializes in meeting the potential of particularly gifted students. They have faculty and resources to meet Sally's needs that, frankly, we do not have here at Germantown."

"But I don't want to be sent to a *facility*," Sally blurted.

"Now, Sally," interjected the principal, "you'd like it at this *school*. You'll be with other students who are more like you."

There it was, thought Sally. They think I'm different. I'm not like my friends. I have *needs*.

"But I don't have needs! I can show you," cried Sally. She couldn't even imagine what it would be like to have to leave her friends. It was bad enough that over the past year she found herself increasingly being removed from classes for special tests and projects. As the principal continued Sally became more and more distressed. It was clear that unless something was done soon, she would be separated from her friends forever.

It was this realization that caused Sally to stop and consider herself seriously for the first time. And it was from this that Sally understood what had to be done. Sally's 'gifts' must forever be kept a secret. It was not until much later that she fully understood what her abilities were actually called. She found that her ability to recall nearly anything that she had seen for even the briefest of moments was called *total photographic memory*. Although she hadn't taken an official IQ test in the fifth grade, she knew that her 'school smarts' were much greater than her classmates. In fact, had she been tested, she would have astounded her teachers by her IQ of nearly one hundred and forty-five.

In a somewhat surprising turn of events, however, two weeks later Sally's recommendation had been reconsidered. Based on the downturn in academic performance over the preceding fourteen-day period it was agreed by her parents and the school that perhaps her evaluation had been a bit hasty.

*\*\**

Tim Kerrigan sat on the back deck of his home working on a cup of coffee and reading the local afternoon newspaper, the *Billings Times*. Over the past twenty years at BSI, he had worked his way up the corporate ladder. Each promotion had come with increased responsibility, increased hours and increased consumption of coffee. He had reached the point with his most recent promotion that his duties would be changing dramatically, and so would his coffee intake if he heeded his doctor. He reached down to pick up the mug of steaming black liquid thinking that the rewards of his new position at BSI could not be fully appreciated if it had to be gained at the expense of coffee.

It had been a June day much like this, Tim reflected, when he had started his first day of work at BSI. After graduating from Harvard Law School, he had stayed in Boston to attend Boston College to get a Master of Business Administration degree. A local hometown boy who graduated as the senior class president at Billings High, Tim had never imagined in those days that he would spend the majority of his career in Maine, let alone in Billings. From an early age, Tim's career ambitions involved obtaining a position in a corporate law firm, perhaps in New York or maybe Washington DC.

After receiving his MBA degree, he spent a year working for a law firm in Manhattan. During this time, he passed the New York Law Bar Exam, thus becoming a fully-fledged attorney at law.

Tim looked up as his wife, Lisa, came out onto the patio and sat down with a book. His year in the New York law firm had really been a turning point in his life he mused. It was the year that he had become thoroughly disenchanted with corporate law. And yet, it was the same year that he had become thoroughly enchanted with a young businesswoman whom he had met as his firm represented her company in a legal dispute. After 'learning the ropes' with his new firm for six months, he was assigned to assist one of the law firm partners in an important case in which a large California advertising company had run afoul with the New York statutes regarding state taxes.

Tim set his coffee down and gazed over at his wife. He never had patience for waiting for what he wanted. He remembered the frustration that year so long ago that he felt as the managing partner waded through mountains of paperwork in preparation for the case. It became very clear that the intricacies of the reality of corporate law were nothing like his education in corporate law at law school. At Harvard he had become enamored with the excitement of the potential for orchestrating momentous decisions with very big consequences. Here in his first law position, however, all he saw was tedious paperwork.

His lack of patience also emerged in force that year in his relationship with Lisa Bradley. She was a young, attractive, talented executive in a prestigious Los Angeles advertising company. She had been sent to New York, along with a company attorney, to deliver tax records and her company's corporation charter documents. There had been a disagreement regarding income that the State of New York considered to be New York taxable income and her company did not. It involved an advertising account that Lisa had managed for a large clothing mail order company that had its home base in upstate New York.

Tim had immediately fallen for Lisa upon their first meeting. That initial day of meetings concluded with Tim offering to show her around the city. She was scheduled to stay over for two days before returning to California. Lisa graciously accepted Tim's offer, and by the time Lisa was ready to return to her home, Tim had made up his mind that this would be his wife.

Over the following six months Tim had flown to California four times, and they were married in a Bradley family church in Long Beach, California just over half a year after they had first met. Tim packed up his things and moved to Los Angeles to a new apartment and to a new life. He had felt no remorse regarding leaving the New York law firm since, for him, the glamour of corporate law had been tarnished to the point that it no longer held any luster.

It took Tim only a week to find a new position of employment. He had noticed that there was a shipyard in Los Angeles and having grown up surrounded by shipyard life with both his parents being employed by

BSI, he felt perfectly comfortable walking into the employment office seeking a job. He was hired in the operations management department and was given the responsibility of reviewing shipyard contracts.

Tim took another sip of coffee and leaned over to his wife who was engrossed in a book that supposedly identified 'the ten secrets to effective marketing'.

"Do you remember the days in LA? You know, it's somewhat amazing how far we have come."

Lisa put down her book and smiled. "I carried you then, and I'm still carrying you."

Those first few years of married life hadn't been that difficult, Tim thought, but he had to admit that Lisa had carried them both, at least financially, for a while. She had been a rising star in her company that had recently gone national and even had hopes for international business. Shortly after their marriage, Lisa had been promoted to the head of marketing after she had landed a million-dollar account with a well-known auto insurance company. It was on her salary that they were able to afford an upscale apartment in one of Los Angeles' suburbs where highly successful young professionals bought condominiums at ever increasing prices. It wasn't that Tim wasn't making a respectable salary, but his entry level position could not hope to compete with the financial demands of the high-speed pace of the upwardly mobile 'best and brightest' in Los Angeles.

Over the course of the next five years, Tim made swift progress up the corporate ladder at the shipyard, never being satisfied with where he was at professionally. Ambition, mixed with a nearly equal portion of talent, opened doors as over the succeeding years he became a project operations manager, and eventually was promoted to the position of department head. Each position seemed to be an opportunity to get further ahead.

But the California lifestyle didn't seem to respect their growing positions of authority and accompanying salaries. It seemed that the more money they made, the more debts they accumulated. It was this condition that finally took its toll on Tim and, when he noticed an advertisement in a professional journal for the position of director of operations at the

21

Billings Shipyard in his hometown, he made a decision for change once again.

At first, Lisa argued against the move. Why would anyone want to leave the center of professional opportunity to move to a place that was at the very border of civilization? Furthermore, even if Tim was able to carve out a successful career at BSI, what would she do? How could she just throw away her hard-earned position and its lucrative salary?

The final acceptance by Lisa was brought about by a ten-second revelation that had occurred to Tim during his interview at BSI. The interview had gone amazingly well. The chief executive officer of BSI was impressed with Tim's academic credentials as well as his general shipyard experience. There was some hesitation regarding his lack of experience with government contracts, but the fact that Tim was a 'Billings boy' tipped the scales in his favor. The position of director of operations involved the day-to-day oversight of project managers and it would mean that he would have the responsibility for ongoing projects in design and under construction, with over five thousand people under his control! He would report directly to the vice president of operations.

As the interview was concluding, Tim had a sense that the job was his. In a moment of inspiration, he turned as he was getting up to leave and said, "Sir, there is one other thing. For me to be able to accept this position, I would need to know that my wife would have an opportunity here at BSI as well. She is a nationally known account executive with an advertising firm back in California. She is interested in starting a marketing group at BSI to explore opportunities for promoting the shipyard to potential commercial shipping customers nationally and abroad." Tim was truly winging it as he had no idea if BSI had any desire to market itself to non-governmental clients, but somehow, the request just seemed right.

There was an uncomfortable pause, but the interviewer responded, "Funny you should mention that. The board of directors has repeatedly criticized our ability to line up commercial contracts. As you may know, except for a few maintenance contracts, nearly every dollar of BSI income is attached to military contracts. The board wants us to diversify. Have your wife send me her resume. I'll take a look at it."

And the rest, as they say, is history. Lisa came on board initially as a marking specialist, and over the past twenty years had built up a successful marketing effort that now included a staff of thirty people. As BSI's marketing director she was now responsible for creating BSI's image and selling it worldwide.

Tim had remained in the position of director of operations for his first five years until his promotion to vice president of operations. As director of operations, he had supervised the shipyard construction workforce as well as the engineering department. His promotion to the position of vice president of operations carried the responsibility of not only the day-to-day working activities in the yard, as was reported by the director of operations, but it also included the project management oversight for projects in pre-construction design as well.

BSI had four members of upper management who held the title of vice president. In addition to the vice president of operations, there was the vice president of finance who was responsible for all aspects of the financial conditions of the shipyard. There was the vice president of administration who was responsible for legal affairs and human resources. And there was the vice president of public relations who was responsible for commercial sector marketing and government relations.

After serving as the company vice president of operations for five years, Tim had been promoted again, this time to the position of chief executive officer, or CEO, replacing the man who had originally hired him. The CEO was the public face for BSI, serving as the shipyard's supreme administrative leader. Each of the vice presidents reported directly to the CEO, who in turn, reported only to the corporate board of directors. In addition to the prestige of the position, the promotion to CEO had also brought with it company ownership through the issuance of BSI stock. Tim could still remember with clarity like it was just yesterday his first board of directors meeting and the thought that someday he would become the board president and have control over not just the shipyard, but the entire corporation as well. And now, at last, as he sat sipping his coffee, he realized that his dream was about to come true.

\*\*\*

Henry Moore sat in the back room of the Billings Electronics Shop. Henry had just completed his sophomore year at Billings High. Well, that is, he had completed all of his courses except English which had ended in an unsatisfactory grade. Much to Henry's annoyance, that unsatisfactory grade resulted in summer school classes.

Henry pushed his thick brown hair back under his cap. It was time for a haircut. Henry was a poster child for all awkward teenagers who lacked both athletic and social skills but who had found their niche in science and technology. In summation, he was a computer geek. At sixteen years old, he was a lanky six foot tall, all elbows and legs, with a genuine heart for others that was shown unmistakably through his smile. He pushed his glasses back up on his nose and concentrated on his task of removing a video card from a laptop computer.

Henry had just had his sixteenth birthday, but it came and went with no recognition or fanfare. Henry lived with his dad who was a welder at the BSI shipyard. His mom and dad had gotten a divorce when he was very young and now his dad was all the family he had. Not that anyone could call his home life much of a family. His dad worked the second shift at the yard, which meant that he was never around between four p.m. and midnight and he slept every day, until noon. Many nights after work and on weekends, he could be found closing down the local bar with the guys from work. When he was around home, he spent most of his time working on the 1978 Pontiac Firebird, which Henry had a suspicion ranked ahead of all else on his dad's list of things that are important.

Henry finished seating the new video card in the computer that he had open on the back room work bench. He had secured a summer job with Mr Riley, the shop owner, repairing and upgrading computers that customers brought in. Henry had a talent for computers. In fact, it was more than just a talent. At age eleven he had built his first computer from parts he had salvaged from a BSI dumpster that contained discarded, inoperative personal computers. By the time he was thirteen, Henry had a bedroom full of high-tech equipment including computers that were more powerful than most found in the BSI engineering department.

Although he excelled at the maintenance and upgrade of computer hardware, Henry's true talent lay in software manipulation and computer code. Unlike acquiring an understanding of English literature, which came at best in fog-shrouded blurriness, decoding computer language and software systems came in bursts of instant clarity.

Henry was forever using words that surfaced from somewhere deep in his memory that sounded just right for the conversation but, in fact, were as out of place as a kazoo in a symphony concert performance. But when it came to computer technology and software systems, Henry always had exactly the right answer. Henry didn't understand why this might be the case, but as his best friend, Sheila Warren, so often said with undeniable succinctness, "Whatever!"

It was this talent that had almost gotten Henry into trouble on several occasions. Finding it easy to enter secured sites by means of programs that he had developed, Henry put this ability to use, mostly as exercises in curiosity. It was a learning experience, however, that taught him that although he might be able to get access to password and firewall protected files at BSI, the Billings city hall, the Paulsen Library, and even at several local banks, it was difficult to do so without being detected. On two occasions, his illegal connection had nearly been traced back to his system. He had only barely had time to reroute his communications path with an algorithm that he had written that randomly switched his connection through servers worldwide, making his point of origin all but impossible to detect.

After testing the computer on which he had just finished work, he powered down the lab bench and headed out to the front of the shop.

"I won't be able to be in tomorrow afternoon, Mr Riley. I have summer school class again."

Mr Riley looked up from the magazine he was reading. Finding Henry had been the best thing that had happened to his business. It was amazing how the kid was able to fix computers. And it seemed that that was all that people were bringing in anymore. The days of repairing televisions, stereos and VCR players were gone forever.

"Make sure you pass that English course, son. Otherwise, you might have to quit school and work for me full time." He smiled and went back to reading.

Outside, Henry grabbed his bike and headed off to his second job at McDonalds. He had not taken on the job for the money, which was minimum wage. The hours were limited, four hours from four until eight p.m. on weekdays, which only translated into enough dollars to allow for a few new clothes each month. The real impetus for taking on the job was the free food that was made available. Work at McDonalds meant free fast food for supper!

# Chapter 2

The quarterly board of directors meeting was not scheduled to begin until two p.m., however, the executive conference room was ready by noon. BSI board meetings were usually conducted with the preparation and formality of any large corporation, but today extra care had been taken. In its one-hundred-year history BSI had evolved from a small, privately-owned shipyard making wooden sailing vessels to a corporate machine that specialized in making high-tech military ships. Its peak had been reached during World War II when the call for navy destroyers turned BSI into an empire of over ten thousand workers. Although the shipyard currently employed less than half of its peak workforce of the 1940s, its workload was sufficiently stable to provide a reliable means of work for what was still a sizeable number Mainers.

Tim Kerrigan walked into the conference room to survey the layout. This would be his last meeting in which he reported the state of the shipyard as the company's chief executive officer and he was sure not going to forget anything in his last report as shipyard CEO.

He walked over to the phone at the conference table and dialed his secretary. "Miss Stanley, are the operations reports ready?"

"You will find them stacked at the side table, sir. I ran fourteen copies," the voice on the phone replied.

Today was going to be the day he had waited for over the past ten years. At the previous quarterly board meeting, the board president of twenty-one years had announced his retirement for health reasons and the board had unanimously decided that Tim should be promoted in his place. With the board's formal vote at this meeting, along with the approval of an additional two and one half per cent stock transfer, his name would officially be placed on the stockholders' ballot as the board's recommendation for board of directors' president. The stockholders' meeting would be held in November, where it was an absolute certainty that he would be elected since the board owned the majority of stock shares and, accordingly, a majority of stock votes. His increase in stock ownership would mean that he would control ten per cent of the company, which made him the largest single stockholder.

His wife, Lisa Kerrigan, would be receiving a promotion today as well from her current position as the BSI marketing director. She was being named as the vice president of public relations and, with her new title, the board had also agreed to put her name before the shareholders for election as a board member.

Tim Kerrigan's vacancy of the position of CEO meant a third promotion was in order. The board had decided that the position would be filled by the current vice president of operations, James Macintyre. Tim had had a few reservations about James taking over as the company's CEO, however, it could not be disputed that James had worked faithfully in his present position and had improved company efficiency by a significant margin in the past five years. More than once, however, it had occurred to Tim that Macintyre had demonstrated a sense of drive that some might call blind ambition. But Tim's newly acquired status as majority owner helped lay to rest any nagging concerns.

The actual change in positions would not be formally recognized until after the corporate annual meeting in November. Due to the current president's rapidly failing health, however, it was decided by the board that the change should be implemented immediately, with the titles for the new positions to be publicly released as 'transitional positions' until after the annual meeting.

\*\*\*

The morning sun streaked through the kitchen window of the Brown residence as if providing a signal for all to begin another day. The red checkered curtains that Sally had bought downtown and had hung up in the kitchen window reminded Steven more of a local diner than a family kitchen. But he imagined that his wife would have approved of the house and especially the kitchen with its generous layout that included a small table in the center with two chairs. She likely would have selected curtains, however, with some kind of fruit on them. Didn't the kitchen in Pennsylvania have curtains with pears, or was it apples? He couldn't quite remember. One more sign that he was continuing to lose hold of the wife that he dearly missed.

Brown gathered his briefcase and headed off to work. On the way out of the front door he turned back and yelled up the stairs, "See you tonight, Sal. I'm off to work." He knew that Sally was still in bed and likely wouldn't be getting out of bed much before ten o'clock. It was summer vacation but since they were new in town Steven hadn't pushed Sally to find a summer job.

He worried about Sally. As much as he loved her, she was truly an enigma. How could anyone who was obviously so bright have so much trouble in school? It certainly was difficult being a single parent, particularly being a man trying to raise a teenage daughter. All he wanted was for Sally to do well and be happy but over the last three years it seemed that she was anything but. He could figure out solutions to the most complex math problems but when it came to his own daughter, most of the time he felt lost.

In spite of the past difficulties, there was something about Billings, Maine that gave him as sense of optimism. He couldn't quite put his finger on it but it had something to do with the strong sense of community in this town. It was a place where people knew their neighbors, and everybody actually cared about each other. They had never lived in a small community. This just *had* to be the place where things came together for the two of them.

This was not Steven's first day of work, but it would be the first day that he would be introduced to the BSI design department that he would be heading. During the previous two days he had gotten a tour of the facility, met with company management, and had filled out endless employment forms in the human resources department.

This was going to be the greatest test of his career, bringing with it both the excitement of a new design challenge as well as a degree of nervous anticipation. Not that he had any doubts about being up to the challenge. But he had worked on government design contracts before and he was well aware of the pressure to meet submission deadlines as well as to meet budget targets.

What would the BSI engineers think of a new boss being brought in from away? It was likely that at least some had been with BSI for a long time and perhaps some of them might be unhappy about being passed over for the promotion to department leader.

Arriving at the shipyard, he eased the car into an open parking space in the enormous BSI parking lot. He pushed the thought that some of his staff might be carrying a grudge against him from the very first day deep inside and headed off to the brick building with a sign that read, Billings Shipyard Engineering Dept.

"I would like to introduce Steven Brown who will be our new lead engineer for the WG-116B Guidance Systems Development Project." James Macintyre stood at the front of Conference Room A in the engineering building with a dozen project engineers and a representative from the Navy Supervisor of Ships staff. "Mr Brown comes to us with eighteen years' experience as an electronics engineer working in the Philadelphia Shipyard, and most recently in Boston as lead engineer in a private consulting firm working for the navy. As you all know, this is a critical project for BSI. It can open doors to new work for the next ten years. The technology that we will be developing will be state of the art and will place the navy in a position ahead of all other nations' navies for some time to come."

Ten minutes more of project hype followed from the transitional CEO that was received by the room full of engineers as mostly a company commercial. At the conclusion, the podium was relinquished to the new lead engineer.

Brown began. "I want to say that I realize that I have some catching up to do. I am generally familiar with the work on the boards so far from my initial briefing. You have obviously made a good start, but we have a long way to go. I look forward to working with you all over what will no doubt be a difficult but rewarding few months ahead. I'll need to meet with the senior project engineers immediately following." With that, he stepped aside to give the podium back to Macintyre.

Short and to the point, thought Macintyre. Just like an engineer. "I want everyone to know that as CEO," he said, intentionally leaving out the 'transitional' prefix, "I will be responsible personally for this project. I will continue to review all design elements and project details and, accordingly, will retain access to all project files."

Brown noticed a look of disdain across the room. He himself couldn't help but be amused that senior management always wanted to make appearances that they were the final design authority, never mind that they rarely understood any of the technical aspects of what they were looking at.

***

July arrived in Maine with a heatwave that brought temperatures into the high nineties. The burst of hot, clear blue summer weather gave rise to the possibility of lazy days spent on white sandy beaches or time spent on the lush green lawns of the nearest golf course. But by the fourth of July, all hopes of such things were replaced with a return to reality and much cooler weather. The annual Fourth of July Days in Billings was the single greatest community event of the year. It included a mile-long parade, arts and crafts tents and band concerts in the park, a carnival for the kids along the waterfront, and a spectacular fireworks display, on the night of the fourth. Over the past ten years, the city council had stretched the event into a week-long festivity with hopes that the invasion of tourists would help the local downtown merchants compete with the large chain stores that had recently arrived in the neighboring town, at least for one week. The first three days of July were exactly what was hoped for. The morning of the fourth, however, brought a cold front that not only dropped temperatures, but it also dropped significant rain showers for most of the day.

Despite the wet morning, crowds were lining up along Main Street by ten a.m. to stake out the best parade viewing spots. The colorful array of umbrellas along the parade route struggled to provide a substitute for the missing hues of blue sky and yellow sun.

Sally Brown stood in front of the local discount store with her father. This was perhaps not the best place to see the parade since the sidewalk at this point widened to accommodate two trees and a bench. The increased sidewalk space attracted a throng of people that stood directly in front of Sally. What made this the spot of choice for Sally, however, was that the store had a large green awning over the front door which, at

31

the moment, was doing a good job of sheltering her and her dad from the latest rain shower.

Sally looked over at her dad and said, "I think I'll go into the store to get a drink. I'll be right out." She walked into the store which mostly sold clothing on the street level and a variety of household items and snack items downstairs. As she walked down the central stairs to the lower level, a man with a large, over-stuffed envelope tucked under his arm hurried past her. As the man passed, he bumped into Sally's shoulder and nearly sent her face first down the stairs. As she caught hold of the handrail, the man rushed on without even acknowledging her.

"People can be so rude," said an elderly lady behind her. "He's probably from *away*," the lady pronounced.

Anger suddenly rose up from deep inside her and Sally turned to speak to the man. He was in such a hurry, however, that by the time she reached the top of the stairs the man was already at the front doors pushing through the crowd to leave. She wasn't exactly sure what she was going to say to the man, but her anger pushed her onward. She needed to let this guy know that rudeness was not all right, and she wanted an apology. As she reached the front doors the crowd seemed to surround her, and it became apparent that there would be no chance to catch up to the man. The parade had arrived and a tractor-driven float with the Billings Municipal Band playing *Stars and Stripes Forever* was passing in front of the store. She looked around but could not see the man anywhere. It was as if he had simply vanished. Then as her hostility began to recede, leaving a much cooler head, she noticed the man across the street disappearing into the throng of people in front of the city hall building who were applauding for three acrobatic clowns.

As she looked for her father, a voice deep inside told Sally that there was something wrong about the man as he vanished into the crowd across the street. It took her only several seconds to realize that when she saw him across the street, he no longer had the large envelope under his arm. Where had it gone? Was the envelope the reason he was in such a hurry? The only mailboxes in the area were two blocks away so he couldn't have mailed it, and besides, due its size, it would not likely have fit in a sidewalk mailbox. Sidewalk mailboxes have such small openings that only the smallest of packages could be accommodated. She looked around but could not see anyone with the envelope.

"Great, you're back. You just missed the start of the parade," her dad said as he came up beside her. He looked at her, and seeing a frown on Sally's face, he asked, "Are you okay?"

Sally looked back at her father and replied, "Slightly jostled, but otherwise okay, I guess."

***

BSI's vice president of finance and chief accountant, Greg Connor, sat in his office listening to a band playing a John Philip Sousa march along the fourth of July parade route. The parade passed by several blocks away from his office, but he was still able to hear the crowd noise and music. He had purposely chosen today to come into the office since it was one of the few days that the shipyard was nearly shut down. He didn't need anyone looking over his shoulder as he checked into something that had been a growing concern for the past two weeks.

It was not just the love of numbers that had inspired Greg at the age of twenty-one to go into accounting as a career. More than his love of math was the immense satisfaction that he derived from taking a complex financial operation and bringing it to closure. So many things in life were left without a precise answer, a precise, and final, *yes* or *no*. Generally, accounting provided just such an answer. Everything had its place and numbers always added up exactly. It wasn't okay to end an annual audit with *about* this much money. It always had to be exact.

And it was this fascination with closure that had first brought the accounting anomaly to his attention. In a review of the contract figures for BSI's new Hamburg Shipping contract, something didn't add up. Actually, the anomaly wasn't in the contract figures, but rather in the accounts receivable, for the project. The contract assigned invoicing and payments due on a monthly basis for stipulated sums relating to the completion of numerous project tasks. The initial invoice had been drawn up and submitted on May twenty-ninth and payment had been received on the sixteenth of June. He couldn't help but smile at the satisfaction of working with private industry that paid its bills promptly, as opposed to the US government that was habitually behind in payments.

The initial invoice was many pages long with multiple tasks identified that were invoiced according to their completion status. Since the tasks were expensed across multiple internal accounts, it was unlikely that any single department head would have caught the inconsistency. The project manager would have been given multiple accounting sheets per expense account and, as long as the income matched the expense lines for each account, there would not have been any red flags.

But Greg Connor was obsessed with closure. The funds received indeed matched all the account line items for task expenses, with one exception. The oddity was that there was a twenty-five-thousand-dollar amount paid, assigned as 'Project Start-Up Equipment Purchases'. This might not have seemed extraordinary except for the fact that there was no such line item included in the May invoice.

And what made this occurrence even more unusual was that he had not been able to identify either the terms in BSI's contract, or any specific expense accounts, associated with 'Project Start-up Equipment Purchases'. The funds had simply been transferred into the special services account and then paid as if it had been a regular invoiced line item. The special services account for the project was managed directly by the company's CEO and generally was used for additional services that might be requested by a client beyond the contract basic services. But in this case, there was no sign of any request for additional services and the notation 'Project Start-Up Equipment Purchases' couldn't be explained.

Greg knew that to be able to find out the basis of these funds he would need to find out what equipment had been purchased and who purchased it. Since the expense account was managed directly by the CEO, this would mean that he would have to gain access to those financial records through the CEO's management files. As the shipyard's chief financial officer, Greg knew that he had the authority to access these files, however, it would undoubtedly raise questions that at the moment he would prefer not to answer without specifics for his concerns. This being a shipyard holiday with minimal staff on site, it would be an ideal opportunity to do some uninterrupted investigation.

After twenty minutes of reviewing standard contract language and management files for the Hamburg Shipping project, Greg ran across a brief letter of agreement that spelled out the specifics of setting up project contacts between the two companies as well as initial procedures to commence project engineering at BSI. Included in the letter was a provision for the establishment of an expense account for the purchase of start-up computer equipment and design software. The provision stated that as additional technical equipment for startup and systems development was required, it would be included in this expense account, to be billed on an expense plus fifteen per cent markup.

Greg was not able to find any other mention of this account anywhere in the volumes of financial documents, nor was he able to find a dedicated expense account that had been set up for its operation. So why had the funds been transferred and then paid under the CEO's special account? Seated at his computer, Greg brought up the financial records that were administered under the direction of Tim Kerrigan. To his surprise, he found that all of these records had been transferred and were no longer accessible through his financial access code. It took him a full minute to get over his surprise and remember that Tim Kerrigan was no longer BSI's chief executive officer. That role had been recently assumed by James Macintyre by executive action of BSI's board of directors.

When Greg accessed Macintyre's financial records, he was able to see a large number of Hamburg Shipping line accounts for various project tasks. Apparently, Macintyre had taken over the supervision in detail of all project accounting which ordinarily would have been performed by the project manager. This was unusual, but perhaps not unexpected for a new CEO who wanted to be certain that the company's first multimillion dollar commercial project finances were maintained in order.

Buried within the various line accounts was the line item labeled 'special services'. Greg accessed the account record and found that it included expenses and reimbursements associated with the initial trips to Hamburg that Tim Kerrigan had made, along with expenses and reimbursement associated with the negotiations held first in Maine in February and then in Hamburg in April when Macintyre had finalized

35

the contract details. The lone item that seemed to be totally out of place was the reimbursement for 'Project Start-up Equipment Purchases'. It existed without the usual expense report detail explaining the request and identifying the specific items purchased according to the corresponding costs incurred. In the place of a standard expense report was a BSI memo that simply stated:

*Funds transferred to Tokushima Industries, Osaka, Japan, approved by T. Kerrigan.*

Dated June sixteenth. This must have been one of the last transactions completed by Tim Kerrigan as CEO before the June board of directors meeting when he was promoted, Greg thought.

Lost in thought, Greg sat wondering about the transaction. He had not heard of Tokushima Industries but that was not necessarily unusual since as chief accountant he was not directly involved with the day-to-day operations of specific contracts. He turned to his computer and did a search for Tokushima. An hour later, he hardly knew any more about the company than when he had begun. The company apparently provided specialized computer equipment and software for control systems. The website, however, gave very few specifics about the company, its ownership or its organizational structure. The company was not publicly traded which meant that it must be privately held in ownership by either individuals or by a parent company.

Greg looked up at the clock and was surprised to see that it was six thirty p.m. He had spent all afternoon researching his concerns, only to end up with more questions than when he had started. Although this was a national holiday in the United States, offices in Japan would be open for business. The current time in Japan would be early morning, but it was likely that someone would be at an electronics company such as Tokushima Industries. Greg picked up the phone and dialed the long-distance number.

After several rings, a person picked up on the other end speaking Japanese, but Greg noticed, not speaking the name Tokushima Industries. Greg interrupted by saying, "Excuse me, do you speak English?"

There was a long pause on the line, followed by a voice inquiring in a Japanese accent, "Who is this?"

Immediately, Greg's suspicions were aroused. He asked, "Is this Tokushima Industries?"

Again, there was a long pause. "Tokushima Industries, can I help?"

Greg spoke slowly into the phone. "This is Greg Connor with Billings Shipyard, Incorporated in the United States. I would like to speak with whoever is handling our contract for equipment purchases."

For the third time there was a long pause. "Please excuse, I do not know that person."

Greg looked with frustration at the phone. "I need to speak with someone who handles contract orders."

He heard some muffled voices on the other end which he could not make out clearly. A new voice came on the line. "The person you need is not here now. Please call back tomorrow." With that, the connection went dead.

This was not normal Greg thought. What kind of company answers its phone this way? Clearly, he was not going to find out the details of this transaction by himself. His head began to ache, and he decided to pack it in for the day. He wasn't going to let this go, however. He resolved to check the July receivables to see if the mysterious account line reappeared.

# Chapter 3

It seemed like the month of July had flown by at light speed. Henry Monroe sat listening to the vice principal as he droned on about *responsibility*. Here it was the middle of August and he should be out enjoying summer vacation like everyone else, but instead, he was trapped in school. It was the last day of summer school. Henry knew that Vice Principal Morton had thought for certain that Henry would fail summer session English. That would have been the end of it, Henry thought. Without passing English, Henry could be sent back to repeat his sophomore year at Billings High. "What an incredibly frightening thought," Henry said to himself.

But somehow, Henry had survived the summer class. He was not sure if it was because he actually passed the final exam, or if Mrs Sheppard had just taken pity on him. Why do they pick such lousy books to read anyway? As Henry sat in the stiff-backed wooden chair in front of Vice Principal Morton's desk, he drifted off into thought. What possible life-skills can be had from reading boring books by Thomas Hardy or George Eliot? *Silas Marner* was so bad that the author had to use a fake name and pretend to be a man rather than admit she wrote the book!

Suddenly, Henry was aware that the vice principal was asking a question. "Do you understand Mr Monroe?"

"Er... yes, sir... I mean no, sir... that is..." stammered Henry, now awake from his thoughts.

"You see, that's just what I was talking about," the vice principal said. "You don't even have the discipline to pay attention. One more screw-up academically, Mr Monroe, and I'll see that your next stop will be anywhere but Billings High."

As Henry left the school, a girl with shoulder length brown hair called out from the sidewalk. "Hey Henry, how'd it go?" Sheila Warren was the only true friend Henry could claim. She had suffered with him through geometry class, and as lab partners in biology class they had somehow managed to dissect a frog without throwing up. What better defines the bonds of friendship if not dissecting animals in the name of science?

Sheila Warren could have been a cheerleader if she had been so inclined. She was an attractive brunette, just over five feet six inches tall, with an athletic figure. The reality was, she wasn't in the least inclined toward either sports or cheerleading. In Sheila's mind, the only thing that represented more of a waste of time than high school sports was standing on the sidelines watching high school sports.

In what some might call a subconscious attempt to run away from her good looks and the teenage lifestyle that such often brought, Sheila did very little in the way of clothes fashion or appearance. She bought her clothes from the discount store downtown and she rarely wore jewelry or any form of make-up. Spending time worrying about what other people thought of how you looked was pointless. Perhaps, Sheila thought, this is why she got along so well with Henry. He was one of the students that did not fit in with the popular culture of high school, which was not a bad thing.

Sheila was an average student academically. Her true passion was writing. Her older sister, Karen, was in her third year at Yale, which, Sheila knew, had set the post-secondary education bar, higher for her than she was likely to meet. But in Sheila's mind, her sister, with all her good grades, had little chance of success in life. Karen never had a sense of focus like that which drove Sheila. Karen had enrolled in the College of Arts and Sciences at Yale without selecting a concentration of study. When at the completion of her second year she had finally been forced to declare a major, she had chosen philosophy. Sheila had to laugh. Perhaps by studying Plato, Nietzsche and Kant, Karen might be able to discover what she actually wanted to be when she grew up!

Sheila, on the other hand, already knew beyond a shadow of a doubt that she was going to be a journalist with a large circulation newspaper in a big city. To Sheila, the world was going to hell in a hand basket, largely because of television and entertainment magazines. No one read anymore. At least nobody read serious journalism. Most people relied on five-minute television sound bites that were more about giving viewers entertainment than about providing real news. And even worse than this, young people were not even relying on television anymore for news, such is it was. Most of her fellow students were 'informed' by reading entertainment magazines that tracked the lives of Hollywood celebrities and presented it as important information that everyone must know. Well, she wasn't going to let serious journalism die. She would dedicate her life to reporting, not what people thought they wanted to know, but what they need to know!

Henry came bounding out of the high school towards Sheila. "I passed!" exclaimed Henry. "I thought Morton was going to exfoliate. He was sure that I wouldn't pass."

"Well, I knew you had it in you," Sheila said, trying hard not to picture the vice —principal without his skin. By now she had gotten used to Henry's routine mangling of the English language.

"I'm waiting for my dad. He's coming by with the car so that I can practice driving. If I can just solve parallel parking, I'll send in for my license."

Henry responded, "Yeah, well I've got to get to work. I've got to fill in this afternoon for one of the regulars over at the golden arches. You know, burgers to make, fries to burn. I'll see you tomorrow." As Sheila's dad pulled up to the curb, Henry started off on his bike.

*** 

It was five a.m. and the parking lot at BSI was nearly deserted. The cool August morning air had a crisp clarity that made everything appear in wonderfully sharp focus. The morning shift would not begin for two hours but the business of the day would not wait for BSI's chief financial officer, Greg Connor. Beyond the normal duties of payroll and project accounting, Greg's mind was occupied this morning with a decision that had to be made. The July and August receivables had both included another twenty-five thousand dollars receivable charged to the 'Project Start-Up Equipment Purchases' line which had been paid to Tokushima Industries. This time, there was no indication of who had authorized the transfer. Greg had to let someone know today about this irregularity. The

40

more he thought about it the more he felt that something was terribly wrong.

As he locked his car, he reminded himself that he had a responsibility to act. Tim Kerrigan had signed off on the original transfer and if something illegal was going on, he could not approach him without concrete proof. He had written a letter to someone else whom he could trust and today he would have to see that this letter was sent.

Lost in his thoughts, he walked toward the west gate, briefcase in hand. A voice surprised him from behind calling his name. "Mr. Connor?"

Startled, he turned around to see a man that he did not recognize, dressed in a long dark coat and a baseball cap.

"Yes, can I help you?"

Two silenced gunshots, barely audible in the early morning air, sounded. Greg Connor looked down in shock at the two red stains that were growing through his jacket in the middle of his chest. Before he could realize what had just happened, he slumped to the pavement. The man bent down to check for a pulse and found none. The first worker's car would not arrive for another hour and, coincidently, the driver would select the very parking space where a body lay in a dark red pool of blood.

The assailant slid his gun into his coat pocket, leaned over and picked up the briefcase. With a quick look around, he walked off into the quiet of the morning.

***

Sally Brown's first thought upon awakening was "Where am I?" This was the same thought she had had nearly every morning for the past eleven weeks since moving into her new home. The early September sun shone through her bedroom window warmly illuminating the foot of her bed in what should have been a welcome start to a new day. But Sally couldn't help thinking that although this might be a new home, a new bedroom, even a new day, the same old life was about to continue from where it had left off in Boston. Here it was again, the first day of school and once again she felt like a stranger in a strange land.

"Well, are you ready?" asked her father when Sally arrived at the breakfast table.

"Ready for what, Dad? Being the new kid in school again?"

Her father looked up from the oatmeal he was making at the stove. "Now don't be negative, Sal. You'll do just fine. I have a good feeling about Billings High. Give it a chance."

"Sure Dad," replied Sally. But she didn't feel the same sense of optimism. At least her father's job was something to feel good about. Who knows, if all went well with his project, the sky was the limit for his career. On the other hand, Sally thought, the sky may be the limit for her dad, but she was likely to be experiencing something a bit lower in altitude on her first day at Billings High.

"Don't forget your class schedule and the floor plan you got in the registration materials. This school may be smaller than Boston Latin, but you still can get lost in any new school. And be sure to take notes in all your classes. I want to hear all about it when I get home tonight."

As breakfast was finished and the dishes were stacked in the dishwasher, Sally returned to her room to get her things. Sally flipped through her registration booklet and a copy of the student newspaper from last year fell out. It listed every conceivable statistic for last year's Billings High sports teams, but only one paragraph on extra-curricular academic organizations. The basketball team had a new coach last year who, despite the team's overwhelming losing record, was 'optimistic about next year's chances'. The football team had won the Eastern Maine Championship and had hopes for a repeat. The swim team continued to set state records and had earned a trip to the New England Regional event... on and on...... sports statistic after sports statistic. "Great," she thought. "I'm enrolling in a jock shop."

With each minute that passed, her sense of foreboding increased. It wasn't just the fact that she would be in a new school filled with people she didn't know. It was more that Sally Brown had a secret. A secret that she did not want to let out, and here she was again in yet another new situation where she would have to build up the protective walls all over again to keep her secret hidden.

At seven fifteen Sally grabbed her bag and walked out of the house. On her way out the door, her dad handed her a five-dollar bill and said,

"Here, take this for lunch. I'm sure they have a cafeteria where you can get something to eat."

Sally took the money and replied with an unmistakable tone of depression. "Thanks, Dad."

As Sally looked back at her father, she saw an expression that Sally wasn't sure was more anxiety or sadness. It was obvious that this move wasn't easy on him either.

As she walked off towards school, she heard her father call out. "Remember, just keep smiling, and everything will turn out fine."

Ah, indeed, she thought. What was the song lyric? Smile and the whole world smiles with you! What a load of crap.

***

As Sally walked through the front doors of Billings High, she was crushed by students pushing past her. Her homeroom was room one-one-two. Her assigned locker was number ninety-eight. Sally had the school's plan in her purse, but she didn't need to look at it.

Sitting on a half-height block wall in the lobby was a group of students who Sally assumed were the school's popular elite. In an instant Sally sized up the four guys and four girls. The guys were obviously from middle income families but were dressed as tough guys from the 'hood'. The girls were likely from similar backgrounds and were dressed for maximum visual impact, exposed midriffs, and skirts that didn't seem to contain enough material to make up a decent sized scarf.

As Sally stood in the lobby reviewing the school's plan in her mind, she heard a comment above the noise of the crowd. "Hey, everybody, check the geek squad." The lobby became immediately quiet and time seemed to stop. All eyes turned to the guy who had spoken. Seated on the block wall with a T-shirt that read *Korn,* he pointed to a guy and a girl in the middle of the crowd.

"Hey, Henry Moron, you ever going to get out of the sophomore class? I hear English II the second time around is really sweet. Look at it this way, you won't need to buy any new reading books." The crowd let loose a nervous laugh.

The girl standing next to the object of attention spoke up. "For your information, Jack, Henry passed English this summer at summer school, so he's *not* a sophomore." Sally thought to herself that the girl was actually attractive, or she could be, if she took a bit more care in the morning getting ready. Obviously neither she nor her boyfriend had much use for looks.

The guy, who apparently was named Jack, and two of his buddies jumped down from the wall and stood in the way of the couple. "So, if Moron thinks he's worthy of the Junior Class, maybe first he should pass the Billings High Cruisers test," said one of the boys who was a head taller than nearly everyone else.

"Good idea, Snap. Let's see how much attention Moron and his girl was paying to Cruiser football last year. Answer these three questions right and you can pass. A wrong answer and we will have to relieve you of those super-cool pants you've got there."

Sally detected a faint groan but was not sure if it came from the guy or the girl. Sally couldn't help thinking, "It's great to see that no matter where you go, high school remains the same everywhere, *might makes right*." She thought that perhaps she could sneak by unnoticed, but it was unlikely. It was more probable that she would be asked to join the pair and losing her pants on the first day of school wasn't exactly the first impression she had hoped for.

"Can... can... Sheila help me?" stammered the boy.

"I don't care who helps you," replied Jack. He glowered at the crowd with an unstated threat that everyone clearly understood to mean, *no one say a thing*.

"Question number one, Who did we beat for the football championship last year?" Jack stood toe-to-toe to the young man while his two thugs stood on either side of the girl named Sheila. The question was met with silence.

"Let's let them chew on that one for a while. Here's question number two, "What was the score of the game?"

Again, silence.

"Okay contestants, Snap here set the single game rushing record in that game. How many yards did he get?"

The silence was deafening.

44

"Is that your final answer Mr Moron?" Jack looked at the others still seated on the wall with a smirk, and said to the tongue-tied couple, "I'm sorry, contestants, but it looks like our flag pole will be getting a new flag to start the year off."

Once again, Sally thought she could hear a groan.

"Wait!" blurted Sally suddenly. She couldn't believe she had spoken. What in heaven's name was she doing?

"Who said that?" barked Jack. "Who has something to say?"

Sally stepped forward.

"Who the hell are you, hot stuff? You want some of this?"

"Perhaps," Sally said more calmly than she felt.

"I don't recognize you. What... are you new here?" Jack asked.

"Hey, maybe she don't know who you are," Snap chipped in.

"Shut up, Snap, let her talk."

Sally stood tall with a false sense of courage and said in her most confident voice, "I'm a transfer student here. I moved here from Boston this summer."

"Well, la-dee-fricking-da!" crowed Jack. "Listen, miss big-shot from Boston, I'm going to cut you some slack because you're new. But if you want to get along here, you need to listen more and talk less," sneered Jack.

"But," Sally continued, "as I understand this exercise in academic excellence, these two can get help from anyone here, including me."

"Why not, Jack, honey," one of the girls on the wall said. "What help could she be? She wasn't even here last year."

"Why not indeed," replied Jack. "You want to help the geek squad? Make it so!"

"Well, in that case," said Sally, "the Cruisers beat Bangor High, the score was twenty-four to twenty, and your Mr Snap here gained two hundred and forty-seven rushing yards."

For a full thirty seconds, no one spoke. You could hear a pin drop. The couple stood in stunned silence. Suddenly a bell rang, and the crowd came to instant life and started moving toward their lockers.

Jack fumed. "This isn't the end of this *Miss Big-shot*. We're not done here." He turned and stomped off with his buddies.

Sally turned to the couple who just now seemed to come back to the land of the living.

"Thanks, my name is Henry Monroe, and this here is my friend Sheila Warren. How did you know those things?" Henry asked in amazement.

"Don't mention it. I'm Sally Brown. I'll see you around," Sally said and walked off toward her home room. As she went Sally reminded herself that she would have to look up the editor of last year's school newspaper and put in a good word about sports coverage.

*** 

Over the years Lisa Kerrigan had found that her employment at BSI had brought a level of excitement into her life that she could never have guessed would have been possible. When Tim had come back from his interview at BSI those many years ago and had informed her of his decision to move to Maine, she had been angry to say the least. What had made her even more upset was his declaration that he had managed to get her a job as well at BSI. How dare he make decisions unilaterally! These weren't just decisions that impacted Tim. They were decisions that would determine her life as well. And what made her most angry was that she apparently had no say in their making.

The transition from being a respected advertising agent working with nationally recognized accounts to being a salesperson for boats… ships… was nearly unbearable. On her first day, she had walked into a position that included an empty metal gray desk and an ancient black telephone that must have weighed five pounds. She had been at her desk for nearly three hours wondering what to do when a disagreeable man came by with a stack of file folders.

The man, who looked to be well past retirement age, shuffled into her room and with great effort let loose the stack of file folders pouring them all over her desktop.

"You must be Lisa Kerrigan," the elderly man growled.

In response, Lisa smiled and began to introduce herself. Before she could utter a word, the man went on.

"I'm your boss. Name is Drake. Wilson Drake. I'm the VP of public relations and you'll be reporting to me."

The man gave a cough that signaled many years of smoking from probably a daily routine of cigarettes by the carton. He pulled out a handkerchief and wiped his brow.

"Damn fool waste of time and money if you ask me. I've been dealing with admirals, senators and presidents for forty-five years and not once in that time have we ever not had a navy ship to build. We sure haven't needed to dirty the yard with the type of commercial scows that litter the seas in the name of free enterprise. We build military ships! And we're damn good at it too."

The vice president paused to catch his breath, and with it he seemed to settle down a bit from his tirade.

"Well, anyway," he continued, "the CEO says we need to do this, so here they are."

Lisa looked down at the pile of scattered folders and said nervously, "What exactly are they?"

With a look of disgust, the man turned and started back to the door. "These are all the files of commercial work that the yard has done since I've been here. Mostly small repair contracts. See if you can identify any prospects for building ships. That's what you were hired to do, right?"

With that, her boss disappeared. It had been a difficult start with no promise of any future. Lisa had quickly realized that she was all alone in this endeavor. Over the succeeding weeks she discovered that no one at BSI really had any desires to pursue commercial shipbuilding at BSI. She had been given a position only to appease her husband so that he would take his job in operations.

A lesser person would have thrown the towel in shortly after arriving. But Lisa Bradley Kerrigan was not a lesser person. In the first week she dove into the files with a sense of purpose and drive that approached fanaticism. She was determined to show this unsophisticated company what real marketing talent could do.

It took a month before she identified a lead on possible work with a commercial company. In one of the files that her vice president had left there was a record of an inquiry from a private company that owned a fleet of tugboats. The inquiry had been sent to BSI ten years ago seeking repair work on diesel generators. At the time BSI was unable to perform the work and the company went elsewhere to implement the repairs. What caught her eye was the manufacturer of the generators that needed work. It was the same generators that BSI were currently installing in navy transport vessels being constructed at the shipyard.

Lisa called her husband and got the manufacturer's name and model number of the generators being installed. She then contacted the tug company who still was in business and, in fact, had grown significantly over the past years. As luck would have it, the current tugs used the same generator as were being procured by BSI and, with a bit of sales expertise, Lisa got the company to agree to generator maintenance work for the next five years.

Initially, upper management balked at the idea of a commercial repair contract. But Lisa brought in three master electricians from the yard who stated that repair work on the generators wouldn't take any new equipment or training since the workmen were already familiar with the specifications for the generators. In the end BSI signed a five-year contract that was eventually expanded to include hull repairs for the company's fleet.

The success inspired Lisa to even more rigorous efforts, and over the past twenty years she had delivered a continuous stream of small commercial contracts that had grown to represent nearly ten per cent of BSI's income. Even the crotchety Mr Drake had eventually come around. At his retirement party ten years ago, he told everyone that the thing that he had most enjoyed about the fifty-five years of service at BSI was Lisa Kerrigan showing up the top execs who had said that commercial work could never be done at BSI. Lisa had come to love that old man and was sad to see him retire.

And here it was that she was finally being promoted to the position of vice president. It was truly a cause for celebration. But it seemed that as her professional life had improved ever so slowly over her years in Maine, her marriage had proportionally gone into a tailspin. It wasn't that her husband begrudged her success in the company. He had always been supportive and had celebrated every achievement with her. But as her professional life at BSI had taken up more and more of her time, so too had her husband's time been monopolized by work. In recent months

Lisa had come to recognize that she no longer shared the relationship with her husband that they had known and loved in the early years. Lately it was like two ships passing in the night, which was a sadly appropriate analogy. They hardly had any time for each other.

In an attempt to recapture that focus, they had decided to go on a vacation last year to Germany. They had started in northern Germany visiting Hamburg and the surrounding countryside. Later they traveled to Berlin, followed by what was supposed to be a romantic trip on a cruise ship down the Rhine River. But years of endless work had taken their toll on both. They both found that they were not able to enjoy the days of vacation without the ever-present cloud of BSI and work looming at the fringes of their minds.

What was worse was that Lisa had begun to detect something wrong with Tim. Something was inside him that was making him different. And it wasn't a good difference.

# Chapter 4

Sally's first class was chemistry with a Mr Wilhelm. She intentionally sat in the row closest to the back wall in the hope that, for the most part, she would remain unnoticed, unlike the student that had just overturned a tray of test tubes when picking up his textbook.

After the first ten minutes of class, it occurred to Sally that perhaps Mr Wilhelm might have been part of the Third Reich. He certainly looked the part, and he had all the compassion of a concentration camp commandant. And most annoyingly, he seemed incapable of pronouncing the letter 'w'. All his 'w's' were replaced with 'v's'.

"You *vill* be quiet in my class, and you *vill* take notes," came directive number twenty-seven from the front. "You *vill* be responsible for your textbooks and you *vill* not write in them. The school has paid good money for these books and you *vill* treat them *vith* respect." The '*you vills*' went on and on...

Sally slipped into her normal background mode. She had already acquired an understanding of chemistry that would challenge most college graduate students. The trick, as always, was to just get by. Don't call attention to yourself. How many times had she gotten herself in trouble by letting her abilities slip out, causing problems? Not this time, she said to herself.

The first period bell rang as Mr Wilhelm was giving his final directives for the day. "You *vill* read chapter *vun* and answer the review questions for tomorrow. I *vill* collect your homework, so write neatly."

***

Henry Moore's first day of classes went a bit less smoothly than Sally's. After the opening salvo had been fired by Jack the Jock and his sidekick Snap, Henry had hoped that his day would settle down into the comfortable routine that normally allowed him to hide as an anonymous member of the crowd. Unfortunately, such was not to be the case.

Henry's class schedule included a general English course, algebra two, American history, business computer applications, French three, and college chemistry. He hadn't worried too much about the English class since his last year's performance had dropped him into a general studies section. He had always done well in math so the second algebra course would be no problem. French was difficult, but nobody understood the French teacher who was born and raised in Quebec. It was the consensus of the student population that she had no idea whatsoever of how to speak English, let alone teach English speaking students French. It didn't seem to matter, however, because everyone in the class always got B's.

Of course, with his computer skills Henry could have taught the computer applications class, so that would be a no-brainer. It was the college chemistry course, however, that looked to be the real challenge. Henry had hoped to sign up for either the environmental science course or the general chemistry course as his third-year science requirement, but when he had finished signing up for his other classes, he discovered that his class schedule would not accommodate either science class. It was with great trepidation that he had filled his last class opening with the only available science course, college level chemistry, which unfortunately was his first period class on day one.

Henry walked into class and picked up a textbook on the front lab table. The question was, why had someone balanced a full tray of glass test tubes at the edge of the table right beside the pile of textbooks? It was like some kind of perverse test and, sure enough, Henry failed. It was amazing how many small pieces of broken glass can be made from a dozen test tubes when they hit the floor. When they started to fall over the edge of the table, Henry made the mistake of trying to catch them in mid-air. This was not only impossible, it resulted in further calamity as his textbook flew from his hand and struck the new chemistry teacher squarely in the chest.

It had been Henry's hope that a new teacher in school would bring the possibility of a chance for Henry to shine. Being new to Billings High this year, here was a teacher who knew none of Henry's past lackluster academic performance. As Henry had entered the room, he had tried ever so hard to project an air of confidence and brilliance as he had greeted the teacher. So much for a positive first impression.

*** 

Sheila Warren's first period class was English writing. Without a doubt it was going to be her favorite class of the year. The episode in the main lobby had left her angry but not even the kind of taunting that was handed out by Jack Tremont and his disciples could dampen her mood of anticipation as she slipped into a front row seat.

"It was the best of times; it was the worst of times."

Mr Sheppard was about thirty-five years old. He was dressed in casual slacks, slip-on deck shoes and a sport shirt that gave him a comfortable, relaxed appearance. Even so, his speaking style contained an air of seriousness that let every student know that English wasn't just a job, but rather it was a passion. He was good looking to the point that before the term ended half the females in the class would have an infatuation that would be impossible to conceal. His saving grace was that the entire student body knew that he was happily married to *Mrs* Sheppard, who was also an English teacher at Billings High.

"Who can tell me why this is considered a classic first line in one of literature's greatest works?" Mr Sheppard stood silently as he surveyed the class. In the back of the class a hand rose tentatively.

The teacher pointed with his pen to the volunteer. "Yes, Mr Crane, isn't it? Enlighten us. But first let the class know which great work contains this famous introductory line."

"It begins Charles Dickens' *A Tale of Two Cities*."

"Excellent, Mr Crane, now tell us why this one sentence has captivated so many readers for so long."

"The boy began with a hesitant voice. "It summarizes the conditions in France at the time of the French revolution. It was both good and bad."

Immediately, Mr Sheppard replied, "Oh course, of course. That's what it says, but why is this first line so great?"

There was a silence that lasted for a full minute while none of the students could work up the courage to meet the challenge being posed.

Finally, Sheila raised her hand. "The sentence is contradictory. It grabs the reader right away by stating something that defies logic. It makes the reader think right from the very beginning. It challenges the reader."

"Ah... there it is! I would say you go to the head of the class, but obviously, you're already there. Dickens uses contradiction not to confuse, but rather to instruct. He engages the reader with a phrase that requires one to read on to understand its meaning. Right from the first line we are drawn into the story with a desire to know more."

Sheila felt a glow of satisfaction that lasted for the rest of the day.

\*\*\*

In addition to chemistry, Sally's class schedule included an advanced placement English course entitled the American novel, pre-calculus, American history, French IV and studio art. BHS juniors were also required to take either a half-credit elective or participate in a non-athletic extra-curricular activity such as band, chorus, math team or debate. Since all the half-credit electives seem ridiculously silly, she elected to go with participation on the math team. Unfortunately, when she arrived at the assigned room after her last class period, a sign was posted on the door that read:

*NO MATH TEAM THIS YEAR. THE SCHOOL BOARD HAS NOT FUNDED THE PROGRAM.*

"Great," thought Sally. "I'll bet the school board found a way to fund the football team."

Just when it looked like she might have to enroll in the only remaining open elective, learning about nutrition, Sally spotted a handwritten sign taped to a door across the hall that read:

*Debate Team Practice.*

Why not, thought Sally. At least Dad will be happy.

Sally opened the door and walked in. Immediately the room became quiet. There were about a dozen students seated with notebooks. At the front of the room were two teachers Sally did not recognize.

Sally noted from writing on the front board that the teacher who was speaking was named Mrs Grabowski, who was apparently a freshman English teacher. She turned to Sally and said, "Greetings. Take a seat. We're always glad to see a new face."

Sally noticed that there were about an equal number of boys and girls, all of whom looked like junior executives vying for a position on *The Apprentice*. All, that is, except for one boy who sat by himself in the back row, the boy that Sally had rescued at the start of the day and who had made a name for himself in chemistry class shortly thereafter. Henry looked as much out of place in the room as the proverbial fish out of water.

Mrs Grabowski continued. "For you new folks, there are three types of debate sponsored by the Maine Forensics Association. The least intensive style is called public forum debate. It involves partners who debate as a team. The debate topics change each month so there isn't a tremendous amount of research required. The second style of debate is called Lincoln-Douglas debate. This is a one-on-one style of debate with topics that change every two months. It is a style of debate that focuses on defending a system of values that you choose for the given topic. LD debate requires a bit more time than public forum in preparing your case. The final style of debate is not for the faint-hearted. It is called policy debate. Only one topic is debated all year and so it requires extensive research. Policy is an evidence-based type of debate, and, like public forum, it involves partners."

The second teacher stood up and spoke. "I recommend that most of you sign up for either public forum or Lincoln-Douglas. I will be coaching those of you who select public forum and Mrs Grabowski will work with the Lincoln-Douglas debaters. I have a sign-up sheet up front here and I need everyone to sign up for their preference. Remember, those of you who want to pursue public forum debate must have a partner."

The group stood and filed to the front of the class to sign up. Sally hung back, standing in front of Henry. "So, what are you doing here?"

Sally asked. "I mean, you don't exactly fit the mold of a young Republican."

Henry looked down at his T-shirt and baggy jeans, feeling a bit self-conscious. "Thanks again for this morning," he said. "One of the conditions of my summer school English class was that I would participate in debate this year."

"Oh," said Sally sheepishly. "I didn't mean any disrespect."

As they got to the sign-up sheet, they both saw that all of the slots for public forum and Lincoln-Douglas were filled.

"Well," said Mr Hollingsworth. "You could both sign up as partners for policy debate. It wouldn't be easy, but I would be willing to help."

"That sounds pretty okay," said Henry.

Sally looked at Henry and thought, "Well if I was concerned about being able to underachieve, Henry should certainly take care of that worry."

\*\*\*

David Walters was a small man who probably had been predetermined to become an accountant at age five. He not only looked like an accountant with his thick glasses perched on the end of his nose, he dressed like one as well, complete with vest and bow tie. He sat behind a large desk made from shipyard finished wood from the early 1800s. The desk included a green blotter and the proverbial jar with pencils. The only thing that seemed out of place in an accountant's world was a copy of the October issue of *Golf Digest* on the corner of his desk. Apparently, BSI's new chief financial officer didn't spend all his time counting beans.

He began his accounting career working in a large CPA firm in Baltimore as an apprentice. He stayed with the firm for five years, mostly working on the financial books for small to mid-sized companies throughout the city. During his employment he made a fair wage, but he never made enough to buy a house or pay off his automobile loan. It became apparent that the principal owners of the company lived appreciably better than he. The answer was obvious, he needed to open his own consulting firm.

Without the capital necessary to start a company, David needed to get a loan. Since banks were less enthusiastic about the enterprise than he was, he needed to seek funds elsewhere. After several phone calls home to his dad, sufficient funds were obtained. The caveat was that he must move back to Maine so that his dad could keep close tabs on his 'investment'.

Ten years later, David had developed one of the most successful accounting firms in Portland, Maine. His staff consisted of twenty dedicated employees. His clientele included companies from Boston to northern Maine. He was comfortably secure in his business and his life, which made the telephone call this past September from BSI easy to reject. BSI had recently lost their vice president of finance, Greg Connor, in a tragic affair that involved some kind of local crime. They were desperate for a new chief accountant but were reluctant to go out of state for someone who probably would not be familiar with BSI. David had assisted Greg from time to time with BSI accounting on a consulting basis.

But the first phone call was followed up by a second, and then a third, each time the financial offer became more lucrative. Finally, the offer became too good to resist and he sold his business to three of his senior accountants and moved to Billings.

Two floors up from the accounting offices, was the office of the CEO in which James Macintyre was pacing back and for as he listened to a call on his cell phone. He resented the tone he was hearing as he looked out his office window. He was now the CEO of a large and important company and that deserved some respect. The voice on the other end became louder. "Listen, I don't care what it takes, the boss wants results. So far all you've done is create a mess that needed to be cleaned up."

The boss, thought Macintyre, that's a laugh. I'm the one who put this plan into motion. I'm the one who takes all the risks.

The voice continued. "There can be no more *incidents.*"

Macintyre responded, "Don't worry, things are under control on my end. You just do your job and report back that another transfer was made last night." With that he abruptly hung up.

He picked up a folder off his desk and went out into the outer office where his secretary sat, typing a report he had dictated that morning.

"I'll be upstairs in the boardroom, Miss Stanley. The meeting is likely to go on for a while, so you can just close up and leave at five."

"Thank you, Mr Macintyre. Don't forget about your appointment with marketing first thing tomorrow."

Macintyre took the elevator up to the fourth floor. It was his third meeting with the board of directors as CEO. The board members would be immersed in self-satisfaction over the bright financial prospects for BSI that had been brought into existence under their administration. It was going to be a meeting where he would have the satisfaction of knowing that BSI's bright financial prospects were finally going to mean something tangible for him as well.

"And now, we can move on to the update on CV1," Macintyre continued. The routine matters of the board had taken up two and a half hours and he had begun to lose his edge. Macintyre brought out his file on Hamburg Containerized Vessel 1 which was the pride of Billings Shipping. Up until last year, BSI had focused a vast majority of its energies on obtaining government contracts for naval ships. The shipyard had built destroyers, cruisers and amphibious assault vessels. In addition, they had performed a regular schedule of naval repair work. Thanks to Lisa Kerrigan's efforts, BSI also had a continuous workload of commercial ship repair contracts as well as a number of contracts with foreign governments for implementing what had become declassified technology systems. This notwithstanding, ninety per cent of BSI's revenues still came from the Pentagon contracts. This had been a long-time concern since a company could quickly find itself without work with the ever-changing mind of congress' appropriations committee. It was a concern that the past three CEOs had been unable to solve, including, thought Macintyre, the recent 'do-no-wrong', now board president, Tim Kerrigan.

The break had come last year when Tim Kerrigan had returned from a vacation in Germany with his wife. In a conversation at the BSI Christmas party, Kerrigan had mentioned that he had attended a social event at the Hotel Vier Jahreszeiten in Hamburg where he met the owner of Hamburg Transport Shipping, a containerized cargo shipping company with a growing fleet. Apparently, the problem was that European ship-building yards were not meeting the aggressive schedule for new ships that Hamburg Shipping had set.

James had seized upon this casual bit of small talk and the very next day he had Lisa Kerrigan place a call to Hamburg Shipping. It took two months of preliminary discussions and a month of negotiations in Hamburg. When it became clear that the two corporations could do business together, it took an additional six months of legal wrangling, but he had managed to deliver the promise of a contract for the complete construction of BSI's first non-military ship in over sixty years. BSI would build an initial containerized vessel within an eighteen-month schedule and, upon successful sea trials, would be given a contract for another six vessels to be built over the following eight years.

Since James was now in charge of shipyard operations as the CEO, he would be responsible for seeing that the tight schedule could be met. The vessel, CV1, would be an entirely new venture for the shipyard and, accordingly, there were many new procedures that had to be developed. The schedule could only be met if everything fell precisely into place. New sources for materials procurement and handling would be required, new construction staging, new fabrication methods. It seemed that BSI would be starting shipbuilding from scratch. And all of this meant new accounting procedures. It had been the board's decision that since every aspect of the contract impacted the success or failure of meeting the schedule, James should serve as the shipyard's primary lead in all aspects for the project, from the initial contract preparation through the execution of final sea trials and delivery to Hamburg Transport Shipping.

This couldn't have worked out better, thought Macintyre as he stood at the boardroom podium. Complete control with no one looking over my shoulder. Sure, it meant that if anything went wrong, he would take all the blame. But as things were unfolding, that wouldn't be a problem.

"Work on CV1 is proceeding according to plans. As you know, the contract for CV1 has been approved and work is now under way to transform yard seven into the preconstruction staging area. Payments have been received through the contract terms for project start-up in the amount of thirty per cent." James Macintyre continued with the report to the board of directors thinking to himself with a smile, things are proceeding according to plans indeed.

\*\*\*

As the days passed at Billings High, Sally found that she was settling into yet another new school routine without much difficulty. It had been nearly a month and there had been no serious incidents. As was always the case, Sally's biggest problem with classes was finding a balance that resulted in acceptable grades, without letting her 'gift' single her out for special attention.

October in Maine presented a surprise for which she had not been prepared. Sally had lived her entire life in areas where autumn meant a change in the color of leaves as well as a change in weather. But she had never experienced anything like this. Over the past week, Billings had virtually exploded with color. Trees were a cornucopia of shades of yellow, red and orange. And what made the environment extra special was the perfect combination of cool, but not cold, temperatures, surrounded by the brightest blue skies Sally had ever seen. Summer may never fully make it to Maine, Sally thought, but autumn arrives in spectacular fashion.

Sally sat in the cafeteria finishing her lunch by nibbling at a paper cup of red gelatin dessert and reading the year's first edition of the school newspaper, *The Cruiser Gazette*. The headline story called for student volunteers to assist with the paper. The article cited a need for people to do graphic layout design, printing, proofreading and reporting. The editor's name brought back memories for her first day of school, — Sheila Warren. Volunteers were encouraged to meet in the computer lab after school. She finished her dessert and folded the newspaper into her bag. It was fourth period and today that meant chemistry with Mr Wilhelm. Oh joy, she thought.

"Today *vill* be a review of electron configuration, chapter three. Get out your books, class, and turn to page forty-nine."

It seemed to Sally that each day, Mr Wilhelm had less and less patience with the class. He certainly didn't seem to enjoy teaching.

"What's his problem?" whispered Sally to Henry Monroe who also sat in the back row, in the corner seat on her right.

"The school was desperate for a chemistry teacher. At the end of last year Mrs Ames retired and I guess they couldn't get anybody any better over the summer," Henry replied.

"And exactly *vhat* do you have to share *vith* the class Mr Monroe?" thundered Mr Wilhelm from the front of the room. All eyes immediately swung around to Henry and Sally. There was a sense of relief from everyone that Mr Wilhelm had apparently selected the day's object of attention, and best of all, it wasn't any of them.

"*Vell?*" Mr Wilhelm repeated.

Henry panicked. His face turned a shade of red that reminded Sally of her lunch dessert. Nothing but silence came forth.

With a sense of guilt for having gotten Henry in hot water, Sally spoke up. "Henry was explaining to me that your electron configuration for chromium on the board is not quite correct."

The entire class sat in stunned silence. This was obviously some form of death wish.

After a moment of disbelief, the teacher responded. "*Vell*, perhaps you might enlighten us all *vith* your brilliance Ms Brown."

It was obvious that there was no turning back now.

"You might want to check the total number of electrons you have shown; I believe you will find that you are missing one electron. Chromium has an electron in its outermost orbit in the *4s* level."

Mr Wilhelm whipped around to look at the board and after several seconds turned back to the class. Now it was his turn to display red, although Sally knew this color had more to do with anger than with embarrassment.

In a quiet voice that contained enough heat to melt chromium, he flatly stated, "You and Mr Monroe *vill* join me in detention this afternoon."

Throughout the room there was an unspoken *'oh-oh'.*"

# Chapter 5

Lisa Kerrigan simply loved her new position at BSI, or at least most aspects of her new position. Her new responsibilities gave her control over all of marketing and development for the corporation. She had spent the last month preparing for the presentation that would be made to shareholders at the annual corporate meeting to be held in November at a hotel conference center outside Hartford, Connecticut. This would be her chance to step out on her own from the ever-present shadow that her husband cast, previously as company CEO, and now as board president. She had great news to present on a new proposal that was being considered by the Coast Guard for the design and construction of a new series of search and rescue ships. The marketing group had been able sell BSI services to Japan for assistance with the development of an implementation plan for adapting navigation technology into Japanese naval ships. And of course, the crowning achievement was the contract with Hamburg Shipping for the construction of commercial containerized shipping vessels. A non-military contract!

But ironically, the best news also contained the one irritating aspect to her job, *James Macintyre*. He had lorded over the Hamburg project from its very start and refused to let Lisa or corporate development participate on hardly any of the project's details. It was understandable that he would want the credit for landing such an important contract. But this could be the start of something huge. With some cooperation, development could use this contract as a stepping stone to pursue other commercial contracts. Lessons learned from the ongoing partnership between BSI and Hamburg Shipping could prove invaluable in promoting BSI in the commercial shipping industry. But the new CEO seemed not to understand, or perhaps care about, the importance of the Hamburg Shipping contract to BSI development. He refused the development staff any participation in the project management or project accounting and he reacted with outright hostility when Lisa tried to intervene.

It was the kind of October day that beckoned one to come outside and enjoy what remained of warm weather before the onslaught of winter. Ordinarily, Lisa would have answered this call by whisking away her husband to go apple picking or to take a walk along the beach. But, in addition to her preparation duties for the upcoming shareholders meeting, she had received an email this morning from accounting to stop by to discuss a confidential matter with the new chief accountant, David Walters. All of BSI was still in shock over the death of Greg Connor, but the accounting staff was particularly in a state of grieving. Lisa felt that although she would rather have taken the afternoon off, she probably owed it to the new senior accountant to see what was up.

The accounting department was located in the main administration building on the first floor. As she arrived at the front door of the chief accountant's suite, James Macintyre came storming out. She stopped short to avoid a collision as Macintyre fumed. "Don't waste your time here. Walters won't be around long." With that he marched off.

Lisa entered the reception area and greeted Janet Stanley. "Mr Walters said for you to go right in when you arrived Ms Kerrigan."

"I understand you just had a visitor," Lisa began.

"How did you know? Wait, let me guess, you probably heard the shouting from your office upstairs."

David Walters looked amazingly calm for someone who just had a run-in with the company's CEO thought Lisa. "What happened?" she asked.

"Mr Macintyre wanted a file that I didn't feel at liberty to hand over to him," said Walters.

"This must be a very special file for you not to want to give it to the CEO. You *were* informed when you took this position that you work for the man, weren't you?"

"Ordinarily I wouldn't have had any trouble with the request, but perhaps you can see my dilemma here," he said as he handed over a file folder with a single sealed envelope inside. On the envelope were the handwritten words:

*CONFIDENTIAL and FOR LISA KERRIGAN ONLY.*

Below the lettering was the signature of Greg Connor.

With a degree of surprise, Lisa asked, "Where did you get this?"

"Once the police released my predecessor's files, I began reviewing them to determine if there were records which needed to be saved. All of the information has been recorded and filed except for a personal file folder that contained some records from his involvement as a board member at the local YMCA, which was returned to his wife. Oh, and also this file folder you now have."

Lisa looked down at the unopened envelope with no idea what it might contain. She had had a good working relationship with Greg Connor but nothing more. She couldn't imagine what confidential message he might have had for her.

Lisa looked up and said, "If the police took all of Greg's files during their investigation, why didn't this envelope get opened?"

"Well, it would have if it had been discovered. But I just found it this morning. The file folder was taped to the underside of my desk drawer. When I opened the drawer, the envelope fell to the floor. That was when I had my secretary send the email to you. Obviously, the police didn't see it when they came to collect the files. Frankly, I wasn't sure what to do with it."

This was beginning to feel more like a mystery novel plot than an ordinary day at BSI, thought Lisa uncomfortably. "How did Macintyre get wind of this?" she asked.

"He stopped by to pick up last month's balance sheet for the Hamburg project, and like an idiot, I had left the envelope out on my desk. Mr Macintyre said that all of Mr. Connor's files had been delivered to him personally when the police order came to have them turned over for the investigation, and that he had taken charge of getting them to the authorities. He wanted to take the file and turn it over to the police."

Lisa looked at him with an inquiring eye as if to say, and why didn't you?

Sensing her question, the accountant said, "It was a problem. I thought that if Mr Connor had something that was so important and so confidential that he felt that it was necessary to hide it, I had better get it to the person to whom it was addressed." And with a sense of finality and relief he continued, "And now it's your problem."

Lisa looked again at the envelope and said, "I'll take this over to Macintyre. That should cool him down a bit. There may be something in this that Greg wanted me to see, but given the circumstances, I think it's more important that the police see it first."

With that, Lisa turned and left. What was actually going through her mind, however, was that it would be a cold day in hell before she let Macintyre see what was in the envelope. When she got back to her office, she closed the door and sat for a moment just looking at the envelope. What could this possibly be, she wondered? Carefully opening it, so that it might later be resealed for the police, she took out a single piece of paper. On that paper was a handwritten note. Lisa began reading.

*Lisa, there is something that you need to know. I trust you implicitly and know that you will do the right thing. I'm sorry but I have no other choice but to involve you in this. For the past few weeks, I have been tracking down a financial irregularity that I cannot resolve. It appears that someone is secretly diverting funds from BSI. So far, more than seventy-five thousand dollars has disappeared through the end of August. The funds are continuing to vanish, and I have not been able to obtain positive proof as to who is responsible. But at this point, I am convinced that your husband is involved...*

\*\*\*

Sheila Warren stood at the front desk in the computer lab.

"Okay, it's great to see everybody here, and it looks like our advertisement in the *Cruiser Gazette* worked. I see a few new faces."

It was two forty-five in the afternoon and the room contained a dozen students who made up the core of the student paper workforce, along with four other first-time students.

"We need to get rolling on our next edition, which means it's time to get down to serious work."

The door opened as Sheila was writing a list of tasks on the front board. Through the door came Henry followed by Sally Brown.

Sheila turned around, and, seeing Henry with Sally, said with a touch of sarcasm, "Nice of you to make it, *Henry.*"

"Hey, we had detention with Wilhelm. We just got out. You remember Sally Brown? She's new here. I convinced her to join us," replied Henry, with an obvious display of pride.

Sheila went on. "Last issue was a great success, but we need to build on the momentum." Sheila looked over at Sally and said, "So what did you think of our paper Miss Sally-who-is-new-here?"

Sally regretted having been talked into coming, but Henry seemed so pathetic in his request to, "Just try it... you'll see... it's fun!"

It was obvious to Sally that there was a thing going on between Sheila and Henry and, unhappily, Sally was being perceived as competition. Given that this was as far from being the truth as Pluto is from the Sun, Sally responded without being defensive. "Well, I thought it had a great design layout, but the articles were a bit weak and they included a few inaccuracies."

"A bit weak...! A few inaccuracies!" stammered Sheila. "Exactly how do you mean?"

Sally stood up to speak. "Now don't take offense. Overall, it was a good effort. But by a bit weak I meant that the articles seemed to lack any significant depth or substance. It's great to inform the public about upcoming events, but you have been given a platform to investigate real issues of the day and to give the student body insight into areas that they otherwise wouldn't have access."

"Yah, right on," chipped in Henry.

Sheila looked over at Henry with a glare. Turning back to Sally she hissed, "And *do* tell us about our inaccuracies."

"Well," Sally continued. "On page one, paragraph two, line three, it was stated that the student relief fund will benefit the recent tsunami victims in Fiji in south-east Asia, however, if you check, you will find that Fiji is not considered part of Asia. And on page two, in the last line, it was written that the lunch menu is being expanded to offer prepackaged salads that contain vegetables including broccoli, tomatoes, cucumbers, carrots, spinach and lettuce. Once again, however, with a bit of research you will find that the *solanum lycopersicum,* better known as the common tomato, is not considered a vegetable, even though the term vegetable has no real botanical meaning and is actually more of a culinary term…"

*"All right!"* Sheila interrupted. "We get the picture."

The room was quiet for what seemed like an eternity when Henry finally broke the ice by exclaiming, "Well, no one can say she only gets our paper for the pictures!"

In spite of her frustration, Sheila couldn't help but be impressed. "So perhaps you would like to join us? We sure could use some reporting help."

"What do you have in mind?" Sally asked, thinking that reporting might help her get to meet students.

"We've been trying to do a piece on new teachers here at school, but we can't seem to find an angle that would be more interesting than just a biographic rundown," suggested Sheila.

Sally thought a few seconds and then offered, "Investigative reporting might produce something of interest by looking into not just who are the new teachers, but why they left their previous jobs."

"Hey that sounds like a great idea," said a girl sitting on one of the desks in the rear of the classroom. "Don't you ever wonder why some teachers don't stay at one school very long?"

Sheila went to the board and wrote down a list of the new teachers this year. Pointing at the girl in the back who had latched onto the idea, Sheila said, "All right, we have three new teachers. Katrina, why don't you start with Miss Greer in the English department? Bill, why don't you take the new history teacher, Mr Kellogg? And Sally… since you already seem to have developed a working relationship with Mr Wilhelm, why don't you do some research on him?"

"And you *vill* be thorough!" commanded Henry from the side of the room. The entire group let loose a hearty laugh.

\*\*\*

"I understand that we may still have a loose end to deal with."

The voice on the phone sounded as though it might have originated from the phone booth immediately next to him, but James Macintyre knew it was coming over a much longer distance. It was ten thirty a.m.

on Saturday and the Maine Mall was already crowded. He looked at his watch and calculated that it would be four thirty p.m. for the caller. He also knew that this was not a call to be taken lightly. The message in his private email account simply had said:

*Tomorrow morning, Maine Mall, phone booths at food court, ten thirty. a.m. Be there.*

This was only the second phone contact that he had had with the caller since setting his plan in motion. The idea was to avoid any possible connection between the two, which meant no direct contact, either by telephone, email, or even regular mail. All contact was to be made through an intermediary third person that had contacted him the week after the arrangements had been made. He did not know who this third person was and had never seen him face to face. The contact had usually been through an email account that he had been instructed to set up. Messages were always brief and to the point, and always were sent from a different email address. The only identifying character that let James know who was emailing was the closing line which always read, nine-four-five-four-three-five-six.

When James had received the email, he had imagined that this was to be a connection with his intermediary contact. He had arrived at ten fifteen a.m. shortly after the mall doors opened for the day. After buying a cup of coffee at the mall Starbucks, he sat down at a table in the food court immediately adjacent to the phone booths.

At precisely ten thirty a.m. the phone on the far right rang. Although feeling a bit self-conscious about answering a public phone, he had a pretty good idea that the call was for him. It took him almost ten seconds to recover from the shock of hearing not the voice of his local contact, but another voice instead. His first thought was that something must be terribly wrong for the risk of a direct contact.

"You know we can't have any loose ends." The caller continued. "We've gotten everything in place, and we are well into this now. We can't have any complications."

Macintyre knew that the 'loose end' involved the envelope addressed to Lisa Kerrigan from Greg Connor that he had seen in David

Walter's office. What he didn't know was how they had found out about it.

"How do you know about the letter?" he asked. "And why are you calling me? I thought we had an agreement, no direct contact."

"I make it my business to know everything that happens regarding our association. And I am calling you to let you know that my local associate has lost confidence in you. He feels that you have been irresponsibly lax and because of your failure to make certain that no one discovers our arrangement, that this should be the end of our relationship. By end of our relationship, he means that you should be dealt with and I should cut my losses while the risk is still manageable."

A sudden panic rose in James' throat. He had already seen how problems were 'dealt with' and knew that if this were not defused, it would definitely not end well. He replied with what he hoped was a steady voice. "Look, this loose end can be easily tied up. I am already in the process of handling it. It isn't anything to be concerned over."

"Fortunately for you, our friend takes his orders from me. I will give you one chance to make this situation go away. I expect results or I will have to let our friend have it his way." The call ended abruptly.

Macintyre stood at the phone several seconds after the call had ended, lost in thought. How had he known about the letter? Was the intermediary contact person spying on him? Or was there another inside person that he was not aware of at BSI? The first thing that had to be done was to get that letter to see what it contained. The problem was, it had likely been given to Lisa Kerrigan and so she might now be a liability. As he drove out of the mall parking lot, it became clear that the issue of Lisa Kerrigan would have to be addressed and addressed soon. Perhaps, he thought, she might actually be able to be used to his advantage if he played his cards right. There might still be time.

As Macintyre's BMW swung out onto the mall access road, a man seated in a black SUV in the outer-most row of cars in the mall parking lot put away his binoculars. He reached for his phone and typed in a text message:

*Our man is on the move. I'll keep you posted.*

68

He hit the send button and pulled out into traffic several cars behind the BMW.

***

Lisa Kerrigan had been in a state of shock since she had read the confidential letter that Greg Connor had left her. Try as she might, she couldn't get past the sentence about her husband. She eventually had tucked the letter into her bag and had desperately tried to ignore it.

It was now nine p.m. on Sunday evening and Lisa could ignore the letter no longer. She sat in her living room alone holding the letter. Tim was away for a two-day meeting at the Pentagon in Washington with the president of BSI's major competing shipyard. They were discussing upcoming legislative proposals before the congressional appropriations committee that would determine the next round of navy ships to be built. He had left in the afternoon to get checked into a hotel Sunday night so that he could get to the seven thirty a.m. Monday morning meeting.

There must be some kind of mistake, she thought to herself for the one hundredth time. She knew her husband and he just couldn't be involved with any 'financial irregularities'. But Greg had been a very intelligent man and an expert accountant. If his accusation about Tim reached the public, Tim would be investigated and his career might well be ended, whether or not there was any substance to the allegation.

She had to read the letter again, starting from where her husband was accused.

*... But at this point, I am convinced that your husband is involved. There are funds that have been entered into the Hamburg account that do not seem to be consistent with the contract. These funds appear in accounts payable but are then not recorded in the balance sheets for the project. In fact, they are transferred monthly to a company called Tokushima Industries in Japan which I cannot get any information on. No one I have talked to at BSI knows anything about Tokushima Industries.*

*At first I thought it was just an entry error, but this same thing has been repeated three times since I first noticed it. I have done some*

69

*discreet checking into the matter and have made some disturbing findings. There are only two people who could divert funds like this. The CEO at the time the project accounting was set up (your husband) and me. Because I was not responsible, that left only your husband. I have traced the initial transfer to the CEO special services account with your husband's name listed as authorized agent.*

*My problem is that I cannot approach your husband without specific evidence of how he might be connected to the money. Perhaps you can discover something from your husband's personal financial records. I strongly suggest that we keep this between ourselves until we find out more.*

*Greg Connor.*

Lisa reread the note again, somehow hoping that the words would rearrange themselves to deliver a different message. There was no way that Tim could possibly be involved in something like this without her knowledge. *Or could he?*

Lisa sat down and looked off into space, lost in thought with Hugo, her cocker spaniel, sitting on her lap. Everyone assumed that Greg Connor had been the victim of a random mugging. The police had suggested that it might have been drug related. For sure Billings wasn't East LA, but lately it was becoming increasingly apparent that the drug culture was making its presence known here in town. The word on the street had been that a young person in need of money to pay for oxycontin had surprised Greg in hopes that he had money in his briefcase. His missing briefcase had never been recovered.

The one thing that was now clear in Lisa's mind was that Greg's murder was not drug related. This reinforced the importance of getting the letter to the police. But this would be like signing the death warrant for Tim's career. She remembered that she had told David Walters that she would deliver the file to James Macintyre, but she knew that this would have the same result. What to do, she wondered?

Hugo jumped off her lap and gave a short bark as the doorbell rang. Lisa folded the letter and put it on the living room coffee table.

She opened the door, wondering who might be calling at this hour on a weekend, particularly since her husband was away. As she looked out, she saw no one in the vicinity of the door. She stepped outside but again saw no one. Thinking that it was probably neighborhood kids pulling a pre-Halloween prank, she turned to go back inside. As she stepped back through the door, she felt a movement behind her, and suddenly felt a painful crack on the back of her head. Everything went black.

# Chapter 6

Lisa sat in her kitchen with two uniformed police officers. It was now one thirty a.m. and her energy was completely drained. She had awoken on the floor of the front hall with Hugo licking her face. For a full ten minutes she sat there trying to remember what had happened, while at the same time suffering what had to be the world's worst headache. When she finally put the pieces of her memory together, she picked up the hall phone and dialed nine-one-one. The police arrived and after a quick check of the premises, she was taken to the hospital in the ambulance that had been summoned by the police.

At the hospital Lisa had been checked over in the emergency room and had been informed by the attending doctor that it appeared that she had suffered a slight concussion and should check into the hospital for overnight observation. Lisa had no intention of spending a night in the hospital, however, and over strenuous objections by the medical staff, and signatures on three release forms signing waivers of medical responsibility, she walked out to the lobby. The two police officers who had traveled to the hospital in their car were waiting in the lobby hoping to get some information for their incident report. She asked for a ride back to her house with a promise to answer questions when they arrived.

Upon reaching her house, they conducted a thorough search looking for anything missing or out of place. After answering what seemed like the same five questions twenty times each, the strain had begun to take its toll.

"Please try to think again, Mrs Kerrigan. Was there anything that you remember that might help identify the man who attacked you?"

Lisa looked up with the full force of fatigue that now could be seen on her face. "Nothing! I've already told you. I didn't see anything."

The police officer who looked barely old enough to be out of high school said, "And there doesn't appear to be anything missing you said."

"No, I can't see that anything is missing. As I said before, we don't keep anything of value here, but what little jewelry I have is still upstairs in my jewelry case. And the jar of change that we keep in the kitchen is still there."

The older officer closed his notepad and said, "Well, if you think of anything else, don't hesitate to call. Here is my card." With that, both policemen turned to leave. "Don't forget to lock your door," he said as he stepped through the door.

Lisa went to the kitchen to get two Tylenol and a glass of water. It was not until she sat down that she realized that through all the excitement she had not called Tim. It was late and there didn't seem to be any reason why she should disturb his sleep, especially now that everything was back to normal. She would call him first thing in the morning and catch him before he checked out of the hotel.

So what was this all about? Who would want to break into their home? And why wasn't anything taken? All that she was left with were questions and the very real sense that her life had been violated. This feeling that someone had robbed her, not necessarily of material things, but more importantly of the sense of security of her personal world, burned deep down inside.

She wasn't going to find any answers tonight, she told herself. On her way to much needed sleep, she passed through the living room. What suddenly caught her attention wasn't what was there, but rather, what wasn't. The coffee table was empty. There was no file folder, no envelope with her name on it, nor was there a letter from Greg Connor.

*** 

Lunch period was almost over when Henry and Sheila strolled into the school library. They saw Sally seated in the far corner and they walked over.

"Hey, Sally, you better pack up or you'll be late to history class," said Henry. "Today we are supposed to announce the person we will be doing our paper on. Who have you selected?"

Sally looked up and said with surprise, "We are?" She loathed these types of assignments which is the likely reason she had put it out of her mind two minutes after it was assigned. As she thought about it the topic flashed back in an unpleasant rush, *write ten pages on the person from Maine who most influenced history.* How juvenile she thought. It sounded more like an essay contest from elementary school than an advanced placement history class assignment. "I haven't decided yet on a person."

Henry looked at Sally with concern. "We were supposed to have out outline done for today, remember? We need to stand up and give a five-minute presentation defending why we have chosen the person we have selected. You really haven't picked anyone yet?"

Sheila looked down at the magazine Sally had been reading. It was a *Time* Magazine from 1983. "You doing some debate research?" she asked, pointing to the magazine.

In fact, Sally had read every current magazine in the school library. Two weeks ago, she had decided to move backwards through history and the librarian had let her get back issues from the library storeroom. So far, she had read all of the old *Newsweek* issues and had now moved on to *Time*. The school only kept issues that were considered of significance. She was still wondering what made this issue worthy of archiving when Henry and Sheila had arrived.

"Actually, I'm just killing time before class," Sally said. As she reached to put the magazine away, a page turned and the answer to why this particular issue might have been saved in a Maine school library presented itself. Rather than put the magazine back on the librarian's desk, Sally tucked it into her bag and started off to history class. Not only was there an article that provided an answer to why the magazine had been saved, but the article might also provide an answer to Sally's history presentation dilemma.

As was most often the case, Sally sat quietly in class perfectly willing to be the last person to speak. She had suffered through what seemed like countless five-minute dissertations on the historical significance of Hannibal Hamlin, Henry Wadsworth Longfellow, Dorothea Dix and, of course, Joshua Chamberlain. As she woke up from her 'background mode' Sally noticed Henry moving to the front of the class. That meant that she would be next.

"The person I have selected as someone from Maine who most influenced history is Percy Lebaron Spencer," Henry began.

Sally let out an abrupt laugh but quickly noticed that she was the only person in the room to react. All of the students, as well as the teacher, Mr Hargrove, stood silently with each mentally asking the question *who?* Sally thought, finally, someone to whom everyone in the room can relate, even if they don't know it!

Henry went on as if he were talking about the best-known man in America. "Without the genius of Mr 'Spencer's invention, we would all be still making popcorn on the stove..."

Sally drew out the magazine she had taken from the library and quickly scanned the article that had caught her interest. By the time Sally finally rose to take her turn, the class had lost its interest in the task. Attention was beginning to focus on the clock and the remaining five minutes of class time.

Sally began, despite the less than full attention of the class.

"The year was 1982. The world's two superpowers were in the height of a cold war that had brought the world to the brink of nuclear war. Then President Ronald Reagan, in a speech in London, referred to the evil of totalitarianism which launched a popular movement across America labeling the USSR as the 'evil empire'. It took the courage of a ten-year-old girl in Maine to look beyond our own self-interests and approach the USSR with a pure heart and a sincere question that should have been on every American's mind, *what are we going to do to prevent a nuclear war?* She wrote a letter to Premier Yuri Andropov that changed the world. The Soviet premier wrote back in answer to the young girl's letter that had been written with such passion and sincere concern that it touched the hearts of people on both continents. A year later the girl received a personal invitation to visit Moscow and she went as America's ambassador of peace. The young girl's name was Samantha Smith, and she was born in Houlton, Maine."

By the time Sally concluded, the class was entranced and not a sound was being made. The quiet was suddenly interrupted by the change of class bell and Sally returned to get her bag amongst the rush of students leaving the room.

"You just got that from the magazine you were reading in the library, right?" asked Sheila on the way out. "That's amazing!"

"Sometimes," Sally replied, "inspiration comes just at the moment that you need it most."

***

Finally, it looked like he was catching a break. How could this be any better, thought James Macintyre as he sat in his office drinking an after-lunch cup of tea. Last night's adventure had gone flawlessly. Lisa hadn't any idea who, or what, hit her. The best part was that there was no way she would report the missing letter. If she informed the authorities about the letter, it would mean bringing suspicion onto her husband. What a break! He had had no idea exactly what Greg Connor might have uncovered, but for Greg to have pointed the finger at Tim Kerrigan was priceless.

It had been a simple matter to gain access to Tim Kerrigan's computer files. Senior management meetings were held the morning of the first Monday of each month and, with the president out of town, it was perfectly normal to have James be logged onto Kerrigan's computer to access and download the status of the previous month's contract negotiations. When the president was away, the CEO would present status reports on contract negotiations to senior management. No one would ever be able to trace the files that he copied onto Kerrigan's hard drive back to him. There would be no record of unauthorized log on to the computer, and James made certain that the files were back dated after loading them.

At the senior management meeting, James couldn't help but notice that Lisa Kerrigan looked like she had gotten no sleep since leaving the office on Friday afternoon. Throughout the meeting, she hardly seemed to be listening, and when she gave her report on development and had briefed management on the upcoming presentation to be made at the annual corporate meeting next month, she showed her power point presentation with very little embellishment.

"It might have been good to see a little more information on how we intend to pursue other non-military contracts, based on our experience with the Hamburg contract," suggested David Walters.

In a hot instant, Lisa shot back with unconcealed hostility. "Well, if Mr Macintyre were a little more cooperative about the project management details perhaps, I would have!"

The room went silent for an uncomfortable moment before James replied with complete calm. "Why Lisa, you know that we all agreed that because the project was a brand-new venture for us, it would be best to have a single point of control. That certainly doesn't mean, however, that you can't have access to project data. Stop by my office tomorrow morning and we can discuss the details."

With that, James went on to other business. Lisa took her seat as the other managers watched her with looks that didn't need to say out loud, *maybe this job is too much for her to handle*.

As she sat through the remainder of the meeting, she hardly heard a word that was spoken. Instead, her mind raced trying to figure out what to do about the missing letter. She was surprised that David Walters hadn't already asked her what she had done with it. Clearly, she couldn't report its theft to the police without implicating her husband. But to do nothing was to turn a blind eye towards the well-being of BSI, and she couldn't do that either. The only answer was that she needed to get to the bottom of this and fast. If Greg had been able to discover the accounting irregularity, it was probably just a matter of time before David Walters discovered it. She needed to find out for herself if her husband was somehow involved in something illegal. The most difficult thing was that until she was sure he was innocent, she couldn't even talk to Tim.

\*\*\*

Lisa started to clear away the supper dishes as her husband got up from the table. He had arrived home late Wednesday afternoon because of thunderstorms that had delayed air traffic at Washington's airport. When he finally got his flight rescheduled, it was two o'clock in the afternoon and so he didn't get back to Portland until four p.m. Since arriving at home he had secluded himself in his study trying to catch up on office work on his laptop. Tim often worked late into the evening at home with his laptop computer connected to his office computer at BSI by means of the Internet.

"I'm going to take Hugo out for a walk," said Tim as he headed into the front hall with Hugo nipping at his heals. "I'll be back in a minute. We'll just go around the block."

When she heard the door close, Lisa dried her hands and walked into Tim's study. As she had guessed, his computer was on. There would be no better opportunity than this, she thought, to see if there was in fact any connection of Tim to the missing money. As she sat down at her husband's desk, she noticed a letter being composed on the screen to Lieutenant Commander Bailey at the US Naval office of procurement services at the Pentagon. She quickly brought up a listing of file folders looking for names or dates that might relate to the Hamburg project.

After a minute of searching, she located a directory labeled Hamburg Shipping. Under the directory were more than sixty subdirectories according to various categories. Her attention was immediately drawn to a subdirectory titled 'Financial'. There were a dozen files which all looked perfectly ordinary. She glanced at her watch and noticed that it had been five minutes since her husband had left. He would be returning soon, she thought with increasing anxiety.

As Lisa was beginning to give up hope, a thought occurred. If there were files that included evidence of impropriety, no one would leave them where they might be easily seen, regardless of the fact that the account is password protected. Such files would either be saved in directories that were not immediately obvious, or they might be saved as hidden files. Being familiar with the company's software, she entered commands to display all hidden files. Only one file came up. When she opened the file, she discovered only a single line of text, Y1721.

Ordinarily, this might not carry any special meaning to anyone, but Lisa instantly knew what the text meant. Last week, when she had been preparing the presentation to senior management, she had needed to access project files on the first non-military project that BSI had undertaken. Since this project had been worked in the early 1950's the project had been archived off site. BSI had a contract with Technology Systems of Maine for secured deposit boxes which were used by BSI.

For the past five years, BSI had been digitizing their older project records for storage on CD recording disks. The digitizing was done by Technology Systems and stored in their deposit vault. Lisa had gone to Technology Systems and, after signing the account register and receiving a box key, she had been directed to box Y1233.

She closed and reconfigured the file on her husband's laptop as a hidden file and brought Tim's letter back up on the screen. Just as the letter popped back into view on the screen, Lisa heard Tim walking down the hall towards the study. She stood up to hear Tim say, "Lisa? What are you doing?"

***

Sally and Henry sat at a table in a classroom in Brunswick High School with their notes spread out all over the table. It was Saturday and they were struggling through their first debate event. They had just completed their third round and were now in the final round, debating the affirmative position for the topic, *The United States federal government should legalize gambling nationwide and assess taxes on casino revenues to help balance the national budget*. They had lost all three prior rounds and were well along the way to making it a perfect score. They were debating the last year's policy debate champions from Cape Elizabeth.

The first negative debater for Cape was standing to speak. "We hardly have to go much further into this debate since it is clear that our opponents have failed to present a workable plan, and as such, their position fails the basic test of solvency. Should the affirmative plan be enacted, the proposed income received would barely cover the added costs of social programs that would be required to help the enormous increase of clinically depressed people who suffer unmanageable gambling losses. My partner and I will definitively demonstrate the association between gambling and depression, and we will identify the amount of federal assistance paid out last year in connection with depression medicines…"

Sally sighed. If they were going to do this again, she was going to have to do something to get Henry better prepared.

On the bus ride home, Sally and Henry were looking over their ballots, reading the judge's comments for each round. All four ballots read nearly the same. "Half your team was incredibly well prepared… Great first constructive, filled with amazing evidence, but the second speaker was not anywhere near as convincing… Only half an effort…"

Henry looked down in the dumps. "Sorry," was all he could say.

"Hey, don't take it so hard," said Sally a little more upbeat than she actually felt. "You just need a little more research on the topic."

Sheila, who had joined the team as a Lincoln-Douglas debater when one of the regulars had dropped out, had faired considerably better with two wins and two losses. She sat next to Henry and offered a sympathetic hand on the shoulder. "Don't let it get to you. Remember, this was just your first time, and you knew that policy debate isn't easy."

Henry looked up. "We got hit with that depression angle both times by the negative side. That sounds so bogus. I wish we could come up with something to counter those statistics."

Sally thought for a second and said, "Maybe we can. Here's an idea. How would you like to go to the Foxwoods Casino in Connecticut to collect some real-world statistics? We could go talk to casino gamblers to get their opinions. We could try to find out if depression is really a by-product of casino gambling. We could find out how many people actually are addicted to gambling and loose huge amounts of money. I'll bet we would find that a vast majority of people in a casino at any given time are infrequent visitors on vacation or are just on a one or two-day getaway. And I also bet that most people set a limit on how much they are willing to lose."

"Man," exclaimed Henry breaking out of the land of self-pity. "A road trip! What a gas that would be. It would be great. I bet we could come up with some great information to use at our next event. Maybe we could even stay overnight at the hotel. I hear rooms are really cheap because casinos make most of their money on the gambling."

"Hold on," demanded Sheila. "Wait just a minute. I don't think seventeen-year-olds are allowed in casinos."

"No problemo," responded Henry. "Give me a few days and I can tap into the Department of Motor Vehicles' main server in Augusta, and voila, we will all have driver's licenses mailed to us identifying us as age twenty-one… with fake names of course."

"No way," cried Sheila. "That's illegal. We could all end up in jail!"

"Who will ever find out? And besides, we'll have them just in case we might need them, and after the trip, I'll go into the system and wipe them out."

Sally had remained silent through the discussion but now spoke up. "Well, if we're going to do this it would be useful to have legal age IDs, and if Henry can get them with false names, there shouldn't be much risk."

Sheila rolled her eyes in surrender. If Sally approved, there would be no turning Henry back. The bus rolled into the high school parking lot and Sheila thought to herself that prison orange wasn't such a bad color. She turned back to Henry and said, "Well maybe, but no gambling! If we go, we're just going to get debate research."

***

James Macintyre sat at his desk looking at his computer with a sense of growing anxiety. The screen showed an unopened email that had been sent at three a.m. It was now seven a.m. and as he looked out his window James saw the shipyard coming to life with the first shift workers getting started at their day's work.

He opened his email to find exactly what he had expected:

*We need to talk. Call me at seven thirty a.m. nine-four-five-four-three-five-six.*

Short and sweet, he thought. This is getting complicated. They were just going to have to be more patient he fumed to himself. They think all I have to do is snap my fingers and they can have whatever they want.

He checked his calendar and called his secretary in the outer office. "Janet, I'll need to postpone my appointment this morning with the union rep, can you take care of that? And could you hold my calls for the next half hour?"

"Yes, Mister Macintyre," was the reply.

He reached for the cell phone that he had purchased just for these special calls. He had purchased the phone with cash and had signed up for a calling plan under a false name and had given a post office box that had been arranged for him as an address. He dialed the number precisely at seven thirty a.m. and heard his contact pick up before the first ring had ended.

The voice said, "You are late with your delivery. I spoke with my employer last night and he wants to know why."

Before James could answer, the voice continued. "And have you taken care of our loose end?"

James felt his temper rising. "Listen, you tell *your employer* that the further we get into this, the more time it's going to take. It's not like I can just snap my fingers and get it done. And, *yes*, the loose end has been dealt with. I've managed to make it go away. That should make *our* employer happy."

"He is *not* happy. There have been too many problems. If you want the next payment, you'd better get that package delivered and soon. You have two days."

James was about to protest when he heard the man hang up. "Pain in the rear end," he said out loud. To make upcoming deliveries, he was going to have to take risks that would put him in further jeopardy. He would just have to make absolutely sure that his plan to have the blame land on others, should something go wrong, be flawless.

# Chapter 7

The Billings High lunch period only allotted twenty minutes for eating, but it always seemed to provide sufficient time for students to finish a quick bite and hang out for a while in the school lobby.

"Man, what a blast it would be to go on the history prize trip to Paris," said Henry as he, Sheila and Sally stood in front of the school bulletin board. A large poster proclaimed a trip to Paris, France during February vacation for the top two winning high school teams who compete in the state-wide history master's competition. Teams must be made up of three members who are either in their junior or senior years in any Maine high school. A handwritten note was tacked to the bottom of the poster that read:

*Billings Competition Today*
*Mr Norris' Room three p.m. sharp!*
*All juniors and seniors welcome*

Sheila looked over with a laugh and said, "Ah yes, Professor Moore, I can just see it now. What did you get in US History last year…? Let me see… I think it was an *A*… no… or was it maybe a *D!*"

Henry's smile vanished and he stood humiliated in front of his two best friends. Sally felt a pang of sorrow looking at the young man who had briefly shown an inner dream only to have it dashed.

"We could enter."

Both Sheila and Henry looked incredulously at Sally.

"Are you on drugs?" Sheila scoffed. "In case you didn't know, my history grades won't get me into Harvard on full scholarship either."

"Maybe so," responded Sally, "but it couldn't hurt to try. I know a little about history so we wouldn't be entirely embarrassed. Why not give it a try? It might be good for a laugh."

Henry brightened. "Come on, Sheila, let's give it a try. What do you say?"

Henry, Sheila and Sally sat in the history classroom with twelve other students, separated into groups of three. The US history teacher, Mr Norris, began with the instructions for the competition.

"We will begin when I say to turn over your papers. On each paper are twenty questions, each with a line for your answer. Be sure to write clearly. If I can't read your answer, it won't be counted. You will be given fifteen minutes. You can work together in your teams to come up with your answers. Correct answers will be credited with a single point each. The team with the highest score will be declared the winner and will be sent on to the state competition. Incorrect answers will not count against you, so if you think you know the answer, a guess is better than leaving a question unanswered. Are there any questions?"

Henry looked around the room. In the front sat three senior girls, Wanda Dutton, Jennifer Smith and Kat Summers. Henry couldn't remember when any of the three girls had ever gotten any grade other than an A. The question most asked at Billings High over the past three years was how the faculty was going to select a class valedictorian and salutatorian from three students, all of whom have identical perfect academic records. Henry gave an inward groan, admitting to himself that this was probably a bad idea. When word got around that he had challenged the 'terrific trio', he was going to be the butt of jokes for weeks to come.

"Okay, teams," stated Mr Norris. "You may turn over your tests and begin."

Sheila turned over the paper and the three read the first question, *'In what year was the Magna Charta signed'* Henry whispered, "What's that?"

After a half hour, Mr Norris announced the results. "You all did very well. You can all be proud of your effort. We have one team with a score of sixteen, two with a score of seventeen, and amazingly enough, two teams with a perfect score of twenty! The team of Wanda, Jenny and Kat scored a twenty and..." he hesitated, "...the team of Henry, Sheila and our new student, Sally Brown, also scored a twenty."

The students all turned and looked at Henry, Sheila and Sally with great suspicion.

Mr Norris continued. "The rules state that in the event of a tie, an oral tiebreaker must be conducted. We will flip a coin to determine who will get the first question. The winner of the coin toss can choose to go first or have the other team go first. The first team to give a correct answer when the opposing team gives an incorrect answer in the same round wins the tiebreaker."

Henry chose 'heads' while Kat flipped the coin. The coin landed on the table with the 'tails' side up. Henry looked apologetically back at his teammates.

Mr Norris turned to the three girls and asked, "Would you like the first question?"

Kat was quick to reply. "No, I think Henry should be given that honor."

Henry and Kat returned to their seats and Mr Norris read the first question. "The category for the first tiebreaker round is European history. In what year was the great fire of London?"

Henry looked at Sheila and Sheila looked at Henry. The three senior girls looked over with a display of smugness that made Henry sick.

Henry, Sheila and Sally sat in silence for a full half minute.

"I need an answer," stated Mr. Norris.

Sally looked up and said, "The year was 1666."

"Correct," confirmed Mr Norris.

Across the room, the three girls glared at Sally.

Mr Norris turned to the next question, 'What was the family name of the last Russian royal family than included Czar Nicholas the second?"

Before the any of the other two girls could respond, Kat stood up and answered, "The Romanovs."

"Correct," confirmed Mr Norris. It was Henry and Sheila's turn to glare.

Mr Norris continued. "The category for the next round is US history. The first question this time will go to our senior girls. "During the Civil War the single bloodiest day of battle saw twenty-three thousand men killed or wounded. What was the name of this battle?"

The three girls put their heads together and talked for a minute. After a decision was reached, Kat stood up and said, "The battle of Gettysburg."

Sally smiled to herself and Mr Norris stated, "I'm sorry, the correct answer is the battle of Antietam, Maryland in 1862. Now, for a question for our second team. If you answer this question correctly, you will win the competition."

After a moment to let the suspense build, Mr Norris read the question. "This industrialist's construction company was responsible for building the Hoover and Grand Coulee dams, the San Francisco Oakland Bay Bridge, as well as over one thousand five hundred cargo ships during World War II. Later he established a foundation for medical care which served as a model for health care systems throughout the US. Who was this industrialist?"

Henry's hopes sank. Not even Sally would know the answer to this. Sheila looked over at Sally with an expression that said, 'It's okay, you did your best.'

The three senior girls collectively gave a giggle of triumph.

Sally sat silently.

Mr Norris said, "I need an answer."

Sally relied, "Fine. The answer is Henry Kaiser. He created the Kaiser Foundation."

Mr Norris looked up in amazement. After several seconds, he quietly said, "Correct. See me up front you three and I will have you fill out the form for you to send in to register for the state finals. The competition will be held on Saturday December tenth at Deering High in Portland."

As the students filed out of the room Mr Norris tapped Sally on the shoulder and said, "Miss Brown, I had no idea that you had such a command of historical facts. You should show some of that expertise in our class discussions."

Sally heard in her mind the faint voice of her fifth-grade principal saying, "Mr and Mrs Brown, I don't need to tell you how special Sally is. She has superior academic *gifts*."

Sally left without responding to Mr Norris, thinking, I must remember to better control my *'gifts'*.

***

James Macintyre carried the large satchel under his arm as he walked from his car that was parked in the municipal lot behind the main street businesses. The routine that he had followed for the past months had led him to a sidewalk bench in front of the Billings city hall. He walked into the local discount store whose rear door opened onto the municipal parking lot. He walked up the open central stair to the upper-level floor and to the front doors on the main street. The instructions called for him to deposit his package under the bench in front of city hall and to walk away immediately. Today would be different.

As he walked out onto the main street sidewalk, he looked around to see if anyone might recognize him. Seeing no one, he moved quickly across the street. It was obvious, he thought, that the recipient of his package must be nearby. Clearly, the package could not be left unattended for long without drawing attention to itself.

It was eleven o'clock in the morning and the usual lunch crowd had not yet hit the street. There were several people down the street in front of the local bookstore, but no one was near city hall. Macintyre walked up to the bench and sat down. As nonchalantly as possible he placed the package below the bench. After a minute he stood up and walked to the city hall building and hid around the corner about twenty feet away from the bench.

In two minutes, a car drove up to the curb and parked illegally in the handicapped space just south of the bench. Macintyre saw a man get out of the car and walk over to the bench. The man sat down on the bench and reached below for the package.

Before the package was retrieved, Macintyre leaned out around the corner and said, "I need to talk with you."

The man froze in place upon hearing Macintyre. It was impossible for Macintyre to identify the man since he could only see him from the back and because the man was wearing a hooded sweatshirt that concealed his face from all angles except head-on.

The man sat back up in the bench. "You have been warned not to make direct contact. Stay where you are. Do not come forward. Whatever you have to say you can do so by email. I will forward an email address for you to make contact."

Macintyre did not move from his position. "To hell with email. I'm telling you here and now, I can't keep providing these transfers by hard copy. It's becoming impossible to make copies of this information. From now on, I need to forward transfers electronically by Internet."

The man spoke with an effort of controlled anger. "You know why that is not allowed. We cannot leave a trail that can be traced. The Internet is too easy to track."

"Then I'll make electronic copies on disks, but no more paper…"

The man interrupted Macintyre. "I'll get back to you. Now back away and leave. If I see you when I get up, our deal will be terminated as will be your payments."

Macintyre moved back around the corner. The man stood up and looked around. Not seeing Macintyre, the man got back in his black SUV with the package and pulled away from the curb.

Around the corner, concealed by a bush, James Macintyre had a pad in hand and was writing down a license plate number, *1367 GH*. With a smile he thought to himself, and now to find out who it is that is forever looking over my shoulder.

***

Lisa Kerrigan stood outside the offices of Technology Systems of Maine in Portland not sure if she really wanted to go inside. There was the fear that someone might find out that she was looking into secured files that she had no business accessing. But there was the even bigger fear that she might find evidence that implicated her husband in something illegal.

It had been a tense moment when her husband had returned home and caught her on his computer. For a split second she had felt a surge of panic when he had surprised her standing at his computer in his study. She immediately recovered, however, and said with a somewhat forced air of composure, "I was hoping that your address list might have your dad's zip code. You know how I can never remember his address. Tomorrow it's been four years since your mom's death, and I thought I would send him a card to help cheer him up." It seemed to work, although she had trouble sometimes reading her husband's inner thoughts, and although he looked doubtful for a moment, he said nothing. That look, however, only strengthened her resolve to find out the truth.

Her new position as BSI vice president gave her the necessary authority to sign out keys to storage boxes at Technology Systems. However, when she made her mind up that she would have to see what was in box Y1721, the thought occurred to her that the Technology Systems records would show that she had accessed the box, which might put her in a dangerous position if there actually was anything wrong going on. It took her a week to devise a plan that would hide the fact that she had accessed box Y1721.

Two days earlier she had set up an account for a new storage box under the pretense that the BSI development department had files associated with the acquisition of non-military projects, including Hamburg Shipping that needed to be archived off site. She had gone to Technology Systems and filed the paperwork to assign another box to BSI. Box Y1801 was assigned by a woman at the Technology Systems office and Lisa had transferred a number of files with relatively unimportant data for Technology Systems to archive into the box.

After two days of working up her courage, she had finally phoned to say that she would be down within an hour to access a BSI storage box. When she arrived, Lisa walked into the front office and approached the security desk. The guard looked up from a cheap romance novel and said, "Can I help you?"

Lisa replied, "I'm Lisa Kerrigan and I have an appointment to access a Billings Shipping storage box."

The guard picked up a phone and dialed. "I have a Lisa Kerrigan here who says she needs to access a box." After a brief silence while the guard listened, he hung up the phone and said, "Please sign in here." He pushed a notebook forward and handed Lisa a pen.

After signing in, the guard looked into her laptop case and, convinced that there was nothing suspicious, he stated, "Third floor." He buzzed the lock on the half-height passage door and turned back to his book.

Lisa walked over to the elevator bank. So far so good, she thought, but the real test was yet to come.

As she exited the elevator on the third floor, a man in his late twenties or early thirties met her. "Good afternoon, Ms Kerrigan. If you will just come with me, we'll get you signed in."

Lisa thought that this might be easier than expected, given what looked like a young, new employee who might be intimidated by power.

When they reach the registration desk, the man took a seat behind the desk and brought forward a security box access form. The young man looked somewhat embarrassed as he said, "I'll need to see some identification, please."

Lisa took this awkward moment to gain establish her authority. She put her driver's license and BSI security card on the table in front of the man with the title BSI Vice President clearly visible.

"Look, I don't have much time here. I have a board meeting at four o'clock and I just need to access a disk in one of our boxes. The trouble is, I'm not exactly sure if the information I need is on a disk in box Y1721, Y1796, or Y1801. I need all three keys, but I'll actually only need to access a disk in one of these three boxes. I'll know it immediately when I see it. Why don't you just give me all three keys and when I see which box contains the right disk, I'll just return the other two keys."

The man looked at bit confused but then said, "That's fine, but I'll need you to fill out three forms, one for each box key."

If this was going to work, Lisa thought, it was time to bring out her nasty side.

"Listen son, I told you I'm in a hurry. I don't have time to sit here and fill out paperwork all afternoon. I only want to access one box. I'll fill out the form for that box when I come out."

Her abrupt tone brought a nervous squawk out of the young clerk.

Lisa delivered what she hoped would be the final blow. "In case you didn't notice, I am the vice president of your largest client. And, if you take the time to do your job, you'll see that I have authorization to access all of BSI's holdings here. Do I make myself clear? Just give me the three keys and I'll return the two I don't need."

The young man was clearly rattled. After a moment's indecision he said, "Box Y1721, Y1796, and Y1801. Yes, ma'am." He opened the locked door behind him and returned with three keys. "Your boxes are in room three-zero-seven, second door on the right."

Lisa took the keys before he could change his mind and marched down the hall. When she got to the door, the clerk buzzed the lock, and she went in.

Inside the room, the lights came on automatically, illuminating a back wall with safety deposit boxes. In the center of the room was a table with two chairs. Lisa quickly took out her laptop and set it up on the table. She went over to box Y1721 and inserted the key with nervous anticipation. When the box door opened and she had slid out the box, she was surprised to see that there was only a single disk inside. She had expected to find many disks which would have made copying them a time-consuming effort. She slid the single disk into her laptop and within thirty seconds the copy was complete. She put the disk back into the box and returned it to its place.

Packing her laptop back into the bag, she exited the room to find the young clerk sitting at the desk.

"It turns out the disk I needed was in Box Y1801 and I got what I needed." She handed the three keys to the man and took a single form. She hastily filled out the information identifying her and the fact that she had accessed box Y1801 on this date and time. The man took the three keys, reviewed the form quickly, and said hopefully, "Is that all you'll need?"

On her way out of the building Lisa smiled to herself with a sense of accomplishment. If anyone were to check, they would see that Lisa Kerrigan had accessed the box that she herself had set up for her department and there would be no record of her looking into the mysterious box Y1721. Now it was time to find out the truth about her husband.

\*\*\*

Steven Brown found himself becoming increasingly frustrated with one aspect of his position at BSI. It was true that he had never been so challenged as he was with his efforts in the development of the new weapons guidance technology system. But this was exactly what he had hoped for. It was exciting to be working with a talented group of design engineers who were breaking new ground in the field of weapons electronics. What Steven had not found so positive was the continuing annoyance brought on by his boss, the CEO, James Macintyre.

What had started out as just an apparent enthusiastic interest on behalf of the CEO in the details of the engineering of the project had turned into an extreme annoyance of management involvement in engineering technical matters. At first Steven had thought it mildly amusing that Macintyre had decided to attend the weekly engineering tech meetings. Macintyre sat with writing pad in hand, taking down notes on what the team was working on, including complex problem solving, with both electronics equipment development, as well as with software design.

Clearly, someone with a business degree would understand very little of what was being discussed and would understand even less the complicated diagrams and schematics that were brainstormed. But there sat the CEO, week after week, feverously taking down notes like a first-year philosophy undergraduate student stuck in a mandatory math class. Every so often Macintyre would interrupt the meeting and ask a question about how a system was intended to work, or how the components needed to be manufactured. These interruptions began as a tolerated annoyance, but over the subsequent weeks, as the design became more involved, Macintyre and his naive questions became an outright irritation to all.

Steven sat at his desk gazing out his window. Things had come to a head at this morning's tech meeting and Macintyre had left in a huff. The team's lead systems programmer had finally had enough of Macintyre's interruptions and had lost his cool. Macintyre had asked about the details of the software development with regards to guidance commands and when the lead programmer answered with specifics that went way beyond Macintyre's understanding, the CEO had asked for an answer in a language other than that spoken by *computer geeks*. The programmer threw his pen at the white board and responded by saying what every engineer in the room felt. He turned to Brown and fumed, "Listen, we've had to put up with insipid questions at these meetings since we began. It's a waste of time and it's counterproductive. Frankly, I don't understand why management should even be at technical design

92

meetings. As long as we deliver the product, the paper pushers should just leave us alone."

As the team leader, Steven squirmed with a sentiment of divided feelings. On the one hand, he firmly agreed with the programmer's assessment. On the other hand, no one can talk to the company's CEO with such an obvious degree of disrespect without expecting disciplinary action. In this case, Steven had a pretty good idea where that disciplinary action would land. As Macintyre stormed out of the room, the words, "Brown, see me in my office in one hour!" echoed off the walls as the group sat in silence.

Steven turned away from the window and returned his attention back to his computer. The meeting with Macintyre hadn't gone that badly he told himself. The team would actually be glad that he could tell them that Macintyre would not be attending any future tech meetings. What bothered him was the request by Macintyre to forward an electronic copy of all technical documents on a weekly basis to the CEO's computer account. This included not only copies of the weekly progress of technical specifications, but also software programs and technical drawings. Brown admitted to himself that this request was certainly within the scope of authority of the CEO, but a small voice in the back of his mind raised an unanswered question as to why management would want to keep such a close eye on the team's work. He couldn't help but feel that it was probably because of a lack of confidence that upper management had in his abilities to produce results in a timely manner. But if that were true, he thought, why not assign an independent engineer who would be able to interpret the technical aspects of the work to report to back to management? Perhaps this had already been done behind the scenes, and management preferred not to let his presence be known to the team.

Whatever the reason, there was little Brown could do about it and with that admission he pushed the send button beginning the transfer of five gigabytes of files to Macintyre's company account.

# Chapter 8

The afternoon closing bell rang and Sally Brown gathered her books and notebook and headed off to the chemistry room. This was not going to be an enjoyable experience. Each of the other school newspaper reporters had already finished their draft copies of interviews with the new teachers at Billings High and Sally knew that she could no longer put off her interview. She had been able to find very little background information on Mr Wilhelm. It was almost as if he had simply materialized out of thin air. None of the other teachers knew much about him. Apparently, he kept entirely to himself and each day after the close of school he returned to who-knew-where.

One week ago, Sally had approached him after class and stated that she was writing an article for the student newspaper on the new teachers at school and she would like to interview him to include in her story. Wilhelm had not even looked up when he pronounced, "I do not think I am available."

Sally stood looking at him in amazement. What did that mean? Not available? She continued. "I don't necessarily mean to take up your time now, I would like to schedule an appointment for some time when you are free."

Again, Wilhelm did not look up when he responded. "No, I am not free. You *vill* have to find someone else to interview. Good day, Miss Brown."

Wilhelm's attitude made Sally more resolved. She clenched her teeth and said, "Fine. I guess you won't mind being singled out as the one new teacher with something to hide so he wouldn't give an interview."

Wilhelm suddenly looked up. After a pause and a look that could stop a charging rhino in its tracks, he said, "See me next Thursday after class in the lab." With no further pronouncements, Sally understood that she had just been dismissed.

At first when Sally entered the chemistry lab, she did not see Mr Wilhelm. Her immediate thought was that he had changed his mind and had not bothered to inform her. As she looked around the room, he suddenly appeared from the small lab prep room at the rear.

"Ah, Miss Brown, I see that you are punctual. Very good. What do you want to know?"

Sally took a seat at the front row lab bench and took out her notebook.

"Let's begin by telling a bit about where you are from."

Wilhelm, sitting on a corner of the instructor's table, replied, "I am from Germany, but now I am from Billings."

This was not going to be easy thought Sally.

"What part of Germany are you from? I presume you were born there."

"I was born in the DDR, but I do not see what this has to do with my teaching here."

Sally decided to change directions and get right to the point.

"How long have you been teaching chemistry and where did you teach before coming to Billings?"

Wilhelm folded the book he was reading and said, "This is my first year at Billings."

As the frustration level grew, Sally asked in an exasperated tone, "I *know* this is your first year here at Billings. My question was, where did you teach before coming to Billings?"

"Before I was a teacher, I had another position."

"And can you tell me what that position was and where you worked?"

Wilhelm thought for a moment and said with a tone of finality, "The only thing that is important is that I am now a teacher here." With that, he got up and left the room.

Sally sat in stunned amazement. The interview had lasted less than two minutes, and she had learned nothing of interest. It only took her a few seconds to decide as to her next course of action. There was no way that she was going to let this pass. If Wilhelm thought she was just some dumb kid that could be brushed off with a few glib remarks he would find out differently.

It was nine o'clock on a moonless night and Billings High was completely dark. Sally had waited outside the school for just over an hour waiting for the last of the janitors to leave the building. Sally looked up into the night sky and said a prayer of thanksgiving for the darkness of night that typified Maine.

The rear door to the school led from a corridor that was seldom used since it connected the main part of the school with only the mechanical rooms. Sally walked quickly up to the door, keeping within the shadows, and slid the door open. The duct tape that she had put over the door latch that afternoon had held, just as she knew that it would, preventing the lock from being secured. So much for Homeland Security she thought as she entered the dark corridor. She had read in the local newspaper that the school district had recently received funds from the federal government to install surveillance cameras and an intrusion detection system at the high school, but she also knew that it was not scheduled to be put in place until Thanksgiving break.

The halls were amazingly dark but there was no way that Sally would turn on a light. For all the days that Sally had walked these halls, they now seemed very unfamiliar. After orienting herself she decided that she would have to trust her memory of the building plan, rather than look for familiar signs along the way. When she finally reached the main corridor, a small amount of light filtered through to the corridor from the windows of the main office that had a view to the outside.

Sally approached the door to the principal's outer office and tried the door only to find that it was locked, as she had expected. Rather than being a dead-bolt lock, the office lock was an old doorknob lock. The pitiful lock and latch, along with ancient wood door and wood frame, would allow even a kindergartener to gain entrance, thought Sally. A minute later, she put away her fingernail file and entered the outer office.

From her back pocket Sally withdrew a tiny LED flashlight and shone it around the room, being careful not to let the light hit any of the outside windows. Several vertical filing cabinets stood in the far corner of the room. Careful not to touch or disturb anything, Sally crept over to the filing cabinets. This would be more difficult than she had hoped since the filing cabinets stood immediately beside a large window to the outside. Sally knew from their position that if anyone passed by and looked toward the office, they would very likely see her, but it was a risk she needed to take. At this point, she thought, there was no turning back.

She shone her light at the first filing cabinet, but she did not find what she was looking for. The second filing cabinet seemed to contain student records which were of no interest. It was the third cabinet that caught her attention, specifically, the third drawer down whose label reach, *Faculty/Staff Files*. She reached over to the drawer and found much to her dismay, that it was locked!

She had not anticipated this. It was bad enough that she had entered the school illegally, but no way was she going to forcibly enter a locked filing cabinet. So close, she thought but this looked like a dead end. Then it occurred to her that it was very possible that the key might be in the office somewhere. What were the obvious places to keep a filing cabinet key?

Sally carefully stepped over to the school secretary's desk in the darkness and opened the drawer under the desktop. Upon finding only pens, pencils and paper clips, she tried the side drawers. Each of them only contained file folders with standard forms and class schedules. She looked at her watch with growing desperation and realized that she had been inside for just over fifteen minutes already. When planning this escapade, she had figured that that would probably be the limit before the risk of being discovered tipped the odds against her favor.

She shone her tiny flashlight around the walls to look for any sign of a box for keys but found none. It was becoming apparent that this evening would end with the same results that her interview with Wilhelm had achieved this afternoon, *none at all*. She leaned up against the filing cabinet and gave a sigh of surrender. As her back rested against the cabinet it tilted slightly backwards and she heard a slight metallic sound behind her on the top of the cabinet. She turned around and put her hand on the top of the cabinet, and miraculously, she felt a set of keys.

With keys in hand, Sally reached down and opened the third drawer. Inside were file folders with the names of all the teachers printed on the top tabs. She flipped to the back of the drawer and thumbed through Walsh, West, and then Wilhelm. She removed Wilhelm's file and was immediately surprised at how thin it was. She opened it up and discovered only a single typed form of some kind inside. The light was too dim to be able to read the form, but she had no intention of staying to read it. She felt her way over to the office copy machine and put the paper inside the top cover. She pushed the copy button and the machine sprung to life from its "sleep mode'." As the copy was being made, the machine made a noise that Sally thought would be heard for miles around, but she took comfort in the fact that she should be out of the building before anyone passing by might be attracted.

The copy machine ground to a halt and the copy was ejected at the end tray. As Sally reached for the sheet her universe exploded. A bright light shown through the corridor window and a voice boomed out "Who's in there?"

Sally froze in a state of absolute terror. The voice called out again as the powerful flashlight was directed into the office, "I know somebody's in there. Come out right now and no one will get hurt."

***

Lisa Kerrigan could not believe what she was seeing on her husband's computer screen. It was evening and Tim had gone off to a Paulsen Free Library board of trustees meeting. This had finally given Lisa the opportunity for some alone time on her husband's computer.

As she sat examining files her thoughts raced back to the information that she had copied from the disk at Technology Systems earlier in the week. She had hurried back to her office after leaving with the copy and cleared her schedule for the next hour to review whatever it was that was so important that it required its own storage box. Surprisingly, the disk from the storage box contained only one file. When she opened the file, Lisa found that it contained a single line of alphanumeric code, 178NM684LC9113JP.

Lisa had no idea what the code might mean. She did not recognize it as being associated with any computer programs at BSI. The mystery had lodged in her mind with no answer for the past week. The frustration of not knowing its significance had only made her more certain that she had to find the truth behind Greg Connor's accusation about her husband.

She did not exactly know when she had first considered the possibility of accessing the restricted company computer files to search for something relevant, but over the past forty-eight hours it had become a certainty that this must be done. The problem was, she did not have access to restricted files. Furthermore, if she attempted to illegally gain access at work and she were to be discovered, it would undoubtedly raise questions that she did not want to have to answer.

The answer came as she and Tim were getting ready for work that morning.

"Don't forget I have a library board meeting this evening," Tim had called out from the dressing room while getting ready. "I don't really have time for it but I can't miss two meetings in a row. I'll have to work tonight at home before the meeting and finish up my report for the annual meeting after I get home. I can access the files I'll need from the office from my laptop here. Don't bother making supper for me. I'll be working in the study."

Lisa waited for fifteen minutes after her husband had left for the board meeting. Assured that he was not going to return, she walked into the study. Tim's laptop computer was in its usual place on his desk. She sat down and happily discovered that he was still connected to the BSI server. With the BSI's president's computer access permission, Lisa could examine any files on the company server.

It took Lisa only five minutes to locate the Hamburg Shipping files. There were hundreds of files but one subdirectory caught her attention. The subdirectory name of 'Kerrigan Files' stood out from all others. No other subdirectories contained any personal names. When she clicked on the subdirectory, she saw two files.

Both files turned out to be encrypted and required a password to be read. Lisa sat and tried several words that came to mind, but none worked. On a whim she decided to try the code that she had gotten off the disk in her husband's storage box, 178NM684LC9113JP. Like magic, the files began to be decrypted.

The first file was titled 'Arrangement Notes'. She opened the file and began reading.

*AN INITIAL PAYMENT WILL BE MADE IN THE AMOUNT OF TWENTY-FIVE THOUSAND US DOLLARS.*

*TRANSFERS SHALL BE MADE MONTHLY.*

*TRANSFERS SHALL BE MADE IN UNMARKED PACKET AT THE SPECIFIED DROP POINT.*

*PAYMENT WILL BE DEPOSITED WITHIN SEVEN DAYS OF MONTHLY TRANSFERS.*

*REGULAR CONTACT SHALL ONLY BE INITIATED BY THE RECEIVING PARTY.*

*FINAL PAYMENT WILL BE MADE UPON REVIEW, TESTING AND ACCEPTANCE OF THE COMPLETED TRANSFER.*

The Second file was titled 'Account'. It simply read:

*BANK OF AMERICA12 376 8900*

This certainly did not look good Lisa thought. How could Tim be involved with an embezzlement scheme? And how could he have done this without her being aware of it?

***

Sally looked out the school office window to the outside and saw a police car parked at the curb. The patrol officer had obviously not turned on his flashing lights or siren when the approach was made. Inside the car was an officer who appeared to be talking on the car radio.

The door to the office was being rattled by the policeman in the corridor and Sally knew that it was just a matter of time until he was able to force open the door lock. She grabbed the copy that she had made and quietly went through the door into the adjoining principal's office. The principal's office was a small office that had doors to both the outer secretary's office as well as directly to the corridor. Sally stood listening and in seconds heard the outer office open and the policeman enter. As the outer office door opened, Sally quietly slipped out into the corridor through the principal's door. The corridor was dark, but Sally had no time to worry about the limited visibility. She hustled down the corridor away from the office towards the side entrance door. When she reached the side door, she turned and saw the policemen now back in the corridor pointing his flashlight down the hall. He was speaking into his radio and as she opened the side door the flashlight beam reached her for an instant. She could only hope that the brief moment in the light had not given the policeman sufficient opportunity to see her clearly.

Sally quickly ran down the side door steps in the darkness and immediately collided with the second patrol officer, sending Sally sprawling backwards onto the sidewalk. The patrol officer was a woman who was knocked onto her rear end in the collision. She sat down hard, temporarily knocking the wind out of her, leaving her struggling for breath. Sally quickly collected her wits and jumped up. She was not hurt other than a slightly bruised elbow, and taking advantage of the patrol officer's incapacity, she ran off cutting through a neighbor's back yard.

Sally ran for all she was worth knowing that if she were to be caught it would be not only embarrassing for her, but it would also be disappointing to her dad. She reached the sidewalk at the next street and pulled up at a streetlight breathing hard. She looked behind but neither saw nor heard anyone following. Just as she began to relax a bit a police car with flashing lights turned the corner ahead with a spotlight shining out into the darkness.

Sally quickly turned up Lincoln Street and began running again. She was a significant way away from her home, but she was only several houses away from where Henry lived. In a split second she made a decision and headed off toward Henry's. When she arrived, she rushed up to the front door and rang the doorbell. As she looked down the street, she saw the police car turn onto the street heading slowly in her direction.

The door opened and Henry's father stood looking out. When he saw Sally, he turned back and yelled into the house, "Henry, another school friend is here." He then turned back to Sally and said, "Come on in, Henry's upstairs in his room with Sheila. You can go on up."

Sally quickly stepped inside as the patrol car moved on by in the street. She entered the front hall and Henry called down from the top of the stairs. "Hey Sheila, guess who's here! It's Sally. Hey Sally, come on up."

When Sally entered Henry's room at the top of the stairs, she saw Henry and Sheila sitting at a desk that was covered in computer equipment. In fact, it was difficult to recognize the room as a bedroom at all with the extent of computer hardware stacked in every available spare space. The room looked more like a large company's data processing server room than a teenager's bedroom.

Henry and Sheila looked up and greeted Sally.

She took a seat on the only exposed corner of the floor and let loose with a narration of the evening's excitement.

Henry and Sheila looked at each other in amazement and Sheila finally said, "Wow! That was close! I can't believe that you had the nerve to break into the school. I'm not surprised, however, that you haven't found much out about Wilhelm. He is such a creep, and he talks to no one about his past."

Remembering the purpose of the evening, she pulled out the copy of the file sheet on Mr Wilhelm. The three studied the single page in amazement as they all read the contents. The paper was a letter from a man named Tim Kerrigan with the title Chief Executive Officer, Billings Shipyard, Incorporated. The letter was dated from April of the current year and it provided a recommendation to hire Mr Gustav Wilhelm as the chemistry teacher for the upcoming year. The letter stated that Mr Wilhelm did not have a Maine teacher's certification, but that Mr Kerrigan would have the State Board of Education approve his position. It further read that Mr Wilhelm was eminently qualified in chemistry. It also stated that Mr Wilhelm would be consulting from time to time for BSI and that in addition to picking up his consulting fees, BSI would also make a donation to the school board to cover the entire year's salary for Mr Wilhelm.

After reading the letter, all three sat in amazed silence.

Sally began by voicing what the others were also thinking. "This is wrong. There is something wrong here. Who is this man? Doesn't the school care that he is a lousy teacher? And what's more, it looks like he has no teaching credentials!"

Henry replied, "I'll tell you what the school cares about. They care that they got a free chemistry teacher for the year."

Sheila spoke up from her silence. "This is big. Think what we can do with this in the *Cruiser Gazette!*"

Sally thought for a moment and said, "Maybe we should get a few more facts before we go public. It wouldn't look good if we made unsubstantiated claims. Remember, we can't very well cite office records that we aren't supposed to have access to."

"I guess you're right," Sheila replied. "Maybe you could contact the State Department of Education to find out more about Wilhelm, like why would the state sanction an uncertified teacher?"

Sally said, "Good idea, I call tomorrow. I'll make it sound like I'm just doing an article for the paper. Maybe I can get them to open up about Wilhelm if it doesn't look like we're suspicious."

Henry had been working on his computer while the girls were talking. He turned and said, "Hey, it's great you showed up, Sally. We're just about to order our driver's licenses!"

Sally looked doubtful. "Look, I know I suggested this, but maybe we should reconsider. How are we ever going to get real driver's licenses that say we're twenty-one?"

"Actually," replied Henry, "it's quite simple. All I need to do is make sure that the necessary information is in the Division of Motor Vehicles' records and then we apply for a replacement license online. The system is fully automated. It will send out licenses in a week."

"But how do you get the necessary information into the records in the first place?" Sheila asked.

"Well, for you, it's easy. You already have a license. Watch this."

Sheila objected. "Hey, wait just a minute. I just got this license, and I don't want to lose it."

"Relax. I've got everything under control," was Henry's response.

Henry entered in several lines of code and the screen on the desk went blank. In less than a minute, the screen brought up a site that was identified as the State of Maine Division of Motor Vehicles' computer server. A menu popped up inquiring which record was to be accessed. Henry typed in Sheila's license number and the screen immediately showed a form with Sheila's picture in the upper right.

"Hey, how did you do that?" Sheila asked. "That's me!"

Henry beamed with pride. "It's really quite simple once to know how to get into the state's main server. That's what took me a while."

Henry started typing over the record fields. "What do you want for a new name? We shouldn't use our own names just in case. How about Brittney Spears?"

Sheila gave Henry a shove and said, "No way I want to be a Brittney! Make me Stella Winslow. I had an Aunt Stella."

After several minutes of typing, Henry had created a new file for a Stella Winslow, aged twenty-one, with an address listed as 235 North Street, Billings, Maine.

Sally looked at the finished file and asked, "What about the address? Is it real?"

Henry said, "We can't use our own addresses because if anything goes wrong, we don't want to be traced. This is the big green house up on North and Middle Streets. The Millers who own the place are friends of my dad. They are away for a month on vacation and dad said that we'd collect their mail for them while they're away. Actually, I go over after school each day and get it. We'll all use this same address."

With that, Henry brought up a blank form. He reached down and pulled out a digital camera from the lower desk drawer. "Here, Sheila, you need to take a picture of me and Sally so that I can set up our records."

Henry stepped over to the side wall where a blue blanket was hung as a backdrop. He stood facing the center of the room and Sheila took his photo. Next, Sally took his place and Sheila took her photo. "I would have dressed for the occasion if I had known it was going to be formal."

After downloading the digital images into his computer, Henry forwarded them into the state's computer database and then returned to the license files he was creating.

"I can paste the photos into these blank forms and set up our records. Earlier today I forwarded our signatures which need to be on the forms."

Sally interrupted. "You forwarded *my* signature? It won't look like my writing!"

Henry continued work as he spoke. "Well, actually, it will look exactly like your writing, since it *was* your writing. I tapped into the school's records and copied your signature from your Billings High application that was on file."

Sally didn't know whether to be angry that her personal information had been accessed or to be impressed by Henry's computer skills.

Henry pasted his photo from the state's database on the license form and filled in the blanks. "I'm going to be Thomas Wright. I've already used that name to get a credit card. I knew we would need one to secure the room at the hotel. I'm twenty-four years old."

Sheila laughed. Who's going to believe that you're twenty-four?"

Henry gave her a sharp glance and said with wounded pride, "I'll be sure not to shave that week."

Sheila picked up the American Express credit card that had the name Thomas Wright imprinted on the front. "How were you able to get this?"

With an air of superiority Henry replied, "Hey, anyone can get a credit card nowadays. They practically beg you to get one. When they find that you don't have any bad credit, and you're older than twenty-one, it's a sure thing."

Sally decided to take the name of Susan Blanchard and was entered with a birth date making her twenty-one years old. When he finished, Henry said, "There, that takes care of that. Now all I have to do is file for replacement licenses online for the three of us."

Sally noticed that the time was now just past eleven o'clock. "I had better get back home or my dad will start to get nervous," she said.

"I'll give you a ride home," Sheila said as she got up.

Suddenly, Sally went pale and dropped back onto the bed. "Good heavens! I just remembered something. Mr Wilhelm's original file is still in the copier at school! What will happen when the secretary discovers it in the morning?"

# Chapter 9

Johann Steiner sat at a dark, dirty table in a back room of Der Schlupfwinkel, a nightclub on Herbertstrasse in the Reeperbahn section of Hamburg. The room was filled with cigarette smoke, loud music and raucous noise coming through the open door leading from the front room. The front contained a large bar with a raised stage that served as a dance platform for an endless parade of mostly naked girls. The bar was crowded with men that included the down and out who spent nearly every Euro, as well as nearly every hour, trying to escape the pain of reality. But the bar also included students from Universität Hamburg, affluent local businessmen, as well as many visiting tourists.

The Reeperbahn section of the city, with its longstanding reputation for its strip clubs and prostitutes, had become a recognized institution throughout Europe. In the eighteenth and nineteenth centuries the section of town had received its name from the quantity of hempen rope produced for the thriving shipping industry. In later years, the district became home to playhouses and theaters that were banished from the city in its more socially and morally restrictive times. Over the years the focus of entertainment changed from the dramatic to the erotic as the district took on an increasingly seedier character.

The Reeperbahn was nearly always crowded on a Saturday evening, but following the Oktoberfest, every club was overflowing with patrons carrying on the celebration in spite of the fact that the actual observance had formally concluded. Ordinarily, Johann Steiner, the lead accountant for the largest shipping company in Hamburg, would not be seen in such a setting. He sat waiting alone at his table in the corner of the room with a glass of locally brewed beer. The back room of this particular establishment was frequented mostly by the prostitutes and their customers. Although legal during certain hours of the day, the police occasionally found it necessary to intervene in the prostitution trade when the usually non-violent activities got out of control, most often due to drugs and organized crime.

Two well-dressed Asian men entered the back room. While the men stood inside the doorway searching the dark room, two ladies approached in hopes of a lucrative engagement. Seeing Steiner, the men quickly waved the women off and moved toward his table. They each grabbed a chair and sat down.

"This isn't exactly an ideal meeting place," said one of the men as he laid his briefcase on the table.

"Actually," Steiner replied, "it's perfect. Where do you go when you want to be invisible? The best place to be is in plain sight, surrounded by a crowd. Besides, no one could follow you here without our noticing."

The briefcase was opened, and a stack of papers was brought out.

"So, tell me. Are they on the right track?" Steiner inquired.

The man who carried the briefcase responded. "They seem to be on to something. The plans are definitely incomplete, but there is great potential here. If they can resolve the control conflicts here and here," the man pointed to a large diagram on the table, "they will have perfected the most accurate, and yet least expensive, missile guidance system ever produced. The work is brilliant in its simplicity!"

Steiner took a sip from his beer and replied. "This is good news. I will be receiving updated progress sets monthly until the work is completed..."

Before he could complete the sentence, a loud commotion was heard through the door in the front room. Shots were being fired and people were screaming. At once, three policemen came through the door into the back room and shouted for everyone to remain in place and not to move. As if the order had commanded just the opposite, everyone in the back room immediately stood up in panic and began to charge past the policemen towards the front, creating absolute pandemonium.

Steiner quickly stuffed the papers back into the briefcase. He yelled over to the others at the table. "We cannot be involved in this. There is a back door in the corridor over there." Pointing to a hall in the far corner of the room, he motioned to the two men. "Get going. I'll contact you by phone."

He hurriedly gathered his things and then forced his way past the crowd to the corridor where his two accomplices had just fled. When he passed through the rear exit door, he saw that the two others had apparently been confronted by two policemen who were stationed to guard the rear exit. They were running off down the street in an attempt to avoid capture and were being pursued by the policemen. Steiner turned the corner and disappeared down the side alley into darkness.

***

Thirty minutes later, control had returned to the inside of the nightclub. Several men were seated at the front bar in handcuffs, along with six ladies of the evening. In the rear room two detectives were questioning the owner of the establishment while two uniformed patrol officers were looking around the room. One of policemen leaned over at an empty table along the rear wall and picked up a piece of paper.

"Gunter, come look at this."

The second policeman came over and looked at the paper. In very large letters stamped across the top of the paper the officer read:

*TOP SECRET CONFIDENTIAL*
*UNITED STATES NAVY SUPIVISOR OF SHIPS*
*DO NOT DISTRIBUTE TO UNAUTHORIZED PERSONS UNDER MAXIMUM PEANALTY OF LAW*

At the bottom of the paper were the words:

*THIS DOCUMENT BELONGS TO BILLINGS SHIPYARD, INC, BILLINGS MAINE*

***

Sally, Henry and Sheila stood in the hall outside the school office waiting for the secretary to arrive. The three had met early that morning to plan their strategy for retrieving the original of Mr Wilhelm's file from the office copier. It was just after seven a.m. as Mrs Cooper, the school secretary, came down the hall. The three carefully hid from sight around the corner while Mrs Cooper unlocked the door. They had all agreed that timing would be critical. If the secretary confronted them prior to opening the office, the scheme would never get off the ground.

As Mrs Cooper went through the door, Henry and Sheila quickly slid in behind her.

"Oh my," she exclaimed. "I didn't see you there. What could you both possibly be doing here at this time of the morning?"

Sheila promptly answered. "We're here to do some work on the school newspaper before classes start. Can you open the computer lab for us?"

Mrs Cooper thought for a moment and then said, "Does Mr Greely know about this? You know how protective he is of his computer equipment."

Henry spoke up with an air of authority. "We're preparing a first draft of this month's newspaper for Mr Greely. You know he's our advisor, right?"

Mrs Cooper gave a sigh of acceptance and said, "Just a minute, I'll get the key." As she went over to the office desk, Henry nervously eyed the paper sticking out from the top of the copier.

"All right, you two, let's go unlock the lab door."

As they started down the hall Sally waited around the corner and began counting to herself to allow time to make sure that Mrs Cooper wouldn't return for some unexpected reason. At the count of thirty she quickly hurried over to the office door. Casting a glance back down the hall to confirm that Mrs Cooper wasn't there, she rushed into the office with her eyes still glued back on the hall, promptly colliding head on with Mr Wilhelm who was just leaving the office.

Wilhelm was hardly shaken but Sally nearly collapsed onto the floor, not so much from the collision, but from the shock of seeing Mr Wilhelm. Where had he come from, her mind screamed in panic?

"Miss Brown. And to what do we owe the pleasure of your company this early in the morning?" he sneered.

"I... I... I was just looking for Mrs Cooper."

"Well, as you can see, she is not here now. I, myself, was just looking for her, but seeing that she is apparently elsewhere, I had to leave a message. You, however, do not belong in the office when staff are not present. I suggest you come back another time."

With that, he ushered Sally out of the office, and he proceeded down the hall toward his classroom. Sally stood in stunned silence, not moving a muscle. When Mr Wilhelm disappeared from view, she quickly went back into the office.

Spotting the copier, Sally removed the file paper that was in the top tray and returned it to its place in Mr Wilhelm's file folder that lay on the top of the filing cabinet. Placing the file back in the third drawer of the filing cabinet, she turned to leave, however, her attention was drawn to the note that Mr Wilhelm had apparently left on the desk for Mrs Cooper. It was a folded piece of paper with Mrs Cooper's name handwritten on the top side.

Temptation overcame good judgment as Sally knew that Mrs Cooper would be returning any minute now. She leaned over the desk and unfolded the paper.

*Mrs Cooper:*
*I will be away attending my sister's funeral next week on Friday, November 21st.*
*Please arrange for a substitute teacher for the day.*
*G. Wilhelm.*

How like Wilhelm, thought Sally, no frills. It was surprising, however, to learn that the elusive chemistry teacher had a sister. If Wilhelm was only taking one day off, he couldn't be traveling too far. That meant that he might have family, or at least people who knew him, fairly close by.

Sally folded the note and put it back on the desk. She peeped out through the office door window, and not seeing anyone, she exited the office and headed off to the computer lab to tell Henry and Sheila the news.

***

110

The Hamburg Davidwache police station on Davidstrasse was in its usual state of noisy activity. People were coming and going as tourists sought directions, vagrants were being released after spending a drunken night of incarceration, and several suspects were being brought in for questioning relating to drug trafficking, which seemed to be ever on the increase.

The station commander, Peter Morgan sat in his office on the telephone struggling to hear over the commotion.

"What was that? Wait a moment please." He put the phone on the desk and walked around to close the door. Returning to his seat he continued.

"I need to be connected to Herr Grant in inspections."

There was a pause on the other end and the voice replied, "Who may I say is calling?"

With an undisguised tone of frustration, he responded, "This is Inspector Peter Morgan with the Hamburg Police."

Morgan had been with the department for twenty-seven years and each time he had found it necessary to deal with Interpol authorities, he had found it an unpleasant experience. The bureaucracy and paperwork of the police department was difficult but getting through the red tape of Interpol was nearly impossible.

After waiting five minutes a voice came on the line with a decidedly English accent.

"Good morning, Inspector Morgan. Sorry for the delay. This is Wayne Coffin, how can I help you?"

"Good day Mr Coffin. Last evening our department conducted an arrest of local organized crime members at a local establishment and in the process a document was discovered under a table in the back room that we feel may be of some significance."

"Can you tell me more about this document?"

Morgan pulled the paper out of his desk drawer and studied it again for the tenth time.

"It is a copy of a typed page written in English with the words printed at the top, *'top secret'* and *'confidential'*. It also has a label identifying it as property of the United States Navy with a warning not to distribute it to unauthorized persons."

The voice on the other end responded with somewhat disinterested concern. "Can you tell me what is on the paper?"

Morgan had told his superior officer that this was a waste of time, but the instruction came down to notify Interpol anyway. Time was better spent tracking down real criminals rather than chasing top secret papers that probably were prepared by a university student as some kind of prank.

"Well, I am not really qualified to interpret the diagram that is drawn on the paper. It looks like some kind of sophisticated electronics diagram, but on the other hand, it may very well be just a diagram for a staubsaugen... er... how do you say... a vacuum cleaner."

"Interesting, well you can just put it in the mail to our district office and we'll take care of it. There isn't anything else on the paper that might suggest what it is?"

Morgan took another look at the paper. "Well, there is a line under the diagram that says *'WG-116B guidance'* and at the bottom of the page is a line that states the page belongs to a Billings Shipyard, Inc located in Billings, Maine, USA.

There was a pause on the other end of the line. The voice suddenly had a note of genuine concern. "Please hold a moment while I look that up."

After another five minutes on hold that seemed like an eternity, a new voice came on the line. "This is Rear Admiral Chester Rand at the United States Pentagon in Washington. Your call has been transferred and we are going to be handling this matter. Please secure the document and a military courier will be sent by shortly to collect it."

Morgan glanced down at the paper again, wondering what was suddenly so important about this complicated diagram. He responded. "That won't really be necessary, I can have an officer drive it down to the American Embassy in Berlin..."

But before he could complete his sentence the vice admiral cut him off. "Listen, just do as you are told. Someone will be by within the hour. Make sure it is put in a secure place." With that the line went dead.

Morgan angrily folded the paper. *Americans,* he thought. They were all the same. They all thought that nothing could ever be done without their involvement. Well, he fumed, I have better things to do. He picked up his phone and dialed an officer at a desk in the outer office. "Manfred, come in to my office please. I have a paper that needs to be taken down to the evidence locker."

Manfred Spear stuck his head in the inspector's office. "You needed a delivery boy?"

Morgan handed over the folded sheet of paper and said, "Very funny. Just take this down and put it away in the locker. An American will be stopping by shortly to pick it up."

Manfred Spear was the department's newest officer. He had graduated from the training academy just last month and had been assigned by headquarters to the Davidwache Station as a patrol officer. In spite of his tender age, there was something about him that gave Morgan a feeling that Spear was, if not well seasoned, at least not entirely reckless, as was the usual case with new recruits. The last thing the inspector needed was another inexperienced trainee but he had taken a liking to him on the very first day.

Spear grabbed the paper and headed for the stairs that lead to the basement. On his way out of the office, he turned back and said with a huge smile, "Thanks boss for trusting me with this top-secret document. Don't worry, I'll make sure it gets to the basement and I'll be sure not to read it."

The evidence locker was located in a dark corner of the basement level where general supplies and other equipment was also stored. The locker was actually just a metal cabinet with a combination lock on the front door. It was attended at all times by a duty officer who restricted access to the locker. The duty officer was usually found seated at a desk adjacent to the locker, most often watching the small television that was set on the desktop.

As a measure of security, Spear, along with the rest of the regular staff, did not know the locker combination. He would hand the paper over to the duty officer and collect a receipt that he would then deliver back to Inspector Morgan. It was a process that he had already performed numerous times in his short tenure at Davidwache. He was looking forward to chatting with the daytime duty man, Richard, who always had an off-color joke to tell. It was a process that Spear had come accustomed to, which was why, when he reached the basement level, he instantly knew that something was amiss. It took a second for him to realize what was of concern but, when it hit him, he knew that this was not right. The television on duty officer's desk was proclaiming the merits of a particular brand of beer, but the officer was nowhere to be seen.

The realization that the situation was indeed very wrong occurred almost simultaneously with his noticing a pair of feet on the floor that extended out from behind the desk. Spear reached for his service weapon, but before he could bring it up to a firing position, a man stepped out from behind a column and fired a silenced round that struck Spear in the center of his forehead. Blackness overtook the young officer before he hit the floor while the folded paper drifted in the air toward the killer.

\*\*\*

Lisa Kerrigan walked into the Billings branch of the Bank of America. The bank was busy with people on their lunch break doing banking errands. She stood in line behind three people and waited her turn considering the approach that might best yield results. When she finally reached a teller, she had reached a decision on what was likely her best option.

"Can I help you?" responded the young female teller with a smile.

"My husband and I have an account here and I would like to get the account balance."

The teller turned to her computer screen and said, "Certainly, can I have the account number and some identification? A driver's license will do."

Lisa had been prepared for the request and handed over her license and a piece of paper on which the account number 12 376 8900 was written. She stood smiling while the girl brought up the account.

"I'm sorry, our records show that this account is listed only in the name of Timothy Kerrigan. Without Mr Kerrigan's permission, I can't release that information."

Lisa reached into her purse without objection and pulled out a fifty-dollar bill. "That's okay, I understand. I guess I'll just deposit this fifty dollars if I may, into the account just to be safe. I hate it when the account gets down and we get a bank charge."

The teller took the bill and tapped numbers efficiently into the system. Lisa stood as nonchalantly as possible, hoping that she wasn't being too obvious. She focused all her attention on the receipt printer on the teller's counter, concentrating on the paper roll where it left the printer. In seconds, the receipt began printing. Lisa was able to see the date, her deposit amount, and just before it stopped printing, a balance amount that looked like either three hundred and fifty dollars or perhaps eight hundred and fifty dollars, it was impossible to tell for sure. The teller tore off the receipt and, with a black marker, scratched out the account balance so that it could not be read. Lisa took the receipt and said, "Thank you for your help."

Outside the bank, Lisa gave a deep sigh of relief as she stood leaning against her car. Whatever the amount, her husband's mystery account did not contain enough money to warrant suspicion of some grand embezzling scheme. You weren't going to get far on less than a thousand dollars. But why, then, was this account set up in the first place in his name, and why was there a record of it in the BSI restricted access files? Could it be possible that there had been more money in the account and that it had already been removed?

# Part 2: Complications

# Chapter 10

Frustration had turned to outright anger. Inspector Morgan had spent the past hour being grilled by both a United States naval commander as well as a man in a black suit representing some American security agency whose name was an indiscernible jumble of English letters. Worst of all, the Hamburg chief of police was standing silently over Morgan as he was being interrogated. Morgan was tired of being asked questions to which he had no answers. Who was the assassin? How did he get past the station's front desk? To where did the man disappear? Morgan just wanted to be left alone to do his job and find the answers but as long as he was being held in this interrogation room, nothing constructive was being accomplished.

The frustration that Morgan felt was focused on the fact that something like this had never before happened under his command. But also chewing at his composure was the attitude of the two Americans. They clearly felt neither concern nor compassion for the slain officers. The fact that young Manfred Spears had been killed within the first month of his duty meant nothing to these men. It appeared that their only interest was the paper that had vanished from the scene. Their uncaring demeanor had brought Morgan to a breaking point.

The chief sensed that Morgan was at the end of his patience and brought a halt to the interrogation by stating that apparently there was nothing more that could be learned and that if any new information surfaced the Americans would be contacted. The Americans obviously did not want to accept this but, realizing that there was nothing that they could do, they left.

After the Americans had left, the chief turned to Morgan.

"I don't have to tell you how bad this is. The mayor will want answers and he will want them fast, not to mention the international pressure that this will draw from our *friends* from the States. You've got one week to come up with something or I'll have to take over the investigation. Make it happen, Peter." With that, the chief strode out of the room leaving Morgan by himself.

When the chief left, Morgan went down to the basement. The forensics team had finished its examination. The bodies had been removed and were delivered to the morgue. Morgan knew that he had two tasks, neither of which did he want to face. He would have to go to talk with Manfred's parents as the next of kin. Following that, he would have to return to the station to conduct a press conference. Before tackling either, he had to find out if the forensics team had turned up anything useful.

When he reached the basement level, he saw Karl Schlimmer, the medical examiner, who was sitting on the desk at the evidence locker talking with the Richard Gross, a department homicide investigator. As Morgan walked over, both men looked up.

"Do we have anything?" Morgan asked.

"Looks like a professional job," replied the doctor. "A single shot dead center between the eyes for both."

Gross added, "It looks like a nine-millimeter. I doubt that we'll get anything from ballistics to trace. I have Williams upstairs talking to all the personnel who were here on the day shift to see if anyone can give us a clue how the killer got in. It looks like he probably got in through the back door as someone was leaving and the door was still open."

Morgan entered his investigative mode, lost in thought for several minutes. At last, he turned back to the senior detective. "So, what about our cameras?" he asked, already suspecting the answer.

Gross replied. "We found that the video cable that serves the outside back entry camera and the camera just inside here had been disconnected. It's hard to know how anyone was able to disconnect the camera without being recorded but the tape doesn't show any people in the vicinity either outside or in the back entry hall just prior to the feed going dead. It sure looks like whoever did this sure knew what he was doing."

Morgan looked around the room. One thing was clear, the perpetrator was obviously not stupid. On the floor in front of the duty officer's desk there was a white outline where the slain officer had fallen. Just at the foot of the stairs was a second outline on the floor where

Manfred had been shot. Morgan walked over to look closer. "Did forensics find anything that might help?" he asked.

Gross replied, "We dusted for fingerprints, but again, I'm not optimistic."

Morgan rubbed his tired eyes and thought for a moment. "Assuming the assailant was here to snatch the paper that I had Manfred bring down, how did he know when to be here and where to get it? He couldn't have coincidently just shown up at the exact moment when Manfred arrived. He must have been here for some time, waiting."

Gross shook his head in agreement. "Even so, we weren't able to find any evidence of the man so we have no idea when he arrived."

The frustration that Morgan felt was beginning to get the better of him. He turned to the medical examiner and said with an undisguised tone of sarcasm, "And can *you* tell me anything relevant?"

Herr Doctor Karl Schlimmer put out his cigarette and said in an even voice, "For instance..."

"For instance," Morgan responded, "do you have any idea of the time when the duty officer was shot? How long had he been deceased when he and Manfred were discovered?"

Schlimmer stood and said, "I'll have to do the autopsy of course to know for certain but examining the condition of the blood at the bullet entry, it looks like he has been deceased for between two and two and a half hours before I arrived."

Morgan glanced at is watch and then said, "And we know that Manfred was discovered ninety minutes ago. That means that the killer must have been here waiting for at least thirty minutes, and possibly for as much as an hour."

Morgan sat down in the duty officer's chair contemplating the facts. There didn't seem to be anything here that would be of help. Everything, except for the chalk outlines on the floor, was in its proper place, just as if nothing extraordinary had happened. That was when he noticed a pencil under the desk on the floor.

If there was one thing that Morgan knew about the day shift duty officer, it was that he was a nut for organization. Everything on the desk, in the drawers and on the room's shelves was not only carefully arranged, every item was perfectly set in place with a level of neatness that screamed compulsive behavior. In fact, hardly a week had gone by that the officer hadn't lodged a complaint against the night shift duty officer's 'slovenly habits' when empty soda cans and wrappers from candy bars were found on the desk.

So why was there a pencil under the desk? The likely answer was that it had fallen to the floor when the officer had been shot. But the duty officer's outline was a meter in front of the desk, which would make it hard to explain how the pencil on the desk had been hit by the falling officer. Perhaps he had been holding the pencil, but why would he be holding a pencil when he was being threatened at gunpoint?

Morgan didn't like details that didn't add up. He looked back at the desk and now couldn't help noticing a small pad of paper on the desk that was situated half on and half off the desk blotter as if it had been carelessly tossed there. This was not something that fitted with the behavior pattern of his duty officer.

Morgan reached over and studied the pad of paper. It appeared as though someone had written something and torn off the top sheet. There were shallow indents on what was now the top sheet where an impression was left from the writing.

Morgan asked the senior detective, "Forensics has photographed the room?"

Gross nodded in agreement as both he and Gustav looked on with curiosity.

Morgan picked up the pencil and carefully rubbed the pencil lead across the top sheet of paper. As the sheet became blackened by the pencil, a string of numbers appeared, each separated by hyphens. Morgan looked at the numbers and quickly recognized the combination to the evidence locker door lock.

Gross looked over Morgan's shoulder and said, "Is that what I think it is?"

Morgan asked the obvious question. "Why would the duty officer need to write down the combination to the locker?" Both Gross and Gustav shrugged.

"The answer," Morgan continued, "is that he wouldn't. My guess is that the killer threatened him with a gun, and he told the combination to the killer. Not trusting his memory, the killer probably wrote it down."

Gross thought for a moment and then said, "That means the killer was able to get into the locker. But when we showed up, the locker door was closed..."

Morgan interrupted. "Nothing was missing from the locker, right? That means that the killer opened the locker and when he didn't find what he was looking for, he closed it again. Likely, he didn't believe the officer when he was told that the paper Manfred was about to deliver wasn't in the locker. That's when he probably shot the officer and decided to wait for the paper to arrive."

"But how did he know when that would be?" Gustav interjected. "How did he know that it would be delivered at all?"

"How, indeed?" remarked Morgan, lost in thought. Suddenly an idea presented itself.

"There actually was only one way for him to know." He turned his attention back to the senior detective, and said, "Get the video surveillance tape of the squad room for the day and meet me in my office."

With that said, Morgan turned and left the room leaving Inspector Gross and Dr Schlimmer looking at each other with puzzled expressions.

*** 

Sally, Henry and Sheila sat in Henry's bedroom planning strategy. It was Tuesday evening the week before Thanksgiving. Henry was handing out driver's licenses.

"Not even the Maine State Police would suspect these. In fact, as far as the system is concerned, there is nothing *to* suspect, they're actually quite valid."

Sheila looked at her license and with concern written all over her face, she spoke up. "I don't know about this. I still feel like this could blow up and we could all get into serious trouble."

Henry put a reassuring hand on Sheila's shoulder. "Look, don't worry. Everything's going to be all right. We're not going to get into any trouble. This is just a road trip to gather information for debate. What could possibly go wrong?"

Sally could think of several things but chose not to voice her opinion. Instead, she passed several sheets of paper each to Henry and Sheila.

"The purpose of this research is to gather statistics that apply to people who are actually present and participating at a gambling establishment. Our debate opponents have been citing statistics from studies that are not based on direct data provided by people in casinos, but rather, they cite statistics from trends reported by government agencies and social service organizations. These statistics are biased since they only involve the experiences of people with very limited conditions."

Sally gave the others a moment to read the plan on the first page of her handout, and then she continued.

"We need to conduct a survey with actual casino guests which I believe will provide more accurate data. Specifically, our hypothesis involves three contentions, first, that most people who gamble at casinos are not addicted to gambling; second, that most people who gamble at casinos abide by a predetermined spending amount; and third, that hardly anyone leaves a casino entirely destitute from their gambling losses."

Henry, somewhat overwhelmed by Sally's explanation, interjected, "But exactly how do we go about getting our data?"

With patience, Sally replied, "We need to conduct a survey of people who are in the casino gambling. To make our survey legitimate, we must survey at least four hundred people."

Sheila exclaimed, "Four hundred people! That will take forever! Why do we need to interview so many?"

"With four hundred participants, if we ask the right question in the correct way, we will have a confidence level of ninety-five per cent with a margin of error of only five per cent. And as for the time required, if we each ask just two questions that take approximately one minute to answer, with about thirty seconds to connect with those being surveyed, that will require no more than three hours and twenty minutes for each of us. If we start at seven p.m., we should be done by ten thirty p.m."

Sally told the others to turn to the second page. "To minimize the effort, we will ask only two questions. You will see them at the top of page two."

On the top of the page Henry and Sheila saw the following:

1. *Have you gambled at a casino more than once in the past year?*
2. *Do you set a spending limit that you do not let yourself exceed when you gamble at casinos?*

Sheila looked up and asked, "Why only two questions, and why these two questions? Will they actually prove anything?"

Sally smiled and thought for a moment. "No, these questions won't actually prove anything. My hope is, however, that the answers we collect will, however, be useful in our next debate tournament. If, as I suspect, we find that a vast majority of people only visit a casino once per year, or less, it contradicts the proposal that chronic gambling at casinos is a serious problem. And, likewise, if we find that a majority of gamblers set a limit for losses that they will not exceed, it would contradict the proposal that gambling lead significant numbers of people to unmanageable debt."

Henry spoke up. "But wouldn't more questions give us more information to counter the opposition?"

Sally shook her head in agreement. "It probably would but we have a problem. I doubt that the casino would give us permission to conduct our survey. In fact, they probably would throw us out if we showed up with pens and clipboards bothering their clientele."

"Point well taken," said Sheila. "So exactly how do we pull this off?"

Sally replied. "This is why I suggested that we limit our questions to just two. We can ask these questions in a seemingly casual conversation with patrons. The trick will be to move around the casino floors getting close enough to people to ask our questions without drawing undue attention. On page three is a map of the casino. Actually, it's a map of three casinos. There are three casinos at Foxwoods that we will be visiting. Henry, you'll begin in the Grand Pequot Casino, Sheila you'll start in the Great Cedar Casino, and I'll take the Rainmaker Casino. After one hour, we'll all change casinos so that the security folks won't get suspicious. After hour two, we'll each move on again. The last half hour we'll join up together and all move through all three casinos."

Sally reached into her purse and brought out six red plastic devices and put them on the bedside table.

Henry picked one up and asked, "Hey, what are these?"

Sally picked one up and held it out. "These are simple counters, you know, like little league baseball umpires keep track of balls and strikes. In our case, we'll push the button on this end for yes and on this end for no. Keep one in each pocket. Your left pocket counter will track the answers for the first question. The right pocket counter will track the answers for the second question. With these hidden away in our pockets, no one will see us recording our answers and so no one should get suspicious."

"Wow!" exclaimed Henry. "You've really thought this through!"

"I wonder if she's thought through how we avoid jail if we get caught in a casino with fake IDs," said Sheila with just a bit of sarcasm.

"If all goes well, that shouldn't happen. But there's one more thing you both need to know. When you walk into the casino pick every fifth person you see to ask questions. Do not ask people who are together. Do not select people that you think might be easy to approach. Pick every fifth person, regardless of who they are or what they look like. Otherwise, our survey will be tainted. It won't be a truly random survey."

The three spent the next twenty minutes reviewing the maps to get familiar with the Foxwoods layout.

After they all had a comfortable feel for the facility plan, Henry shifted his focus to his computer and began tapping at the keys. After a few minutes he announced, "Well our room for Friday night has been booked."

Sheila looked surprised and then turned to Henry. "Tell me you didn't hack into the casino's reservation system!"

Henry looked back with a feigned expression of hurt feeling. "Oh, course not. I booked us a room. We may have to actually pay for this out of our own pocket, unless of course, we get lucky at the slots."

Sally immediately spoke up. "No! There will be no gambling. That's not why we're going. We need to promise each other that we will not gamble."

Both Henry and Sheila became serious. They both voiced a, "we promise", simultaneously.

There was a silence that followed for a full minute as each recognized the bond that this endeavor was forging between friends. To break what was becoming an air of awkwardness, Henry asked, "Are you both square with your parents about taking time off for this trip?" He knew well that none of their parents would sanction this teenage insanity. He casually mentioned, "My dad won't even know I'm gone. I've been gone before for four days and Dad never had a clue."

Sheila said, "I told my folks that we were off to a debate tournament at the University of New Hampshire and that I needed the car to give you both a ride. So, we're set for a ride."

Sally said, "As luck would have it, my dad is going out of town in connection with his work. He won't even be around. He's leaving Thursday and won't be home until Sunday noon. We should get back long before he returns. He'll never find out."

***

The charter plane circled over Bradley International Airport in Hartford, Connecticut once and came in for a smooth landing. Aboard the plane, James Macintyre was working out the final details of his talk. The preparations for the annual corporate meeting had taken up most of his time over the past two weeks and he was glad that it was finally time to get on with it. It was Wednesday November nineteenth. The actual meeting wouldn't begin until Friday, but BSI's senior management group had been sent ahead to supervise the set-up and organization of the meeting site.

For the past three years the annual meeting had been held at the Foxwoods resort casino and hotel complex just outside Hartford which had proved to be an ideal location. Being close to New York City, Hartford was convenient for several of the BSI board members who worked on Wall Street. It was also convenient for the management team whose flight from the airport in Portland, Maine was a short twenty minutes. Foxwoods included fine hotel arrangements, numerous meeting rooms, and excellent dining facilities. And of course, no one complained about the on-site entertainment which included not only all forms of gambling, but also evening shows with top name stars.

The annual meeting was scheduled to include Friday morning informational meetings to be held with clients associated with the shipyard's current major projects. After a lunch held in one of the casino's fine restaurants, a social time was scheduled to let guests try their luck at the tables. Friday evening included box seats offered to the most important clients and major stockholders at a concert in the Fox Theater with the world-renowned violinist, Anne-Sophie Mutter, in concert playing a selection of Mozart's sonatas. On Saturday morning the management team would meet with the entire board of directors to review the final details for the afternoon general stockholders' meeting. The stockholders' meeting, which would be held in the grand ballroom, was where official corporate business would be conducted with stockholders present. The activities concluded on Saturday evening with a private formal dinner for senior management, members of the board of directors, government officials and other important stockholders.

As the airplane taxied on the ground towards the general aviation flight terminal, Macintyre stood up and went to the front of the plane.

"People... people... if I could have your attention, please. I just want to briefly go over your assignments before we leave the plane. I'm sure that you all know your responsibilities. Lisa, you and David Walters will be meeting with the representatives from Hamburg Friday morning in the Aspen room to present our progress on the CV1 project. You will need to make arrangements to make sure that the room is set up for your presentation. Be sure to check in with the hotel event staff when you get in."

Lisa Kerrigan looked up from her laptop and gave a nod with a strained half smile. She had initially been insulted that the vice president of finance would be assigned with her. It showed a lack of commitment to their first significant non-military contract in decades. The assignment meant that there would be no BSI shipbuilding technical support for her as she made her presentation. But as time went by, her confidence grew, and she began to feel better about her role. If there was one thing that private industry valued, it was cost control and fiscal responsibility. It might not hurt to have the shipyard's best financial expertise in the room.

Macintyre continued. "Bill Gleason, as vice president of operations, you will be meeting with Navy Secretary Rogers and Admiral Thompson along with the naval Supervisor of Ships director, Tom Trask. You will be reviewing our current destroyer contract. You will be meeting in the Monterey room. Be sure to make a strong pitch for BSI as the lead shipyard for the next contract round. The board will want an update Saturday morning on our prospects for the contract extension."

Without waiting for a response, Macintyre continued. "John, you will be in the Palm Springs room to meet with the legal team from Washington."

John Phillips served as the vice president of administration and as the shipyard's legal counsel. He had the unenviable task of meeting with attorneys from the judge advocate general's office who were representing the department of the Navy in an investigation of an accident that involved the injury of a navy seaman who died while on sea trials on a BSI destroyer last year. The sailor had slipped on a wet deck, and in what was considered by all as a freak accident, he had hit his head and had died from the impact. The family had brought a wrongful death suit against the navy. It was pretty well accepted that the accident had no legal merit. Since the ship, however, was technically still in the ownership of BSI at the time of sea trials, BSI was required to participate in the defense.

Macintyre shuffled a number of pages. After finding his place he looked up. "I will be meeting with the Pentagon representatives to review the WG-116B Guidance Systems Development Project. I will be meeting in the Cancun room."

Bill Gleason stood up at his seat and said, "Jim, don't you think it might be prudent to have some support in your presentation? The technology project is the most important contract we have, considering its potential for future work. I could keep my talk short so that I could join you..."

Before Gleason could finish, Macintyre interrupted with a tone that bordered on hostility. "No, that won't be necessary! I can handle the presentation. You don't need to lecture me on the importance of this contract."

The group went silent with embarrassment. Realizing that his response had been a bit heavy-handed, Macintyre lowered his tone and said, "Really, Bill, I can do what needs to be done. Thanks for the offer though, but you're needed with our largest construction contract. Besides, Steve Brown, our lead engineer for the project, will be arriving Thursday and he will be with me to address any technical questions."

# Chapter 11

Molly Burgess, the Foxwoods chief of security, stood behind three security staff members who were seated in front of an array of video monitors in the surveillance room high above the Foxwoods' casino floor. All were studying the video camera that displayed one of the blackjack tables in the Grand Casino. Billy Styles, seated in the center chair, was a gray-haired man approaching retirement age. He had served on the Foxwoods' security staff longer than any other staff member, including the newly hired chief of security, *Ms.* Molly Burgess. In fact, he had twenty years more experience in casino security than did his supervisor who had come on board just last week. The management had told him that he had been considered for the position as chief but there were those who felt that the position needed someone who would be around for a long time. It was common knowledge that Billy had his sights set on retirement and likely would be around for at most only one more year. Being passed over for the promotion was just fine with him. He surely didn't need the headaches that came with the job, particularly in his final months.

"A bit early to be 'tying one on'," said Billy. The group's focus was centered on a man seated at table twenty-seven. The man was dressed in a wrinkled sport coat that gave the appearance that he had slept in his clothes. As the security team looked on, they saw the man ordering yet another drink from a waitress who disappeared with his order. Clearly, he had had enough already. The man could barely sit in his chair without falling and he was beginning to attract attention from other patrons at nearby tables.

Molly glanced at her watch which showed it to be ten minutes after two p.m. It was indeed early to be well past drunk, but she knew that this was not necessarily unusual. She spoke into her headset microphone, "Table twenty-seven, go."

Within seconds, two well-conditioned security men appeared on the screen and escorted the man away from the table towards the casino exit. The man protested but he was in no condition to put up any significant resistance.

As Billy turned toward Molly to speak, she interrupted him saying, "I want you to pull that waitress. Give her notice and send her to the bursar to settle her pay. I want her gone immediately."

Billy simply nodded. Everyone knew that there were strict rules against serving guests who were inebriated. What he had wondered was whether the new chief had the stomach to take the action. His question had been answered before he had been able to ask. Chalk one up for the rookie, he thought.

The man on Billy's left had been watching a monitor that had been aimed at another of the blackjack tables. He pointed to a young man who was seated at a table with no open seats. "Check out this guy. Any thoughts?"

After watching three dealt hands Billy said, "Maybe."

Molly stared at the man wondering, *maybe what?* The man appeared to be in his early twenties. He was dressed in a shirt that proclaimed YALE on its front pocket. As Molly watched, there did not seem to be anything out of the ordinary with him. He did not appear to be drinking, nor was he socializing with anyone else at the table. The only thing that caught her attention was the size of his winnings. The typical twenty-something came and went in a relatively short amount of time, usually just after having lost all of his money. By the look of his stack of chips, Molly could see that this player had been playing for some time.

The dealer gave a casual, but knowing, glance at the hidden ceiling camera. "That seals it," Billy announced. The other security staff nodded in agreement, which was followed by an unmistakable sense of expectation from those seated. All three turned in unison to look at Molly after she had said nothing for several seconds.

Molly was not sure who she was angrier at, her staff for putting her through this test, or for herself for failing it. She stood in silent anger staring at the monitor.

Billy broke the silence by turning back to the camera just as the young man was seen to have a losing hand, with the dealer taking up more than one thousand dollars in chips. "Looks like the boss may be right," Billy said. "Let's wait one more hand to see. Maybe we were a bit hasty in calling this guy a counter." The next hand saw another significant loss for the young man.

Billy looked over his shoulder at Molly and said, "Good call. We were about to jump on this guy for card counting but you must have seen something we didn't. Well done." The others both sighed in relieved agreement.

The com radios interrupted that moment with the announcement that the Billings Shipyard guests were about to arrive, and that Molly was needed at the front entrance to secure their arrival. Molly tapped Billy on the shoulder and said, "Why don't you take the lead on this. Bring along two others. I'll be down in a moment after I make sure that the executive floor is ready." On the way out of the room, Billy called on his radio for a replacement in the surveillance room.

Outside the room, Molly stopped Billy and said, "Thanks. I appreciate the recovery ops you did for me in there."

With a knowing smile, Billy just shrugged and said, "I thought you were just keeping us honest, boss."

\*\*\*

Lisa Kerrigan turned off the television in her hotel room. It was now seven thirty in the evening and she realized that she hadn't had anything to eat since nibbling on a stale sandwich that had been served on the flight from Maine. She had checked into her suite immediately upon the arrival of the BSI management team and had spent the remainder of the afternoon in her room reviewing her notes and preparing for Friday morning's meeting with Hamburg Shipping. A group of the other managers had arranged to meet for dinner that evening, but Lisa had politely declined. Her husband, Tim, wouldn't be arriving until early Friday evening along with several other members of the board of directors.

Lisa knew that tomorrow would be a busy day of preparation. She would be spending the morning with David Walters reviewing the current financial figures for the Hamburg project. In the afternoon, she would join David in the Aspen room for a trial run of their presentation. It was essential that they had their materials set and that she had her talk well-rehearsed. Confidence was always a key to keeping a client satisfied. This was especially true, Lisa knew, when there was a woman at the helm. She was going to be so well prepared that there would be no doubt that she was in control and there were no aspects of the project that she couldn't address.

Recognizing the importance of her day tomorrow, Lisa admitted to herself that starving herself for the weekend was probably a bad idea. She grabbed a sweater from the closet and, after a brief stop to fix her hair, she stepped out into the hall in search of one of the many restaurants.

Walking down the hall in the direction of the elevators, her thoughts drifted back to her husband. She had been busy over the past few days with preparations for the annual meeting. This business had kept her from dwelling on the thing that lay just below the surface of her consciousness like a shark patrolling in shallow water. Was it really possible that her husband was involved in some nefarious scheme to illegally embezzle funds from BSI? As many times as she had convinced herself that this was entirely absurd, thoughts of the mystery bank account and Greg Connor's letter came front and center into her mind demanding explanation.

As the elevator opened at the hotel main level, Lisa was lost in suspicious thoughts about her husband that she had been able to suppress over the past days. She started for a moment trying to think things through and was awakened from her distraction when a man standing outside the open elevator said abruptly, "Miss, remove yourself from the lift... now."

Lisa looked up with a mixture of embarrassment at being caught in a self-absorbed moment, and irritation at the man's rude comment. The man was dressed in what looked to be a well-tailored, gray suit. Except for his coarse comment, one might expect him to be an investment banker or perhaps a company CEO. As Lisa exited the elevator, she saw a second man with closely cropped white hair and sunglasses, standing behind the man in the gray suit. The second man was dressed in black pants and a black sweater which were in stark contrast to his white hair. The second man looked somewhat apologetically at Lisa but said nothing as they moved passed her.

A thought drifted into Lisa's head that had been burned into her memory years ago by her mother, *Money doesn't make up for bad manners.* In high school she had gone to the senior prom with the senior class president, Alexander Rothschild IV, who, aside from being the most popular guy in school, was also by far the wealthiest. Lisa's family, by contrast, was not exactly poor, but they had to work hard for everything that they had. That fateful night when her date had waited in the living room for Lisa to finish last minute preparations, he had remarked to her mother that he hoped that Lisa's prom dress was appropriate. It wouldn't do to be seen with a date who wore second-hand clothes. When Lisa returned from the prom early, she told her mother that Mr Rothschild the fourth wasn't exactly well behaved. Her mother had simply responded with those words of wisdom that had stuck with her from that day forward.

\*\*\*

The central corridor at the main level of the hotel that contained the BSI Suites was labeled the 'Pequot Trail' in deference to the resort operators. The Foxwoods resort was constructed in 1986 by the Mashantucket Pequot Tribal Nation, and one of the three interconnected hotels was named for the owners, the Grand Pequot Tower. In addition to its other two connected hotels, The Grand Cedar Hotel and the Two Trees Inn, the resort also was home to six casinos with more than seven thousand slot machines and four hundred gaming tables. The BSI meetings on Friday were booked for the tenth-floor business rooms in the Grand Pequot Tower, and Saturday's annual stockholders' meeting would be held in the Grand Ballroom on the main level of the Pequot Hotel. Accordingly, the BSI accommodations were always booked in this hotel to allow for immediate access to all the weekend activities.

Lisa strolled along the main level corridor trying to get her bearings. A short distance away the corridor opened up to a cafe area with an oriental restaurant named the Golden Dragon. Never being able to pass up a good oriental meal, Lisa walked in and sat at an open table. From her position she was able to see the crowds moving back and forth through a long main corridor, coming to, and going from, the adjacent large casino floor.

The sweet and sour chicken had just been served when Lisa looked up to find a middle-aged man standing at her table.

"Lisa Kerrigan?" he asked.

Surprised by the sudden appearance, she didn't answer immediately as she sat uncomfortably wondering who this man might be.

"Excuse me Ms Kerrigan, my name is Peter Ashley. I'm with the US Department of the Navy." He opened a wallet that displayed an identification card. Lisa leaned over and read, *Lieutenant. Commander Peter E. Ashley, United States Navy.*

The man gave her time to read the ID card and then asked, "Do you mind if I join you? This is about official business."

Having recovered a bit, Lisa motioned to the open chair. "If you are active US Navy, on official business, why aren't you in uniform, Commander?"

The man smiled. "Let's just say that I do not necessarily want to call attention to myself."

Lisa thought about this for a moment, wondering what the navy would want with her. "Exactly what is your role in the navy?" she inquired as she sipped a cup of tea.

The man hesitated and then quietly replied, "Actually, I'm with naval intelligence and I'm here on an investigation."

With that pronouncement, the blood drained from Lisa's face. Could it possibly be that Tim is indeed involved with something illegal and that it is connected to the navy? All of her worst fears began to circulate in her mind.

The shock on Lisa's face must have been obvious. "Are you all right Ms Kerrigan?" Ashley asked.

"Yes... Please call me Lisa." She quickly composed herself and went on. "What is it that you need from me?"

Ashley flagged a nearby waitress and ordered a cup of tea. "Would you like some more tea?" he asked.

Lisa smiled at the waitress who couldn't be much more than twenty years old and said, "I'm fine thank you."

When the waitress left, Ashley leaned forward and spoke quietly. "I would like your help. But before I go any further, I need to have your assurance that anything we discuss will stay between us."

Lisa nodded without verbalizing a reply.

"I'm investigating an incident that may involve people at Billings Shipping. I'm sorry but I can't disclose the specifics of the investigation at this time, but I believe that you may be able to help us."

A million thoughts raced through Lisa's mind as Ashley spoke. How much should she say? What if she said something that proved to be incriminating to her husband? But on the other hand, if Tim was involved in something illegal, she had a responsibility to cooperate. And perhaps worse, what if the navy thought that she was involved in some way?

She settled on saying the obvious. "Well, I'm not sure how much help I can be if I don't even know what this is all about."

The waitress arrived with a pot of tea and a cup for the commander. After she departed Ashley turned back to Lisa.

"Ms Kerrigan... er, Lisa... how much do you know about Billings' contract with the navy for the WG-116B guidance system?"

Lisa's first thought was that this was a curious question. Greg Connor's accusation had been in connection with the Hamburg Shipping contract. As far as she knew, there was no connection to any of BSI's other ongoing work.

"Actually, I'm not very familiar at all with that contract since I have no direct connection with the work. My focus at BSI is the acquisition of non-military contracts."

"I understand that, which is why I am speaking with you. Since we know that you have no official connection with that particular contract, we are comfortable in assuming that you are not involved as a person of interest in our investigation."

Lisa quickly shot back, "It's good to know that I'm not a suspect since I don't even know what the accusation is."

The commander paused and then continued. "As I mentioned, I am not at liberty to divulge the details of our investigation, however, I can say that certain details of this project... certain *classified* details, have shown up where they do not belong." He let this information sink in for a moment and then went on.

"Can you tell me who has access to the classified documents for the WG-116B project, specifically to control schematics?"

At this point Lisa was thoroughly confused. Her husband couldn't be involved. As the president of the board of directors he did not have access to day-to-day details of projects, so he certainly couldn't have been responsible for technology leaks. Even in her role with non-military projects, however, Lisa fully understood the gravity of letting classified documents out of company control.

Lisa took another sip of her tea and thought for a moment.

"If you are investigating a breach of security at BSI, surely you must already know who has authorization to view classified documents. Why are you asking me?"

"You are correct. We know who has been granted authorization at BSI. What we want to find out is who else might have been able to access the released documents. We thought you might be able to help us discover any suspicious activity that might be going on and report back to us."

Lisa responded in shock. "You want me to spy on workers at BSI?!"

***

On the sixth floor of the Pequot Tower, two men were talking quietly in a guest room. A man in a tailored gray suit was sitting in a chair at a desk located in the far corner of the room. The room drapes were drawn and the only light that was on in the room was the recessed down-light at the entrance door. The seated man's face was cast in deep shadow so that he could not be clearly seen. A younger man with white hair was standing by the door. A single briefcase lay on the bed between the two men.

The seated man pointed to the briefcase and said with a pronounced German accent, "Open the case."

The other man reached over and opened the case. Inside was a nine-millimeter berretta with a silencer, one large envelope, as well as a business size envelope.

"Open the large envelope."

Inside was an eight-by-ten photograph. The picture showed a portrait showing a face that had obviously been taken at a great distance but had been enlarged.

"This is your mark. The gun is untraceable. This needs to be taken care of by Friday evening. Be sure to be discreet. I don't want any loose ends that can be traced back to either of us."

Pointing to the remaining envelope, the man continued.

"The second part of your task that needs to be done is in that envelope. You will find a hotel room key and a coat check tag. There are also instructions that identify the guest who will be staying in the room. After the subject arrives and checks in, hide the tag in the room where it will be found when the room is searched. Be careful not to be seen. You must complete the first part in such a way that implicates this second man so that the room will be searched."

The man at the door folded the photograph and put it, along with the hotel room card and coat check tag, in his pocket. He took the silencer and put it in his other pocket and then slid the gun in his belt under his sweater. "What about the payment?" he asked.

The seated man waved his hand in dismissal. "You do your jobs, and the payment will be made. As soon as I know that your tasks have been completed, I'll have the money wired to the account we arranged."

With that, the man adjusted his black sweater and left.

\*\*\*

Thursday morning arrived with a frigid wind that seemed more appropriate for late January than mid-November. The sky was a threatening shade of gray which held the promise of an early snow for southern New England. The effect of the weather for those at the Foxwoods Resort was that visitors who might otherwise be out and about traveling to coastal tourist spots or the city of Hartford had all decided to stay indoors for the day. It was the sort of day that the casino operators loved.

James Macintyre pushed his way through the crowd in the hotel front lobby on his way to the racetrack betting area in the adjacent Rainmaker Casino building. Macintyre glanced at his watch and saw that it was ten forty-five a.m. He cursed under his breath at the throng of people who seemed to be stuck in place in the lobby, apparently not knowing what to do or where to go next. Pushing through to the entrance to the Rainmaker Casino, he quickened his step.

When he awoke this morning the message on his cell phone had simply said for him to go to one of the betting carrels in the Ultimate Race Book lounge at ten thirty a.m. and wait to be contacted. He had spent the last forty-five minutes with the resort's chief of technology systems reviewing the details for presentation equipment that would be required for the weekend. The morning had not started off well when he had been given the news that the audiovisual cabling in the Monterey room had been experiencing problems and that the LCD ceiling projector would not be available for that room. Macintyre had immediately flown into a rage and had informed the man that all of the audiovisual equipment would be operational by tomorrow morning or the resort owners would be meeting with BSI's attorneys. A contract had been signed, he had reminded the man whose name tag read, *Chief of Information Technology*, and if every piece of equipment promised was not fully functional, he would be held personally responsible.

Now fifteen minutes late, Macintyre hurried in frustration toward the race betting lounge. It wasn't bad enough that he had to orchestrate every little detail of this weekend he told himself, he now had to deal with this. Before leaving Maine, he had been informed by his contact that there apparently was some problem with the information they had just received. His first response had been one of panic that perhaps there was a flaw in the work being prepared by BSI and that a defect had been discovered, rendering the project useless. But he had quickly learned that the problem had nothing to do with BSI or his end of the deal. Hearing this news was like having a weight suddenly removed from his shoulders.

But upon listening further, he had been warned that there may be an issue with the government representatives being sent to review the WG-116B Guidance System project. Questions may be asked, and Macintyre was warned to be tight-lipped. In fact, he was not being given any details for the reason that it was important that if he were to be questioned, he should be able to answer truthfully that he knew nothing. It was for this reason that he had arranged to be alone as the BSI lead for the WG-116B briefing with the Pentagon officials. If suspicious questions were going to be asked, Macintyre wanted to be sure that no other BSI members would be around to ask why.

Macintyre arrived at the Ultimate Race Book lounge. The space was filled with betters, some parked in front of a fifty-foot-high projection screen that displayed a live horse race being run somewhere in England, while others were seated at many of the two hundred carrels that each had a video screen and electronic betting consoles.

Macintyre took a seat at one of the carrels and waited for his cell phone to ring. After a minute he heard a voice coming from the carrel next to his.

"You're late Mister Macintyre."

James sat in shocked amazement. How could his contact be here? Before he could move to see who was seated next to him the voice barked a sharp command. "Stay seated and don't move! Don't take your eyes off the screen. Just sit there and look like you're just another pathetic looser looking to get rich."

Macintyre sat transfixed. He had expected to hear by phone any updates on the 'situation', but he never imagined that he would be met personally. So much effort had been taken to avoid any direct personal contact. He strained to hear the voice over the crowd background noise.

"Mr Macintyre, I am here to remind you of our agreement. You are being very well compensated, and we expect you to live up to your end of the agreement. If you get any thoughts about backing out of our arrangement and confessing your deeds to the government representatives in your briefing tomorrow, you should understand that we would not let that happen. It would end poorly for you, were you to attempt this. We will be watching and listening to you very closely."

Macintyre's blood pressure rose above its already elevated level. Whatever was going on, this must be serious. As far as he knew, everything had been proceeding without major problems. The issue with Greg Connor had been taken care of, and his backup plan of implicating Tim Kerrigan through his wife was comfortably set in place.

Macintyre's voice contained an obvious tremor. "Look, I don't know what is going on, but if there is something I should know about the

WG-116B project you'd better tell me before I get face to face with Pentagon officials and have to make up stories on the spot."

There was a lengthy pause in the next-door carrel and Macintyre began to wonder if the man had left. Just before he was about to look around the side of the carrel, the man continued.

"One of the data sheets that we received has unfortunately fallen into the hands of Interpol. We are not certain, but it is entirely likely that word has been transmitted back to the US government."

Macintyre immediately lost control. "Crap! What do you mean it fell into the hands of Interpol? Those sheets had 'BSI' and 'Top Secret' stamped all over them. And you aren't certain that the government has gotten word? Well, I'm certain! I might be arrested, and you didn't even bother to tell me what was going on?"

"Calm down Mr Macintyre. No one has any idea how this paper got out of BSI, which means, no one knows you are involved in any way. As long as you maintain your control, everything will be all right. By the time anyone understands what is happening, it will be too late to do anything about it."

Macintyre shifted uneasily in his seat. With equal parts of frustration and panic, he croaked, "What am I supposed to say when the FBI asks me how classified documents could get out of BSI's control?"

"I doubt seriously if the FBI is involved. My sources tell me that the Navy Department is keeping this to themselves. They really don't have any idea how this happened. In the worst case, there will be a few questions that need to be answered, but I'm sure that you will be able to show the navy the many security measures that are in place that will prevent any further leaks. Perhaps you might offer to develop an increased security program with maybe even naval oversight to soothe those concerned. After all, no one can possibly suspect that you are the source. Put in place any measures that they require, as long as you maintain access to the files with no way that anyone can trace the leak to you."

Macintyre hung his head with worry and despair. How could something this simple get so messed up, he thought. As if his contact was reading his mind, the voice continued. "We understand that this calls for efforts above and beyond our original expectations. When you return to

142

your room this afternoon there will be an envelope at the front desk waiting for you. In it you will find a generous gift for your hard work and loyalty. I think you will be pleased."

After a minute of silence passed, Macintyre stood and discovered the carrel next to him was empty. He looked around the lounge but could not pick out any familiar faces in the vast crowd of people who were cheering horses on the home stretch on the giant projection screen. In frustration, he headed for the hotel lobby. He glanced at his watch which told him that he now had just one hour to get the rental car that he had arranged for today upon his arrival and head to the Hartford airport to pick up Steven Brown.

As he headed to the hotel concierge desk, he couldn't suppress the feeling that he was being watched, although there didn't seem to be anyone taking any special interest in him that he could see. In the far corner of the lobby a man stood studying a casino map. As Macintyre stepped up to speak with the concierge, the man put the map on a nearby table and turned to exit through the front doors, adjusting the gun tucked under his sweater as he went.

# Chapter 12

The weather Friday morning showed a promise of relief from the bitter cold and wind. The sky had continued to darken Thursday when Steven Brown had reached the Hartford airport and by the time he met up with James Macintyre for a ride to Foxwoods, it had begun to snow. The temperature had dropped to twenty-four degrees and the snowflakes were tiny dots of frozen ice crystals. It was the kind of snow that New Englanders knew would not be stopping anytime soon. Whenever giant white flakes lazily drifted down from the sky like a scene from a Christmas card, it was inevitable that it would not amount to great depth. By contrast, tiny flakes driven by a strong north-east wind meant it was time to break out the shovels. The snow had lasted throughout the afternoon and night but as dawn broke Friday morning, the clouds were moving off with a hint of blue sky returning.

Steven Brown stood outside the hotel lobby entrance drinking a strong cup of black coffee. It was good to begin the day with a breath of fresh New England air he thought to himself. The six inches of newly fallen snow seemed a bit out of place for November, but it made everything clean and bright.

It was eight thirty and already there was a steady stream of guests arriving. Hotel porters rushed to meet taxis and arriving cars as guests were escorted into the hotel. The guests were no doubt looking forward to getting an early start to the weekend away from their daily work routine, hoping for success in the casinos. He couldn't help but wonder, however, if the joy and smiles he saw on the faces would still be there as these visitors left on Sunday with far less money in their pockets.

Brown finished his coffee and headed back into the hotel. His meeting with Macintyre and the Pentagon officials would begin at nine a.m. in the Cancun meeting room on the tenth floor of the Grand Pequot. He glanced at his watch and decided that he had plenty of time to stop back at his room to pick up his briefcase with his notes and then get to the meeting.

As he walked toward the elevators he couldn't help wondering once again why he was here. Clearly, annual meetings were management functions, in which he had very little interest. As far as he knew, there were no other members from the technical staff present. When he had received the memo stating that he would be attending the meeting he had immediately phoned Macintyre to inquire why he had been instructed to attend. Not only did he have nothing to contribute relevant to management meetings, but it would also mean valuable time away from the engineering team. And they were at a critical point in the project. It appeared that a breakthrough was imminent that would solve the remaining design issues. If these issues could be addressed satisfactorily, construction could begin on a working prototype. He was needed to do the work he was hired to do, not put on a show for management types who weren't able to understand anything that he might have to say.

Arriving at his room, he pulled out his room card and reached to insert it into the electronic door lock. Just as the card was inserted, the door flung open and a man came rushing out, running squarely into him and knocking him on his seat onto the floor. The entire event took no more than four or five seconds, but it put him into a state of shock that stopped time and removed him from reality. As his senses returned, he found himself somewhat dazed, sitting in the hall up against the wall opposite from his room door. His heart was pounding so wildly that he thought that it might be about to jump out of his chest.

After he took a minute to collect himself, he stood and entered his room. Who in the world was that, his mind screamed? Obviously, this was not a hotel staff member. But why would anyone break into his room? There was nothing to steal. He walked over to the closet and checked his clothes. Everything was in its place as far as he could tell. He inspected his briefcase that lay on the bed and could find nothing missing. The money that he had brought he had kept in his wallet which he had with him at all times.

He sat on the bed and reached for the phone. He would have to call hotel security to report this. But as he dialed the front desk a thought occurred to him and he put the phone down. Exactly what was he going to report? Someone had broken into his room, but there was no sign of forced entry. The person had gotten in but had not taken anything. In fact, there was no sign that anyone other than himself had been in the room. Worst of all, not only couldn't he identify the man, he couldn't even give a description. It had all happened so fast that he didn't get a look at the man other than seeing a blinding flash headed right at him.

It was clear that reporting this incident would not lead to any results. His bedside clock showed that it was now eight fifty-five a.m. He had five minutes to get to the Cancun room. If he called security, he'd be lucky to get to the meeting by ten. That wouldn't do. The last thing he needed was the wrath of James Macintyre. He grabbed his briefcase and headed out the door.

When he reached the Cancun room, he arrived just in time to see a group of naval officers being seated at the table. Macintyre waved impatiently to Brown, motioning him to come to the front to sit at the head of the table with him.

"Good morning," began Macintyre. "We're here to review the Billings Shipyard contract for the WG-116B Guidance Systems Development Project. Perhaps it would be best if we began with introductions. For those of you who do not know me, I am James Macintyre, the chief executive officer for Billings Shipyard. I also serve as the project principal-in-charge for the WG-116B project and I will be giving today's presentation. On my left is Steven Brown who is our lead engineer on the project. If there are any technical questions that I cannot address, Mr Brown will be available."

Brown wondered to himself with amusement exactly which technical questions Macintyre might actually *be* able to address, but he kept a smile off his face.

There was a brief pause and the first naval officer spoke. He was a decorated career officer in his mid-sixties who had an unmistakable air of command about him. He was an imposing figure of just over six foot in height with square shoulders and a remarkably fit figure for his age. His face displayed a sense of seriousness that left little doubt that this was a business trip with a purpose, not a pleasure junket to a casino.

"I'm Rear Admiral Chester Rand with US Naval Operations at the Pentagon. I have assumed the lead for this project and will be reporting directly to the secretary about its viability."

The word 'viability' gave Macintyre a sour feeling in his stomach. This was the first that there had been any question by the navy as to the project's merits or technical feasibility. Furthermore, he had never had such a senior ranking member attend what should be a routine briefing.

Beside the admiral sat a familiar face.

"Good morning, James," the officer said with a considerably less threatening tone. "I'm Commander Bart Hicks with Naval Warfare Systems Command. I am serving as the project coordinator for the Department of Defense."

Commander Hicks had made several visits to the shipyard and Macintyre always felt that he was a strong supporter of BSI.

Seated beside the commander was another familiar face to Macintyre. The man spoke up with a strong southern accent.

"Hello. I'm Captain Davidson, navy Supervisor of Ships."

Davidson had an office across the street from the shipyard in the office building that the staff of the supervisor of ships occupied. He was a Mississippi native which made him as about out-of-place as anyone could be in a coastal Maine community. He had made the adjustment well, however, and his southern charm had made him popular with everyone at the shipyard.

The final naval officer at the table had been sitting quietly the entire time with his hands folded on the table. Macintyre had no idea who this person was, but his sixth sense did not give him a good feeling. The man was in his late thirties and was an imposing figure who was obviously in good physical shape. He sat erect and had hardly moved a muscle during the introductions, spending the entire time studying Macintyre. At last, he spoke up with a no-nonsense intensity.

"I'm Lieutenant. Commander Peter Ashley. I've been temporarily assigned to help with project coordination for Naval Command."

Macintyre looked on in silence expecting more. When no further explanation was offered, he asked, "Exactly what is your role, Commander? Who are you representing?" When the commander did not respond right away, Macintyre added, "Just so that we have an accurate record of today's meeting and those attending."

Without moving, the commander replied, "I'm reporting to Admiral Rand. My duties are to provide an additional set of eyes for the navy to assure that the project stays on a proper course."

It was a vague answer, but Macintyre knew that he would be getting no further details for now. He resolved to speak with Commander Hicks after the meeting to see if he could find out more.

Macintyre proceeded with the project update displaying a sense of calm that he did not feel inside. There were several general questions about the details of the project schedule and about materials procurement that he was able to handle without trouble. Questions about the status of the guidance software and a date for prototype testing were fielded by Steven Brown to the apparent satisfaction of the group.

Just as the meeting was coming to its conclusion and Macintyre began to feel a sense of relief at having encountered no difficulties, the admiral spoke. "Mr Macintyre, would you please brief us on security measures that are in place regarding the handing of classified information on the WG-116B project."

It was if time had stopped for Macintyre. A sudden panic gripped his heart and started it beating wildly. In a concerted effort to present an appearance of control and nonchalance, he responded. "Well Admiral, certainly security on classified projects at BSI is of the utmost concern. We strictly follow all Department of Defense protocols and regulations. All project team members are required to receive security clearances..."

Before he could continue, the admiral interjected. "Yes, yes, but what would you say if I told you that copies of classified information from Billings Shipyard have been discovered in Europe on the open market?"

Macintyre flushed as he struggled to retain control. "Well, I would have to say that that is not possible. We have the strictest security measures in place to keep that very thing from happening."

The admiral waved his hand and said in a tone of dismissal, "Mr Macintyre, let me assure you that it *has* happened, and that the Department of Defense is taking active steps to find out *how* it happened. Let me also assure you that those who are found to be responsible will be prosecuted for treason and, at the moment, the US attorney general's office is looking into the appropriateness of taking action against Billings Shipyard."

Macintyre paused and thought, so the bomb had been dropped. He looked over at Steven Brown who thankfully had the sense to remain quiet. At some point, he realized, he would have to take care of Brown now that he had heard about the leak.

Thoughts of his meeting this morning returned. His mind replayed the statements, *They really don't have any idea how this happened... no one can possibly suspect that you are the source.* The admiral was on a fishing expedition hoping to discover something but, in truth, he had no idea about how the leak happened. For that matter, how did anyone know that the leak actually was at BSI? After all, copies of the very documents that might have turned up are all kept in files at the Pentagon. How could anyone know that the leak wasn't in fact on the navy side?

With more resolve, Macintyre responded. "This is a serious situation indeed and I want you to know that BSI will conduct its own investigation as well. If there are additional security measures that need to be put in place, be assured that we will attend to them. As for accusing us of leaking classified information, I am certain that neither your efforts, nor ours, will show that BSI had any culpability in this matter. I welcome any investigation that the DoD will undertake, and we will cooperate fully to find answers."

Then as a closing shot, Macintyre paused for effect and then stated with firmness, "I trust you will be conducting an investigation with equal thoroughness of your own staff connected with the project."

\*\*\*

Lisa Kerrigan sat at the head table in the Aspen room. By her side was David Walters who was running a laptop as Lisa gave her PowerPoint presentation on the CV1 Containerized Vessel Project for Hamburg Shipping. Representing Hamburg Shipping were six men and one woman, all of whom were seated around a configuration of tables that had been arranged in a U shape, facing the screen at the front of the room.

Lisa pointed to the screen with a laser pointer. "The next slide shows the timetable of the project with milestone dates indicated in red. As you can see, the project commenced on April first. As of the end of September, the first stage of the project had been completed, which means that we are approximately thirty days ahead of schedule."

Lisa looked around the room. The Hamburg Shipping delegation was all shuffling through the handouts that she had prepared, keeping one eye on the screen. The company president was unable to make the trip and so the group was headed up by the financial officer, Johann Steiner. It took several minutes after the delegation had been first seated and introductions had been made that Lisa recognized Hamburg Shipping's financial officer as the man with whom she had had the unpleasant encounter at the elevator when she had first arrived. He didn't acknowledge the incident, however, and Lisa hoped that perhaps he didn't recognize her.

Of all the delegation, Steiner seemed to be the only member that was not impressed with the presentation and BSI's results to date, which worried Lisa. He sat stoically as each slide was shown without taking any notes. Lisa could not help wondering if his silence meant that there were problems about which she had yet to hear.

When David Walters took over the presentation to review the project accounting, Steiner seemed to come to life. Initially Lisa thought that since he was the financial officer his interests must lie wholly with the project costs. But when she asked a question about invoice amounts for expenses, Steiner ignored her and directed his response to Walters. It was then that she realized that his problem wasn't with any details of the project, but rather was with the fact that a woman was in charge.

Ordinarily, Lisa would not have let this slide without challenging the obvious display of male chauvinism, but she was resolved not to let it get the better of her. Her effort to control her temper was not due to the fact that this was an important client of BSI and an insult might jeopardize a key account, although she admitted to herself that was probably true. Her resolve for discretion came more from self-interest.

When she had been informed that she would be put in charge of the briefing for the Hamburg Shipping project she had realized that this might be an excellent opportunity to try to find out something about her husband's bank account from the Hamburg side. If she could speak with the financial officer alone, she would be able to ask him about Tim's role in setting up the project financial arrangements, and perhaps shed some light on why he had a secret bank account charged to the project. Creating a relationship of antagonism over the role of women in business didn't seem like the best approach to getting the information that she wanted.

After the presentation concluded and all the questions had been answered, Lisa spoke to the delegation members as they were gathering their things.

"In your package of information, you will find a ticket to this evening's performance in the resort theater. I believe that you will be especially entertained as the concert will feature the renowned German violinist, Anne-Sophie Mutter. The performance starts at nine p.m., that is, at twenty-one hundred hours. Feel free to enjoy the resort this afternoon at your leisure. Charge any expenses to your room and BSI will be taking care of the bill. You are welcome to attend our annual stockholders' meeting tomorrow afternoon, and there is a closing banquet to which you are invited tomorrow evening."

The group nodded in appreciation and began leaving. As Steiner stood to leave, Lisa walked over.

"Herr Steiner, could I please speak with you a moment before you leave?"

Looking somewhat surprised, he responded in perfect English, but with a heavy accent. "Certainly, should I call our group back?"

Lisa quickly said, "No, this is a matter that I would like to discuss privately with you. Could we perhaps meet for a cup of coffee? I would appreciate just a few minutes."

Steiner looked over at the woman of the delegation who had remained in the room. He spoke with a tone that was more of a command than a polite statement. *"Gertrude, gehen Sie nach zimmer und erwarten mich."*

The woman immediately turned and left the room. Steiner then turned back to Lisa and said, "There is a cafe in the main hall on the ground level."

Lisa waved at David Walters and said, "David, leave the equipment. I'll be back shortly to pack up. You can take off for lunch. I'll catch up with you later this afternoon to review our notes." With that, she and Steiner headed out toward the elevators.

After they each had gotten a cup of coffee and had secured a table, Lisa decided to get right to the point. Johann Steiner was obviously not one for small talk.

"Do you know any reason why the president of BSI would have negotiated a separate bank account in the contract with Hamburg Shipping?"

Steiner took a sip from his coffee and said after a moment, "By president of BSI, do you mean your husband?"

Lisa was a bit flustered, but she refused to let Steiner intimidate her.

"It has come to my attention that... Tim... had a bank account established into which funds from the Hamburg account were deposited. Do know about this account?"

"What kind of account are we talking about? Is it a business account or a personal account?"

Lisa did not want to divulge more information than was absolutely necessary because of the possibility that this information could be used against her husband if legal actions were ever to take place.

"I have been reviewing the project accounts and in so doing I have discovered an account that I am not able to trace in the contract agreement. The account is drawn on a US bank."

Steiner thought for a moment and then said, "I would have to know more to be able to find out the details. Can you give me a bank account number and dates of activity?"

It was a risk giving out this information, but Lisa just had to find out the truth. "The account number is 12 376 8900. It is drawn on the Bank of America. Somehow I think it has something to do with payment for some kind of transfers."

Steiner gave no indication that he had any knowledge of the arrangement. "Have you asked your husband about this account?"

"I haven't talked to Tim about it, frankly, because there is some question about its legality."

Steiner finished his coffee and put his cup down.

"Well, Ms Kerrigan, as Hamburg Shipping's financial officer, I am familiar with all of the payments made in connection with the Billings contract and I am not aware of any unrelated accounts."

With that Steiner got up and left with no further explanation, leaving Lisa wondering. Why hadn't Steiner seemed surprised at her question? Why hadn't he said that he would look into the matter? On the other hand, he certainly should know all the payments that have been made and, if he was unaware of the account, perhaps it wasn't directly connected with Hamburg Shipping. She had hoped that this opportunity would shed some light on the mystery, but here she was just as confused as ever.

# Chapter 13

It was one fifty-five p.m. on Friday afternoon and Henry stared impatiently at the clock in his last class of the day. Sheila had driven her parent's car to school that morning and he and Sheila were going to meet Sally after school in the parking lot. Sally had found out that it would take about four hours to drive to the Foxwoods Resort from Billings and the plan was that they all would leave immediately after school. If all went well, they should be arriving no later than six thirty p.m.

Following the afternoon announcements Henry bolted from the classroom to his locker to get his bag with a change of clothes. As he rounded the corner at full speed, he collided with Mr Jackson the vice principal who seemed to be traveling with equal velocity in the opposite direction. Brushing himself off, Mr Jackson looked down at Henry who had landed on the floor. Mr Jackson snarled, "In a hurry Mr Moore? You know that running in the halls is not allowed. Perhaps an hour in detention would give you a chance to slow down a bit and contemplate the necessity of school rules."

Henry stood up as a crowd of spectators began to gather. Before he could catch his breath to speak, Jack and his faithful entourage of Snap and three girls stepped forward. Jack straightened and spoke to Snap with a most responsible air so that all could hear. "It's about time one of our teachers began to enforce the rules. Some people think that rules don't apply to them but our rules are for the good of all and should be obeyed by all."

Snap added, "Yo, Jack… right on bro!" Jack turned back to face his groupies with a look of smugness. The girls stood gazing at Jack in quiet admiration.

Having found his voice, Henry pleaded. "Please Mr Jackson, I have somewhere really important to go to. I promise, I won't run in the halls ever again."

The vice principal looked at Henry with loathing and said, "You're lucky that I too have an appointment, or I would personally see that you would be spending time in the detention room this afternoon. See to it that you walk in the halls in future." With that he pushed on down the hall.

Having received his reprieve, Henry breathed a sigh of relief. He picked up his books and walked off to his locker. Upon passing Jack he mimicked in whining voice, *"...rules are for the good of all..."* which resulted in an arm punch from Jack that was well worth the pain, Henry mused.

Outside in the parking lot, Henry found Sheila and Sally waiting at the car. Sheila waved as she saw Henry and said impatiently, "Hey! What took so long? We need to get on the road if we're going."

Henry threw his bag in the trunk and said dismissively, "I had a brief chat with Mr Jackson on the way out, but I'm here now so let's get out of here."

The Warren family had two automobiles. The regular family car that Sheila's parents drove was a new, red Toyota Prius. It was a small car that was fun to drive and it still had the 'new car smell'. The family's second car was a tired 1993 Chrysler Concorde. It had one hundred and forty-seven thousand miles and it now only had the smell of the pine tree scented car freshener that hung from the rear-view mirror. This was the car that Sheila was allowed to drive, and it sat expectantly in the high school parking lot with its passenger front door open and its engine idling.

Henry jumped in the front. Henry stretched his legs in the spacious front foot well and proclaimed, "This is a classic. You know they don't make this model anymore."

Less enthusiastically, Sheila replied, "There's probably a reason they don't make this boat anymore. I wanted to get the Prius, but my dad said no way."

Still lost in the moment, Henry said, "This is the original year. I bet it's worth something. It was a bold design move for Chrysler."

As Sheila pulled out of the parking lot she answered, "Well I think it looks like an old lady car."

From the back seat, Sally spoke up as her mind subconsciously pulled up data from a deep recess.

"Actually, the Concorde model was based on the 1987 concept Lamborghini Portofino. Chrysler introduced what it called the 'cab-forward' design, which was characterized by the long, low-slung windshield and relatively short overhangs. The wheels were pushed to the corners of the car, creating a much larger passenger cabin than the contemporaries of the time."

Henry and Sheila looked at each other in amazed silence, which was eventually broken by Henry. "Yeah, right."

The drive went faster than expected as the previous day's snow had been almost completely cleared from the roads. The overhead sign read *'Route 2 Norwich exits 15 miles'*. It was just six p.m. and Sheila reached over to wake Henry who had the incredible ability to sleep in a car just like he was home in bed. Henry had dozed off when they had gotten back in the car at the rest stop just south of Providence and hadn't stopped snoring since.

As Henry came back to life, he glanced at his watch. "Hey, we've made pretty good time. We should be there soon."

The words had hardly left his mouth when a billowing cloud of steam abruptly came up from the front of the car, enveloping the windshield. Visibility instantly went to zero and Sheila panicked as she was now driving sixty-five mph totally blind. Suddenly, horns blared all around them as the car began to swerve out of its lane toward the median divide. Instinctively, Sheila hit the breaks, which resulted in the car screeching to a stop in the fast lane of the three-lane interstate highway. As the car skidded to a stop, the cloud of steam lifted from the windshield allowing the passengers to see that they had spun one hundred and eighty degrees and were now facing an oncoming SUV coming at them at full speed with its horn sounding violently.

At the last second the vehicle swerved around them, narrowly missing another car that was in the middle lane. Other cars were veering wildly to miss the stopped Concorde in what looked more like a video game than reality. The entire episode took less than ten seconds but to Sheila, Henry and Sally, it felt like an eternity. Sally came to her senses first and yelled at Sheila to drive the car off the road into the median

156

grass area. When Sheila didn't respond, Sally reached out from the back seat and grabbed her shoulder. "Sheila! Move! Get us off the road!"

Like coming out of a trance, Sheila grabbed the wheel and stepped on the accelerator a bit too heavily. The car lurched forward and the steam cloud, which had only gotten worse, once again covered the windshield. Fortunately, it was a short distance to the median area and Sheila was able to get the car off the road by looking out the side window. Once the car was safely off the road, Sheila shut the engine off. For a full minute, the three sat in stunned silence.

Miraculously, no other vehicles had collided. The traffic pattern had resumed its normal flow as if nothing had happened, leaving the Concorde behind as a wounded, dying animal that was beyond help.

The three got out of the car. Sally looked at the front of the car and said, "It probably is a damaged radiator hose."

Sheila looked at Henry expecting him to be the resident auto-mechanic. He replied with total lack of conviction. "Um… right. That's exactly what I was thinking."

Sally looked over at Sheila and said, "See if you can get the hood open. Maybe we can make a temporary fix."

Sheila looked back with a blank expression. After a moment, she walked to the front of the car not having a clue as to how to get the hood open. Sensing her confusion, Sally called over to Henry who was standing beside the driver's door. "I think you'll find a handle under the dash below the door side of the steering wheel."

Henry opened the door and pulled the handle that said 'hood'. The hood popped opened a bit and Sally reached for the hood latch at the front. The moment the hood was lifted, a spray of water and steam came out. The engine compartment was entirely soaked.

After several minutes, the steam subsided providing an opportunity to inspect the damage. Every inch of the engine compartment was filled with complicated looking equipment that made any likelihood of affecting a repair doubtful. The hoses looked fine but there was water everywhere.

Sally straightened up and backed away from the car. "We need to call for help."

Immediately, Sheila cried, "Oh no! We can't call my dad. He'll kill me if he finds out I took the car. What are we going to do?"

At that moment a car pulled off the side of the highway and an older man ran across to join them.

"Looks like you're having problems. Are you all right? Can I help?"

Sally gave a silent prayer of thanks and said, "We're fine. Our car just broke down. Do you know of any place around here we can call to get it fixed?"

The man pulled out his cell phone. "I live a few miles from here. Probably the closest place with a tow truck is in Norwich. I know a place just off the interstate. Let me look up their number."

He scrolled through telephone numbers and finally said, "Here it is. Ace Auto Repair. Let me give them a call."

He placed the call and let them know that a wrecker was on the way and should be arriving in about thirty minutes. After reassuring them that everything would be all right, the man jumped back into his car and took off. The three got back into the car to wait in the relative warmth.

At about six forty-five p.m. a tow truck arrived with flashing orange lights. A man got out of the cab and walked over. He was the stereotypical repair mechanic dressed in insulated overalls that had copious grease stains. He was somewhere between twenty-five and thirty-five years of age, made difficult to judge by the two-day growth of beard and the amount of grease on his otherwise exposed face. "What seems to be the problem?" he asked."

Once again, Sally took charge. "It looks like some kind of coolant problem. The radiator and hoses look fine, but as you can see there is a significant leak."

The man directed his flashlight at the engine compartment that was still dripping wet. After about five minutes of standing around in the cold evening, the three were joined by repairman. He pronounced only two words as if that explained everything, "Water pump."

Quietly, Sheila started to cry. Henry put his arm around her shoulders to comfort her.

Sally asked the obvious question. "What will it take to fix it?"

The man stood chewing on either gum or tobacco, it was not exactly clear which, for a while considering the question.

"I'll have to tow it to the garage. This is Friday, you know. My guys have gone home for the weekend. And I'm not sure if I can get the parts right away."

Sally sensed that they were being played in some sort of game in which they were about to be announced as the losers.

With all the resolve and confidence she could muster, she stated, "Look we're on the way to Foxwoods and we need this car fixed. Can you do it or not?"

"Sure, little lady, but if you need it in a hurry, it's going to cost extra, that's all I was sayin'."

Sally, afraid to ask, plowed forward anyway. "How much and when can it be ready?"

The man took out a small notepad and wrote down some figures. Sally guessed that this was more for show than actual calculations.

"The tow will be seventy-five dollars. The repairs will be two hundred and ninety dollars. I'm doing you all a favor here with the price, seein' as you're in a tough jam and all. I'll need the seventy-five dollars up front for the tow, along with a hundred-dollar deposit for the work."

Sally snapped back. "Our car isn't sufficient security for the work? If we skip out on you its value would more than cover the cost of repairs."

The man chewed for a while and said, "It's registered out of state. Taking possession of an out of state car means paperwork that is a big pain in the rear end. It'll be one hundred and seventy-five dollars. Take it or leave it. I need to get back to the garage."

Sally saw that there was no negotiating with the man so she moved off to talk with Sheila and Henry. She explained the situation and then asked each how much money they had brought.

Sheila went back to the car and retrieved her purse. Holding it in the headlights of the tow truck she brought out one hundred and fifty dollars. Henry had pulled out his wallet and counted one hundred and thirty-five dollars in his hand. Sally did a quick computation. With her one hundred and fifty-five dollars, the total came to four hundred and forty dollars.

Upon hearing the news, Sheila despondently addressed the others. "Look, the hotel room costs two hundred dollars. We need to pay this guy one hundred and seventy-five dollars upfront. The remainder of the repair cost will be one hundred and ninety dollars. There's no way we have enough money for all this."

Suddenly Sheila brightened. "Henry, you have a credit card!"

Henry shuffled his feet and looked down at the ground in distress.

"Actually, I never really planned on *using* the credit card. I put the Millers' address down on the card application. I got the card while they were still away for the month on vacation. They're back now. If I charge anything, the bill will end up in their mailbox and I'll never be able to get it to pay it. I just wanted to use the card to secure the hotel room when we check in. I expected we would pay cash for the room in the morning when we check out."

Sally had been listening quietly. Seeing that the tow truck driver was getting impatient, she made up her mind. Turning to Henry she said, "Give me twenty dollars."

Henry was not sure what was up but he did as he was told. Sally took the money and walked back to the driver.

"How do we get in touch with you?" she asked.

The man fished out a filthy business card that read, *Ace Auto Repair*. The name on the card was Leon Munson. There was a local telephone number. Sally took the card and said, "We'll call tomorrow afternoon at four p.m. I expect you'll be finished by then." With that she handed over the one hundred and seventy-five dollars.

It took Leon only five minutes to hook up the Concorde to the tow truck. When it was completed, he approached the three. "How you three g'tting' over to Foxwoods?"

The question landed like a bombshell. In all the excitement, no one had thought about how to get to the hotel.

Sheila spoke up with pleading in her voice. "Could you give us a ride? We all could squeeze in the cab."

Leon immediately shook his head and said, "Sorry, no riders. Company policy."

There was a pathetic silence for several seconds and a change seemed to come over Leon's face. "Look, I'll call a cab for you. You can get to Foxwoods from here. It'll cost you about seventy-five dollars."

\*\*\*

160

Molly Burgess stood in front of the weekend senior security crew in the security meeting room. It was six p.m. and the shift had just changed for Friday night duty. Molly looked over the staff and thought to herself that there probably wasn't one of them that had an ounce of faith in her skills.

Molly was thirty-five years old which made her by far the youngest chief of security at any major resort facility with casino gambling. She had graduated summa *cum laude* from Harvard with an undergraduate degree political science. Upon graduation she enrolled in Northeastern University's program of Criminology and Justice Policy and, after two years and a summer, she received a Ph.D. at age twenty-five.

Having had enough of academic life for a while, she applied for, and received admission to, the FBI Academy in Quantico, Virginia. After seventeen weeks of rigorous field training, she was assigned as a special agent at the Las Vegas Field Office. Her crowning achievement occurred in her ninth-year assignment to the local criminal apprehension team. Having worked on a case involving organized crime at a Vegas casino for three years, Molly was given the team lead assignment in a joint FBI and Drug Enforcement Agency sting operation that was put in place to apprehend a money laundering operation. The operation involved a drug money scheme where funds were being brought into the casino and were being lost in amounts that would not attract undue attention each day at craps tables and in slot machines. The money was then returned by having blackjack dealers, who were paid off by the syndicate, using rigged decks to pay out winnings to the mob's players. It was a steady in and out routine that never resulted in excessive house gains or losses, which allowed the operation to go on unnoticed for years.

For a year Molly had gone undercover at the casino working on the casino's security staff. The sting operation had finally been set up to trap the blackjack dealers and syndicate players. The day of the sting, Molly had uncovered the fact that the chief of security at the casino was also involved. Just as her team had entered to make arrests, she had caught the chief erasing video surveillance records of the dealers. Without the video files as evidence, the FBI's case would have been shaky at best. In the ensuing conflict in the security surveillance room, gunfire had taken place, resulting in one of the regular security officers being shot and killed, and the security chief being shot, but not fatally wounded.

161

Molly had been decorated with an award of commendation from the FBI director himself and had resigned the very next day. Through the year of undercover work, she had gotten to know the security officer, Sean, who had been killed in the raid. They had developed what was becoming a serious relationship and now Molly couldn't help feeling horribly depressed over his death. She didn't know what she could have done differently, but deep down in her heart she felt that somehow, she was to blame. This sense of guilt, along with the overwhelming sense of grief over the loss, made a career move necessary. She had to get away from Vegas where memories of her time with Sean popped up around every corner. She had considered a transfer to another Bureau office, but the thrill of the FBI and field work had been forever tarnished. All she wanted was to move to some out-of-the-way place with a relatively quiet job, and just exist for a while.

The problem was, she had very little employable experience. After two weeks of trying to identify a job possibility with no results, she finally admitted to herself that her only two skills were the operations of gambling casinos and her security background. She was not excited about employment as a casino security staff member since such positions did not pay well and they often included shifts that were not conducive to establishing a regular day-night routine.

As if in answer to her problems, she discovered an advertisement for the position of chief of security at a resort casino in Connecticut. Although not exactly a small facility, Foxwoods would not carry the same pressures as one of the major casinos in Vegas or Atlantic City. And, as chief, she would receive a decent salary and would be able to keep regular working hours. And perhaps best of all, she thought, what could be more out-of-the-way than a small town in Connecticut?

At her interview for the position, Molly discovered that Foxwoods was a much bigger enterprise than she had imagined, and this part of Connecticut was not exactly 'out-of-the-way'. But the interview went well and within the week she had been notified that she had gotten the job.

Now, standing in the security meeting room in front of twelve senior officers for her weekend briefing, she understood something that had not occurred to her when she had applied for the position as chief. She would be leading men and women who, no matter what credentials or awards she had received, would only give her respect when she had earned it.

Molly quickly looked over the weekend schedule and began.

"As you all know, we have a busy weekend scheduled."

Looking up from her schedule, Molly spoke to two men in the first row.

"Jim and Pete, you will be heading the detail for the theater this evening. We have a high-priced violinist from Germany staying at the MGM Grand as tonight's performer. She has her own security detail so Jim you will need to coordinate the operation with their security head. His name is Gunter Schmidt. He will be checking in at seven thirty. You should meet with him as soon as he arrives. The violinist and her accompanist will be arriving by the back entrance at eight p.m."

Molly took a breath and continued.

"Needless to say, this is one of our premier events and we need to make sure that nothing goes wrong. No one gets past the security posts backstage without a pass. That means no one."

The two security officers nodded in understanding.

"The performers will be leaving by the back at precisely ten forty-five. Make sure their limos are in place by ten thirty."

This was one of the special entertainment events for the year and Molly knew that the performance of her crew would be watched closely by the resort manager. The violinist was a world class concert master who had performed internationally. This event had attracted people from as far away as Washington DC and Molly knew that the house would be full of important people.

"I don't want even the smallest of disturbances tonight. Pete, make sure that we have people in the theater before the crowd is admitted. Any sign of trouble and I want it stopped immediately. Use a firm hand but don't draw any undue attention."

Pete looked up from his notes and responded, "Yes, boss."

Looking back at her notes, Molly went on.

"This Wednesday the first of the Billings Shipping executives arrived to prepare for their annual corporate meeting this weekend. They spent the day Thursday pretty much by themselves getting their presentations together. This morning they held business meetings in the

Pequot tenth floor meeting rooms and tomorrow the big corporate meeting. Tomorrow, from nine a.m. until eleven a.m., the Billings board of directors will meet in the Mezzanine conference room. At one thirty p.m. the general stockholders' meeting will begin in the Grand Ballroom."

Molly handed out a sheet of assignments.

"Billy, you'll be heading up security for the Billings meetings tomorrow. You all have your assignments that I just handed out. Any problems contact Billy immediately. Don't wait until a minor issue becomes a major problem."

Looking over at Billy Styles, Molly smiled.

"I have no idea who comes to annual stockholder meetings, but you can bet that there may be disagreeable stockholders. Screen everyone that gets into the ballroom. We're not taking any chances."

Billy nodded and then asked, "What about the Billings management group or the board members? Do they have any special security teams that will be on site?"

Molly replied, "No. The security is entirely being left up to us."

***

Responding to a quiet knock, the door to a room on the sixth floor was opened by Johann Steiner. Outside the room was a man who was quickly ushered in. Inside, both men took a seat at the table in the corner of the room.

Steiner poured a cup of coffee for himself and asked, "When did you get in?"

The other man said, "I arrived just before noon. I checked in and got situated. I tried to find you at lunch but you were not in your room. Is everything set with your contract help?"

Steiner nodded. "I gave him the assignments yesterday. I let him know that he had until the end of today. I need you to keep tabs on the situation for me. Make sure our man gets the job done. If it looks like he has any trouble I want you to be there."

The younger man replied, "I'll be here until Sunday. How did this morning go?"

164

"She brought up something interesting that I want you to check into. She asked about a bank account set up in her husband's name."

"Was it the Tokushima Industries account? How could she have uncovered it?"

"If their accountant Connor could discover that account, we have to be prepared that perhaps she might have also."

The man answered, "We plugged that hole."

"Maybe so, but I want you to find out why she thinks we set up this account and how she discovered it. Let me know when you get an answer."

With that, the younger man rose and headed out of the room. He took the elevator down to the main level and walked over to the hotel entrance lobby. When he arrived at the desk, a pretty young clerk looked up and asked, "Can I help you, sir?"

"I'm looking to speak with a guest who is staying at the hotel. He is a US naval officer. His name is Commander Peter Ashley."

The clerk smiled and replied, "I cannot give out room numbers of our guests, but I could ring his room for you if you would like."

The man nodded and said, "Yes."

The clerk typed the name into her computer and, after finding the name, dialed the number. The man watched carefully and noted the room number that was dialed. The room phone rang four times before the clerk decided that no one was in the room to answer. She turned back to the man to say that no one picked up but the man was no longer standing at the counter. In surprise, the clerk looked around for the man but, apparently, he had just disappeared. Looking over at the bell captain who had just walked up to the counter, she remarked, "That was strange. A man just asked me to ring a room for him and then just walked away. How rude!"

The captain leaned on the counter and said, "Yeah, I saw him take off. He seemed like he was in a hurry. I checked him in with his bags around noon today. He was a piece of work. Not exactly a model of politeness and no tip. Not one of your more friendly Germans. I think I remember his name was Wilkins, no wait a minute, it was Wilhelm... Gustav Wilhelm."

165

The clerk grabbed a pen and jotted down a note saying, "Well, I'll put a note in the message box for Commander Ashley that Mr Wilhelm was looking to speak with him."

# Chapter 14

The taxi pulled into the resort entryway. Henry, Sheila and Sally hopped out and Sheila opened her purse. The cab driver flipped the meter handle. "That'll be seventy-six dollars fifty."

Sheila gave a sigh and paid the fare with four twenty-dollar bills.

Henry watched and, after the taxi left, he cried, "You gave that guy a three fifty tip! We can't afford tips. We can't even afford to get our car out of hock."

Sally said, "Don't sweat it. I have a plan. We need to go in and secure our room."

The trio walked inside as Henry ran along mumbling, "Plan? What plan?"

When they reached the lobby desk, the clerk looked up with a smile and said, "Can I help you?"

Henry stepped forward and said with a deeper voice than normal, "Yes, miss, I have a room reserved for the evening."

Sheila looked at Sally and rolled her eyes.

The clerk said pleasantly, "Could I have your identification and a credit card?"

Henry took out his wallet and casually slipped his license and the credit card towards the clerk. "I'm sure these will do."

The clerk took a moment to look at the documents and then processed the room. "How many keys would you like, Mr Wright?"

Henry stood in confused silence. Why would he need more than one key?

Sally stepped up and said, "Why don't you get three keys, *Thomas*?"

Not recognizing his name, Henry looked with a puzzled expression. All sense of confidence had been lost. Sheila kicked him in the shin and he suddenly regained his composure. "Er, sure, three keys would be great."

The clerk shook her head and said with a chuckle, "Would you and your party like help with your bags?"

Henry looked down at his worn backpack which looked a bit sad, and said, "No thanks, I think we can manage."

The clerk gave Henry a smile and said, "Have a good stay, Mr Wright."

When they reached their room, Sheila dropped her bag on the bed and, looking at Henry, said, "Real smooth Mr Wright."

Henry glared back. "Look, we're checked in, all right? We're doing fine."

Sally hung up her coat in the closet and took control. Spreading out a resort floor plan that she had picked up at the front desk, she began.

"It's now already seven thirty but if we get started, we'll get as much data as we can. Between now and say... eleven p.m. If we need more data, we might be able to stay tomorrow and finish up in the morning. I say tonight, Henry, you begin in the Grand Pequot Casino, and Sheila, you begin in the Great Cedar Casino. After an hour, you should switch places. Ask your questions but don't attract attention."

She handed out the plastic counters. "Keep these in your pockets. Remember, use your left pocket counter to track the answers for the first question, and the right pocket counter for the answers to the second question."

Looking at Henry, Sally asked, "You remember the questions, right?"

Henry made a face and said, "Yes, Mom, I remember. The first question is, Have you gambled at a casino more than once in the past year? And the second question is, Do you set a spending limit that you do not let yourself exceed when you gamble at casinos?"

Sheila took her counters and then asked, "Hey wait a minute. You said Henry will be in the Grand Pequot Casino and I'll be in the Great Cedar Casino. Where are you going to be?"

Sally took a breath and said, "I'll be getting our money to get the car back."

Both Henry and Sheila gave a startled look. Henry was first to react.

"Exactly how to you plan to do that? If you get caught stealing, remember we don't have bail money."

Sally laughed. "I'll try to keep that in mind. Actually, I shouldn't need it if all goes well. I'll be in the Rainmaker Casino at the blackjack tables."

Sheila interrupted. "Wait a minute, Sally, we all promised no gambling. You know that gambling can only lose what money we have left."

Sally knew that the explanation wouldn't be easy, but she also knew that the others would not let her use the remaining money without knowing that it she would be taking a reasonable risk.

"I have a certain ability that will tip the odds in my favor when I play cards. Perhaps you have heard of card counting."

She waited for a response, but when Henry and Sheila both gave none, she continued.

"The game of blackjack, or twenty-one as it is sometimes known, is actually a study in probability mathematics. Ordinarily at any casino, the house maintains an advantage in the game of blackjack because the ratio of low cards to high cards favors the low cards. When relying on the chance of the draw to exactly match the point total of twenty-one, the fact that there are fewer tens and face cards than low point cards, results in the probability that the player will lose to the house. Card counting is simply a system of keeping track of the number of cards by type that remain in the deck, and when it can be determined that the ratio of tens and face cards to low point cards is greatest, one bets with the odds now in the player's favor."

Henry sat in amazement as he listened. When Sally finished, he spoke up. "But it would take a genius to be able to memorize all the cards that had been played at a blackjack table with several players. How could anyone do that?"

"Actually," Sally replied, "it is simpler than that. All you must do is assign a point system to cards. One of the simplest systems is to assign a value of one point for cards with numbers of two through six, a value of zero for eights' and nines', and a value of minus one for tens and face cards. As the game proceeds, you just keep track of the running total. The total will tell you when to bet."

With enthusiasm Henry offered, "Hey, anyone could do that. We could win easily if we can just keep track of the numbers!"

With a fierce look of skepticism, Sheila said to Henry, "Look, it can't be that easy or everyone would be doing it and casinos would go broke."

With patience, Sally responded. "It turns out that Sheila is right. Casinos make card counting more difficult by using multiple decks. A blackjack deck that includes six decks of fifty-two cards requires a bit more computation."

In fact, the counting system that Sally had in mind was even more complex than she had described. The Zen Counting system assigned card values between negative two and positive two which greatly increased the probability of success in her favor, but which required significantly greater skills of memorization.

As Henry considered the prospect of keeping track of cards from six decks, he came to the realization that the task might be a bit beyond his abilities. He spoke up with a tone of resignation. "So, with six decks it really can't be done by us."

Sally smiled and said, "Well actually, I've done a bit of reading on the subject, and although I admit that I haven't actually put my reading to a real test, I am confident that I can use card counting to make back the money that we need. What I need from you both is your trust. I will need some of the money we have to get started."

Henry immediately grabbed his wallet and put his money on the bed. Sheila hesitated but after thinking for a moment emptied the money from her purse on the bed saying, "I'm still not entirely on board with this but I'll admit that I can't think of anything else."

Sally counted the money. "We have one hundred and eighty-five. If we get something to eat before we begin this evening that will probably bring us down to about one hundred and seventy. The hotel room will be two hundred dollars. We will need about thirty-five for gas and tolls for the trip home, about another thirty for meals tomorrow. We are also going to need another eighty dollars for the cab ride to get the car and one hundred and ninety for the rest of the repair bill. That means we are short by at least three hundred and sixty-five dollars. To be safe, that means I'll need to win around four hundred dollars. That should be reasonable."

Henry's excitement returned. "Hey, can I watch while you win us the money? I've never seen a card watcher!"

"That's card *counter*, you moron, and no, you can't watch," Sheila pronounced emphatically. "We came here for a reason and we're going to get your data on gambling, not hang around watching people lose money!"

Sally broke the tension by gathering one hundred dollars from the bed. This is about what I will need to do my work." Turning to Sheila she said, "Why don't you take the rest of the money with you?"

Henry began to protest but when he saw the look on Sheila's face he mumbled under his breath, "Yah, Sheila, why don't you take the rest. I might lose my head and end up at the craps tables counting dice."

With that, the three left the room in search of a place to eat supper.

*** 

Seated in a restaurant booth, Peter Ashley pulled out a folded piece of paper and slid it across the table to Rear Admiral Chester Rand. The waitress arrived with a plate for the admiral with a cut of prime rib that was so large that it could hardly be contained on the plate. She set a plate of broiled haddock at Ashley's place and asked, "Can I get you something else to drink?"

Rand motioned to the two empty glasses and said, "Two more beers if you would please."

The waitress grabbed the glasses and headed off to the bar.

Rand began attacking his meal and, after savoring several bites, he put his fork down and picked up the paper.

Ashley motioned to the paper and said, "This is a list of all unauthorized personnel who might possibly have had access to the BSI documents. Ms Kerrigan was cooperative, but she wasn't able to provide any real positive leads. This is just a list of possibilities. I'll check them all out, though."

Ashley went back to nibbling at his meal. After the beers arrived, he asked, "What did you think of Macintyre's response this morning?"

The admiral thought for a moment and then said, "At first I had a suspicion that maybe he knew more than he was letting on. But afterward I wasn't so sure."

Ashley nodded in agreement. "There's something about the man that I don't like. I can't say that there's anything particularly wrong, but I just don't get a good feeling from him."

The admiral gave a nod of agreement. "We need to review the BSI security system. I think it would be best if you would head up to Maine on Sunday and spend the week seeing what you can find out. I've spoken with Bill Davidson with the navy's Supervisor of Ships. He will make arrangements for your access to the shipyard."

Ashley took the paper back and put it away. "I want to speak with the project lead engineer, Steven Brown, tomorrow. I didn't get any idea that he is involved in anything, which might mean he's innocent, or it might mean he's particularly good at deception."

The admiral said, "That's a good idea. I also want you to squeeze Macintyre a little harder. See if he responds to some pressure."

"Will do. And if I'm going up to Maine, I also want to get with Lisa Kerrigan again to have her set me up when I arrive to get access to personnel files of all the senior project staff."

Across the restaurant, a man with pure white hair sat by himself nursing a cup of coffee as he read a newspaper. As the admiral and Peter Ashley stood up to leave, the man folded his paper and motioned for the waitress to get his check.

\*\*\*

A thirty-two-year-old security staff member stood at the entrance to the Grand Pequot Casino. Deb Creighton watched as guests poured into the casino area. It looked like most of these folks were looking to play slot machines she thought. It wasn't hard to tell. It seemed to be an older crowd with a high number of married women who always seemed to prefer playing quarter machines. The buckets of quarters were another clue.

It was seven forty-five p.m. and as the crowd filed in after the dinner hour, her attention was drawn to a person who stood out as dramatically as a page from a book from her childhood that asked, *who doesn't belong here?*

"Excuse me," she said as she motioned to a young man. "Could you show me your ID?"

Henry walked over and pulled out his wallet. He handed over his newly printed driver's license to the security lady wondering if she would run a check on the name. The lady looked carefully at the license and then back at Henry.

"Is this your current address, Mr Wright?"

Henry looked down at his shoes as his insides began to squirm.

"Yes, it is."

Holding onto the license, Deb asked, "And what would that address be?"

Without thinking, Henry blurted out his home address. "112 Lincoln Street, Billings, Maine." He stood in silence for a moment wondering why the security lady did not give back his license when he suddenly realized his mistake.

"Er... that's where I *used to* live. But I just moved to a new house... er... apartment. My new address is 235 North Street." He looked sheepishly at the security lady and mumbled, "Yeah... 235 North."

Deb could hardly contain her laughter. She had seen her share of teenagers with fake IDs trying to get into the casino, but she had to admit to herself that this one took the cake. If this kid was twenty-one, she would eat not just her hat but her shoes as well. But there was something cute about this guy, and if his ID were fake, it was as good as she'd ever seen. She studied the license again and then gave it back.

"Have a good evening, Mr Wright."

Henry took his license back and moved quickly into the casino with a word of relief. "Thanks."

As Henry walked into the casino, Deb radioed the security office. "Check on Maine license 9870954."

After several minutes, her earpiece sounded. "Maine license 9870954, Thomas Wright, twenty-four years old, 235 North Street, Billing, Maine. Is there a problem?"

With a somewhat surprised tone, Deb responded. "Thanks, Aaron, no problem, I just needed an ID check. Thanks."

Henry surveyed the casino floor that was crowded with people. The center area contained gaming tables including tables of blackjack, craps and roulette. At most tables there were a crowd of people focusing their full attention as they served up an endless stream of chips. Across the floor, above the din of the crowd, ringing bells could be heard along with squeals of delight, as nearby players collected an outpouring of coins from slot machines that made one think that winning was just a moment away for all.

Between two blackjack tables stood a woman that looked to Henry to be about the age of his grandmother. She seemed to be taking a break from the action so Henry decided to get his evening started. He walked over and said, "Hi! Winning much?"

The woman looked at Henry and smiled. "Well, you know, you win some and you lose some, but mostly you lose."

Henry tried to sound casual, but he couldn't help feeling like a police interrogator. "Have you gambled at a casino more than once in the past year?"

The woman was somewhat taken aback by the question, but after a second, she replied pleasantly. "No, this is my husband and my first trip here. We've never been to a casino before. We live in Vermont and we don't travel much. Yesterday was our anniversary and we just decided on an impulse to get away for a long weekend. I wanted to go to New York, but Chester, that's my husband, was set on coming here. So here I am!"

Whoa, thought Henry, more than I needed to know! At this rate, I'll only get to interview three people before the first hour would be up. Nevertheless, he pushed on.

"Sounds like you haven't won the grand jackpot yet. Did you set a spending limit that you won't allow yourself to exceed when you came?"

Again, the woman gave Henry a quizzical look, but she seemed happy to be talking with someone. Obviously, thought Henry, her husband had abandoned her seeking his fortune on his own.

The woman nodded her head and said, "Absolutely! My husband and I agreed that we would not lose more than fifty dollars each. I don't know how Chester's doing, but so far, I'm only about five dollars down.

174

You know, sonny, you really won't win money by gambling. You should be saving your money, not giving it away here."

This really *is* my grandmother, thought Henry! I'm getting the 'you should be saving your money' talk. Having gotten his answers, he turned to move away to find another subject, saying, "Well, have a good time, and happy anniversary." Henry put both hands in his pockets and clicked each counter once.

Over in the Great Cedar Casino, Sheila was also finding it tough going. She had gotten past the security greeter at the entrance with just a smile. She moved over to the slot machine area that was laid out in a circular space. At first, she just stood taking in the layout. Having gotten a feel for how the space worked she began connecting with random people asking the rehearsed questions. After about half an hour she had surveyed twelve people. Before she could reach the next person, a guy walked up to her. Sheila thought that he was probably a college student from one of the nearby colleges or universities, and by his somewhat disheveled look it appeared that he had already had a few too many drinks.

"Hey there cutie," the guy said. "You here by yourself?"

Sheila thought, sure, I always go to casinos alone looking to meet guys. Instead, she smiled politely and said, "Actually, no, my boyfriend is in the men's room and he'll be right back."

The man put his arm around her shoulder, spilling some of his drink that he held in his other hand. "Hey, how would you like to join me at the craps table while your beau is occupied? I'm on a winning streak."

Sheila tried to wriggle out from under his arm but it proved to be not so easy to disengage herself. While she struggled, she hissed, "Listen, bud, let go of me or I'll call security."

Looking hurt, the guy stammered on. "You don't want to do that, honey. I just want to have a good time and you look kind of lonely."

Sheila began to worry about making a scene and attracting attention that she did not want. Just when she thought she would have no other option than getting physical, a voice spoke up behind the guy.

"Let go and move on or I'll call security."

Sheila turned and saw Sally standing with a grim look of determination. The guy also looked at her and after a moment of decision, he let go of his hold on Sheila and, as he walked off, he snarled, "Whatever. I've got better things to do… your loss."

Sheila breathed a sigh of relief. "What are you doing here? Not that I mind much."

Sally smiled and said, "The blackjack tables in the Rainmaker Casino were all full. I thought that I would try my luck here. Why don't you go over to the Rainmaker to continue collecting data? I'll stay here. When Henry shows up, I'll send him over to catch up with you."

Sheila didn't argue. A change of venue wouldn't be a bad idea she thought. Saying thanks again and so-long to Sally, Sheila headed off to the Rainmaker Casino.

Sally walked over to a blackjack table that had three open chairs. She stood watching until the dealer re-shuffled the deck and then sat down to play. She handed five twenty bills to the dealer and received her chips which she stacked neatly.

*** 

At eight thirty p.m. Molly Burgess stood outside the entrance to the Fox Theater watching men and women dressed in formal attire enter the theater. As she watched she spoke into her radio. "Pete, this is Molly. Can you meet me out front please?"

In less than a minute, Pete Stryker arrived. Molly nodded and asked, "Did everything go okay with the private security team?"

Pete put away his radio and replied. "Mr Gunter Schmidt won't win any popularity contests, but he seemed prepared and capable. The violinist and the guy who plays the piano, along with an entourage of twenty support folks, arrived on time and we escorted them to the green room suites. I left Jim backstage to keep an eye on things."

Standing in the foyer not twenty feet from where Molly and Pete were surveying the crowd, was a group waiting for someone to join their party. James Macintyre stood with Steven Brown and all of the Pentagon members who had attended the WG-116B briefing, except Commander Hicks, who was apparently running a bit late. Macintyre took the opportunity to make sure that Admiral Rand knew how, with Macintyre's expert guidance, the project was proceeding on schedule and was close

176

to completion of the first phase. The admiral listened politely, but without participating.

With no sign of Commander Hicks and the show not due to start for another fifteen minutes, Peter Ashley announced that he was going to the men's room. More out of a desire to escape Macintyre's ranting than a need to relieve himself, Steven Brown turned and simply said, "Me too."

On the way to the restroom Ashley said with a smile, "It must be fortunate to have such a gifted manager on the project. With all that Macintyre does, I'm not exactly certain what is left for your engineers to do."

As the two men walked along, a man with closely cropped white hair stepped out from behind a nearby potted plant and followed them toward the men's room. As the man approached the restroom door, he drew his gun out from under his sweater.

# Chapter 15

Henry glanced at his watch and noted that an hour had gone by. He had managed to survey twenty-seven people and was feeling good. It was time to go find Sheila. He casually walked out and headed to the Grand Cedar Casino. He entered the casino without incident, which gave him a bit of relief as he couldn't help but remember how his entrance into the Pequot Casino had gone. He looked around for Sheila without success. He was wandering through the crowd looking for Sheila when instead he saw Sally seated at a blackjack table.

Looking up and recognizing Henry, Sally subtly shook her head and gave him a look that said, *not now*. Henry stopped at the table and watched without giving notice that he knew Sally. At Sally's place there was a large stack of chips, all of which were piled on the table as a single bet.

Sally sat studying the cards in front of her. Henry noticed that each of the eight players had two cards face up while the dealer had one card face down and one facing up for everyone to see. He generally understood that the object was to get a total of twenty-one with the cards, but he wasn't exactly sure of the details of the game. The dealer's face-up card was a queen of clubs. Sally's face-up cards were a two of hearts and a three of hearts. Oddly enough, Sally seemed to be paying more attention to the other players' cards than her own.

Sally was sitting in the chair on the end of the table, which meant that she would play last. Henry saw that she was watching intently as each player took their turn. Henry saw the first player ask for an additional card but had apparently got a bad one because he turned his cards over and the dealer took his chips away. The second and third players suffered the same fate. The fourth player decided not to ask for a card and he was able to keep his chips. This, he thought, seemed to be the smart move. Why would anyone ask for more cards if it meant you would lose your chips?

The fifth and sixth players each asked for one more card but apparently, they both got good cards because they were allowed to keep their chips. The seventh player asked for not one card, but two cards, which resulted in what Henry knew would be the obvious result, losing his chips!

When it came to Sally's turn, Henry wanted to scream out, *Don't ask for another card!* It seemed to Henry that Sally was caught in a trance. She sat motionless as if in a daze, lost in thought. At last Sally seemed to awake. She motioned for the dealer to give her a card and Henry's heart sank. The dealer gave Sally a three of spades. To Henry's horror, Sally immediately asked for another card. The dealer obliged without showing any sign of interest. The third card showing was a six of diamonds. Henry quickly added up the cards that were showing, eleven. Sally then asked for yet another card which turned out to be a nine of spades. That meant that Sally's cards added up to a total of twenty.

It was with great relief that Henry saw that Sally had decided not to take any more cards. The dealer flipped over his face-down card to reveal a nine of diamonds and announced, "*Nineteen*", as though it resolved all questions which, as Henry saw, it apparently did. Both of the other two players who still had chips disgustedly turned their hidden cards over and gave up their chips to the dealer. Without any emotion, the dealer counted out a stack of chips that equaled the stack in front of Sally and slid them over to her place.

Sally stood up and pushed the chips into her purse. She left two chips as a tip for the dealer and walked over to speak with Henry.

As Sally approached, Henry exclaimed, "That was awesome! How did you know it was okay to keep asking for more cards?"

Sally frowned and said, "Shhh... we don't want to attract any attention. I have the distinct feel that I was being watched. They don't like card counters at casinos, and I was probably pushing my luck. Anyway, we have five hundred and fifty dollars, which should be more than enough to get us home."

Henry looked at Sally with a new sense of respect. "You know you really are amazing." Continuing, he remarked, "As for being watched, it was probably more than a feeling. Right above the dealer at the ceiling is an IP digital camera."

Sally began to turn around, but Henry put a hand on her shoulder.

"Don't bother looking. You probably wouldn't see it anyway. It's only the size of a pencil eraser. It's probably fed by a multi-mode 52.5-micron single strand fiber optic cable back to a local network node. You probably didn't see it when you were playing, but it's a sure thing that they were seeing you."

Sally cursed herself for not figuring out that there would be surveillance cameras everywhere. "We'd better not be seen too long together. I sent Sheila to the Rainmaker Casino. Why don't you stay here and continue collecting data? I'll go to the Rainmaker Casino and begin my survey. When I find Sheila, I'll send her back to the Grand Pequot Casino."

Henry agreed and Sally started off back to the Rainmaker Casino. Everywhere people were mingling, shuffling between gaming tables and back and forth to slot machines. The hall wasn't any less crowded when she exited the casino floor. She found herself in the middle of some commotion just outside the entrance to the resort's theater. There were casino security people everywhere pushing the crowd back as it appeared that someone was being arrested.

\*\*\*

As Peter Ashley and Steven Brown entered the men's room, they saw that all of the urinals were occupied except one. Coming through the door first, Ashley walked over to the open urinal as Brown made his way back to one of the enclosed toilet stalls.

As Ashley stood at the urinal, the white-haired man entered and waited against the lavatories, concealing his gun under his arm. Before Ashley had finished, all the others in the room had made their way out, leaving only the man and Ashley in the outer restroom area. Standing directly across from Ashley, the man raised his gun and aimed at Ashley's heart. As the trigger was pulled, the sound of a muffled *THWACK* filled the room, but it was not a sound that would have been audible outside. As Ashley looked down in surprise at his chest, he had

180

just enough time to see a growing red stain appear on his white shirt before he dropped to the floor unconscious.

The gunman quietly walked over to the toilet stall which was occupied by Brown and slid the gun under the toilet partition. He then turned to leave. As the man walked casually out of the room, he peeled off his set of gloves and put them in the waste receptacle by the door. Looking around to see that no one was paying any particular attention to him, he walked away toward the resort main lobby and the exit doors.

***

Steven Brown had heard the silenced gun go off, but not ever having owned or shot a gun before, he didn't exactly know what the sound might be. He didn't think anything unusual was going on until he heard the gun sliding along the floor into his stall. He zipped up his pants and stared down at the gun, not knowing what to make of it. At first, he couldn't identify the object as a gun. So often when an object is seen totally out of its expected environment, it takes on an unrecognizable nature. After a moment he leaned down and picked it up, and for the first time understood what it was. This understanding, however, only resulted in a rush of questions that flooded into his mind. As his engineering brain tried to sort through the questions to form a logical framework for answers to be developed, he heard a man cry out in alarm at the urinals. Brown opened the toilet stall door, and carrying the gun in his hand, he saw a man standing at the lavatories and Peter Ashley lying on the floor in a pool of blood in front of the urinals.

The man was yelling for help when he saw Brown with the gun. The man instantly turned white and stammered, "Please… please don't shoot me. I have a wife and three kids."

***

Molly and Pete were standing at the Fox Theater entrance looking for any problems when simultaneously they heard a yelling coming from the men's room down the hall. Molly's first thought was that a scuffle had likely broken out between two guys who had more than their quota of

181

drinks. Not thinking that it warranted any special attention she motioned to Pete. "Why don't you go and see if you can help whoever seems to have a problem with his equipment."

Pete gave a nod of agreement and headed down the hall. Just as he arrived at the restroom door, a man came rushing out in a panic yelling, *"There's a man in there with a gun. Don't go in!"*

This stopped Pete in his tracks. He grabbed the man saying, "Hey, slow down there. What's going on?"

The man pointed back to the men's room and he blurted out somewhat incoherently. "A guy in there just shot somebody... He's got a gun... I don't know. I think the guy's dead... There's blood everywhere."

Pete grabbed his radio and spoke calmly with a voice that concealed his apprehension. "This is Stryker. We've got a code red situation at the Fox Theater restrooms. I need all available officers in the vicinity here for backup on the double."

It wasn't five seconds before Molly Burgess was at Pete's side. She immediately took control. "What do we have?"

Pete held onto the man who had exited the restroom. The man was beginning to regain some control.

"This guy says that there's man in the men's room with a gun and that at least one person is down."

Molly quickly assessed the situation as she gave instructions. "Pete, keep this crowd back. I want the hall evacuated immediately. Keep the people in the casino area out of the hall. Move everyone in the hall out to the main lobby. Go!"

She grabbed her radio and called the security office. "This is Chief Burgess. I need a nine-one-one call for state police assistance. Let them know we have a suspected armed conflict in progress and for them to enter at the Grand Cedar entrance. They'll be met on arrival."

At that moment four other casino security men arrived. Molly ordered two of them to assist Pete with the emergency evacuation of the connecting hall. She turned to the other two and said, "Jim is backstage at the theater. Coordinate with him. I want the theater sealed immediately. No one is to come out. Have everyone sit tight until I give the okay."

The two rushed off and Molly turned her attention back to the door of the men's room. She drew her service revolver and started toward the door. She flattened herself against the wall beside the door and took a deep breath. At that moment Billy Styles, along with three security members, came running down the hall.

"Boss, you okay?" Billy shouted.

Molly answered back, "Yea, I'm fine but we may have a guy with a gun in here with possibly one or more down and who knows if he has hostages."

The security team took cover behind a metal table that they tipped on its side with their guns drawn and aimed at the door. Billy took up a position against the wall on the other side of the door. "What's your plan?" he asked.

Before Molly could answer, the men's room door opened, and Steven Brown came staggering out in a dazed state holding the gun loosely in his hand. He looked at the security team with their guns drawn and, as if coming back to life, said, "Don't shoot!" He dropped the gun on the carpet and Billy grabbed his arms from behind. In a split second, Billy had him in handcuffs.

Molly immediately rushed into the men's room and found Ashley on the floor lying in blood. After checking to see that no one else was in the room, she radioed the security office to have them call for an emergency med-flight helicopter. She then called for the resort physician. Kneeling down at Ashley's side, she felt for a pulse. To her relief there was a faint heartbeat but she could tell that the wound was serious and his life would depend on how quickly help would arrive.

\*\*\*

James Macintyre and the Pentagon contingency had gone into the theater shortly after Brown and Ashley had headed off to the men's room. Commander Hicks had arrived, and the group had decided to get to their seats knowing that Brown and Ashley would be in shortly. The house lights dimmed in the theater and the audience sat in expectation of the entrance of Anne-Sophie Mutter and her accompanist. The grand entrance never happened.

Moments after the house lights had dimmed, they came back up. A man came on stage and announced that there had been an 'incident' out in the hall and that the ushers were to see that everyone remained seated until the situation was resolved. No one was to leave the theater.

They waited for twenty minutes when Macintyre's impatience won out over his self-control. He leaned over to the admiral and said, "This is ridiculous. We paid good money for this facility for our annual meeting and I expect better treatment. I'm going to see what's the matter."

He stood up and slid down the row to the aisle. Immediately an usher came up to meet him. She said politely, "I'm sorry, sir, we need to have everyone stay in their seats for a little while longer. It won't be too long."

Macintyre wouldn't have any of it. He barked back at the usher. "Look, you may not know who I am, *miss*, but I'm James Macintyre the CEO of Billings Shipyard. In case you didn't know, that's the company that paid a major share of the cost for this performance tonight and I expect some answers why we aren't seeing it. And don't tell me it's because of some *incident*. I want to know exactly what's going on here."

The usher was immediately flustered. She looked back at the security man standing at the rear theater doors and then back at Macintyre. "You should probably speak with that man at the rear doors," she said.

Macintyre marched up the aisle under the curious gaze of everyone in seats along the aisle. When he got to the security officer he said curtly, "I'm the CEO of Billings Shipyard. What's the hold up here?"

The security officer could see trouble brewing and did not want a scene that would heighten the level of anxiety that was already present in the audience. He leaned over to Macintyre and said quietly, "Keep this to yourself, but someone was just shot in the men's room. We've got the guy who did it, but the state police are here, and they don't want the crowd here to contaminate the crime scene. I understand that the restrooms have now been taped off and people will be dismissed shortly."

Macintyre grunted, "It better be shortly." And with that he returned to his seat. When he arrived back at his seat, he announced the details of the situation.

Instantly, Admiral Rand said in a worried voice, "Wasn't Peter Ashley in the men's room? And your engineer Steven Brown was with

184

him. Come to think of it, neither of them ever made it to their seats." The admiral stood and headed toward the back of the auditorium. At that very moment, a man came out on stage and began to speak.

"Ladies and gentlemen, I am terribly sorry to have to announce that tonight's performance will have to be cancelled."

There was a loud groan from the audience and many people started to object. The man on the stage raised his hands and the audience quieted down.

"Unfortunately, there is nothing we can do about the circumstances. There has been an accident just outside the theater which is why it was necessary to keep you all here while the situation was attended to. We recognize that you have all been terribly inconvenienced and we sincerely apologize. As a token of our appreciation for your understanding, the ushers have been given vouchers to hand out to each of you on your way out. The vouchers are redeemable at any of our casinos for fifty dollars in casino chips. Of course, you will also be reimbursed for your tickets for tonight's performance."

There is nothing quite like the perception of 'free money' to calm the soul, and so for the most part, the audience left in good spirits.

The admiral had reached the rear doors first and spoke to the security officer. "My name is Rear Admiral Chester Rand with the Department of Navy. One of my officers was in the men's room and perhaps was involved in the shooting."

The security officer looked with surprise at the admiral when he used the word 'shooting'. Then he remembered his conversation with the man from Billings Shipyard and he realized that bad news truly travels fast. He took out his radio and called Molly Burgess.

"This is Brian Herbert. I've got an Admiral Rand with the US Navy here who says that one of his officers was in the men's room at the time of the… the *incident*."

The radio came to life and Molly spoke. "Send him up to the security office."

Rand was ushered into the security office to discover at least twenty-five people standing around, including casino security staff, Ledyard Connecticut police officers, the New London County deputy sheriff as well as Connecticut State Police. In the back of the room were the people who were obviously in charge. Rand worked his way to the back of the room. Standing over a man who was seated in a chair was a woman who was introduced as the chief of security, Molly Burgess. Standing beside her was a captain with the state police.

Rand shook hands with Molly and was about to introduce himself to the state police officer when with total shock he saw that the man who was seated in the chair in handcuffs and leg shackles was BSI's engineer Steven Brown!

Rand recovered and spoke to Brown. "Where's Commander Ashley?"

Molly looked at Rand with surprise and asked, "You know this man?"

Rand answered, "This is Steven Brown, an engineer with the Billings Shipyard in Maine." Turning back to Brown he asked again, "Where's Commander Ashley?"

Brown looked up and with sadness in his voice as he said, "The commander was shot."

The state police captain held up a hand to Admiral Rand and turned to face Brown. "Mr Brown, you have the right to remain silent, and anything that you say may be used against you in a court of law. You have the right to an attorney to be present and if you cannot afford one, one will be appointed for you at no cost. Do you understand these rights which I have just read?"

Brown was obviously still in a state of shock. Looking somewhat dazed he said, "Yes, I understand my rights."

The officer asked, "Do you wish to waive your rights to an attorney during questioning?"

Brown nodded and replied, "I didn't do anything wrong. I don't need an attorney."

The admiral interjected. "Listen, I don't know what's going on here, but Mr Brown, you should seriously think about calling a lawyer, even if you didn't do anything wrong. I'm sure that BSI has an attorney."

The officer gave the admiral a menacing look and said to Molly, "Please have the admiral escorted to the outer office. We'll call him when we need him."

After relating the details of what he knew of the shooting, Brown lapsed into a moment of silence. The state police captain gave him a second to catch his breath and then asked, "You expect us to believe that you didn't shoot this guy Ashley? There is a witness that saw you with the gun in your hand standing over the victim. There wasn't anyone else in the room. Exactly who would you have us believe did the shooting? A ghost?"

A look of panic began to surface in Brown's face. "Listen to me!" he pleaded. "I didn't shoot anybody. I was in the toilet stall when it happened. I told you, someone slid the gun under the toilet partition and I just picked it up. When I came out to see what was going on, there wasn't anyone around... at least until that other man walked in."

Leaning over to look Brown directly in the eyes the officer said, "I don't know how you think you're going to get out of this, but we're not idiots. In case you don't know it, Connecticut has the death penalty, and if this man dies, I'm personally going to see that you get put on death row."

For the first time, Brown began to realize that being innocent wouldn't necessarily save him from harm. He looked up and said with a sense of resolve, "I want to talk with a lawyer."

The state police officer straightened and said to the sheriff's deputy, "Take him down to the New London County lock-up. I'll get in touch with the district attorney." Turning to a lieutenant with the Ledyard Police Department he said, "Have your detectives coordinate with Sergeant Wilson who is downstairs interviewing people who were in the vicinity when the shooting took place. I want your reports on file by tomorrow at nine a.m. You can tell your chief that the state police will be taking the lead on this since the crime occurred on a site administered by the Connecticut Gaming Policy Board."

With that, the sheriff's deputy lead Brown out of the room with a Ledyard police officer in front and two casino security staff members at his sides.

The police captain watched as Brown was led away and then yelled to Molly who was at the door, "Now bring in the admiral."

A security staff member was pushing people along saying, "It's okay, everybody. Just a minor disturbance. You'll all be able to return in just a few minutes. Right now, we need you all to head out to the main lobby."

Sally was caught up in the movement of the crowd. Suddenly, as if by cue, the crowd stopped, and everyone looked back down the hall toward the theater. A group of security men were escorting a man who had his hands cuffed behind him. The man was being pushed along and he had his head down so that people couldn't get a good look at his face. One of the security staff pushed an opening in the crowd ahead of the man who was obviously being taken away for perpetrating some sort of crime. As the man reached the area in front of Sally, the man raised his head.

There was a noisy clamor that arose from the crowd as everyone wondered aloud what the man might have done. The security staff pushed ahead through the crowd as a voice could be heard above the commotion, speaking a single word, "Dad!"

# Chapter 16

Henry and Sheila sat in the main lobby with Sally who was visibly distraught.

"I thought you said your dad was working this weekend," said Sheila. "Why would he be here at a gambling casino? It couldn't have been him."

Sally thought for a moment, and replied. "He said he had to go out of town for the weekend on business. What if he meant he was coming here for a business meeting?"

Henry put a reassuring hand on Sally's shoulder. "Look, we're all tired. The thing with the car messed up all of our heads. I'm sure the guy looked like your dad, but really, there's no way your dad would be here, let alone be in handcuffs being taken away by the police. Come on, you know your dad better than that. That just wasn't him."

Sally took a breath and tried to relax. Had she actually seen her father? Or, more likely, was her tired mind just playing tricks on her? She had to admit that she had only gotten a very brief glance at the man, and although at the time she had been sure it had been her dad, now she was having doubts.

Henry saw that Sally was beginning to show signs of calm. In an inspired moment he added, "Besides, if BSI was having a business meeting here, it would be easy enough to find out. Let me just go ask the person over there at the hotel desk."

The two girls agreed that this seemed logical, and it also seemed to be a way to bring closure for Sally. Henry stood and walked over to the front desk. There were several people in line checking into the resort and Henry took his place in line. He certainly understood that Sally might mistake someone in this crowd for her father, particularly given her fatigue. It was now approaching eleven p.m. and he too was beginning to feel the strain of the long day. This would only take a moment and afterwards he was sure that they would all agree to call it a night.

Between them, they had been able to gather about two hundred responses in their survey which, although it was well short of the four hundred target, should be sufficient to give them an idea of the results. What was more, Sally had been able to win enough money to pay for the hotel room and get their car out of the shop. Now, he thought, when he was able to put to rest the notion that Sally had seen her father being arrested, he could call it a successful day.

That was when he saw it. At first, he couldn't believe his eyes. But after he read it a third time, he let out a soft cry, "*Oh-oh…*"

A lady in her seventies who stood behind Henry stepped around and said, "Sonny, are you all right?"

Henry just stood transfixed looking at an electronic sign on the wall behind the desk clerk and replied more to himself than to her. "I don't think so." The sign continuously scrolled a lighted message: *Welcome employees and stockholders… Billings Shipyard, Inc.*

\*\*\*

Molly Burgess decided to let the questioning go on without her. The man from Billings Shipyard who had come out of the restroom with the gun had been taken away. The single witness had been questioned thoroughly and had given his formal statement. She doubted that she would learn anything useful by listening to an interrogation of other people from Billings Shipyard or their guests, particularly since it seemed that none of them had been present at the scene during the shooting. Molly decided that she would leave the further questioning up to the state and local police and seek answers herself elsewhere. After all, this was *her* casino, and although the police had every right to run the investigation, she also had a right, and a responsibility, to investigate on behalf of the casino. There was no doubt that the resort managers would be interrogating her tomorrow as to how casino security could have let something like this happen.

She grabbed her radio and called, "Billy Sykes, this is Molly."

Billy replied immediately. "Yes boss, what's up?"

Molly answered, "Billy, I want you to find the manager on duty and get a key card for the room checked out to a Mr Steven Brown. As soon as you find out the room number, let me know. I'll meet you there."

Molly knew that it was just a matter of time before the detectives investigating the case wanted to search both the victim's and the gunman's rooms. She figured that with the interrogations going on, and the questioning of guests as they looked for a possible second witness, she might have another ten to fifteen minutes alone in the room.

Billy radioed back and informed her that Brown was checked into the Grand Pequot, room seven-one-three. On her way to the room, Molly could not help but wonder why someone would shoot a man in a public restroom and then just walk out of the room with the gun as if nothing had happened. Something surely didn't add up. It was a long shot, but perhaps she might be able to find something in the room that might be a clue.

Arriving at room seven-one-three, Molly saw Billy standing in the corridor outside the door with the key card. "Did the manager say that the police had asked to get into the room?" she asked.

Billy replied, "Nope. He just wanted to make sure that you had legal cause for entering a guest's room without permission. I assured him that it was a matter of dire safety to the other guests. He didn't want to know more."

Molly took the key and entered the room. At first glance there did not seem to be anything unusual about the room. The bed was neatly made and there weren't any suitcases, books or clothing in sight. She turned to Billy and said, "Don't touch anything. The police will be here soon enough, and I don't want them accusing us of messing up a crime investigation."

She stepped into the bathroom and saw a toothbrush, deodorant, comb and electric shaver laid out on the lavatory counter. Moving back into the room, she went over to the closet and opened the door. Inside was a suitcase on the floor along with a briefcase. Hanging on the rod were three pressed shirts two pair of slacks and several ties.

Taking out a pair of plastic gloves from her pockets she put them on and reached into the pants pockets only to find them empty. She then carefully took the briefcase and laid it on the bed. Thankfully, the briefcase did not have a lock and she was able to open it. Inside were airline tickets, several papers and a notebook along with a calculator. The papers included notes of a typed meeting agenda for a meeting that was held earlier in the day. Another paper included handwritten notes that apparently had been taken during the meeting. At the top of the sheet were names of people who had likely been in attendance. Molly turned to Billy as she laid the paper out on the bed and said, "Copy down these names."

She quickly went through the rest of the papers and thumbed through the notebook. The notebook contained handwritten pages of engineering calculations that she was unable to decipher. After reviewing the briefcase contents, she carefully replaced it and returned the case to the closet.

"So far," she said, "I don't see anything here that looks suspicious. It certainly doesn't look like the room of a man who is about to commit murder."

Billy smiled and asked, "And exactly what does a room look like that contains a man who is about to commit murder?"

Molly grimaced and said, "You know what I mean."

She walked over to the bedside drawers and opened the top drawer. Inside was the usual collection of hotel papers that included restaurant menus, a notepad, tourist information, casino plans, and of course, a Gideon's Bible. She opened the next two drawers to find socks, underwear and a pair of pajamas with a cute snowman design. Holding them up, Molly said in a sarcastic tone, "Here is what we were looking for, the same pajamas that Charles Manson wore just before his murder spree."

Billy laughed and said, "We'd better get out of here. The police will be looking to search this room and I'd rather not be here when they arrive."

Molly turned to place the pajamas back in the bottom drawer when her eye spotted something inside. It was a Foxwoods hotel coat check key. She picked it up and said, "Wait just a minute. Why would this guy have something left at the coat check room?" She turned it over and read the number, *thirty-eight*. Just as she was turning to put it back in the drawer, her radio sounded.

"This is Darrell the manager. I have a police detective here asking if he can get into Pequot room seven-one-three."

Molly quickly put the coat check key and the pajamas away and responded to the call. "I'll have security waiting at the door for him. Send him up."

Turning back to Billy she said, "Why don't you stay here and let the detective in. Don't say anything about our having been here first. In the meantime, I'm going to check out this coat check. First thing tomorrow, I think we should talk to the people who were in Mr Brown's meeting this morning to see if anyone can shed some light our mystery man."

Billy stepped out into the corridor and shut the door. "What if the detective finds the hotel coat check tag?"

Hurrying toward the elevators, Molly called back, "By the time they get to the coat check room, I will already know what's there. Call me when you're done here." And with that, she disappeared into the elevator.

***

Johann Steiner sat in his room drinking a glass of Gewurztraminer white wine from a bottle he had ordered from room service. Across from him sat Gustav Wilhelm. Steiner took a sip and asked, "Well, from all the commotion I saw earlier this evening, I assume our friend was successful in his task?"

Wilhelm folded his fingers together in his lap and replied, "Amazingly so. I had been watching him, discreetly of course, since this afternoon. Just before twenty-one hundred hours, he went to the theater area dressed in a tuxedo. He waited at the fringe of the crowd that was entering the theater and when the subject retired to the restroom, our friend went in after him. It was the most astounding stroke of luck that the shipyard engineer went in with the subject, and after our friend departed from the restroom, it was he who was arrested."

Steiner smiled with satisfaction. "Excellent. And now we wait for the rest of the puzzle to be completed. You should stay to see that our friend's second task was completed as well. Contact me when you have any news."

Wilhelm stood and left the room.

It was midnight and Lisa Kerrigan sat completely stunned with the rest of the BSI senior management group in the mezzanine conference room. Lisa had not planned on going to the evening concert with the others since her husband had been due to arrive at nine p.m. After picking up Tim at the Hartford airport they returned to the resort in the midst of the mayhem and confusion. It had taken twenty minutes for them to find out what had happened and then another half hour to locate James Macintyre.

Tim Kerrigan addressed the tired group. "I want to bring you all up to date on the facts as we now know them. As near as I can tell, at approximately nine o'clock this evening, Steven Brown, our lead engineer on the WG-116B project went to the restroom just outside the theater. He was with our group who were attending the evening's performance with the Pentagon representatives. At the same time Brown went to the restroom, a Commander Peter Ashley of the US Navy also went along."

Looking up at James Macintyre, Kerrigan said, "In a moment, perhaps James you might be able to tell us the role that Commander Ashley serves on the project for the navy."

Kerrigan then continued. "As I have been informed by casino security, during the time that both Ashley and Brown were in the restroom, Commander Ashley was shot and now remains in critical condition at Hartford Hospital. Moments after Ashley was shot, a casino guest entered the restroom to find Steven with a gun in his hand, standing over Ashley. The man who had walked into the rest room... let's see... a Mr Brooks from New Haven Connecticut... left the restroom and alerted casino security. When Steven exited the restroom, he was immediately arrested without further incident. After answering questions, he was transported to the county holding facility in New London."

Bill Gleason spoke up. "Does Brown have legal representation?"

Kerrigan put down his notes and said, "Yes, as soon as I was able to find out that Brown was being formally charged, I had John Phillips head over to New London to meet with him."

Lisa had been silent since arriving but now she could no longer contain herself. "This is absurd. Does anyone here seriously think that Steven Brown actually tried to murder Commander Ashley? What possible reason would he have? And what's more, why would he choose to do it during a time when there were hundreds of people around?"

Lisa's mind was in a state of turmoil. Should she mention her Thursday meeting with Peter Ashley? Clearly this must be related. Commander Ashley had mentioned that classified documents had been leaked on the WG-116B project. But there was no way that Steven Brown could be involved. She didn't actually know him that well, but whenever they had talked, it seemed clear that the project was part of his heart and soul. It just didn't seem possible that he was involved in sabotage. But if not him, who? It certainly was true that the lead engineer had access to all the files, and what's more, the position didn't have significant oversight, giving him the opportunity.

Lisa's thoughts were interrupted by James Macintyre who had been speaking to the group. Macintyre was talking about Commander Ashley.

"During the project briefing, Commander Ashley was introduced simply as being on temporary assignment as a liaison to Admiral Rand. Frankly, I didn't pay much attention to him during the briefing as he didn't have anything to say."

Lisa was surprised that Macintyre did not mention the security breach. Had Commander Ashley not brought it up during the briefing? That seemed unlikely, but surely there was no reason that Macintyre would bring it up if it had not been discussed.

Tim Kerrigan stood up and brought the meeting to a close.

"Tomorrow morning, we will be meeting with the board of directors at nine a.m. We'll have an update from John Phillips then regarding Steven Brown. For now, I suggest that you all get to bed. Tomorrow will be a full day."

***

Back at their room as they got ready for bed, Lisa Kerrigan was torn between her desire to confide in her husband about the meeting with Ashley and the announced security leak, and her nagging suspicions about her husband and the mysterious bank account. She decided that she needed to find out more before she opened up.

"Honey, I stopped in at the bank last week and, like I do half the time, I forgot our savings account number. Anyway, I got in a line with a new teller... you know how they keep hiring younger and younger tellers... well, anyway, I wanted deposit a check. I asked the teller to look up our account and I gave your name. Funny thing, she came back with not just our savings and checking accounts, there was a third account in your name. Since it was in your name only, I couldn't get any details. What's up with that account?"

Tim Kerrigan came out the bathroom with his toothbrush. "A separate account? I don't have any separate accounts. It must have been some kind of mistake. I'll look into it when we get back." He turned and went back into the bathroom.

Lisa thought angrily to herself, what did she expect? If it were something underhanded, he wouldn't admit to it, and if it truly was just an innocent mistake, he probably wouldn't know about it since she did the family banking. He was either being very cool about it, or she was being very foolish.

\*\*\*

Steven Brown lay on a bunk in a holding cell in the county lock-up. He wasn't sure what time it was but it had to be well past three a.m. he thought. Brown lay on the bunk wide awake as he reviewed in his mind what had happened.

When he had arrived, he had been led to a processing room where he had been fingerprinted and photographed. Following the processing, he had been given a prison orange jumpsuit to change into and had been brought to an interrogation room where he was chained to a metal table. After an hour wait, John Phillips, the BSI chief legal counsel and vice president of administration came into the room. Phillips took out a pen and a notebook and sat down.

"We don't have much time. The district attorney and state police will be here shortly to start questioning. Listen to me carefully, Mr

Brown. When the DA arrives and starts asking questions, if I say not to answer the question, then don't. Don't volunteer anything."

Brown asked, "Are you going to represent me... legally?"

Phillips responded. "I am not a criminal attorney. I'm just here to represent you during the initial statement that is being taken. Tomorrow, we will see about getting you local legal counsel with criminal experience. Don't worry. BSI will be working with you to straighten this situation out."

Brown asked, "Don't you want to know if I did it?"

Phillips answered without hesitation. "I assume that you're innocent. That's my job. Now tell me what happened."

Moments after Brown explained what had happened at the resort, the door opened, and two men came in. Brown noticed that one man was dressed in a shirt and tie and casual slacks. The other man was a state police officer. The man in the tie took the seat at the end of the table and set a recorder on the table. The state police officer stood by the door.

The man with the tie introduced himself. "My name is Brandon Dupree. I am the assistant district attorney for New London County."

John Phillips introduced himself and said that his client would be willing to answer all questions except those that were purposely aimed to incriminate his client.

Dupree agreed and then asked Brown to describe the events. He then very carefully related the events from the time that he had decided to go to the restroom to the time when he had been grabbed by casino security.

Dupree listened, taking notes from time to time, and then began his questions. "You said that a man must have come into the restroom while you were in the toilet stall. Did you hear the man come in?"

Brown looked over at Phillips who nodded, and he answered, "No I didn't hear him come in."

"All right, when you and Mr Ashley entered, were there any other men in the room who might be able to verify that you went into the toilet stall?"

Brown thought for a moment. "There were two men standing at the urinals with their back to me, so I guess, no, they wouldn't have seen me go into the stall."

"Can you describe either of these men?"

Again, Brown thought for a moment, and said, "Not really. I mean they were just ordinary guys. They were both dressed in black suits or tuxedos. I suppose they were going to the performance in the theater."

"So there wasn't anyone who could confirm that you went into the toilet stall, as opposed to staying behind the victim, waiting to shoot him."

John Phillips quickly spoke up. "Don't answer that."

Dupree waved his hand in acceptance and continued. "Let's go back to the shooting. When you heard the noise that turned out to be a gunshot, why didn't you go to see what was going on?"

Brown shook his head. "I heard the noise, but it didn't sound like a gunshot. I didn't know what it was. I figured it was just something ordinary."

"Then, you say that someone slid the gun under your stall. Surely that wasn't ordinary. Why did you pick the gun up?"

"I don't know. At first, I wasn't sure what it was. I just picked it up. I don't know why."

"So, you're saying that you picked up the gun and then came out of the stall. If you didn't shoot the gun, where was the person who did? How could the person who slid the gun under the toilet partition not still be in the room?"

"I don't know. There just wasn't anyone there... at least until the other man came in."

"What did you do, exactly, when you came out of the toilet stall?"

Brown twisted his hands under the strain that was increasing proportionally with his fatigue. "I saw the commander on the floor, and he was bleeding. I went over to see if he was okay."

"Well, obviously, he wasn't okay. Why didn't you put the gun down?"

"When I got near the commander, I could see that he had been shot. That was when I guess I panicked. I went into shock I guess."

Dupree then shifted in his chair. "Okay, let's pursue another subject. How well did you know the victim?"

Brown seemed relieved to be able to leave the thoughts of the shooting. "I only met him for the first time this morning at a project briefing with the navy."

198

Dupree reviewed his notes for a moment and then asked, "So you are aware that Commander Ashley was conducting a United States Navy investigation of BSI for a serious security breach on the very same project which you are the acting senior technical engineer?"

There was a silence in the room. John Phillips gave Brown a look of shocked surprise. Brown hung his head and softly said, "Yes."

The questioning went on for at least two hours. Brown was made to answer the same questions two and three times. The questions covered not only the events surrounding the shooting itself, they also included everything about his role on the WG-116B project. The questions also probed his personal life, even extending to inquiries about his daughter.

When the questions were completed and Dupree left, Brown spent another hour with John Phillips. He wanted to hear as nearly as possible, word-for-word what Admiral Rand had said about the security leak. This seemed to Brown to distress Phillips more than the murder accusation. After Phillips finished, he told Brown that he would be held at the county jail tomorrow and Sunday. A bail hearing would be set for Monday and as soon as the time was set, he would let Brown know.

The gravity of the situation had settled around Brown by the time Dupree had finished. Dupree had informed him that these charges would not just go away. The evidence against Brown was not particularly good. In addition to multiple witnesses who had seen Brown holding the murder weapon, a pair of gloves that were Brown's size was found in a waste receptacle inside the restroom. It was a safe bet that the right-hand glove would have trace evidence of gunpowder from the murder weapon. Dupree also made it clear that Brown's story would definitely not convince the DA's office to let him go.

As Dupree stood to go, Brown grabbed Dupree's arm. In a voice of desperation, he asked, "Will you get in touch with my daughter, Sally, back home? You need to call her and let her know what's happened."

Dupree looked back with compassion. "I'll see that she is taken care of."

\*\*\*

Sally, Henry and Sheila were in their room with the lights out. Sally lay awake in one of the two beds. Sheila was sleeping in the second bed, and Henry was snoring, curled up on the sofa. Sally was reviewing the facts in her head. Her dad was away on business. BSI was having a business meeting here at Foxwoods. She had seen a man that looked very much like her dad being arrested. They had learned that a man had been shot in one of the restrooms.

The three had decided to stay at the resort, at least through lunch on Saturday. Sally had pleaded to be given an opportunity to find out more about what had happened. She had to find out if her father was the man who she had seen earlier. One bit of bad news was that she had not been able to reach her dad's cell phone. It was apparently turned off and the best she was able to do was leave three voice messages.

When the desk clock flipped to five a.m., Sally gave up trying to sleep. She couldn't get the image of her father's face as he was being led out of the casino out of her mind. She quietly dressed and slipped out into the hall as the others lay asleep. She needed to find a place to sit and work out the details.

As Sally exited the elevator at the main level, she was surprised to see that there were still a significant number of people milling around. She walked to the main lobby and took a seat in one of the lobby chairs. Seated in a row of chairs behind her were two young girls who apparently were casino employees. They were engaged in conversation to which Sally didn't pay much attention until she heard one of the girls say in the middle of their conversation, "… and I know it was connected with what happened tonight."

The second girl responded. "You know, Kate, I heard that some guy was murdered. He was shot dead. So, if this is connected to the murder, you'd better just do what our security queen says."

Sally heard the other girl named Kate say something that she couldn't quite make out. Then she heard, "… she didn't have a coat check key, but she just said for me to go get it. When I went out back to get the coat, it turned out to be just an envelope. As I grabbed it, it fell to the floor. And guess what was inside?" Money! Ten one-hundred-dollar bills!"

The other girl said, "What'd you do? You didn't take any, did you?"

"Of course, I didn't. I put the money back in the envelope and brought it out to the queen. She took it away and then brought it back a minute later. She said just put it back and to call her if anybody comes to pick it up... even if the police come for it."

The second girl thought for a moment and then offered, "Well, you just have to know that this money belongs to the killer. Why else would she have you put it back? I bet you were being watched all night to see if the killer had a partner who would come for it. It sounds just like a *CSI* show I saw on TV last week."

Kate nodded and said, "Well maybe, but no one came for it. Not the police or anybody else. All night long I expected that the guy who gave it to me would show up. He was a nasty man. I hardly understood him. He had this German accent and he looked real mean."

The second girl spoke up. "You don't think he was the killer, do you? That would explain why no one came for the money... that is if he was working alone. I heard the killer was hauled off to jail."

Just at that moment, a young man arrived, and the girls rose out of their seats and they all went off together through the front doors, talking as they went.

Sally stood and walked over to the morning hotel clerk at the front desk. He was a young man in his late twenties. Sally looked around and noted that the desk was quiet, she presumed because guests had not yet begun to arrive given the early morning hour. The young clerk was sitting behind the counter shuffling through papers. When he saw Sally a look of appreciation came over his face, having been given a break in the boredom.

Sally smiled back and began a conversation. "I heard there was some excitement here last night in the Pequot Casino."

The clerk, whose name tag read Trevor, took the bait. "Well, I wasn't on duty last night, but when I came in this morning, I heard that some guy was shot in the men's room outside the theater. They took the guy away in an ambulance. I guess he was still alive when he left but who knows how bad it was."

Sally gave an expression of disapproval and said, "Who would do such a thing? I mean right out where he must have known he would be caught... they did catch him, right?"

Trevor nodded and replied, "Yeah, they got him all right. He was a guest staying here I heard. They caught him red-handed. I heard he came out of the men's room still holding the gun. They dragged him out of here and took him off to county lock up. Man, he can't be long for this world. He'll get the needle for sure!"

Sally shuddered and then asked, "You don't know who the shooter was, do you? You said he was a guest."

Trevor was clearly enjoying conveying his sense of authority to this pretty young girl. "I don't know the guy's name, but I did hear he was staying in room seven-one-three. The entire day shift was told that room is off limits. It has been sealed like a crime scene. So is room two-three-three, the room that the man who was shot was staying in."

The clerk beamed with his special knowledge showing Sally that he was a person 'in the know'. A moment later Trevor dropped the pen he had been holding and exclaimed, "Wait a minute! We can find out who the guy was. All I have to do is look up the room. Hold on a second..."

Trevor tapped on the computer for a minute and then said, "It was a Steven Brown from Billings, Maine."

Sally had been hoping against hope that the name would be anything other than her father's. When she heard her father's name it was like an enormous weight had been applied to her heart. After a moment to collect her wits, she asked, "So they're pretty sure that this guy is the one. Who is the head of security here?"

Sally thought she saw a look of fear cross Trevor's face.

"Our security chief is a battleax of a woman. There would be no doubt about getting the shooter with Molly Burgess around. She runs this place like a prison camp."

Sally thought to herself... *ah yes... the security queen.*

Having gotten what information, she could she leaned over the counter and said, "Hey Trevor, it was great to talk with you. Maybe I'll see you again later. Got to run."

With that, she headed back up to her room to wake Henry and Sheila.

# Chapter 17

Molly Burgess sat in her office behind a desk that was cluttered with papers. Seated in a chair in front of the desk sat Billy Styles who was nursing a giant-sized cup of black coffee. Both had left the building around one thirty a.m. after seeing that everything was back to normal. This morning, their faces showed that neither had gotten much sleep.

The readout on the digital clock on her desk flipped to seven thirty a.m. Molly sat in silence, deep in thought. At last, she spoke to no one in particular. "The state police crime crew must be blind."

When she had arrived that morning thirty minutes earlier, she had been surprised to see Billy in the security office typing at a computer. He admitted that he couldn't sleep and that he wanted to get an early start on preparing the incident report for the in-house inquiry that would be launched by the casino owners.

Molly's thoughts drifted back to last night.

Last evening when Molly had left Brown's hotel room, she had hurried to the coat check room. When she arrived, she called to the check clerk, a young girl of not more than twenty-five or twenty-six she guessed. Looking at the girl's name tag she read the name *Kate*. "Listen, Kate, I'm Molly Burgess, the head of security here. I need you to get whatever is assigned to check number thirty-eight and bring it here."

The girl hesitated for a moment but apparently something in Molly's no-nonsense look made up the girl's mind. She went into the back room and returned with a business envelope that was closed, but not sealed. Molly took a tissue out of her pocket and picked up the envelope without leaving fingerprints on it. She stepped back into a corner of the hall where she wouldn't be seen.

Inside the envelope were ten one-hundred-dollar bills and a folded piece of paper. The paper simply had a single typed line that read, *Peter Ashley, room two-three-three*. She quickly returned the money and the note to the envelope and brought it back to the coat check room.

Molly handed the envelope back to the coat check girl and said, "If anyone comes to get this, I don't want you to mention that I was here, understand?"

The girl nodded her head and replied with a solemn tone. "Yes, I understand."

Molly gave the girl a moment to let her understand the seriousness of her request. "That even means the police. When someone comes to get this, whoever it is, the police or anyone else, I want you to call me at this number immediately after they leave." Molly wrote out her personal cell phone number and slid it across the counter to Kate.

Molly had returned to her office and had filled Billy in on the contents of the envelope she had found at the coat check room. Billy told Molly that the state police captain, along with officers from the Ledyard Police Department and the county sheriff's office had all arrived at Brown's room. He had let them in and had been directed by the state police captain to wait in the hall while the room was searched. After about thirty minutes, he had been informed that the room would be sealed until a crime scene investigation unit could go over the room more thoroughly. Both Molly and Billy had stayed until one thirty a.m. The phone call Molly expected never came.

Molly awoke from her thoughts and turned to Billy. "So, what do we do now?"

Billy thought for a moment and said, "Perhaps we can help the process. Let's put a request in to inspect the room as part of our in-house investigation. The official CSI unit will have finished their work and I doubt that the police will care if we take a look. All we have to do is suggest that the coat check key be used to see what *isn't* still in the room."

Molly replied, "I don't see any other options. Let's see what happens."

She grabbed the phone and dialed the state police. After announcing herself, she was connected to Captain Russell.

"Captain, I am required to submit my own report to the casino owners and as part of my investigation I would like to look at Steven Brown's room."

There was a brief silence before the captain answered. "That room is part of an official crime investigation."

"I understand that, Captain. All I want to do is look around. I have investigation experience as a member of the FBI's Las Vegas Bureau."

"Listen, *Ms* Burgess. The only reason I'm cutting you any slack at all is because we know of your background. But let's not forget, this happened on *your* watch."

"You don't need to remind me, *Captain*. I'm just trying to do my job here. Are you going to let me into the room or not?"

There was no answer for several seconds. Just when Molly thought that she wouldn't be allowed in, the captain spoke. "I'll send over an officer. Wait for him to arrive. And I don't need to tell you, *don't touch anything.*"

When the state police detective arrived, Molly, Billy and a state police patrol officer entered Steven Brown's room. The room looked the same as when Molly and Billy had last seen it. It was as if nothing had been disturbed but Molly knew that the state police investigative unit had been over the room with a fine-tooth comb. Molly pulled on latex gloves and walked around the room as if it was a new experience. After twenty minutes of looking around, Molly looked in the dresser drawers. When she came to the drawer with the pajamas and the coat check key, she pulled out the key.

Turning to the state police officer, she asked, "Did the crime scene crew look into this? What's in the coat check room?"

The officer pulled a small notebook out of his pocket and flipped several pages.

"Actually, I don't believe anyone went down to see."

Molly looked at Billy and then back to the officer. "*Excuse me?* You're saying that you found this key, and no one thought it might be important enough to see what might be in storage? Do you think maybe we should go see?"

The officer was clearly flustered. After several incoherent mutterings he said that he needed to call the captain. When he reached the captain on his cell phone, the yelling on the other end could be heard all the way across the room where Molly and Billy were smiling to each other.

The officer hung up and he said meekly, "The captain said we should go check it out."

***

Sally, Sheila and Henry sat in the main lobby across from the coat check room. When Sally had returned to her room, she was in such a state of excitement that she could hardly contain herself. She immediately woke Sheila and Henry, who were decidedly less enthusiastic. Sally quickly explained the conversation that she had overheard.

It was now eight thirty a.m. and the trio sat watching the coat check room. Wiping the sleep from his eyes, Henry said, "I still don't get it. What's so important about knowing that your dad had money checked in the coat check room? And from the sounds of it, it doesn't even look like it was your father they were talking about anyway… it was some German guy."

Sally stood up unable to remain calm. "That's just it. I checked at the front desk and I found out that the head of security is a woman. Her name is Molly Burgess. That had to be the security queen the girls were talking about."

Sheila interrupted. "I'm with Henry on this. I just don't see what's so…"

Before she could finish, Sally raised a hand and continued. "Let me finish! The chief of security… Molly Burgess… is certain that my dad is guilty of shooting that guy in the men's room. She must have found some connection to dad and the envelope that was left in the coat check room. But here's the thing. She must think that the money was a pay-off, and she hopes that whoever left it will come back and get it now that they know that my father isn't coming to claim it. We know that the person who left the money had a German accent. If this guy can be caught, he can be forced to admit that my father isn't involved."

"So why don't we just go tell the security lady what we know and get your dad off the hook?" Henry asked.

"Because telling the security chief that someone else is involved without proof will get us nowhere. She must already suspect that. Anyway, it wouldn't clear dad from suspicion. We know that my dad is innocent and that means that someone else is guilty. My guess is that now that dad has been framed for the shooting, the German will come back to try to get the money. And I want to be here when he arrives to see who he is. When he arrives, we'll spot him."

"And then what will we do? Shouldn't we just leave all this up to the resort security people?" Sheila asked.

"The coat check girl said that they were to call the security chief if someone came by for the envelope. That sounds to me like security doesn't really think that anyone will actually ever come for the money. They probably think it was put there and dad was going to get it later when he left. I don't think that they seriously think that it will be retrieved. Otherwise, they would be here watching the coat check room themselves."

Henry asked, "So why are we here then?"

Sally answered. "The security chief doesn't think that the person who left the money will ever come back because she thinks that that person who hired my father got what he wanted, that is, the targeted man was shot. And as for the money, the person doesn't care about it. But we know that that's not really the case. The money was left by someone to implicate my father and it appears that that isn't going to be necessary since my dad's already been arrested. I believe that the person may think that since the police didn't come to check out the money, they either didn't find the connection, or they didn't think it was important. In that case the person may come back to retrieve the money rather than just abandon it."

Looking around the vacant lobby, Sally continued. "And as you can see, there is nobody doing surveillance here but us. I want to be here when whoever comes by checking on the envelope, and then I want to follow that person and find out who it is."

Just as Sally finished her words, two resort security officers and a state police officer arrived at the coat check room. Sally, Sheila and Henry moved through the lobby to stand close enough to hear what was being said, being careful to avoid suspicion.

The two resort security officers, a man and a woman, both wore jackets that read 'Foxwoods Security' across the pocket. As Sally moved into position, she could hear that the woman was engaged in conversation with the coat check clerk. The clerk was an older woman who said something that Sally couldn't hear. Sally took a step closer, to hear more clearly. Sheila and Henry stood by her side talking about losses at the slot machines with pretend intensity to deflect suspicion.

The Foxwoods security woman was speaking. "… it's check number thirty-eight. We'll wait."

The coat check clerk disappeared to the back and, after a moment, she returned with an envelope in hand.

The police officer took the envelope and looked inside. The three glanced past a column and saw the police officer slide a piece of paper out of the envelope. After he read for a short time, he slid the paper back into place, saying, "This will have to be turned over as evidence."

They heard the resort security lady, who Sally now assumed was the 'security queen', Molly Burgess, say, "What did the paper say?"

"It contained only a single name with a room number, *'Peter Ashley, room two-three-three'*. There also was a considerable amount of money in the envelope. I'm not going any further with this. We shouldn't even be looking at this. I'm going to get the DA to get an official search warrant for this, based on finding the coat check key in the suspect's room. As soon as the warrant is issued, the captain will be back to take possession. In the meantime, this goes back, and it shouldn't be touched."

Sally, Sheila and Henry moved back to the seats across the lobby. As they sat down, they saw the resort security lady head back into the resort and the police officer head out the door, talking on his cell phone as he went. As the resort's chief of security crossed the lobby on her way back to the security office, she passed by the three who all were trying to look inconspicuous. When she was just a few feet away she stopped for a second looking directly at Sally. For a brief moment in time Sally's heart stopped beating. Just as she thought that the security queen was going to say something, she continued on her way. When the three were alone again, their breathing resumed.

Sheila asked, "What do you make of that paper with the name on it?"

Sally shook her head saying, "I don't make anything good of it. I'll bet you last night's winnings that the name, Peter Ashley, was the man who was shot."

Henry whistled. "Whoa… that can't be good." When the girls looked at him and didn't answer he added, "Well, it can't be… right?"

Sally's face showed a deep expression of concern. "Now that the police have the money, the connection to my father that brought them here must be considered as serious evidence, rather than the set-up job that it really is."

Sheila replied, "If this guy Peter Ashley is the one who was shot last night, you are probably right. Your dad is being framed all right for murder. The question is why."

"The more important question right now is by who," offered Henry.

Sally nodded and said absently, "Actually, it's by *whom*, but you're right Henry. We need to find out who is doing this."

Henry's face took on a puzzled look. "I thought you said it was whom, not who."

Sheila thought for a moment and then added, "First of all, we have jumped to the conclusion that the person shot, was this Peter Ashley. That may not be necessarily true. He may just be some person your dad knows, and the money is simply connected with the business that brought him here."

The investigative reporter in Sheila began to take control. She took out a small pad of paper from her purse and began writing. "We need to write down in separate lists what we actually know to be true, what we think is true, and what we do not know. That may help us figure out what to do next."

Sally agreed enthusiastically. "Let's do that. On our list of what we know, let's start with the fact that my father is definitely here. Let's add to the list of items we *think* we know that we think he is here on business."

Henry, now caught up in the process added, "And let's say we know that your dad was arrested for shooting someone, and on the list of things we *think we know* we'll put that he is innocent."

Both girls gave a dumbfounded look at Henry. Sheila was the one who spoke. "Listen, Sherlock, I think we all *know* that Sally's dad is innocent."

Henry replied somewhat indignantly, "Yeah... I meant to say that."

Trying to avoid a confrontation, Sally continued. "Okay, on the list of things we know, we need to add that Dad was apparently in the men's room when the man was shot. Trevor, the desk clerk, told me that Dad was caught coming out of the men's room with a gun in his hand."

"Does anybody else get the feeling that this isn't looking good for your dad?" Henry said.

Sheila shot Henry a menacing look, but Sally seemed to ignore the remark.

Sally went on. "On the list of things we don't know, is the question, if Dad was in the men's room when the person was shot, why doesn't he just tell the authorities who did it?"

Sheila wrote down the question and then spoke up. "There are only three possible answers to that question. First, he didn't see who did it for some reason. For instance, maybe he had been knocked out by the guy before the shooting took place."

Henry interrupted. "Or maybe he was doing a number two in a stall with the doors shut."

Once again, both girls gave Henry a look of disapproval.

Sheila went on with her thought. "Second, he did see who did it and told the authorities, but for some reason they don't believe him. Or, third, he did see who did it, but for some reason he won't say, perhaps to protect the person."

Sally said, "That's good reasoning. We will need to find out which of the three is correct. Let's get back to our lists. We need to put on the list of things that we think we know is that the man who shot was Peter Ashley."

Sheila jotted that down and said, "And, under the list of things we don't know would have to be, who is this Peter Ashley and does he have a connection with your dad."

Trying to redeem himself, Henry chimed in. "On the list of things we know, is the fact that there is an envelope with Ashley's name and money in the coat check room. On the list of things we don't know, is why."

Sally added, "And on the list of things that we now know is the fact that the authorities think that the envelope is connected with Dad somehow."

Looking up, Sheila put her notepad away and said, "Well, I think I can confirm one of the items on our 'think we know' list, that is, was it

Peter Ashley who was shot? I'm going to go over to talk to the desk clerk, Trevor. He looks like he just went on break."

Pointing to the clerk who was standing outside the office door, reading a newspaper, Sheila said, "I'm going to see what I can find out."

Sally stood and said, "Maybe I should go talk to him. He already knows me from our talk earlier this morning."

Sheila shook her head and said, "No, if you ask him more questions, he might get suspicious. He's never seen me."

With that, Sheila walked across the lobby toward Trevor who was balancing a cup of coffee in one hand and a folded newspaper in the other. When Sheila reached him, she began her act.

"Excuse me, sir."

Trevor looked past the newspaper wondering who might have addressed him in such a respectful way. When he saw Sheila, he immediately went into, what was obvious to Sheila, his charm mode.

"Yes, my dear, can I help you?"

Sheila smiled for the full effect and asked, "I'm looking for a guest... actually my uncle. I am not sure what room he is staying in. Is there any way I could find that out? His name is Peter Ashley. I don't have his cell number and I was supposed to meet him here, but I don't see him."

Trevor gave a sly wink and said, "Well, you know, we aren't supposed to give out that information, but for someone as nice as you seem to be, maybe I could bend the rules. Why don't you come with me to the front desk and I'll see what I can do?"

Sheila followed Trevor to the front desk and watched him slide up to a terminal at the back counter. Beside him was a girl with a resort jacket who was also on duty for the day at the front desk. After a moment, Trevor turned around and said, "We do have a Peter Ashley registered as a guest. If you would like, I could ring his room for you."

The girl who was working beside Trevor looked up and said, "Peter Ashley? A man came in yesterday looking for Mister Ashley. He wasn't in at the time, but I put a note in the message box to let Mr Ashley know that the man had come by. If your guest is going to see him, perhaps she could let him know that this person stopped by looking for him. Just a second, I'll see if the message is still there."

When Sheila returned to Sally and Henry, they were eager to hear the news. Henry asked, "Well, did you find out if Ashley was the person who got shot?"

Sheila stood in a dazed silence for a moment, and then replied in a voice that didn't exactly sound connected to the here and now. "No, I forgot to ask."

Henry jumped up. "You forgot to ask! How could you forget in the two minutes it took to walk over to talk to the guy?"

As if coming out of a trance, Sheila told the two, "You both better sit down. You're not going to believe what I'm about to tell you."

Henry and Sally remained standing, both with a look of confusion on their faces. Sheila took a seat.

"The girl who is behind the counter heard Trevor mention Peter Ashley's name. She said she was on duty yesterday when a man came up asking for Mr Ashley. She said that she told the person that Mr Ashley was not in and then the person walked away. She took down a note, however, and left a message at the front desk for Peter Ashley that a man had come looking for him."

Losing patience, Henry spoke up. "That's all fascinating, but what does all that have to do with Sally's dad?"

Sheila, now a bit more composed, continued. "Well, the girl wrote down the name of the man who was looking for our Mr Ashley. And who on earth do you think the man was?"

The other two shook their heads signifying that they had no idea.

"Believe it or not, the man's name was Gustav Wilhelm!"

Henry gave a blank look. "So…"

Sally sat down rubbing her head. "You've got to be kidding!"

Once again, Henry said, "So…"

Sally looked up at Henry and said, "You *vill* not forget my name Mr Moore!"

Suddenly, it dawned on Henry. "No… No… It can't be. Not Wilhelm from chemistry class. Not the chemical Nazi! What's *he* doing here?"

"What indeed," remarked Sally.

Sheila had watched the shock of realization cross their faces. Now she sat down and took control. "Look, we need to try to understand this.

It's obvious that Wilhelm has a German accent. Is it possible that he is somehow connected? Could he be the man who put the envelope in the coat check room?" She pulled out her notepad and wrote down a question under the heading, *things we do not know*.

Sally thought for a moment and then said, "It seems highly improbable that we would come all the way here from Maine to find that Mr Wilhelm would coincidently be here as well. But, let's not forget that it is equally improbable that my father would also be here. I do not believe in such radical coincidences. The two circumstances must be connected."

Henry, who had been watching a television on a wall of the lobby, shook Sheila's arm and pointed to the screen. "Hey guys, listen to this."

A reporter on the screen was talking behind a news desk. "…and the police have released the identity of the man who remains in critical condition as Lieutenant Commander Peter Ashley of the United States Navy. Authorities have not commented on the shooting other than to say that they have a man in custody and that there will be a news conference later today at three p.m."

Henry turned back to the others. "Well, I guess we know now that it was Peter Ashley who was shot."

# Chapter 18

Tim Kerrigan sat at the head of the long conference table. The rest of the BSI board members were seated along the two sides of the table, each giving their full attention to the chairman of the board. The BSI senior management members occupied seats around the perimeter of the room. Lisa Kerrigan had arrived early at the mezzanine meeting room and had selected a seat where she would be close to her husband. Much to her chagrin, James Macintyre had arrived shortly after and had taken a seat immediately beside her, one seat closer to Tim.

"We still don't have many details," Kerrigan began. "I was informed earlier this morning that there will be a bail hearing scheduled on Monday which may mean that Steven Brown might be released sometime during the week."

At the far end of the table sat the senior member of the board of directors, Mr Clarence Jordan, the president of a large national bank in Manhattan and a member of several other corporate boards. At the age of seventy-eight, Mr Jordan had acquired a reputation for impatience, and it didn't take long for that reputation to be confirmed once again. He set down his pen and interrupted Kerrigan's update.

"Yes, well, this is all well and good, but we need to know if this incident will have any impact on the company. Does the loss of this engineer in any way jeopardize the WG-116B project? And can someone please tell me how did this engineer get hired in the first place? Doesn't your company do personnel screening of prospective employment applicants?"

Tim Kerrigan gave Jordan a patient look with a smile, as he continued.

"Our lead engineer for the WG-116B project was hired with not only impeccable credentials, but also with a thorough security background check. I have every belief that he will be exonerated from these charges and this incident will not impact our work on the project. Our CEO,

James Macintyre, has been involved with the oversight of the project since it began and will be taking over Mr Brown's duties while Mr Brown is... *being temporarily detained*."

Turning to the CEO he suggested, "Perhaps, Mr Macintyre, you might say a few words about the project."

Macintyre rose to his feet with an air of self-importance that reminded Lisa of Alexander Haig, the secretary of state under the Reagan administration. She half expected Macintyre to begin with the statement that was made by the then secretary of state who, shortly after the president had been shot and had been taken to a hospital, told the White House press corps, "As, of now, I am in control here..." even though the vice president was clearly the next in line for command. Macintyre saying that he was in control of the technical aspects of the WG-116B project would have been as ridiculous now as Haig's statement was then.

After a brief pause for dramatic effect, Macintyre began. "The WG-116B project is on schedule and on budget, and I do not see anything with the current situation here created by Steven Brown that will negatively impact BSI's progress."

Looking over at the board president with a smile that seemed to suggest that they were the best of friends, Macintyre spoke on. "As Tim has said, I have been involved with the project every step of the way. There isn't any aspect of the work that I will not be able to handle, including direction of the project engineering tasks. As far as the navy is concerned, it will be business as usual."

It was clear that Macintyre fully intended to go on expounding on his own abilities, but Clarence Jordan interrupted. "Maybe so, but who's going to deal with the press? Those clowns will turn this annual meeting into a media circus event if they can!"

Kerrigan waved Macintyre to sit down, which he did reluctantly with an obvious look of disappointment. With continuing patience, Kerrigan replied, "There is no way that I will let any item that is not on our published meeting agenda be introduced at the annual meeting. The incident will not have any part in our annual business procedures."

Shuffling through papers in front of him, he then turned his attention back to the board. "I have asked John Phillips, our vice president of administration and the shipyard's legal counsel, to put together a statement to be issued. John and I will be meeting with the press immediately after the annual meeting to deliver our statement. The statement reads as follows."

*Billings Shipyard would like to express our sincere regret regarding the incident that took place last evening here at the resort when a US Naval Officer, Lieutenant. Commander Peter Ashley, was shot and was taken to a local hospital where he is currently being attended. A BSI engineer, Mr Steven Brown, who was here participating in the preparations for our annual meeting, has been taken into custody in connection with the shooting.*

*BSI offers our sympathy and prayers for Commander Ashley and his family. We will not comment on the details of this incident since not all the facts are yet known. If you have any questions regarding what happened, we suggest that you contact the local authorities who are in charge of the ongoing investigation."*

Having read the statement, Kerrigan concluded. "I hope this brings to a close the matter of Steven Brown. We need to move on to review our actual business for this afternoon's meeting."

As the meeting finished, Lisa rose in hopes of attending the directors' lunch with her husband. But as the crowd made its way to the private dining room that had been reserved, Lisa saw Clarence Jordan at Tim's arm, lecturing him on the 'correct' procedures for running the annual shareholders' meeting. It was clear that Tim would have his mind entirely occupied during lunch, and therefore he wouldn't be much company. Lisa decided that yet another business lunch was not what she wanted anyway and headed off to the elevators to find some brief solitude before the afternoon meeting.

As she stepped out of the elevator at the main level, she surveyed the lobby full of hotel guests and casino gamblers. It occurred to her that people who come to this kind of resort seem to come to escape the everyday world in which they live. It's like time is suspended while they are here, allowing them to briefly step outside their responsibilities and care. For a brief moment in time, they are able to become something else… something perhaps that hides deep inside and does not allow itself to be seen in the routine of the normal life. When the responsibilities of work or family can be temporarily pushed away, it seems to leave that something else free to surface.

As Lisa looked around it occurred to her how sad it is that so many people have such an overwhelming need to escape their ordinary lives, even if just for a brief time. The question arose in her mind whether she spent a majority of her time simply *coping* or if, in fact, she was able to truly enjoy life as she lived it. She thought that she had been enjoying her life, at least until recently when the BSI accounting impropriety had been discovered by Greg Connor and her suspicions had been raised about Tim. And now there was this business with the naval officer, Peter Ashley, who the night after soliciting her help in finding a security breach at BSI, was shot.

As Lisa headed off to find a quiet corner to perhaps have a cup of coffee and a sandwich, her attention was suddenly drawn to the far corner of the lobby. Standing in the corner behind a large lobby plant that looked more like a small tree than an indoor plant, stood James Macintyre. He was standing with his back to the lobby, speaking on a cell phone. Lisa's first reaction was to quickly move away to avoid the inevitable confrontation that would include condescending instructions on how she was to give her brief report at this afternoon's meeting. But seeing Macintyre, Lisa couldn't help but wonder what could be so important that the CEO wasn't at the directors' lunch. His absence would undoubtedly be conspicuous.

Lisa walked through the lobby to a point on the opposite side of the plant which concealed Macintyre. She decided that if he were to discover her standing behind him, she would tell him that she was simply waiting to ask him if he had any additional news about Steven Brown. A feeling of guilt arose in her for eavesdropping, but her curiosity as to why BSI's CEO would be making a phone call rather than talking with BSI directors took command of her. Listening through the plant, she picked up what was a very agitated conversation.

"...no, *you* listen! I want no part of this! I didn't sign on for a shooting. You tell him that I want to talk with him this evening."

There was a pause and then Macintyre spoke, obviously straining to keep his voice quiet so that he would not attract attention. "Don't give me that crap. I *know* he's here at the hotel. I spoke with him here in person! Look, you just get him to call tonight. I'll be waiting."

With that, Macintyre abruptly closed the cell phone and spun around to leave. Standing five feet away, he saw Lisa Kerrigan looking at him with unconcealed shock.

***

Gustav Wilhelm sat watching Johann Steiner pack. When he had arrived, Wilhelm had been ushered in and told to sit. He had waited for direction for several minutes but when Steiner did not speak, Wilhelm finally took the initiative.

"*Was möchten Sie mir zu tun?*"

Steiner folded a shirt and put it in the suitcase that lay on the bed. "What I want you to *do* is go immediately back to Billings."

Steiner continued folding clothes. "We have now resolved the unfortunate problem with the misplaced document in Hamburg. The American Navy's investigator is now out of the way and we have implicated the Billings Shipyard engineer. But I want you to put a final piece of insurance in place that should relieve any suspicion that might have been placed on Herr Macintyre."

Steiner took out a handkerchief and reached into a drawer in a bureau beside the bed. Careful not to touch the envelope and leave fingerprints, he slipped it into a plastic bag and handed it to Wilhelm.

"It's probably just a matter of time before the police decide to search the engineer's house in Billings. I want this envelope to be there when they arrive. In it is another piece of evidence that will point to the engineer's guilt, both in shooting the investigator, as well as being the security leak at the shipyard, should we find that necessary."

Wilhelm took the envelope and put it in his jacket pocket. "What are you going to do about Macintyre? He demanded that you speak with him this evening."

"I'll deal with our frightened rabbit later. Now I am off to New York. I have a flight at six. I'll call him when I get back home. You must get back to Billings before the police move in on the engineer's house. And

I need not tell you to be very careful not to leave any sign of your presence in the house."

Wilhelm nodded and rose to leave. As he reached the door, Steiner spoke quietly. "Keep a close watch on our rabbit, *mein freund*. And see that he makes the next delivery on time."

*** 

Sally, Sheila and Henry had decided on a plan. Sheila and Henry would go pick up their car and Sally would remain at the resort to try to find out more about the presence of Mr Wilhelm. Sheila had called Ace Auto and had found out that the repairs to their car would be completed by noon and that the bill would be two hundred and eighty-five dollars. Figuring the hundred-dollar deposit that they had given the tow truck operator, an additional one hundred and eighty-five dollars was needed. Guessing that the cab fare to the repair garage would be about eighty-five dollars, Sally had given Sheila three hundred dollars from her winnings from the previous evening. As Sheila and Henry rode off in the taxi, Sally began working in her mind how to confront Mr Wilhelm and how to determine the extent of his involvement with the framing of her father.

As Sally walked back into the resort, her cell phone rang. She pulled the phone out of her pocket and looked at the display to see the calling number. The number had a two-zero-seven area code which meant that it was a Maine caller, but Sally didn't recognize it. It wasn't either Henry or Sheila and so it wasn't anyone that she wanted to speak with. She closed the phone and let it go to message.

Sally decided to first check with the hotel front desk to see if she could find out Mr Wilhelm's room. Arriving at the front desk she asked, "Could you please telephone a guest for me? His name is Gustav Wilhelm. I'm sure he's staying here but I forgot his room number."

The girl at the front desk typed the name into the computer and then replied, "I'm sorry, it looks like Mr Wilhelm has checked out. I'd say you just missed him. The record shows he checked out not more than five minutes ago."

Sally frowned. If he had just checked out, she must have missed him while she was saying goodbye to Sheila and Henry as they got into the taxi! Suddenly, the thought of the taxi leaving gave Sally an idea. She quickly turned around and darted out of the lobby. As soon as Sally got outside, she could see one of the resort parking garages approximately fifty yards across from the entrance drive. Sally raced across the lawn in hopes that she might get lucky. As she ran, a million reasons why this wouldn't work went through her mind. It was certainly possible that Mr Wilhelm hadn't parked in this garage. Or even if he did, he might have had the valet service pick up his car and have it delivered to the hotel entryway. Or most likely of all, Sally was simply too late to catch him.

As Sally reached the garage out of breath, she saw that the garage exit was located at the far end away from where she stood. With a grunt of frustration, she started running again toward the exit. As she came within view of the exit booths, she stopped dead in her tracks with shock. Idling at one of the exit booths was Mr Wilhelm in his car, handing a parking garage ticket to the attendant. Sally quickly pulled out her cell phone and raced toward the booth. Just as the car started up and sped through the raised gate, Sally lifted her phone and took a picture.

The entire event since she had entered the garage took less than ten seconds. Afterwards she wasn't even sure if she had managed to get the car in the picture. Totally out of breath, she leaned up against the bumper of a parked SUV. After a moment of taking deeps breaths, she looked at her phone and brought up the picture. She saw a clear image of Mr Wilhelm's car with the license plate easily readable, along with the sign overhead at the garage exit which read, *Thank You for Visiting Foxwoods. Come Again Soon!*

***

For a split second, James Macintyre considered simply walking past Lisa without speaking. But he quickly realized that if she had been standing behind him for the past minute, she would have heard every word of his phone conversation and he would have to deal with it. Her initial look of shock was turning into a look of accusation, which confirmed the worst for Macintyre. He decided to go on the offensive.

"What are you doing, Lisa? Are you in the habit of eavesdropping on people's conversations?"

Lisa was momentarily caught off guard, but she quickly recovered. "I was coming to see why you weren't at the directors' lunch. What did you mean that you didn't sign on for a shooting? What exactly *did* you sign on for? Are you involved in Peter Ashley's shooting, James?"

Macintyre shot back an angry look. "This isn't any of your business."

Seeing that Lisa wasn't going to be satisfied, Macintyre forged on. "I'll tell you what I can, but you need to promise to keep this confidential. This is a matter of the highest security. Can you assure me that you can keep this under cover?"

Suspicion rose in Lisa's mind, but she wanted to hear more. "That depends. Tell that you aren't involved in anything illegal."

Macintyre continued without hesitation. "Before we came down here, I was contacted by Naval Intelligence in Washington. I was asked to look into a breach of security regarding classified documents at BSI. I can't tell you exactly the details of the security breach but there was some reason to suspect Steven Brown."

Lisa stood dumbfounded. Could this be possible? Certainly, her conversation with Peter Ashley confirmed the matter of the security breach. But Ashley hadn't mentioned anything about Steven Brown. In fact, she had gotten the impression that he was looking for someone who might not have had been granted authorization to BSI's classified work.

"So, who were you speaking with just now?" she asked.

Macintyre sensed that he had convinced her. Confidence was building. "I was trying to speak with my contact in Washington. He wasn't in and I was getting the run around from some low-ranking administrator. When I asked to have Admiral Rand meet with me, I was told he wasn't here."

Lisa experienced a mixture of acceptance and suspicion. Macintyre's story seemed to square with what she knew, but somehow, she felt very uneasy.

Macintyre finished by saying, "I need you to keep this to yourself. The issue of the security breach cannot be made public. I don't want you even discussing it with anyone else at BSI, including your husband. Understand?"

Lisa couldn't believe that Tim didn't already know about the situation, but Macintyre's comment raised a new suspicion. Did Macintyre think that her husband was involved in some way? Was that why he didn't want her to talk to Tim?

Lisa spoke quietly. "I understand."

Macintyre nodded and headed back to the elevators leaving Lisa by herself to ponder what she had just heard.

\*\*\*

The BSI attorney, John Phillips, sat in the interview room at the New London County lock-up. Across from him sat Steven Brown in leg irons.

Phillips began. "I've just come back from a meeting with the District Attorney. I won't sugar-coat it. The charge is first degree murder. I've managed to get the arraignment scheduled for ten o'clock Monday morning."

Brown hung his head. "What exactly is an arraignment?"

"The arraignment is when we will be entering a plea. Obviously, we will be entering a plea of not guilty. We should be able to establish a reasonable bail given that you have no prior record and have an established life and steady employment in Billings."

Brown hung his head with fatigue. Sleeping in his cell had not been a possibility. "I'm worried about my daughter, Sally."

"I had Denise Witham, my secretary back home, call Sally earlier this morning but so far she has not answered. Don't worry. Denise will reach her. I told Denise to go over to your house and bring Sally back to her house until we get you home."

Brown had met Denise on the first day he had arrived for work at BSI. He remembered how he had felt like a complete outsider until he met the administrative vice president's secretary at the office of human resources. She had welcomed him with such a genuinely warm smile that it had immediately chased away his concerns. Denise was in her early sixties and she seemed more like a kindly grandmother than a lead corporate secretary. After only a minute of meeting her, however, one couldn't help but get the impression that maybe all those big-shot

222

executives think they are in control, but in fact, BSI would collapse without Denise Witham behind the scenes.

"Thanks, John. I appreciate what you're doing for me," Brown said.

"Steven, I need to tell you that although I am confident that we will be able to establish bail, it won't be a slam dunk. In these instances, the prosecutor will undoubtedly argue strongly against releasing the defendant to travel out of the area of jurisdiction while awaiting trial."

Concern suddenly appeared on Brown's face. "You mean they might release me on bail but not allow me to go home?"

Phillips quickly responded. "We're going to try to make sure that doesn't happen. But I want you to understand all the possibilities. I'm having an attorney that I know from New Haven who specializes in criminal law come up this afternoon to speak with you. His name is Myron Feldman. He will want to go over the facts with you in preparation of Monday's hearing."

Brown nodded and then asked, "Is anyone trying to find out who actually shot the commander?"

Phillips looked down at the table in silence for a moment. "We're doing what we can."

***

Sally, Sheila and Henry sat in the very back row of the seating in the Foxwoods Grand Ballroom. Sheila and Henry had returned from picking up the car mid-afternoon. After meeting up with Sally, they had decided to go to the Billings Shipyard annual meeting to see if they might learn something more about the arrest of Sally's father. When they arrived, the meeting was well underway. Not hearing anything but boring business discussions, the three had decided to leave when the elderly man sitting next to Henry leaned over and said, "You guys must be waiting for the press conference, right?"

Henry gave a quizzical look and asked, "Press conference?"

The man set his meeting information packet on the floor under his chair and leaned back in his chair, looking back at Henry. "I live right here in New London and never would have come to this boring meeting except that the noontime news said that BSI was going to hold a press conference right after the annual meeting to talk about last night's shooting. I hear it was a BSI engineer who shot the guy. I want to hear what they have to say about that!"

***

The three had suffered through the remainder of the business meeting and were now listening attentively as the BSI chairman of the board of directors stepped to the microphone. The front three rows were occupied by members of the press. Tim Kerrigan read the brief press release and then opened the floor to questions. The press instantly started shouting questions until Kerrigan pointed to a lady in the front row.

"Can you tell us what Steven Brown's connection to the victim was? Was Commander Ashley involved with the BSI project that Brown was working on?"

Tim Kerrigan looked down at the press who seemed to be more of a lynch mob than a body of reporters looking for the truth.

"We have no knowledge that Lt. Commander Ashley was directly involved with any BSI projects."

A shout of questions arose from the press members and Kerrigan again pointed to a person in the front row.

"If the commander was not involved with any BSI projects, can you tell us what he was doing here at your annual meeting?"

Kerrigan replied, "You would have to ask the navy about the commander's assignments."

Again, a shout arose from the press. This time, Kerrigan pointed to a television reporter who stood off to the side with a cameraman at his shoulder.

"Ken Malone, Channel Six news. Mr Kerrigan, given that multiple witnesses identified Steven Brown with a smoking gun in his hand as he emerged from a room that contained no other persons other than a United States Naval officer who had been brutally shot, can you explain why your company is using its own legal staff... supported by stockholders' money I might add... to represent such a heinous criminal? Is it because you feel you need to try to mitigate the negative effect that this crime will have on your corporation?"

224

Sally Brown rose to her feet in an uncontrolled rage and yelled, "Whatever happened to being presumed innocent, you media leech!"

Before the cameras could be re-aimed to capture whoever had just made this outburst, Sally stormed out of the room, followed by Sheila and Henry close at her heels.

# Chapter 19

The drive back to Billings was painfully quiet. Sally had wanted to stop by the New London County lock-up where she had learned that her father was being held, but both Sheila and Henry had voted against that plan. Sheila reminded Sally that none of them had permission to be in Connecticut, and if they showed up at the county jail, Sheila and Henry's parents would very likely be notified. Sheila added that there was nothing that any of them could do at this point to help Sally's dad, and if all went well, Sally should be able to see him on Monday when he would certainly be released on bail.

At first, Sally had protested but, in the end, she gave in to reason. She wanted desperately to comfort her father and tell him that she knew that he was innocent, but in reality, if she showed up when he thought she was safely back home, the result would likely be that his anxiety would only be increased. A disobedient daughter was not what he needed right now.

As the trio passed over the bridge into Maine at Kittery, Sheila broke the silence. "So, what do we do now?"

Sally had been formulating a plan ever since they left the resort.

"The one solid lead we have is Mr Wilhelm."

When Sheila and Henry had returned to the resort after picking up the car Sally had told them about seeing Wilhelm at the garage. Henry had been skeptical at first but when Sally showed them the photo on her phone, he recognized the car.

Sally continued, "We know that he was at Foxwoods when the shooting occurred."

"And," added Sheila, "we know that he had some connection with the naval commander, Peter Ashley, who was shot since I found out from the hotel clerk that Mr Wilhelm had been looking for Peter Ashley."

Henry, not wanting to be left out of the process, added, "And don't forget that whoever left the money at the coat check room had a German accent. That sure sounds like our chemical Nazi!"

Sheila asked Sally, "But what do you have in mind? We can't exactly confront him with what we know and ask him if he shot Peter Ashley."

Sally thought for a moment and then replied, "I'm not sure how Mr Wilhelm is involved. It's hard to believe that he is a murderer…"

Henry interrupted, "You didn't see his comments on my last chemistry lab."

Sally continued without acknowledging Henry. "If Mr Wilhelm is involved, it must be connected with my dad's work somehow. Remember that his teacher's file included a letter of recommendation from BSI to the state board of education, and that BSI is paying his salary this year. I intend to talk to my dad when he gets home to see if he knows anything about Mr Wilhelm."

***

An hour and one half later, the three turned into Sally's driveway. It was ten o'clock which was considerably later than they had planned on arriving home. Sheila looked at her watch and said, "We need to get going. I will have some explaining to do at home as it is. Are you going to be all right?"

Sally jumped out and grabbed her bag from the back seat.

"I'm fine," she responded. "I'll call you both tomorrow."

As Sheila and Henry drove off, Sally got her keys out to unlock the front door. The house was dark, which was not a surprise knowing that her dad would not be home. She stepped into the front hall and picked up the mail from the floor where it had been deposited through the main slot in the door. Seeing nothing but advertisements and what looked like bills, she tossed the mail onto the hall sideboard and headed into the living room where she fell into the overstuffed chair in the corner with a heavy sigh. A million thoughts raced through her mind. After fifteen minutes, the strain of the past two days finally caught up with her and she dozed off, thoroughly exhausted.

Sally awoke to the sound of her cell phone ringing. The morning sun came streaming through the living room window which made her squint from the brightness as she reached for her phone. Her back ached from the overnight in the chair. Glancing down at the phone display she saw that she had four messages from the same number that was now calling. Knowing that she couldn't avoid the call forever, she took the call.

"Hello?"

An obviously relieved voice of a woman spoke. "Miss Brown, this is Denise Witham. I work with your dad at BSI."

The woman sounded pleasant enough, but Sally wasn't sure what to say so she just listened.

"I've been trying to reach you, dear, but I was beginning to think that maybe you'd lost your phone. You know I do that all the time. Usually, I have to call myself to find it."

Sally felt a bit embarrassed, but she spoke up. "My phone battery went dead, and I just found my charger."

"I know how it is, dear. Sometimes I wish cell phones had never been invented."

There was a brief pause and then Denise continued. "You know that your dad is in Connecticut on business. He has run into a problem which may keep him there longer than he anticipated, and I was asked to give you a call."

Cautiously, Sally asked, "What kind of problem?"

Denise paused as if considering her answer and then said, "I know that you are a very bright young lady and so I'm going to be direct. There was a shooting at the hotel where your dad was staying, and the police have detained your father. Your father didn't have anything to do with the shooting, but he was in the wrong place at the wrong time and the police have arrested him."

Sally tried to act surprised. "They arrested him!"

Denise sensed Sally's concern. "Don't worry, dear. I know that he will be cleared soon. In the meantime, he will have to stay in Connecticut through at least tomorrow. I can come over and stay with you if you would like until your dad comes home."

Even though Sally already knew more details than Denise probably did, talking about it again brought a new round of emotional pain. Choking back her emotions she replied, "No. I'm fine. And as you say, I'm sure that Dad will be back soon."

Denise spoke as if she had guessed that Sally would decline her offer. "Well, listen dear, my number is 555-1278. You can call me anytime. I know that you can take care of yourself for a while, but I'm hoping that you will let this old grandmother look in on you later. Your dad worries about you. If it's all right, I'll just stop by to meet you tomorrow morning on my way to work before you go off to school. And if you need anything, just call."

"I will," Sally said. She couldn't help but smile. "And I leave for school at seven thirty so you can stop by around seven if that's not too early."

Denise said, "That's not too early for me, hon. I've been getting up for work at BSI at six thirty every morning for thirty-five years. Just don't ask me to be awake after nine o'clock in the evening!"

After finishing her call with Denise, Sally dragged herself upstairs to get a shower and get changed. Coming down later she walked into the kitchen to make a cup of coffee and have a piece of toast. As she sat drinking her coffee her thoughts focused on how she could find out Mr Wilhelm's involvement in the shooting. After twenty minutes of planning, Sally began to feel the loneliness of not having her dad at home. She cleared away the dishes and, lost in thought, she wandered into her father's study. She wasn't sure why she was in the study but somehow she took comfort in being here as if it provided some kind of connection to her dad.

Sally sat at her father's desk and rested her head in her hands. It seemed ironic that there is a tendency not to value that which you have until it is taken away. Her dad had worked hard at being a good father, which hadn't been easy without a wife present to help out through the years. And Sally had to admit that she hadn't exactly been an ideal child.

Sally reflected on her father's strengths as she sat. He was not someone who panicked easily. In fact, he was almost always in control and so many times Sally had drawn strength from the fact that he always seemed to have answers to every problem. There was little doubt that this situation would be no different. Clearly this was a difficult circumstance for her dad, but Sally knew that he would come through as the gifted analytical engineer that he is.

Sally looked around her father's study. It reflected the fact that he was very organized with everything in its proper place. No pen or pencil, no piece of paper, or no book lay out of its place. No book out of place except for that one, Sally noticed. She looked across the room at the bookshelf on the opposite wall. In stark contrast to every other book in the bookshelf, one book on the top shelf was sticking halfway out. As Sally walked over out of curiosity, she saw a white envelope projecting from the top of the book.

Sally pulled the book off the shelf and read its title, *Engineering Circuit Analysis* by William H. Hayt, Jr. and Jack E. Kemmerly. She pulled out the envelope and immediately noticed that it was not sealed. Knowing that this was an invasion of her dad's privacy, Sally nevertheless opened the envelope and read the single sheet of paper that she pulled out.

*Mr Brown,*
*The schematic was received.*
*The down payment will be left at the coat check room under tag # thirty-eight. When you complete your task, the remaining funds will be forwarded per our agreement. The gun will be delivered to your room.*

Sally sat down in a chair beside the desk in shock. This couldn't be. There was no way that her dad was involved. But this note would erase any doubt from the minds of his accusers. It was obvious that this was much more serious than Sally had imagined. Someone was making sure that her father would be framed and that there would be no questions asked.

Why would someone want to implicate her dad? And who had put this note here? Whoever it was had broken into their home and had planted this note knowing that it would be found. Sally calmed her nerves and cleared her mind. What did she learn from this? First, this was about more than just a simple shooting. The first line of the note spoke about a schematic. Sally knew that her father was working on a navy contract at

BSI that required a top security clearance. How often had her dad come home and answered Sally's questions about how his day went by saying, 'I'd have to kill you if I told you!' Clearly, someone had received a schematic and it was likely that this was some kind of diagram that was highly classified and had been stolen from BSI.

The second thing that was obvious was that whoever was behind this had been both at Foxwoods as well as here in Billings. That could be Mr Wilhelm, but it seemed unlikely that he could be working alone. He had been in school on Thursday and it seemed like there had to be someone in place at Foxwoods to set this up well in advance. Mr Wilhelm might have planted the evidence in the coat room Friday. He might even have been in the men's room when Peter Ashley was shot, but how would he have known that both Mr Ashley and her dad would be together that night? It seemed like he must have had advanced help with surveillance, if not with the operation itself.

The third thing that the note pointed to was that the naval officer who was shot, Commander Ashley, must have either known something about what was going on, or he was about to find out. Unfortunately, the news report just before they left Foxwoods said that Commander Ashley was still in intensive care and had not regained consciousness.

The final thing that Sally had to admit was that her father was in even bigger trouble than she had thought. This was meant to be the proverbial final nail in his coffin. That was undoubtedly based on the assumption that the police would be coming here soon to search the house.

Sally picked up her cell phone and called Henry. On the third ring, Henry picked up.

"Henry, we need to get together right away. Can you get Sheila?"

"Funny you should mention her. Sheila is right here making me erase our fake IDs from the state computer records. Just a suggestion, but you probably shouldn't use your ID again."

"Listen, can I come over? I need to have you hang on to something for me. I need to get it out of the house immediately."

As Sally waited for Henry to speak, she looked out of the front window to see two police cruisers pull up in front of the house, one from the county sheriff and the other from the Billings Police Department.

Sally jumped up and headed for the back door.

"Got to run. I'll see you in a few minutes."

With that, Sally folded the note and put it in her right shoe. She then walked to the garage to get her bike and walked it to the front of the house. When she got to the front yard, she saw three police officers standing on the front porch.

"Can I help you?" she inquired with as much calm in her voice as she could muster.

The Billings chief of police came down the walk to speak with her.

"Sally Brown?"

Sally tried to relax as she replied, "Yes."

The chief smiled and said, "Sally, I'm Chief Wilkerson. I'm here with Sheriff Trent. We have a warrant to search your home. Are you aware of the fact that your father is being held in connection with a homicide investigation in Connecticut?"

Sally looked directly at the chief as she said, "I know about the investigation. And I also know that if you have a search warrant, I can't stop you from going into our home."

The chief looked sympathetically. "Is there anyone inside, Sally?"

Sally shook her head. "No one is here other than me and I am on my way over to a friend's house to study for a history exam tomorrow. If you want to search the house suit yourself. The front door is unlocked. I'll be back by noon. Will you be done by then?"

The chief said, "Yes, we should be done by noon."

Sally got on her bicycle and peddled off to bring Sheila and Henry up on the new developments.

***

The courtroom was full. Steven Brown was led into the room in handcuffs. Ahead of him was his Connecticut attorney, Myron Feldman, along with John Phillips. They sat at the front table awaiting the entrance of the judge. After several minutes, the bailiff called for all in the courtroom to stand and announced the Honorable Judge Aaron Winston.

After the preliminary instructions were given and the charges were read, the judge asked how the defendant would like to plead. Without

232

hesitation, Myron Feldman stood and spoke so that all could hear. "Your Honor, my client enters a plea of not guilty."

With the plea officially entered, the terms for bail were then argued. The New London County district attorney rose and began his motion.

"Your Honor, the victim was shot in an act of the most violent and heartless way. The victim was shot with no regard other than self-interest by the perpetrator. Your Honor, the State moves that bail be denied and that the defendant be held awaiting trial. The risk of flight is great given that the defendant has no ties to Connecticut. Furthermore, he has been employed less than a year by Billings Shipyard in Maine, and he has no significant connection to that area either."

Steven looked across at John Phillips and whispered with great concern. "I'm going to be released, right?"

Phillips didn't respond vocally, but he gave Brown a nod that to Brown didn't seem to have much conviction. Following the district attorney's motion, Myron Feldman stood.

"Your Honor, Steven Brown is a nationally respected engineering professional. He was selected by the Billings Shipyard to head one of their most important contracts and the company stands behind Mr Brown's integrity. Billings Shipyard has submitted an affidavit stating that they will take full responsibility for Mr Brown if he is released on bail. The company's confidence in my client's innocence is such that they will be bearing all costs of litigation. We request, Your Honor, that a reasonable bail be granted and that our client be released to return home to his job under the recognizance of Billings Shipyard corporate attorney, John Phillips."

Myron Feldman paused a moment and then continued.

"The State has maintained that my client has no significant ties to Maine, however, I point out that he is a single parent with a daughter who is enrolled in her junior year in high school. Mr Brown's wife passed away from cancer and he has raised his daughter as a single parent for the past four years. I suggest that my client indeed has a significant tie to his home in Maine, that being the desire to be present for his daughter."

When both the prosecution and defense finished, the judge looked down on Steven Brown to pronounce his decision. Brown thought that it had been impossible to read the judge's face during the motions, but as the judge now looked at him, Brown suddenly felt discouraged.

"This is a most heinous crime. There can be no doubt that there was intent to murder with no mercy for the victim. I have listened to the arguments from both sides and I must admit that I am uncomfortable with the defendant's lack of longevity with either his employment or residence in Maine. It is acknowledged that the defendant's employer has offered to stand on behalf of the defendant should he be released on bail, however, the facts of the defendant's current situation must be weighed. It is the court's opinion that the risk of flight is deemed to be of significant concern and, therefore, the defendant is hereby remanded into the custody of the County of New London awaiting trial without bail."

Continuing, the judge checked a calendar. "Jury selection will be scheduled to commence on December twelfth."

# Part 3: Revelations

# Chapter 20

Station Commander Peter Morgan with the Hamburg police sat at his desk in the Davidwache stationhouse. He stared at the ceiling trying to regain his composure. The chief had just told him that he was being put on administrative leave pending an internal investigation. Morgan stuffed his anger deep down inside and tried to consider the facts with the objectivity and analytical expertise that he had spent his entire career developing. At least an administrative leave meant that he would continue drawing his salary. It was the first week of December, with the Christmas holiday fast approaching, and he didn't relish the thought of going home to his wife and telling her that he was being suspended. As bad as things were, however, at least he wouldn't have to add that there would be no money coming in over the holiday. They had just bought a new house in one of the more upscale sections of the city and they were now beginning to experience the joys of much more room, a two-car garage, and the pain of a much larger monthly mortgage. Things were tight enough financially without his difficulties making it worse.

It had been an emotional roller coaster ride over the past month. It had all begun when his daughter, Jane, had announced that she was leaving the university to travel by herself. He and his wife had tried to convince her that there would be plenty of time to travel and see the world, but now was not the time. They pleaded that she needed to finish her degree, which she was only a semester away from receiving. But Jane would have none of it. She was determined to set off to who knows where in search of who knows what.

And then there was the matter of his suspension. It began with what was supposedly a routine crackdown on organized crime in the city, but it had quickly grown into something much more complicated. He thought back to what had been the first sign of trouble. It had been the raid on the nightclub on Herbertstrasse. The operation had been planned a full month in advance. Information had been obtained from a Reeperbahn prostitute that this nightclub was a regular meeting place for the local crime syndicate. It had taken weeks of undercover work to provide a usable lead that finally identified the date for a meeting that involved several local crime bosses and a major drug supplier from Amsterdam.

The operation had been planned to the nth degree. When the evening finally came, there were undercover officers stationed in the nightclub and a strike team ready and waiting across the street in a vacant building. The crime bosses were seated at a large table in a corner of the front room that was separated from the main nightclub by a two-meter-high partition. When the two drug dealers arrived, they were seated at the table and drink orders were taken by a waitress who was actually a Hamburg undercover police officer. Twenty minutes after the meeting had begun, it was deemed that enough incriminating dialogue had been recorded by the concealed microphone under one of the seats and the strike team was ordered to move in for the arrests.

It was supposed to be a routine, controlled arrest without incident. What it turned out to be was anything but. When the strike team entered the nightclub, officers immediately headed for the table in the corner. Before they could reach the table, however, shots were fired at them from behind the screening partition. The crowd panicked and, instead of control, there was complete pandemonium. What made matters worse was that the criminals were relatively protected by the heavy wooden screen and they showed no hesitation to make an armed last stand. In the confusion, three civilians were shot, one seriously. Three of the mob bosses, along with one of the drug dealers, were killed. Fortunately, none of the strike team was injured.

During the hearing conducted by the police internal affairs division, it was determined that what had been considered by the operation commander as comprehensive planning was, in fact, seriously deficient. The judges cited both the inadequate protection of the public and the lack of consideration of the criminals' use of firearms as being elements of negligence on the part of the operation command.

Morgan sat smiling. It was amazing how internal investigation judges had such brilliance in stating the obvious, particularly after the fact. Fortunately, he had only been responsible for the part of the investigation that turned up the lead that had identified the meeting details. The strike operation itself had been run by headquarters.

Morgan now sat deep in thought. At the time of the investigation, no one had given any thought whatsoever to what eventually turned out to be the most important element in this strike operation. At the time, it just didn't seem important.

When the strike team entered the nightclub that evening, three officers had been assigned the task of securing the room at the rear and the back door exits. When the first shots were fired the three officers were far enough into the front room that they were able to quickly move into the rear room to avoid the gunfire. Later, the officers would state that by the time they entered the rear room the few people who were there were panicking and were trying to exit through the rear doors. According to the officers' testimony, at least two men fled through the doors. Two of the officers pursued those leaving the scene while the third officer secured the back room and tried to keep anyone else from leaving. It was later admitted by the officers that, given the confusion, it was impossible to tell if others beyond the two that were seen leaving had also exited the nightclub through the rear doors.

The pursuing officers ran after the two men who had been seen leaving, but they were not apprehended. The internal investigation hearing did not consider this incident worthy of consideration.

Additionally, in apparently yet another unrelated incident, a document had been discovered on the floor of the rear room that appeared to be a classified document of an American shipyard with some connection to the United States Navy. The document was noted in the incident report, but it was not brought up at the internal investigation hearing.

The day after the nightclub operation, the chief had ordered Morgan to contact Interpol and have the international authorities deal with what possibly was a classified document. At the time, Morgan himself had felt that spending time on the document was a waste of time. After all, how would a top-secret document wind up on the floor of a nightclub in the Reeperbahn? When he had contacted Interpol and informed them about the document, however, he had been immediately connected with a naval military officer in the States who seemed to take a keen interest in it.

That was when things took a serious turn for the worse, and Morgan's life had been sent spiraling out of control. Morgan hung his head in sadness as he remembered the day when his duty officer, as well as his newest recruit, young Manfred Spear, had both been slain. What had previously been considered as a document of little importance had cost the lives of two of his police officers.

It had been Morgan who had come up with the lead that proved critical to the murder investigation. Standing in the basement level at the evidence locker, he had realized that the killer who had made off with the classified document must have had an inside contact. There was no way that an outsider could have known that the document was being held at the stationhouse and, furthermore, it was more than coincidence that he had been waiting and ready exactly at the time when Manfred Spear arrived with it at the evidence locker that fateful morning. Additionally, an inside contact would explain how the killer had been let into the rear door of the stationhouse and would therefore have not been seen by the front desk officer.

Morgan had surmised that for the killer to know that Spear was on the way with the document, he must have been warned by phone from someone on the floor who had seen and heard Spear as he was leaving. As Morgan thought back, he remembered that Spear had spoken about taking the document downstairs as he had left his office.

After reviewing the surveillance video tape of the squad floor just prior to the murder, Morgan discovered that only one of his officers was on the phone as Manfred Spear was seen leaving with the document. Only Inspector Leo Krauss, whose desk was located within five meters of his own office, was seen in the tape placing a call, and it was a call that lasted less than fifteen seconds.

Rather than detain the detective for questioning, Morgan had taken the responsibility to break department policy by keeping the information under wraps. He assigned the homicide investigating officer, Inspector Richard Gross, to head up a surveillance detail to see if Krauss would make contact with the killer.

Morgan sighed and thought to himself that although he had bent a few rules, if he had it to do over again, he would do nothing differently. They had nearly been successful in identifying the killer but, as things so often have a way of happening, just when Morgan thought he had everything well in hand, disaster struck.

Morgan turned back to his computer and started writing a summary of the events for the investigation report. His first sentence said it all:

*What appears to be an isolated incident of theft and homicide at the Davidwache stationhouse is, in fact, one of a complex series of connected crimes that can now be understood to have far reaching consequences beyond this city, with international implications.*

\*\*\*

The day that Lisa Kerrigan had arrived home following the BSI annual meeting she had made a decision. The questions were driving her to distraction. She could no longer concentrate. First there were the suspicions about her husband that had been raised in the letter by BSI's financial officer, Greg Connor. Then, to reinforce these suspicions, the letter had been stolen from her home. Just when she had thought that perhaps her suspicions had no merit, the revelation that BSI was involved in a serious security breach was brought to light by Peter Ashley.

And then, there was the matter of James Macintyre. She had heard him on the phone talking about the shooting of Commander Ashley. But was what she heard an indication that Macintyre was somehow involved in the shooting, or was he actually part of the investigation as he claimed?

Lisa decided that she had to take action to find the answers that she so desperately needed. It had taken a day for Lisa to formulate her plan. Now here it was two weeks later, and she couldn't believe what she had found. It was midnight and she was sitting in front of her computer in her office. She had decided to go back to the beginning and consider the letter that Greg Connor had written. She had wracked her memory to remember the contents of the letter.

When she had first read it, the allegation against her husband had captured her full attention. But as she reviewed its contents in her mind, she remembered that Greg had mentioned a company that had shown up in the project Special Services account line item that he could not identify with the Hamburg Shipping contract. As she remembered, the company had an Asian name and was associated with the purchase of start-up equipment.

It had taken her a week of investigating the project accounting files but her diligence had finally paid off. The Project Start-Up Equipment Purchases account in the computer files did not include anything relating to a deposit made to a Special Services account. Neither was there anything indicating that a payment had been made to a firm located in Asia. Just when she had felt that this was a dead end, she decided to check the paper files. All of BSI's revenue and expense records were computerized and stored as electronic files. Lisa knew, however, that although nearly everything was received and transmitted electronically, there were still some transactions that took place by mail or by paper fax. These items were scanned and were then added to the electronic record. It was BSI policy to keep the paper copies until project closeout.

Her investigation of the paper project accounting files turned up a piece of paper that wasn't in the computer files. It was a copy of a transfer of funds in the amount of twenty-five thousand dollars to Tokushima Industries, Osaka, Japan, approved by her husband on June sixteenth. At the bottom of the copy were the handwritten words, *check this — GC*. It was clear that the handwritten note was made by Greg Connor. Lisa had no idea why there was no electronic record of the transfer since the paper copy had been stamped 'Scanned/Entered'.

Lisa had wondered why her husband would have been directly involved with routine funds associated with project start-up. Ordinarily, this was something that would have been handled by the project manager, not by the company's chief executive officer, which he had been at the time.

The problem was, she couldn't confront her husband with the question. If he was somehow involved with something illegal, she had no proof and he would simply deny any accusations. After thinking about it for a day she finally decided that if answers were to be obtained, she would have to get them through Tokushima Industries. Unfortunately, she couldn't exactly ask them point blank if they were involved in criminal activities either. A search of the company on the web provided few details about the company but it did provide an email contact address.

242

Lisa decided that the best approach would be to send an email under the name of her husband. Given that she didn't have a clue what might be going on, she decided to be cryptically brief. Setting up an email account on Hotmail, she sent off a one-line message to Tokushima:

*"Things have gone wrong. What can you tell me? Email at this address."*

It had been just an hour before Lisa received a reply.

*"We have no problem. Safeties are in place and are working. We expect you to tie up loose ends when finished."*

The reply sent Lisa into a fit of depression. Clearly something bad was going on, and whatever it was, it certainly looked like Tim was somehow involved. The email seemed to point to the security leak, but it didn't say so explicitly even though it was hard to deny the obvious. But in her heart she knew that Tim would never do anything illegal or damaging to BSI. As her mind raced, she couldn't blank out the overriding question, *What was going on?*

***

Sally, Henry and Sheila walked along a sidewalk in silence. Just ahead, Mr Norris turned as they all reached the entrance door to Deering High School. "I'll sign us up at the registration desk and pay the entry fee. You three can wait in the lobby. I'll be back in just a minute."

It was December tenth, but Sally couldn't have said what day it was. Since returning from Connecticut, time seemed to have become a blur, each day simply melting into the next. When Sally had returned home from Henry's house to show Henry and Sheila the note that she had found, the police had finished their search and had left. The following day after school, the chief returned to her house with Denise Witham, whom she had met that morning before leaving for school. The chief told her that her father's request for bail had been denied and that he would be held in Connecticut until a trial could be held. He said that that could be a number of weeks, so that afternoon she had moved into the spare room at Denise Witham's house around the corner. The chief had made it clear that, as a minor, Sally would not be allowed to live alone while her father was *away*. Both the chief and Denise had reassured Sally that the arrangement was temporary until her father was cleared, but here it was weeks later, and Sally was losing patience with 'temporary'.

It wasn't that living with Denise was all that bad. She was like the grandmother that she had never had the benefit of knowing. But Sally was in a constant cloudy day state of mind knowing that her father was wrongfully in jail awaiting trial and there was nothing that she could do about it. She had tried to explain the situation to Denise, but she was handcuffed by her inability to divulge that she and her friends had been there. Denise had simply given her a hug saying, "I know things will be all right."

Sally, Henry and Sheila had tried to follow up on their only lead. They had all taken turns doing surveillance of Mr Wilhelm but, so far, they had not witnessed the chemistry teacher making any clandestine rendezvous with nefarious characters. In fact, he hadn't done anything suspicious at all. They had finally reached the conclusion that they would have to pursue other clues.

The three had wanted to meet this Saturday to formalize a plan on what to do next but, on Friday at lunch period, Mr Norris, the history department head, had stopped by their table to remind them that the state history competition was tomorrow. With all that was on their minds, they had completely forgotten about their qualifying for the state competition. The prize, a trip to Paris, had seemed like such a dream fantasy when they had decided to enter the school contest. Now, however, it didn't seem important at all. Before Sally could say that they really didn't want to enter the state competition anymore, Mr Norris spoke up saying, "I hope you three will honor your commitment to represent the school. I know from Mr Hollingsworth that the three of you have dropped out of debate. I expect that you will show more perseverance in this endeavor. I'll pick you up tomorrow morning at seven thirty here out front of the school. Don't be late. We will be returning around four o'clock in the afternoon."

*** 

During the ride down to Portland, Sally, Henry and Sheila had been quiet. Mr Norris had explained the rules and had let them know what to expect. There were going to be twenty-four school champions entered. The competition was set up to be a head-to-head competition between teams for the first three rounds. After round one, the winning twelve teams would advance. At the end of round two, the six wining teams would advance. The end of round three would determine the three finalists. Round four would pit the three finalists against each other to determine first, second and third place. The top two teams would win the grand prize which was a chartered trip during February school vacation week to Paris, with tours of the Louvre, Notre Dame Cathedral and Versailles.

When they entered the school a student representative from Deering High ushered Sally, Henry and Sheila to the cafeteria to wait with the other competitors for the event's opening address that would be delivered by the governor of Maine. After checking in at the registration desk, Mr Norris arrived at the cafeteria and Henry asked the question that both Sheila and Sally had thought silently to themselves. "If we bomb out in the first round, do we have to stay for the entire day?"

Mr Norris frowned. "It would be polite to stay and support the winners and give them congratulations. It wouldn't be a very good show of Billings High sportsmanship if we left early."

Henry looked back at Sheila and mumbled, "I tried."

The cafeteria was crowded with students who were all anxiously rehearsing questions with textbooks open and papers strewn everywhere. Sally looked over at Henry and Sheila and the three suddenly felt conspicuous at their bare table with no prep materials.

Henry smiled sheepishly and said, "So look, a priest, a rabbi and a minister walked into a bar…"

Sheila rolled her eyes and gave Henry a look that clearly said, *enough already*.

Sally looked at the envelope that Mr Norris had given them just before he had headed off to the judges' lounge. Inside the envelope was a piece of paper with the words, *Billings High School — Team F*. Mr Norris had explained that each team would be given a code rather than identify their school so that the judges would not have any bias in their decision. Henry glanced down at the paper and laughed. "Hey, that's not fair. Everyone will know that it's Billings by our grade… F!"

After fifteen awkward minutes of waiting around with nothing to do, the governor arrived, followed by all the teachers who would serve as judges. It was an uninspiring talk, thought Sally, who could barely keep her mind from drifting to her dad's troubles. Following the governor's talk, a teacher posted a piece of paper on the wall. Immediately, every student in the room except for Henry, Sheila and Sally rushed over to the wall. Students slowly filed out of the room and, when nearly everyone had departed, the three walked over to read the notice. It was a listing of team parings for round one by code. After searching for a moment, Sally pointed to the middle of the list, *Team C vs. Team F, Room two-two-seven*. Resigned to their fate, the three walked off in search of Room two-two-seven and their first opponent.

Room two-two-seven was a physics classroom with lab benches. Two of the front benches had three chairs each aligned facing the teacher's desk at the very front of the classroom. At the teacher's desk sat a woman who apparently would be the judge for the round. Team C had already taken their seats at one of the benches. They were three guys who looked like they were auditioning for a role in a teen geek movie. As they walked to their seats, Sally heard Henry say to one of the geeks, "Nice pants, dude. Way to spring plaid from its prison on the golf course."

Sheila shoved Henry into one of the open seats as she and Sally surrounded him on either side.

The judge closed the door and began to review the rules.

"There will be no books, laptops, cell phones or papers allowed. I will ask questions of each team. All team members may consult on an answer, but only one person may answer for the team."

Both Henry and Sheila looked at Sally with an unspoken nod.

The judge continued. "You will have fifteen seconds to give your answer. A correct answer will count as one point. An incorrect answer, or failure to answer within the fifteen seconds, loses a point. Questions will be asked alternating between each team with Team F receiving the first question as was determined in advance by random selection. At the conclusion of twenty questions, the score will be tallied and the team with the highest score will be counted as the winning team. In the event of a tie score after the twenty questions, additional questions will be asked of each team until one team answers incorrectly while the opposing team answers the same question correctly."

The judge looked up from her paper. "Are there any questions?"

Henry immediately replied, "Is that our first question?" Which drew a sharp kick on the shin from Sheila.

The judge gave Henry a disparaging look. "Seeing no questions, I will begin with the first question for Team F. The subject category is ancient history."

The judge looked up at them and asked, "Are you ready?"

Sheila nodded.

"The largest of the three great Egyptian pyramids at Giza dates from the fourth Egyptian dynasty. For which Egyptian pharaoh was this pyramid built as his tomb?"

Henry looked at Sheila. Sheila looked at Sally. Sally counted off seconds quietly in her head.

At the count of fourteen, Sally spoke. "Cheops, son of Seneferu."

The judge reset her stopwatch and said, "Correct, one point for Team F." She marked a point on the board behind her under the heading Team F. She then turned to the opposing team and said, "The category is ancient history. Are you ready?"

The geek in the blue plaid pants grinned widely and nodded.

"The war that was fought between Athens and Sparta from 431 BC to 404 BC is known by what name?"

Team C huddled together in whispered murmurings.

Henry began whistling softly the theme music from *Jeopardy*. Immediately the judge stood and said, "That's a fault for Team F. When a question has been asked, the opposing team must remain quiet! I will deduct one point from Team F and award the point to Team C." She turned and wiped away the one point on the board and added a point under Team C.

Sheila put her head down on the table in exasperation. Henry reached out and put a comforting hand on her shoulder, which she fiercely brushed away. Henry, looking like a hurt puppy, softly said, "Sorry."

The judge continued. "The second category is nineteenth century European history. Is Team F ready?"

By lunch they had completed the first two rounds. The first round had actually gone quite smoothly. After losing their first point with Henry's musical accompaniment, they had answered each question correctly, while Team C struggled with only ten correct answers. The second round went nearly as well with twenty straight correct answers, and the opposing team, Team A, missing on their last three questions.

After lunch the three headed off to Room one-two-four and round three. It was a round that had each team matching each other question for question. On the twentieth question, their opponents incorrectly identified the only bachelor US president as Millard Filmore, and Sally was able to correctly identify William Taft as the only incumbent US president to run for re-election and end up third in the Electoral College count. From there it was off to the final round four.

This round would determine the three winning positions and, although Henry and Sheila wouldn't admit it out loud, they were beginning to get excited about their success. As the trio entered the room, they saw that it wasn't an ordinary classroom, but rather was the school's auditorium. Seated in the audience were all of the event's contestants who had failed to make the finals, along with coaches, friends and family. On the stage were three tables for the three final teams, all facing a table with a panel of three judges.

Seated at one of the team tables were two girls and a guy and a sign that identified them as Team Y. They obviously went to a school in a very affluent community where parents showered their kids with great amounts of money and even greater expectations for success. Henry leaned over to Sheila as they stood at the rear of the auditorium looking at their opponents and whispered, "Wanna bet that there are three brand new Beamers out in the parking lot?"

Seated at the second team table were three guys who looked nearly identical, each with dark unkempt hair, round Harry Potter glasses, and badly sweat stained white shirts, each with a bundle of pens in their shirt pockets. The three looked the exact image of the definition of *nerd*. Sally

248

couldn't help feeling a bit sorry for the three. Each sat transfixed in a state of barely controlled panic. The sign on the table read Team Q.

Before Henry could comment, Sheila put up a finger and simply said, "*Don't!*"

The three walked down the main aisle of the auditorium with all eyes fixed on them. They climbed the stage steps and took seats at the table identified as Team F.

As soon as the three were seated, the lead judge rose to speak to the audience.

"Welcome to the state of Maine finals of this year's history prize competition. Let me say to all of you who competed today, *well done!* Although you may not have made it to the final round, your academic achievement in being named your school's most knowledgeable history students is a tremendous accomplishment. You all deserve a round of applause."

The auditorium erupted in a moment of applause, after which the judge turned to the three final teams.

"For the three finalists today, we express our sincere congratulations and wish you the best in this final round. The rules for this final round are a bit different from the previous rounds and so I will take a moment to explain the format. A question will be asked of the first team, which will be Team F, as was decided in advance by random draw. If Team F answers the question correctly, a new question will be asked of the next team in turn, Team Y in this case. If, however, Team F answers the question incorrectly, and the next team, Team Y, is able to answer the question correctly, then Team F will be eliminated from the round. If Team F answers incorrectly and Team Y is unable to answer the question correctly, both teams remain and a new question will be asked of the third team, Team Q. The round continues sequentially until we have only a single team left as the champion."

The explanation of the fine points of the rules went on for what seemed an eternity, however, when they were finally all announced, the round began. It continued for twenty-seven questions, with each team answering correctly until the twenty-eighth question, when it quickly all fell apart.

For the twenty-eighth question the lead judge announced, "This question is for team F. The category for this question is early American history."

Sally had brought a bottle of water with her from lunch, and although she didn't exactly feel like there was any pressure, she felt that she needed a drink. Sally grabbed her bottle and took a drink and the water slid down her throat the wrong way. The next thing she knew she was coughing uncontrollably. After several seconds, the judge asked if she was okay. Sally couldn't speak but held up her hand to signal that she was going to live. The judge immediately issued their question as Sally fought to get her voice back.

"In 1734, the publisher of one of America's earliest newspapers, the *New York Weekly Journal*, was arrested for writing negative articles against the governor of New York. The publisher was brought to trial and won his landmark case that helped establish the right of freedom of the press. Who was this early American newspaper publisher?"

Sally was now struggling to control her coughing and clearly was unable to speak. Henry looked at her with unconcealed panic. If they got this question wrong, he had no doubt that team Beamer would send them packing. Seconds ticked by as Sally fought to get a coherent word out without success. As the judge began to put her stopwatch down, Sheila blurted out, "John Peter Zenger!"

The lead judge, with an obvious surprise, responded, "Correct."

Henry grabbed Sheila and whispered excitedly, "That was awesome!"

Sally's coughing fit, along with Sheila's last minute saving answer, seemed to have an effect on the other two teams, breaking the rhythm of the stream of correct answers.

The judge turned to Team Y and continued. "The category is Greek history and this question is for Team Y. This ancient Greek playwright wrote over one hundred and twenty-three plays, however, only seven exist in their completed form today. He wrote about Oedipus who fulfilled the prophecy that he would murder his father and marry is mother. Who was this famous Greek writer?"

The team put their heads together in what appeared to be, for the first time, a moment of confusion. After several seconds of whispered argument, the team responded with somewhat less than their accustomed confidence, '*Euripedes*'.

The judge looked back at her note card and then stated, "I'm sorry, that is not correct. Team Q, if you can answer the question correctly, it will eliminate Team Y from the competition. Do you want the question repeated?"

The audience sat in stunned silence.

One of the boys of Team Q, Sally didn't see which, and therefore couldn't tell which one spoke since they appeared to be clones of each other, answered, "*Sophocles!*"

The judge immediately responded, "That is correct. Your correct answer means that Team Y is eliminated from the final round. Let's all give Team Y a round of applause."

The two Team Y girls stood with obvious dejection. They both were working hard to control their disappointment. Their male companion, however, seemed to be more relieved than disappointed. All three exited the stage as the crowd continued their applause.

As the clapping died down, the lead judge spoke. "We are now left with two teams. It only remains to determine the order of first and second place. I am pleased to say, however, that both of these teams will be awarded the trip during February vacation to Paris, France."

The crowd again erupted in applause. The boys of Team Q couldn't contain their enthusiasm. They were giving each other awkward high-fives when the lead judge called the room to order. Sally, Sheila and Henry sat in quiet composure looking over at the opposing teams' continued celebration.

Sheila leaned over to Henry and Sally, nodding toward the Team Q boys. "Look at those geeks. This is probably the only good thing that's ever happened to them."

Sally smiled. "This is certainly their fifteen minutes of fame."

Sheila gave a look to Sally that was clearly understood. Sally nodded back in unspoken agreement.

After control had returned to the room, the lead judge issued the next question to team F.

"The category is history of the Renaissance. "One of the greatest minds of the Renaissance, this famous inventor, painter and sculptor, was the creator of the fresco painting *The Last Supper*. Who was this Renaissance artist?"

Sheila quickly answered, "Vincent Van Gogh."

# Chapter 21

Christmas arrived in Billings, Maine with a surprise snowfall. Being located a short distance up-river from the Atlantic coast, Billings typically received less snow each winter than areas inland due to the warmth of the nearby ocean. But this year was the exception. There had been that early snow in November, and now steady snow began falling on Christmas morning. By the following day more than twenty-four inches had fallen with no sign of let-up.

The snowplows were making a valiant effort to keep the roads and sidewalks clear but, with each hour of snowfall, the effort fell further and further behind. Work had been scheduled to resume at the Billings Shipyard the day after Christmas for the early shift, but with the yard blanketed in snow, the work day had been postponed by management until the second shift in hopes of better clearing the parking areas.

James Macintyre trudged through knee-deep snow as he approached the BSI administration building front entrance. Ordinarily he would have stayed home today knowing that the yard would be largely vacant. But this wasn't going to be an ordinary day.

The day that he had returned from the annual meeting he had received a phone call from Steiner. He had wanted to speak directly with him that last day at the annual meeting, but he had received a message from the hotel's front desk that Mr Steiner had to leave unexpectedly and that he would be telephoning Macintyre later that day. The phone call hadn't come until eight o'clock that evening just after he had returned to Billings. Steiner had made it very clear that he would allow for no more screw-ups. The next shipment was due by the end of December and he had been warned that things had better go without a hitch. No one would be looking any further into the issue of security leaks now that the blame had securely been placed at the feet of Steven Brown. There were no excuses now and Macintyre had been told that he had better hold up his end of the bargain... or else. He didn't want to think what the *or else* might entail.

Arriving at his office, Macintyre hung up his coat and took off his LL Bean boots, leaving a pile of melting snow in the corner. The administration building was vacant with the lights off in all but the hallways. Macintyre had initially been concerned that perhaps another brave soul might have made their way into work in hopes of getting something accomplished in the quiet of the snowy morning. When he arrived at the building, however, his worries evaporated as he saw the empty parking lot, only partially cleared of snow.

He sat at his desk and turned on his computer. This was going to be a piece of cake he thought. It was almost as if after all the turmoil of the past month this transfer had been made purposely easy as a reward for all the trouble that he had endured. Macintyre looked out the window at the falling snow and smiled to himself. What could possibly be better than a nearly empty shipyard for what he needed to do?

It only took a moment for the directory for the WG-116B Guidance Systems Project files to show on his computer screen. Entering the classified password, the restricted files began to be displayed. The project management scheduling documents indicated that the current project status was listed as eighty-five per cent complete. This meant that there would likely only be one or two more transfers required, after which payment in full would be forwarded. Macintyre sat back, caught in a momentary daydream of life to come. By this time next summer, he would be comfortably situated in a villa in Cancun, Mexico. He didn't have dreams of excess. Just a modest place overlooking the ocean, he had thought. The benefit of the value of the US dollar versus the Mexican peso would easily allow for a comfortable living for many years to come.

He couldn't wait to see the face of Tim Kerrigan when he handed in his resignation. That would be a real shocker. Everyone, including Kerrigan, thought for sure that he would be next in line for the position of president of the board of directors. They'd all be in for a surprise, he thought happily. No more long days and nights sacrificing his life so that others might benefit. From now on, it would be life dedicated James Macintyre!

Returning to his computer, he started the process of copying files onto a portable memory drive. The process would take at least ninety minutes, but that didn't matter today. No one was here to poke their noses into his office to see what he was up to. Better yet, no one was in the engineering building to wonder who might be accessing classified project files. As the files began uploading to the remote disk, Macintyre opened his desk drawer and took out several brochures describing available real estate in Cancun.

*\*\*\**

It was nearly ten o'clock when Macintyre had finished sealing the large manila envelope. In addition to copying the files, he had also printed out what seemed like endless pages of technical specifications and diagrams. It was beyond him why the client required both electronic copies as well as printed copies of much of the information, but so be it. What did he care how they wanted the information? It was true that the printing had always been a much tougher proposition since he had to access the printers well after hours to assure that no one saw what he was doing. But today, with no one in because of the snowstorm, printing was no problem.

Putting on his boots and coat, Macintyre checked around to make certain that there was no telltale evidence that he had been in this morning. He grabbed the over-sized envelope and stuck his head out the door to make sure that no one was in the building. Seeing that all the offices were still dark, he slipped out into the hall, locking his door behind him. Heading toward the front doors whistling 'Let It Snow' to himself, he checked his watch. It was quarter after ten. He had plenty of time to make the drop at ten thirty in front of the city hall, he thought. He opened the doors to the winter wonderland outside, oblivious to the fact that one of the office supply room doors inside had opened a crack and a pair of eyes watched him as he exited the building.

*\*\*\**

Lisa Kerrigan could not bring herself to believe that her husband might be involved in some illegal activity. Greg Connor's suspicions were centered on the Hamburg Shipping Contract. And somehow, Tokushima Industries was connected as well, either to the Hamburg contract, or to both the Hamburg and the navy WG-116B contracts. But so far, regarding Tokushima Industries, there were only suspicions, not facts.

But there were other facts that needed to be considered. Peter Ashley had said that there definitely was a security leak at BSI. There didn't seem to be any way of finding out more about the Hamburg situation, but she *had* been asked to participate in the WG-116B investigation. With Peter Ashley still in the hospital not yet having regained consciousness, she had had no further contact about the navy's inquiry. But perhaps she could do a little investigating on her own. And just perhaps, in the process, she might be able to take her mind off her suspicions about Tim.

The question Peter Ashley had raised was, who might have been able to access the classified documents? She remembered that Ashley had been most interested in discovering who might have accessed the documents without proper authorization. But she knew that this would be nearly impossible. BSI's security protocols and security measures were the best that could be had. Once at a company gathering, she had heard the information technology department head say that their electronic data was more secure than that at the Pentagon.

So, if it wasn't possible for unauthorized access of the classified files, only those with authorized access need be considered. The list of suspects included all of the engineering staff who were assigned to the project, as well as some of the accounting staff. Of them, only a small handful would have authorized access to more than the small portion of the project files on which they personally were involved. Only the lead project engineer, Steven Brown, and the project manager would have full access.

Steven Brown was in jail for the shooting of Peter Ashley. Certainly, it was possible that he had been the security leak, and the fact that it appeared that he had shot Commander Ashley certainly seemed to point to his guilt. But something about this seemed wrong. Perhaps it was because it was just too obvious. Wouldn't everyone immediately suspect the lead engineer if technical documents were stolen? After all, not only did he have full access to all the files, but he would also have been one of the few people who would have understood them. And wouldn't it be totally insane to shoot the navy's investigator in public where it would be impossible to conceal what he had done? From her few encounters with the lead engineer, it was clear that he wasn't the least bit insane.

With Steven Brown taken off the prime suspect list, that left only the project manager. In this case, she knew that James Macintyre had taken on the responsibilities of project management. She knew this because it was somewhat unusual for the company's CEO to take such an active project role, but she knew from management meetings that he had insisted on this assignment. And that was curious indeed.

Considering his unusual involvement in the project, along with the strange phone conversation that she had overheard, she had no doubt that James Macintyre was worth looking into. She didn't exactly know what to do, but she was sure that that it would be worth keeping an eye on him for any signs of suspicious behavior.

*** 

The day after Christmas, Lisa awoke to a white blanket of snow on the ground and a steady downfall of new snow in the air. Checking her cell phone, she read the automatic text message that the yard would be closed for regular duties until the second shift. This, she thought would be an excellent opportunity to check out James Macintyre's office to see if there might be any incriminating documents. The yard would be deserted of all but essential personnel and she would almost certainly be able to slip into his office undetected.

She rose at her usual six thirty a.m. and put on the coffee for her husband. His routine allowed him to start his day at a later hour than hers which let him sleep in on most days until the unimaginable hour of eight o'clock. Still, she wouldn't trade her schedule for his since he spent many late evenings either at the office or in his study working on overseas communications in time zones that didn't begin until well past midnight Eastern Time.

After a leisurely shower she entered the kitchen to find Tim at the table drinking a cup of coffee and reading last evening's paper. Lisa went over to get a cup from the cupboard and poured herself a cup of coffee.

"You're up early this morning," she remarked.

Looking over at Lisa, Tim turned the page of the paper and said, "You know that the yard is down until second shift."

Lisa put two pieces of bread in the toaster and sat down.

"I heard. I thought that I might go out for a walk this morning and enjoy the snow for a bit. I love it when there is a new snowfall."

Tim nodded without comment and continued reading.

By the time she had finished her toast and black coffee and cleaned up the kitchen, it was almost nine thirty. Tim had adjourned to his study and so Lisa bundled up in a white New Zealand wool sweater and her winter overcoat and headed out into the winter storm. No way was she going to take her car in this mess. Anyway, it wouldn't do for anyone to see her car in the parking lot while she was in the middle of her clandestine endeavor.

Walking proved to be a bit more physically challenging than she had imagined with the amount of snow on the unplowed sidewalks, but she was able to trudge along. There was always something magical about the eerie quiet that a fresh blanket of snow creates. Early in the morning, with pure white snow on the ground and snow collecting on her eyelashes, it seemed that the whole world had been reduced to a magical fantasy with the sounds of the real world muted in the distance. Even the usual glut of macho guys in pickup trucks with plows who always seemed to be caught in a frenzied search for driveways and parking lots to plow had not yet arisen to the day. The beauty of the stillness made her lose herself for a moment, forgetting the knot in her stomach that had formed when she had finally decided to risk playing James Bond.

She awoke from her pleasant dreams when she arrived at the BSI administration building. Curiously enough, there was a pair of recently made footsteps in the deep snow leading to the front door. Looking up to the building Lisa could see that the parking lot was empty and that all the office lights appeared to be off. Instantly, apprehension arose with the concern that someone might be in the building. But who could that be? Perhaps it was just a security guard who wanted to check that the front door was locked. Or perhaps, it was the very person she didn't want to see...

Lisa wiped the snow off her face and continued down the sidewalk. If she was going to play James Bond, she would have to be careful not to get caught. If someone was indeed in the office building, she would be more likely to go unnoticed if she entered by the back door. Circling around the building she headed up the back steps and entered quietly. For several minutes she stood without making a sound at the end of the hall. When she finally convinced herself that there was no one in the building she walked down the hall toward James Macintyre's office. This was highly likely going to be a wasted effort she thought, but you never know.

As she approached his office she suddenly stopped in her tracks. The light was on inside and she thought she saw movement. In a frozen state of panic, Lisa watched with horror as the light was turned off and the door began to open.

The only thing in her mind were the words repeating over and over again, *Bond... James Bond.* As Macintyre's door opened, she awoke from her frozen state just in time and quietly ducked into the adjacent stock room, closing the door quickly behind her. She was certain that she had been seen, but the person continued down the hall toward the front door. Very carefully Lisa opened her door a crack and saw James Macintyre exiting the building with a package under his arm.

Lisa stood in confused silence for several moments. Why was James Macintyre here? Was he indeed trying to get some work done in the quiet of the morning? Or was he, like Lisa herself, taking advantage of the empty building to do something that required no prying eyes? She had come to see if there was something that could be found in his office that would answer her questions. But this just didn't seem right. On an impulse, Lisa hurried to the front door and peeked out. Macintyre could be seen struggling against the depth of the snow along the sidewalk, heading towards the center of town.

Lisa buttoned up her heavy coat and headed out into the cold. At least the falling snow seemed to be letting up, she thought. But she would have to be careful not to be seen. Just then a city snowplow turned onto the street and Lisa hurried across to the other side. If she was careful, she could probably stay out of Macintyre's sight by keeping the plow truck between her and him.

Lisa followed the truck to the end of the street and, as fortune would have it, it turned and headed in Macintyre's direction. When she had gotten to the main street, the plow turned down Center Street, leaving

Macintyre in full view. Quickly she ducked into a doorway of a cafe, hiding behind an entrance column. Like nearly all of the businesses along the street, the storm had apparently kept the cafe workers from getting in to open up and the main street still slept in solitude.

Macintyre could be seen standing in front of city hall. It appeared that he was waiting for someone as he stood looking up and down the street. The thick blanket of pristine snow looked like a Christmas card with only Macintyre and his footsteps in the snow to show that anyone was alive in this picturesque downtown scene. Just as Lisa began to drift off into the beauty of the morning, her peace was interrupted by the sight of someone walking up Center Street towards Macintyre.

It was obviously a man, but she could not see his face since it was wrapped in a woolen scarf. When Macintyre saw the man, he hurried down the street to meet him. Lisa did not dare to get any closer for fear of being seen and so she held her place. The two men spoke together briefly, and Macintyre could be seen handing over the package under his arm to the other man. It was impossible to hear what they were saying at this distance, but it appeared that the other man didn't have much to say to Macintyre anyway. After receiving the package, he abruptly turned and headed off in the direction that he had come. Lisa had expected Macintyre to return to BSI, but instead, he walked off down the main street away from the yard.

Lisa was left wondering what to do. Her choices were that she could go back to Macintyre's office, follow Macintyre, or follow the man with the package. Searching Macintyre's office was probably not a good idea at this point since it was almost a certainty that someone would be arriving at the administration building soon. Following Macintyre also didn't seem prudent since if she were seen by him, she would have some uncomfortable explaining to do. The most interesting proposition seemed to be following the unidentified man. She needed to be getting home soon from her 'walk' or Tim might become suspicious. Luckily, the man was headed in the same direction as her house and so, she rationalized, that following this man would be taking her in the right direction. Also, if he were to see her, she would be nothing more than just another person out for a walk in the snow. But above all, she had a burning need to know what was in the mysterious package.

She tried to walk casually along the sidewalk as she headed up the Center Street hill. At the top of the hill the man passed by a lady out walking her two dogs. Lisa smiled, happy not to be the only other person out in view of the man. He turned toward the high school and after continuing several blocks he entered an apartment house. Lisa waited for a minute and saw a light come on through the side window of what was probably a first-floor apartment. She then gathered up her courage and walked up onto the porch.

On the porch she saw three mailboxes labeled, three-zero-one — Landers; two-zero-one — Hansen; and one-zero-one — Wilhelm. So, she thought, it would seem that our mystery man has a name. She quickly left the porch and walked around to the side of the building. There was a driveway between this apartment house and the adjoining house that also looked like it contained apartments. The side window where the light had been turned on was relatively close to the ground. Under the window was a stack of snow-covered boards that lay up against the wall.

Carefully, Lisa stepped onto the boards and hoisted herself up to be able to see through the window. Inside she could see the man that she had been following, sitting at a table in a small dining room. Before him on the table was a stack of papers and what looked like a portable computer hard drive. Also on the table was the package envelope that had obviously been torn open. Lisa looked for several seconds hoping to get a better view of the papers as her eyes adjusted to the lesser light in the room.

The man was studying the papers and one fell off the table and landed on the chair closest to the window. Lisa looked at the paper and in amazement saw that the paper was an electronic diagram of some sort. But most shocking was the fact that the paper had a Billings Shipyard logo in the title block. She couldn't believe what she was seeing! She stood transfixed in amazement.

That was when the man reached down for the paper and looked up into the frozen face of Lisa Kerrigan peering through the window.

\*\*\*

The Steven Brown trial in New London had begun three weeks ago and was now in recess for the holidays. The court was scheduled to reconvene on the second of January with the defense presenting its case. The proceedings had begun with jury selection which took a week. The following week, both sides presented their opening statements and then the district attorney began presenting expert witness after expert witness who testified that the murder had taken place at point plank range, that the single shot had inflicted a critical wound, that Steven Brown was indeed caught holding the murder weapon, and that there were no other people in the vicinity. It had been a frustrating affair for Steven as he had to sit quietly while the prosecutor's witnesses testified.

Steven suffered through the questioning, knowing that the picture that was being painted was not a picture of the actual happenings. He did not know who had shot the naval officer, but it certainly wasn't him. He was particularly frustrated with his own attorneys who permitted the prosecution to set up the crime in the minds of the jurors without any significant objections. He knew that he had competent attorneys, but he would have like to see a little more participation on their part in his defense.

\*\*\*

On morning of December sixteenth, Steven Brown had been ushered into the courtroom and was seated beside the BSI counsel, John Phillips, and the defense attorney, Myron Feldman.

The bailiff stood and announced, "All rise for the Honorable Judge Aaron Winston."

After the judge had reminded the jury of their duties the trial resumed. With a dramatic flair, the district attorney called Steven to the witness stand.

He only vaguely heard those well-known words from countless law shows on television. "Do you solemnly swear to tell the truth, the whole truth, and nothing but the truth…" The situation seemed surreal as he stood before a packed courtroom with the crowd of onlookers, the jury and the judge, all obviously anxiously awaiting his breakdown and confession on the witness stand.

Once seated, the district attorney walked over with a gun in his hand.

"Do you recognize this, Mr. Brown?" he asked.

Steven looked at the weapon and responded. "Well, I'm not certain, but it looks like the gun that was used to shoot Peter Ashley."

The prosecutor turned to the jury box and smiled.

"Indeed, it is, Mr Brown."

Waiting a moment for dramatic effect, he continued.

"And could you tell us if this is your gun?"

Looking back with defiance, Steven replied, "No, it isn't my gun. I do not now own, nor have I ever owned, a gun."

"Well, that's very interesting, because you see, your fingerprints were found to be on this gun. In fact, no other fingerprints were found on the gun other than yours. How do you explain that Mr Brown?"

Myron Feldman spoke up. "Objection Your Honor. Calls for speculation."

The judge simply replied, "Objection sustained."

The district attorney paused for a moment and then continued.

"Our criminal investigation team has testified that only your fingerprints were found on the weapon. Would you please tell the court how that came to be?"

Steven knew where this was headed, and it wasn't going to sound good.

"I picked it up when I saw it in the toilet stall that I was in while I was in the men's room."

The prosecutor immediately spoke. "So let us get this straight, this isn't your gun, it just magically appeared in your toilet stall. That's quite some toilet, Mr Brown. Or perhaps it was the casino's policy to not only provide each stall with an ample supply of toilet paper for personal use, but also with a handgun for personal safety."

The audience and several members of the jury broke into laughs.

Myron Feldman shouted above the laughter. 'I object, Your Honor!"

Judge Winston banged his gavel and spoke with such authority that the room instantly quieted. "Objection sustained."

Turning to the prosecutor, the judge remarked, "I will expect you to keep your sense of humor under control."

The prosecutor gave the judge a contrived look of apology and then turned back to the witness.

"We have heard from expert testimony that the weapon here, exhibit three A, is not able to be traced since its serial number has been removed. So, we may not be able to determine its owner. How convenient, wouldn't you say?"

Myron Feldman exclaimed with a degree of accusation. "Objection, Your Honor. Calls for the witness' opinion."

"Sustained," responded the judge.

The prosecutor smiled and walked over to the jury box. While facing the jury he asked, "Mr Brown, I understand that you are the lead project engineer at Billings Shipyard for a current navy contract. That is correct, isn't it?"

Brown answered with a simple, "Yes."

"Can you tell us about the details of that project? Exactly what does it entail?"

Brown shook his head. "Actually, I'm not at liberty to divulge the details of the project."

The prosecutor whirled around to face the witness. "Indeed! In fact, isn't it true that the reason you are not at liberty to discuss the details of the project is because the project is highly classified by the government and that the project involves national security?"

Once again, Myron Feldman spoke up. "Objection, Your Honor. I fail to see the relevance of this line of questioning. We're here to determine Mr Brown's role, if any, in the shooting of Peter Ashley, not to discuss details of his work assignments."

The prosecutor approached the judge's bench. "Your Honor, the details of Mr Brown's work are highly relevant, and if you would allow, I can show how his work provides motive."

The judge leaned over the bench and said, "I'll allow the question to stand. But I want to see a connection soon or I'll terminate the line of inquiry."

Turning back to the witness the prosecutor asked, "Mr Brown, isn't it true that your current project assignment at Billings Shipyard is classified by the United States Government and is restricted to authorized personnel only with a top-level security clearance?"

Brown nodded.

"Yes or no, Mr Brown."

Brown answered defiantly, "Yes, the project is classified."

"And isn't it also a fact that the United States Navy was at the time of the shooting, and is still currently, in the process of conducting an investigation of Billings Shipyard regarding a security breach that allowed highly classified documents from your very project to be stolen?"

Brown looked over at his attorneys in frustration, but no help was forthcoming.

When he didn't answer immediately, the prosecutor asked, "Mr Brown?"

"Yes, it is true that there is an ongoing investigation into possible security leaks at BSI."

"And Mr Brown isn't it also true that you are the only person, other than the highest executive officers of the company, who has authorized access to all the technical details of the project being investigated by US Naval Intelligence?"

With an air of defeat, he replied, "Yes."

"And, Mr Brown, you were aware of the investigation prior to the shooting of Lieutenant Commander Peter Ashley, isn't that correct?"

"I found out about the investigation that morning at a briefing on the project we were giving to navy representatives."

"And you knew that the lieutenant. commander was the chief investigator?"

"I became aware of that fact, as I said, at the morning briefing."

The prosecutor waited for a dramatic pause and then continued.

"So, let me summarize, if I may. You work on a top-secret project for which only you and your company's very top officers have full access to. There has been a security breach and highly classified documents... documents that are critical to our national defense... were somehow brought out into the public. The US Navy instituted an investigation, and just hours after you find out about it, and find out the identity of the chief investigator, the investigator is nearly fatally shot. And, oh yes, you just happened to be... not only the only person with a connection to the investigator... but the only person, period... in the vicinity of the crime.

And, let us not forget that you were found holding the attempted murder weapon which you cannot prove wasn't yours…"

Myron Feldman interrupted. "Objection, Your Honor! Is there a question for my client here, or is the prosecutor just making a closing statement?"

The judge looked over at the prosecutor and said, "Counselor, please stick to questioning the witness."

"Absolutely, Your Honor."

The prosecutor then walked over to the exhibit table and picked up an item in a small, sealed clear bag. Bringing it over to Brown, he asked, "Do you recognize this?"

Looking carefully at the item, Brown handed it back. "It appears to be a coat check key from Foxwoods."

The prosecutor turned to the court clerk and said, "Let the record reflect that the witness referred to exhibit twelve B, the coat check key found in the defendant's hotel room at the Foxwoods resort."

Returning the key to the exhibits table, the prosecutor continued. "Do you admit that this key, found in your hotel room, was yours?"

Brown stammered, "That key isn't mine! I have no idea where that key came from, but I surely didn't get it."

"But surely you aren't suggesting that this key belonged to someone else who just happened to put it at the back of one of your drawers in your room?"

"Objection, Your Honor. My client already stated that he had no idea where it came from."

"Sustained."

The prosecutor gave an angry glance at the defendant's table and then continued. "Let me ask in a different way. You say that you have no idea where the key came from. Do you know how it came to be in your hotel room?"

Brown hesitated a moment before speaking. "When I returned to my room from having a cup of coffee just before the morning briefing with the navy, I saw a man coming from my room. Before I could open the door, he came bursting out and nearly knocked me over. He might have planted the key."

"Did you see who this man was? Did you speak with him?"

"No, he rushed off down the hall, and I was in a hurry myself."

"Did you report this to the hotel security?"

Again, Brown hesitated. "Well... no. I didn't have time to make the call and it didn't look like anything had been disturbed in the room. I thought he might have been a hotel steward."

The prosecutor turned to face the jury once again. "A stranger enters your room and flees before you can find out who he is. And you didn't even bother to notify security. And now you say that this was how the key came into your possession. We are left with no way to identify this person, or even verify that he was real. Another convenient occurrence, wouldn't you say, Mr Brown?"

"Objection!"

The judge pointed a finger at the prosecutor. "Counselor, one more editorial remark and I will find you in contemp. Stick to relevant questions."

"Certainly, Your Honor."

The prosecutor turned and went back to the exhibits table, this time picking up an envelope. Bringing it to Brown he asked, "Do you recognize this envelope and its contents?"

Brown looked at the outside of envelope and then inside.

"No, I do not recognize this."

The prosecutor turned to the court clerk and said, "Let the record indicate that the defendant referred to exhibit eighteen E."

The prosecutor then held the envelope high so that the jury could see it.

"This envelope was discovered at the Foxwoods Resort coat check room. It was checked under the number thirty-eight; the same number as the coat check key found in the defendant's room."

Turning back to Brown, he asked, "So you say that you do not recognize this envelope. Nor do you recognize the contents, correct?"

Brown responded, "No I do not."

"Well let me identify the contents of this envelope that was found checked into the hotel by a key found in your hotel room for the benefit of the jury. It contains one thousand dollars in one-hundred-dollar bills.

It also contains a piece of paper with the words Peter Ashley, room two-three-three."

There was a gasp from the audience and the judge banged his gavel saying in a loud commanding voice, "Order!"

# Chapter 22

The cell phone rang twice before Gustav Wilhelm answered.

"Yes?"

Wilhelm listened as the caller spoke in German.

"Why didn't you get the item put in place? I understand from my contacts that it hasn't been entered as evidence at the trial."

Wilhelm heard the displeasure in the voice.

"I planted the item in his home just as you suggested. I do not know what happened. I saw the police search the house. Apparently, they didn't find it. However, I placed it so that it couldn't be missed."

"That means that it must have been removed by someone before the police arrived. That is not a good thing."

"If this is the case, it could only be the daughter who found it. I doubt that she will be a problem. She knows nothing."

"Nevertheless, you had better take care of this just to be sure. And what about the bank account that frau Kerrigan spoke of. Have you found out anything?"

Wilhelm looked across the room at an unconscious Lisa Kerrigan who was tied up in a chair with her head drooped forward.

"I am pursuing this matter at this very moment. I will have answers shortly."

"Good." And the line went dead.

\*\*\*

Lisa had nearly fallen off the stack of boards in shock when she saw Wilhelm staring at her through the side window of the house. Realizing that she had been discovered, she jumped down and started running up the driveway. As she rounded the front corner of the house, she caught a glimpse of the man coming out through the front door. In her panic she lost her footing in the snow. Lying face down in the snow she scrambled to get to her feet. The deep snow made her efforts feel like she was moving in slow motion. Just as she was upright, she felt someone grab her arm and spin her around. She swung a fist out in defense but missed wildly. The effort knocked a clump of snow from the top of her head into her eyes, temporarily blinding her. Before she could get her vision cleared, she felt a sharp prick on the side of her neck and, within seconds, blackness descended.

She awoke in a dream-like state, not sure where or when she was. As she tried to clear her mind, she could tell that she was tied to a chair with a gag in her mouth. At first the questions that circled in her mind kept her from grasping the reality of the situation. But eventually she was able to remember her struggle outside as she had tried to flee from the man, and panic set in.

Lisa struggled against the ropes that held her tight. Her hands were tied behind the back of the chair and her feet were secured to the front legs. In addition, there was a rope wound around her waist that was so tightly secured to the chair that it felt like it was cutting into her skin right through her blouse.

Looking around she saw that she was in what was likely the bedroom of the apartment. The room was unusual in that, although there was a bed and a side dresser, there were none of the typical mementos of personal life anywhere to be seen. There were no pictures, no magazines or books, no objects of sentimentality collected over the years of someone's life that offered a portrait of their personality. It was as if she were in a low budget motel room without the ubiquitous awful prints hanging on the walls.

Her concentration was interrupted as the man entered the room. He was relatively tall, she guessed perhaps six-foot two or three, and was in his mid-forties. He was dressed in gray wool slacks and had a knit cardigan sweater that made him appear more like Mr Rogers than a psycho criminal kidnapper. In his hand he carried a second chair which he set opposite her. Taking a seat, he looked at her for a minute without speaking, apparently trying to decide what to say. Finally, he spoke, with an unmistakable German accent.

"Ms Kerrigan, I am going to remove the cloth from your mouth and if you make any sound other than answering my questions, I will shoot you."

He removed a gun with a long silencer from beneath his sweater and set it on the bedside table at his right. Lisa was frightened by the casualness with which he had spoken the threat. There was obviously no question that this man would do exactly as he had said, as if shooting a person was no more out of the ordinary than shaking someone's hand.

The man reached out and removed the gag from her mouth. It had been tied so tightly that her face hurt even after it was removed. She blurted out, "Who are you? What do you want with me?"

The man reached over to touch the gun and Lisa immediately stopped talking.

The man calmly replied, "That's better. I will ask the questions. You will only speak when I tell you."

He shifted in his seat and then began.

"What do you know about the investigation by your government into security matters at Billings Shipyard?"

Lisa sat for a moment gathering her wits before speaking. She needed to collect all the information she could about this man, so that if... no *when*...... she managed to get free, she could provide a detailed report to the police. Already she knew from his accent and from his use of the words 'your government' that this man was not American and was likely German.

"I do not know anything about any investigation."

The man's face took on a hateful expression. "Wrong answer, Ms Kerrigan. I'll only give you one more opportunity to tell me what I want to know. You are of no consequence to me. If you do not cooperate, the authorities will find you floating in the river, the unfortunate victim of some terrible accident."

Lisa tried to keep the fear in her gut from reaching her face. Clearly, this man was connected with the security breach that the naval officer, Peter Ashley, was investigating. Looking at his cold, hard demeanor, she couldn't help but wonder, was this the man who shot Commander Ashley?

She forced herself to remain calm and responded. "I was contacted by a naval intelligence officer, Peter Ashley, and was made aware that there was an ongoing investigation. I told him... and I am telling you now... that I do not know anything about a security problem at the shipyard. I do not work on any classified projects."

The man continued. "Who else knows about the investigation?"

"At this point, all of the senior executives do."

The man asked, "And what are the details of the investigation? What exactly are the investigators looking for?"

Lisa replied with a tone of frustration. "I told you I don't know anything about classified projects. I only know that allegedly there was some kind of security leak on one of the navy contracts. I don't know any details because I am not involved."

The man seemed to be satisfied with her answer. After a moment he went on.

"What do you know about a bank account that your husband set up at the Bank of America? Account number 12 376 8900."

Lisa sat in stunned silence trying to absorb the meaning of the last question. How could this man know about the unexplained account? She had only discovered the account herself by looking at her husband's personal computer files on BSI's secured server. No one could possibly know about it other than Tim and herself. And what could possibly be the connection between this mysterious account and the security investigation? This mess was getting way too complicated! There was the letter from Greg Connor that implicated her husband, the alleged security leak with the navy contract, and this mysterious bank account. Were they all connected in some way?

Lisa's mind raced through the possibilities. Could it possibly be that the money being routed through the Hamburg Shipping contract was connected to the WG-116B security leak? My client contacts with the Hamburg Shipping contract are German. This man asking questions about the security breach is German. And he knows about my husband's secret bank account. What if the people behind the Hamburg Shipping financial impropriety and the naval security leak are the same people? But what could one possibly have to do with the other? Assuming, however, that there is a connection, this man must be the connecting link.

Suddenly, an awful truth came rushing into Lisa's mind. This man had killed Greg Connor! It all made sense. The police had said that Greg's murder had been a random act of violence, perhaps drug related. But Lisa knew, as well as did the entire population of Billings, that this was unlikely. Billings was a small community and random drug killings just didn't take place here. Lisa had always thought that the killing must have been somehow connected to the shipyard, but she couldn't figure out how. The letter that she had received from him was the obvious connection, but her subconscious had kept her from linking Greg's death to the shipyard because it would then mean that her husband might somehow be involved in not only financial wrongdoings, but also murder.

This man was obviously part of the security breach that Peter Ashley was investigating. If he was also connected to the Hamburg contract, he must have shot Greg to stop his nosing around into the Hamburg account finances and, perhaps, uncover the connection to the WG-116B leak. And, she thought with horror, he might very well have shot Peter Ashley. She was being held by a cold-blooded murderer and unless a miracle happened, she would become his next victim!

***

Davidwache station commander, Peter Morgan, typed furiously as he recorded the events that had led to his suspension from active duty. He tried to be impartial as he wrote, but the anger that burned inside sent billows of smoke into his mind, threatening to cloud his objectivity.

*In my investigation of the murder of officer Manfred Spear and officer Gerhardt Frank, the station evidence duty officer, I deduced that the perpetrator had to have received a telephone call from within the stationhouse. He had apparently been alerted to the fact that officer Spear was on his way to the evidence room with the classified United States Navy document that had been recovered in a raid on the nightclub in the Reeperbahn. After reviewing the day's security surveillance tapes, it was discovered that Inspector Leo Krauss was the only person seen to be on the telephone at the time of the phone call. Furthermore, the same surveillance tape showed Manfred Spear carrying the classified document down the hall, just past the desk of Inspector Krauss.*

*I fully admit that I did not follow department policy by not reporting this finding immediately as part of the investigation. At the time, however, I believed that there was not sufficient evidence to confront Inspector Krauss with a formal charge. It was my opinion, and mine alone, that the best course of action would be to put Inspector Krauss under twenty-four-hour surveillance to see if he would lead to us to those responsible for the theft of the classified document. And, in so doing, it was my hope that incriminating evidence would be found to implicate Inspector Krauss in the murders. I felt that if I reported my suspicions, it would be impossible to keep Inspector Krauss from finding out, and he would then be sure to distance himself from the other responsible persons.*

*I assigned Inspector Richard Gross, the lead homicide investigator on the case, to begin the surveillance of Inspector Krauss. Around twenty-three-hundred hours that evening, I received a phone call from Inspector Gross. He had followed Krauss to a third-floor office at 157 Braunstrasse. Inspector Gross reported that he could hear voices inside talking heatedly but could only make out certain words. The conversation was about money and a secret paper. Inspector Gross felt that there was sufficient cause for an arrest and requested backup.*

*I immediately went to the Braunstrasse address and when I reached the third floor, I saw that one of the office doors was open. Before I could get to the door, I heard a gunshot. Upon entering, I saw a man with a gun standing over a body. The room was relatively dark, and I did not see the man with the gun clearly. I did not see anyone else in the room, but I was only there for a brief moment before someone hit me over the head from behind and I lost consciousness. When I awoke, there was no one in the room and there was no evidence of the shooting.*

Inspector Morgan took a break from typing. He couldn't help but become overwhelmed with emotion as he recounted the events that lead to so many deaths, *deaths that he might possibly have prevented.* After getting a cup of strong black coffee, he continued typing.

274

*I did not know at the time what had happened to Inspector Gross. I tried his cell phone but got no answer. When neither Inspector Krauss nor Inspector Gross showed up for work the next day, I put the department on high alert and instituted an all-points search for both. I simply stated that they had been working on a case lead and had not reported in on schedule.*

*I investigated on my own the office on Braunstrasse. I found that the office had been leased for six months under an assumed identity. The landlord could not identify the man who had taken the lease. Money had been transferred into his bank account in advance for the six months, and the landlord saw no reason to run any checks on the tenant. The landlord did, however, state that the man who had met him to arrange the lease drove away in a white van with the name of Hamburg Shipping on the side. He said that he remembered this because he had hoped that perhaps there might be future lease arrangements coming with the largest shipping company in the city.*

*I went to the offices of Hamburg Shipping but the person I spoke with could find no record of leased property on Braunstrasse. When I pressed further, I was directed to the company's chief financial officer, Mr Johann Steiner. I interviewed Steiner but was unable to obtain any useful information. Nevertheless, it was clear to me that Steiner knew more than he was letting on.*

*I then put in place a wiretap on Steiner's office and home phones. I understand that this action was not authorized and as such was not legal. Late in the evening of November twenty-third, a phone call was made from Steiner's home phone to a cell phone registered to an untraceable name in the United States. The call was cryptic in nature, but Steiner was heard to say that, "the problem", has been taken care of and that there should be no further trouble getting out the remaining documents. In the call, Steiner mentioned the name Herr Macintyre.*

*One week later, the bodies of Inspector Gross and Krauss were discovered beneath dock fifty-seven at the harbor. It was determined that the cause of death in both cases was a single gunshot to the head.*

When the bodies of his two inspectors had turned up it was impossible to keep his investigation to himself. Morgan had reported his activities to the chief of police. Ironically, it didn't seem that the driving force for his suspension had been his unauthorized activities, nor even the deaths of the officers under his command. What had touched off the worst barrage of outrage were the suspicions raised against Hamburg Shipping, not only one of the city's largest and most powerful companies, but also one of the city's most politically influential forces.

The company had not raised a complaint when Morgan had initially visited, but when the chief himself contacted the company as a follow up to Morgan's report, the hammer had been dropped. It had been made clear that in no way was the reputation of Hamburg Shipping to be tarnished based on the misguided efforts of a single police inspector who was operating outside of his authority. This point had been driven home by the fact the chief was reminded that there was absolutely no concrete evidence linking Hamburg Shipping to the murders in any way, and if Inspector Morgan wasn't adequately disciplined, the inspector chief would lose Hamburg Shipping's most considerable support in the future.

***

Christmas hadn't seemed like Christmas at all to Sally without her dad at home. The trial was dragging on and Sally was in a blue funk of depression. What made it worse was that it had been decided that she would not be allowed to attend any of the trial hearings. She had been told that her father had explicitly ordered that Sally be kept away.

It wasn't like Denise Witham hadn't tried to make the most of the holiday for Sally. She had decorated the house with the world's most gaudily trimmed tree and had placed battery operated white candles in each window. On the front lawn there had been a plastic Santa with three small plastic elves and a reindeer with a blinking red nose. None of the usual holiday festive decorations, however, could turn this awful time into a celebration for Sally.

Somehow the unhappy school vacation weeks managed to slip by and now it was the first day back at school. Sally, Sheila and Henry sat in the cafeteria during their lunch break. None of them were eating, however. Instead, Sheila sat writing in a notebook. She looked up and said, "Let's recap what we have."

276

Looking over at the food counter that was stacked with slices of pizza, Henry replied, "Or let's recap what we don't have... *food!*"

Sheila shot a frown in his direction. "Look, go get something to eat if you want. You're not being a help anyway. Surely eating is less important than helping free Sally's dad."

Henry bowed his head apologetically. "Sorry. Go on. Read what we have."

Sheila flipped a page in the notebook and began.

"This is what we know. Let's start by organizing the facts by the people involved. First, there's Peter Ashley, the victim. A naval officer, Peter Ashley was shot at the annual meeting of BSI. That connects him to BSI, presumably with the navy contract that Sally's father was working on. We don't know much more about him other than what was written in the newspaper account of the trial that introduced the fact that he had been investigating some kind of security leak at BSI regarding the project."

Sally spoke up. "That suggests that we're dealing with industrial espionage. I don't exactly know what my father was working on, but it involved something to do with a new form of technology to be used in the next class of navy destroyers. I think it was somehow related to weapons guidance."

Sheila thought for a moment and then asked, "So who would want to steal top secret naval weapons technology? Likely it would be either another government, or someone who works the black market for arms, selling pirated weapons or weapons technology to terrorists."

Henry exclaimed, "Great! Now we're going after terrorists! Maybe I could tap into the state police system and authorize us to carry concealed guns! Wouldn't it be great if we could all go to school packing heat!"

"Let's stay on track, please," Sheila replied.

Continuing, Sheila said, "Next we have Lisa Kerrigan. She is a vice president at BSI. She was also at the BSI annual meeting when Peter Ashley was shot. As we know from the reports all over the news, she went missing the day after Christmas and hasn't been seen since."

Henry added, "To borrow a phrase from a great flick, I think Lisa Kerrigan sleeps with the fishes."

Sally looked over at Henry and said, "Actually, *The Godfather* was about local syndicated crime, not international terrorism. But you may be right. Crime statistics show that the longer a person is missing, the less likely it is that they will be found alive."

Sheila slowly shook her head. "I don't know... if she has been murdered, you would think that the body would have turned up by now. But there are several interesting facts about Ms Kerrigan beyond the fact that she works at BSI. From what little I have read, she wasn't involved with Mr Brown's navy contract. But, her husband, Mr Tim Kerrigan, is the head of the BSI corporate board of directors, which means that she might very well have had access to classified information through him."

Sally added, "That means we should probably add *Mr* Kerrigan to the list of interesting persons."

Sheila went on. "And isn't it interesting that Lisa Kerrigan's primary project at BSI is a contract to build ships for a German company."

Sheila flipped through her notes until she found the name of the company.

"It's called Hamburg Shipping... definitely a German connection... which brings us to our next person."

Henry jumped in, speaking a little louder than he should, "You mean our chemistry Nazi!"

Sheila looked around in embarrassment as students at the next table interrupted their meal to glance over at their table. Looking back at Henry with an accusing expression, she quietly admonished, "Shhh! you idiot. Be a bit more discreet, will you?"

Ignoring Henry's outburst, Sally continued. "We know that Mr Wilhelm was hired to teach at Billings High with a recommendation from none other than Lisa Kerrigan's husband, Tim Kerrigan, who was the company's chief executive officer at the time. That makes a connection between Mr Wilhelm and BSI. The question is, why would the CEO of BSI recommend a teacher who doesn't seem to have any real teaching experience?"

"And why," asked Sheila, "would he be at the BSI annual meeting?"

Henry, speaking in a whisper, said, "Man! Wouldn't I like to see our esteemed chemistry professor locked up! You just gotta know that he's behind this whole mess somehow."

Sheila flipped through a few pages in her notebook again. "And don't forget the fact that the Foxwoods desk clerk told me that there was a message in Peter Ashley's box at the hotel that Mr Wilhelm was looking for him."

Sally nodded. "I can't help but wonder why the authorities haven't gone after Mr Wilhelm based on that message... or at least questioned him."

Henry suggested, "Perhaps they never found out about the message. After all, we only found out about it when Sheila thought to talk to the clerk. After the excitement, the message might just have been thrown away."

"Perhaps so," Sally said. "The other thing to remember is that I heard the coat check attendant say that the person who left the envelope in the hotel coat room... you remember... the envelope with the money... the person who left it had a German accent."

Henry piped in. "That settles it! Wilhelm's guilty. It's off to the pokey. There'll be no fourth Reich now!"

Sheila took a swipe at Henry. "Be serious. Even if we think Mr Wilhelm is connected, we can't prove it."

Sally sat thinking for a moment and then said, "We've been watching Mr Wilhelm, but so far we haven't been able to document anything to help. I think we need to take a more active approach."

Sheila put down her pen with a worried expression.

"Er... what exactly do you have in mind?"

"Look, we're all sure that Mr Wilhelm is somehow involved. In fact, he seems to be the key to figuring out how to prove that my father is innocent. We need to search his apartment to see if we can find the evidence that we need. Even if we can't find any incrementing evidence about the shooting of Peter Ashley, at least we might be able to find out more about his connection to BSI."

Henry perked up. "Cool! Count me in for a little B and E!"

When neither Sally nor Sheila responded, he clarified, "You know... B and E... *breaking and entering.*

Sheila turned to Henry. "I know what it means! And I know that it's illegal. We would get caught for sure."

Sally responded. "Not necessarily. If we went while he was teaching, we would be able to look around with no fear that he might be there."

Before Sheila could object Henry enthusiastically exclaimed, "I'm ready! Why wait? Let's go right now. There's no time like the present. Wilhelm has a period four general chemistry lab this afternoon."

Sheila shook her head. "No way, guys. This isn't only illegal, it could be dangerous. What if Mr Wilhelm is the murderer and he somehow figures out that we broke into his house. We could be next!"

Henry quickly replied, "So we have to be careful so that he never finds out. Listen, I know we can do this."

Sheila gave Sally a look of desperation in hope for a return to reason. Sally, however, voiced exactly what she didn't want to hear.

"I agree that searching Mr Wilhelm's apartment has its risks. That's why I want to do this myself. I don't want either of you to get into any legal trouble. But I can't just sit here and do nothing. I have to try to find something that will help my dad."

Sheila hung her head in defeat. After a moment she looked up at Sally with what she hoped would convey confidence. "Okay, you're right. We need to do something, and Mr Wilhelm seems to be the key. But you're crazy if you think we're going to let you do this alone. You know that we live by the musketeer's credo."

Henry beamed. "Right, I loved that show. I watched the Disney channel every day when I was a kid…"

Sally gave a laugh. "I think Sheila was referring to Alexander Dumas' *The Three Musketeers*, not Walt Disney's *Mouseketeers*."

Turning red, Henry mumbled, "Yeah, I knew that. I was making a joke."

Sheila broke the embarrassing silence that followed. "Sure. It's all for one and one for all. And I agree, if we're going to do this, let's get it over. I agree with Henry. Let's go right now."

The trio slipped unnoticed out of the building as the crowd of students headed off to the next period at the end of lunch. Henry said that he needed to pick something up from his house that he had been working on before heading over to Mr Wilhelm's apartment. The three jumped into Sheila's car and took off out of the school parking lot heading to Henry's.

280

"What's so important that we needed to stop by here?" asked Sheila as she pulled into Henry's driveway.

Henry leaped out of the car and ran into the house without responding. A minute later he came running back to the car and slid in the front seat with a small bag in his hand.

"Again, I ask," inquired Sheila pointing to the bag that Henry stuffed into his pocket. "What's so important that we needed to make a detour to your place to get?"

Henry grinned and said, "Oh, it's just a little piece of technology I've been working on. I thought it might come in handy. You wouldn't understand. It's pretty complicated."

Sheila made a face back at Henry. "Thanks, Mr Wizard. I'll just go back to being the dumb chauffer."

From their surveillance of Mr Wilhelm over the previous three weeks, they knew that his apartment was only a few blocks away from the high school. Arriving at the three-story house where he lived, the three looked at each other and then marched with determination up to the front porch.

Henry peered through the front window into the apartment. "It looks dark in there," he announced.

Sally rang the doorbell to apartment one-zero-one. When no one came to the door, the three went around to the back of the building. In the back was a set of steps leading up to an open deck. The deck had a wooden set of stairs that led up to the upper apartments. The first-floor apartment had a door that led directly onto the deck.

Henry tried the door and found that it was locked. Turning to the others he said, "There is some good news and some bad news. The good news is that there doesn't appear to be an alarm system. The bad news is that we may have to break down the door because there is no way we're going to get past the lock."

Sheila gave a groan.

She turned to Sally to object, but Sally had disappeared around the corner of the building. Sheila walked back to the side driveway and saw Sally on her hands and knees in front of a stack of boards.

Henry came around to the side to join Sheila just as Sally announced, "Hey, I think we might be able to get in here. There's a basement window that has been modified to allow for this dryer vent panel. Come take a look. It's behind these boards."

Sheila and Henry quickly came over to where Sally was moving the boards and saw the window with the dryer panel. After several attempts they were able to slide the widow sash up just enough to pull the dryer vent panel out through the window opening.

Henry volunteered. "Let me go in and unlock the back door for you."

The window opening was small, but Henry was able, with a great deal of pushing from Sheila, to get through into the basement. Landing with a thump, Henry let out a yell.

"Are you okay?" Sheila asked with concern.

Henry replied, "Yeah, I'll live, but next time it's one of you who gets to do the acrobatics."

After a moment, Henry shouted up, "Let me find the light switch... hang on just a minute."

It took several moments for the basement lights to come on. When it looked like Henry had things under control, Sally and Sheila headed to the back door. They waited for what seemed to be an extremely long time before hearing the door lock unlatch. The door opened and Henry stood motionless with a panicked look on his face.

Sheila looked at Henry and exclaimed, "Henry... are you okay...? What's the matter?"

Henry tried to calm himself and responded in a shaky voice, "You'd better come see this. This is worse than we'd imagined."

# Chapter 23

On the morning of January second, John Phillips and Myron Feldman sat with their client Steven Brown in the holding room adjacent to the New London County superior courtroom awaiting the start of the trial after the holiday break.

Myron Feldman began.

"I think it's time to face reality. I'm sure you can tell that the trial is not going well. Unfortunately, the prosecution has a strong case. I'm set to begin our defense today, but I think that you might want to consider options."

Steven Brown shifted uncomfortably in his chair. "What kind of options?"

John Phillips spoke. "We spoke with the district attorney last week and I think we have come to a reasonable compromise. If you agree to plead guilty, based on a temporary loss of sanity, the DA will allow for a lesser sentence. It still will be attempted murder, but they will recommend a life sentence with allowance for parole. I'm sure you know that Connecticut still allows the death penalty for capital crimes such as murder or attempted murder. If you are convicted of attempted premeditated murder, at best it will mean a life sentence with no hope of parole, and at worst, I must let you know that it could mean the death penalty. By agreeing to a guilty plea, you will receive a life sentence, and with good behavior, you could probably be released in ten to fifteen years."

Steven jumped out of his chair and shouted, "I'm innocent! I won't say otherwise."

Myron Feldman pointed a finger and said in a heated voice, "Listen, you don't seem to get it. As things are going now you may very well be convicted of the highest of the state of Connecticut's crimes. And if that happens, you may very well face death by lethal injection. On top of which I happen to know that the federal prosecutor is already preparing charges against you for treason. And even if you escape conviction of attempted murder, conviction by a federal court of treason can mean execution as a traitor to the United States. You'd better start cooperating with the authorities or what little hope you have now for any semblance of an ordinary life will go up in flames."

Steven sank back into his chair. After a moment of silence, he spoke in a whisper. "I thought you were going to prove my innocence, not make a deal that lets everyone think that I'm guilty."

"We tried. But there isn't anything that we can hang our case on. You were the only person seen leaving the men's room and you were holding the murder weapon. There's only so much we can do."

Steven thought for a moment and then said, "No. I won't say I'm guilty when I'm not. I owe that to my daughter. I want you to go in there and do what you can. But I will never say that I shot Peter Ashley, and I will never say that I sold classified technical information. That's final."

\*\*\*

Sally and Sheila followed Henry into Mr Wilhelm's apartment. They followed him into what was obviously a bedroom. At first the girls didn't see anything untoward. Then Sally noticed a stain on the carpet on the floor.

Henry pointed to the stain and said one word, "Blood."

Sheila responded. "Don't get carried away. That could be anything."

Henry walked over to the closet. "You think so? Well check this out."

Opening the closet door, he reached inside and pulled out a woman's white wool sweater. It was obviously blood stained.

Sally and Sheila stood dumbfounded for a full minute. Finally, Sally responded. "It certainly looks like blood. But we have no way of knowing whose it is or what the circumstances are of how it came to be."

Henry said in a nervous voice, "Well maybe this will help you understand the circumstances." He quickly tossed over what looked like a credit card and it landed on the floor in front of the girls. Instantly they recognized what they saw. It was a BSI identity card with a picture of Lisa Kerrigan.

Henry said, "I found it under the sweater."

Again, the girls stood in amazed silence. This time Sheila was the first to come out of the shock of what they had found.

"We need to put this back... exactly as you found it."

Henry objected. "Why? Shouldn't we call nine-one-one? We need to have the cops drag Wilhelm's sorry butt off to prison."

Sheila held up her hand. "Wait a minute. Think about this for a second. If we call the police, it may well put Mr Wilhelm behind bars for a while, but without a body, they wouldn't be able to make murder stick. He could just say that he found the sweater and ID out on the sidewalk."

Sally added, "Listen, we know that he is connected to the shooting at Foxwoods and now we know he probably either kidnapped or maybe even murdered Lisa Kerrigan. Unfortunately, without any proof, our knowledge alone won't help my father. We need to look around and see what else may be here."

Sheila gathered up the ID and sweater and put it back in the closet.

Henry and Sally turned to inspect the rest of the apartment with Sally heading to the kitchen. Upon entering the living room, Henry immediately saw a laptop computer on a coffee table. Sitting down, he powered up the computer.

After finding no other items of interest elsewhere Sally and Sheila entered the living room to find Henry bent over the laptop working diligently. Sheila asked, "Hey, what do you have there?"

Henry didn't look up but spoke as his fingers flew over the keyboard. "This is a goldmine. Give me just a second and I'll have what I need."

After a minute, Henry pulled out a USB drive from the computer and said, "Let's go. We need to get out of here. And we need to make sure everything is just as we found it. We don't want our esteemed professor to know that someone was here."

Just before leaving, Henry grabbed the bag that he had brought from home. Reaching inside, he pulled out a small black box about the size of a deck of playing cards. Looking around the living room, Henry made a calculated decision and placed the object on the fire place mantel, partially hidden behind a mantel clock.

Back at Henry's house, Sheila and Sally sat expectantly waiting to hear what Henry had discovered. He popped the USB drive into his computer and began explaining.

"At first I couldn't get past his password, but I was able to use my superior computer skills to crack into his files."

Henry looked up expecting the girls to be duly impressed. Not seeing anything but impatience, he continued.

"There wasn't much of interest in his root directory, but I struck pay dirt when I tapped into his emails. I found several emails that I traced from a German company, namely *Hamburg Shipping!*"

Sally interrupted. "Say, isn't that the company that Lisa Kerrigan was working with at BSI?"

"Precisely," answered Henry.

Sheila asked, "Who were the emails from at Hamburg Shipping. Is there a name?"

"Unfortunately, there is no name, per se, but there are initials, *J.S.*"

After taking a drink of soda, Henry excitedly went on.

"Most of the emails don't say much that I understood, and I haven't actually read all of them yet but, while I was copying the files, I took a look at the most recent email. Check this out."

Henry swung his screen around so that Sally and Sheila could read the copy of the email that he had brought up.

*G.W.*

*This is a most troublesome event. I do not like having your acquaintance sent to me, but I agree that she might be useful at some point. If what you say is true, the situation was indeed becoming critical. She arrived without incident and we are taking good care of her. I trust that you can tidy up things on your end. There should be no connection of our friend to your business but be certain to take care to see that our rabbit does not panic and run.*

*We are nearly at the conclusion of our endeavor. See that all goes well from this point on.*

*J.S.*

Henry remarked, "This was written last week. And I think it's pretty clear what this is saying."

Sheila read over the email a second time and then said, "Do you really think that this is talking about Lisa Kerrigan? It sounds like Wilhelm somehow shipped her off to Germany."

Sally agreed saying, "And if our reading of this is correct, maybe Ms Kerrigan is still alive. I wonder if she stumbled across the truth of what really happened, and they had to *take care of her.*"

"If so," Sheila said, "this confirms that Mr Wilhelm is at the center of everything. He must be behind the shooting of Peter Ashley and the espionage plot at BSI. He must also be behind the abduction of Lisa Kerrigan."

Henry nodded in agreement. "So, the question is, what are we going to do about it?"

Both Henry and Sheila turned to Sally for an answer. Thinking for a moment she replied, "Somehow, we need to get evidence that Mr Wilhelm is behind all this. It definitely would be too dangerous, however, for us to confront him directly."

\*\*\*

James Macintyre sat in his office at BSI worrying about what he was going to do. It was now three weeks since Lisa Kerrigan had mysteriously disappeared and there was no sign of what had happened to her. She had gone out of her house the day after Christmas and was never seen again. Macintyre sat remembering that day and the incredible snow fall that had blanketed the city. Tim Kerrigan had said that Lisa had wanted to go for a walk in the snow since the BSI offices had been closed due to the weather. A missing persons' report had been filed the next day and the police had questioned nearly everyone in Billings as part of their investigation, but no one seemed to know what had happened to her. It was like she had just dropped off the face of the earth.

Alien abduction thought Macintyre with a smile. That must have been it. Little green men from Mars had come down and made off with a human for study of our species. Little did they know, he thought humorously, that they had grabbed such a meddlesome crank. Actually, he was glad to be rid of her. In many ways, this had solved a problem that seemed to be getting out of hand. It had started when he had caught her at the annual meeting eavesdropping on his phone conversation. He didn't exactly remember what he had said on the call, or how much she might have heard, but ever since that day she had been suspiciously nosing around.

Now she was out of the picture, thankfully. But as things often have a way of happening, a problem solved can create new problems. The police just would not seem to let up. They had come to the office the day after the disappearance and had questioned people at the shipyard looking for leads. He had expected that as the company's CEO he would have to answer questions, but he hadn't anticipated how difficult it would be. After all, he didn't know anything about what had happened and so he had thought that the questioning would be finished after just a few minutes. What had transpired, however, wasn't simple questioning, it had been more like an interrogation.

A Billings police detective, along with the county sheriff, had spent two hours in his office asking questions as if, somehow, they thought he had been responsible. They wanted to know everything about the projects that Lisa had been working on. That had been a bit troublesome since Lisa's primary project was the Hamburg Shipping project and they wanted to know her contacts in Hamburg. At first, he had been reluctant to give the name of Johann Steiner since he didn't want to involve his German connection in any more difficulties. After considering the matter for a moment, however, he realized that they could easily obtain warrants to search the company files and they would find the contact names that they wanted anyway. Not being seen as cooperative would only make it look like he had something to hide.

He felt that he had handled the Hamburg Shipping inquiries successfully and had not caused any undue suspicions in that regard. But then questioning turned to his own work and that's when things got really sticky. They wanted to know all the details of the WG-116B contract. At first, he had declined to answer their questions citing the fact that the project was classified under US Naval authority. But this had only made their questioning more intense. They had wanted to know about the shooting incident at Foxwoods and how that tied to the BSI navy contract. They wanted to know all about the navy's investigation into the security breach and his own supposed involvement in the matter.

After what seemed like an eternity of questions and answers and more questions, he had wilted a bit under the strain. He finally broke down and emphatically told the police officers that the BSI navy contract had nothing to do with Lisa Kerrigan's work at BSI, nor did it have anything to do with her disappearance. With that he curtly told them to leave.

Unfortunately, that didn't end the matter. Just as he had feared, the police had obtained warrants to search the BSI files for the Hamburg Shipping contract as well as the WG-111B contract. Even though many of the navy contract files were withheld under the protection of national security, the investigators wouldn't let go. After a week of the investigation, it was as though they had reached the conclusion that Lisa Kerrigan's abduction, and that was what it was now being called, was unquestionably connected with BSI, and in some way to him personally.

Macintyre sat brooding over the recent event. What irony, he thought, that something totally unrelated to his endeavors over the past nine months might bring the whole thing down around his ears. The police had no real evidence linking him to any impropriety regarding the leak of classified documents, but every day they kept asking more questions and digging deeper into the history of the project. It was just a matter of time before something was uncovered that he wouldn't be able to explain.

And now it was time for another monthly delivery of documents. Macintyre sat looking at the large envelope that lay on his desk. In twenty minutes, he would have to walk into town and make the delivery. How did he know that the police weren't having him under twenty-four-hour surveillance? What if he were followed and they caught him in the act of transferring the package?

He had collected a tidy sum each month for his efforts. The money had been wired into his bank account and it was his dream that the money would set him up for life in Cancun. But the reality was that it would be the very considerable bonus payment that would be paid upon delivery of the final documents that would make this happen. He could skip out now, but the amount of funds in his account wouldn't be sufficient to support the lifestyle that he dreamed of.

There was no question of what he had to do. He had to make the delivery. If all went well, he would only need to make one more delivery. Next month the final designs for the guidance system would be completed and he could deliver the information that would make the system operational. Then he would get his bonus and he could retire from BSI. There was a risk that he was being watched, but he had no choice. He had to finish what he had started.

***

The trial of Steven Brown continued with the defense presenting its case and then the prosecutor taking an opportunity to redirect questions of witnesses who had testified. Closing statements were finally made on January thirty-first. The prosecutor delivered an eloquent speech, citing the irrefutable evidence, that pointed to Steven Brown's guilt of attempted murder in the first degree.

"Ladies and gentlemen of the jury. I could list the events of this case item by item, all of which point with unquestionable clarity to the guilt of the defendant. But I will not take up your precious time by repeating what you already know to be true. Instead, let me just say that Mr Brown has been caught with the proverbial smoking gun in his hand."

The prosecutor paused a moment for dramatic effect and the resumed, building to a climax.

"In spite of the obvious truth that the defendant was the only person seen in the men's room with Peter Ashley, and he came out holding the murder weapon, Mr Brown still maintains his innocence. Why is this? I'll let you decide. Could it possibly be that the highly classified government project on which he served as the lead engineer has been found to have had a serious security leak? Classified documents from Mr Brown's project, classified documents, I might add, that involve our national security, were stolen from the Billings Shipyard engineering department that Mr Brown leads. These were classified documents that, other than the company's most senior officers, only Mr Brown had access to. And Peter Ashley, the special investigator assigned by the navy, was

290

about to reveal the truth. And now, if the defendant is found to be guilty of attempted murder, it will likely serve to help convict him of an even more serious crime, *high treason to the United States of America!"*

The prosecutor let this statement sink into the jury's collective mindset before closing.

"Can this case be any more straightforward? Multiple witnesses have testified that the defendant was in the men's room with Peter Ashley, giving Mr Brown opportunity. He was caught with the murder weapon in his hand, giving Mr Brown means. And the naval investigator, Peter Ashley, was about to reveal details about the theft of classified materials from the project on which the defendant alone had full access to, giving Mr Brown motive. It is your responsibility, ladies and gentlemen of the jury, to see that this most heinous crime of cold-blooded attempted murder is brought to justice. I urge you on behalf of the victim and his family, and on behalf of the people of the state of Connecticut, to find the defendant guilty as charged."

When the prosecutor took his seat, Myron Feldman stood to make the defense's closing statement.

"That was a wonderful story delivered by the prosecution. The trouble with that statement is that it is only a web of supposition and circumstantial evidence. As such, it is only a story... a fictional story."

"It is true that my client was in the men's room with Peter Ashley when the shooting took place. But is that evidence that my client was the shooter? Did anyone actually see him pull the trigger? The answer is *no!"*

"And we have heard that no one can say that they saw someone else coming from the men's room following the shooting. But is that evidence that there *wasn't* someone who left the men's room and wasn't seen? Did anyone testify that they were intently watching the men's room doorway checking to see each and every person who came out? The answer is *no!"*

"And we know that my client came out of the men's room holding the gun that was used to shoot Commander Ashley. But is that evidence that he used the gun? Does holding a gun necessarily mean that the holder shot the gun? Once again, the answer is *no!"*

Every member of jury sat intently listening to the closing statement. No one showed any sign of agreement or disagreement. Myron went on, explaining why the prosecutor's case held no merit.

"The prosecutor has no concrete evidence of my client's guilt. And, I must add, neither is there any credible finding for motive. The prosecutor would have you believe the story that Steven Brown was involved in acts of treason and had to silence Commander Ashley to keep from being exposed. This is a work of fiction… and not very good fiction at that. First, please understand that there is no evidence whatsoever linking my client to the security leak at Billings Shipyard, although as I have shown, evidence doesn't seem to matter to the prosecution. Second, at the time of the shooting, Commander Ashley had only just been assigned to investigate the security matter at Billings. The prosecution would have you believe that the commander had completed his investigation and was on the brink of revealing his findings, when the truth is that his investigation had not yet even begun!"

Myron went on to close his statement with a passionate plea to the jury to find his client innocent of the charges. The jury was then given its instructions by the judge and was sent off to deliberate. When, after three hours the jury had not reached a verdict, they were sequestered overnight. At two o'clock on the following afternoon the trial was reconvened, and the jury pronounced its decision.

The jury foreman rose and read, "In the matter of Steven Brown versus the state of Connecticut the jury finds the defendant… *guilty* of attempted murder in the first degree."

There was an audible gasp heard from the audience and the judge called for order. Myron Feldman and John Phillips both leaned over to Steven and offered their apologies. Following restoration of order in the courtroom, the judge rendered his sentence.

"Steven Brown, you have been convicted of attempted murder in the first degree. This is a capital offense in the state of Connecticut. Given the circumstances of this case I feel that it is my responsibility to levy the maximum sentence commensurate with the seriousness of this offense. I therefore pronounce judgment as granted by the authority of the state of Connecticut and sentence you to execution by lethal injection. I hereby order you to be placed into the custody of the state where you shall be held until the date of your execution."

*   *   *

Sally, Sheila and Henry were all seated in the living room of Denise Witham's house. Sally was struggling to keep her composure while her two friends sat in silence. On the table in front of them sat a tray of cookies and a pitcher of hot chocolate. Mrs Witham, seated across from Henry, tried to break the mounting tension as she spoke to Henry.

"Wouldn't you like some more hot chocolate, son? And feel free to have another cookie."

Henry started for the tray of cookies but a look from Sheila brought him up short.

It was February second, a clear, bright Saturday morning that certainly would have made Punxsutawney Phil scoot back underground into his hole on Gobbler's Knob in anticipation of six more weeks of winter. Although the sun was streaming through the living room windows, the atmosphere inside was anything but bright and cheery. Billings' chief of police, Stan Wilkerson, seated beside Mrs Witham, had just delivered the news of the conviction and sentencing of Sally's father.

"Of course, there is always the possibility of appeal," the chief said. "Although the sentence is for..." he hesitated, trying to find an alternative to the word *execution*, "... capital punishment, it is not a certainty by any means that the sentence will be carried out. There hasn't been a case where capital punishment has been carried out in Connecticut since 2005."

Trying to sound helpful, Henry added, "Yeah, and who knows, he could get a pardon from the governor."

Sheila gave Henry a kick in the shin with a look that screamed, *don't be helpful!*

Sally sat silently in a state of disbelief. Her father couldn't have been found guilty. Couldn't they see that he isn't capable of shooting anyone? How could the justice system fail so miserably?

There wasn't anything that she could think of to say. Apparently, neither could anyone else as everyone sat staring that their shoes. Finally, Sally stood and said to Sheila and Henry, "Let's go over to Henry's house and work on our chemistry homework. I need to go do something and sitting here thinking about Dad is getting me down."

In relief that there wasn't going to be an emotional meltdown, Mrs Witham replied, "That sounds like a great idea. I'm spending the day in the kitchen baking and when you get back, I'll have one of my famous apple pies ready for you."

When the three reached Henry's house they rushed up to his bedroom. Sally and Sheila plunked down of the floor while Henry took a seat at his computer desk. Sheila pulled out her notebook from her bag and said, "Well, now we know if Sally's father is going to get out of this, it's going to be up to us."

Sally nodded, thinking for a moment, and then added, "It's not like we don't know who the primary culprit is. Now what we have to concentrate on is getting proof of his involvement."

Henry was tapping keys on his computer with his back to the girls. After a bit he stopped and turned around in his chair.

"It's really creepy going to chemistry knowing who Wilhelm is and what he has done. I can't concentrate. On the last quiz I couldn't remember the difference between molarity and molality. I bombed it for sure."

"Well," Sally replied, "it's important that we don't give anything away. We sure don't want him suspecting that we know what he's up to."

"That's just it," Henry said. "We really don't know what he's up to. We know he kidnapped Lisa Kerrigan, and he most likely shot that navy guy, but we don't know what he's up to… that is… we don't know what he'll do next."

Sheila jumped into the conversation excitedly. "You're right! We're always reacting to something that has just happened. And because that's the case, we never seem to get any evidence of what was done. Somehow, we need to be *pro*-active."

Henry gave a big smile and, with confidence, he announced, "Funny you should say that, because that's just what we're gonna do. I've got an idea that once and for all should trap our chemistry Nazi so that his goose will be sauced."

Sally laughed for the first time all morning and said, "I think you mean his goose will be *cooked*. But what do you have in mind?"

Henry spun around to his computer, talking as he brought something up on the screen.

"You remember that I was able to trace the incoming emails on Wilhelm's computer from the mystery person 'J.S.'? Well, I've been able to hack into the server that forwarded the email and we can send Wilhelm an email that he will think came from Mr, or Ms, J.S.!"

Shelia gave a questioning look. "You mean the email wasn't sent by Hotmail or yahoo?"

"No, actually it was sent with a dot-*net* extension from a service provider located in Hamburg. It wasn't easy to track down the provider because there wasn't any mention of it on the web. But I was able to back-track the message and identify its origin. Once I had that, it was a piece of pie to hack into their server!"

Sheila still wasn't clear on Henry's suggestion. "So even if we could send Mr Wilhelm an email that he thought came from this J.S. character, what would we say? I don't see how we could get him to confess."

Sally added, "And even if he did confess in an email, it wouldn't be admissible as evidence in a court of law…"

Henry shook his head and held up a hand. "Wait, you guys are thinking way too small. Check this out! I've been working on my end of my special project and last night I was finally able to get it working."

Henry turned to let the girls see his computer screen which showed what looked like a live video of someone's living room. The resolution was poor, and it was difficult to make out details of the room clearly, but the scene showed a wide-angle view of a room with chairs, a coffee table and a desk with a laptop computer.

Sheila frowned and said, "Wait a minute, buster. I'm not interested in some YouTube sleaze video of some nerd's house."

Henry shook his head and said, "No, just wait a second, you'll see."

As if on cue a man could be seen walking into the room. He was standing relatively close to the camera with his back facing it, so it wasn't possible to see much.

Suddenly the man turned around and sat in a chair.

"Holy crap!" exclaimed Sheila in shock. "That's Mr Wilhelm and that's his apartment!"

Sally stood to take a closer look. There was no doubt, however, who was in the video. In a moment he reached over and grabbed a newspaper that was lying beside the chair. Through the computer's speakers, the turning of the paper's pages could be clearly heard.

Henry reached over and tapped several keys on his computer and the screen went blank.

Henry looked back at the girls who were now standing in dumbfounded shock.

"I don't want to use up the batteries. The camera has super powerful lithium cells, but the case had to be small so I could only fit in a miniature power supply."

Sheila was the first to respond. "How on earth did you... I mean... how did you..." she stammered.

Henry, looking like he had just solved the answer to preparing cold fusion at low cost, interrupted, "You remember that day we broke into his apartment? Remember I had to go by my house to pick something up? Well, I brought my special project along to test it and now it finally works!"

Sally sat back down on the floor and asked, "Exactly how does it work"

The only thing that Henry enjoyed more than fooling around with high-tech equipment and computer systems was talking about it. Unfortunately, while he had ample opportunity to pursue the former, he had little occasion to engage in the latter. Enthusiastically, he launched into a detail-by-detail description of his latest creation.

After several minutes of tech-speak, Sheila interrupted. "How about you give us the explanation for dummies? You know I hate it when you start talking capacitors and diodes."

Somewhat deflated, Henry summarized. "I was able to join a video camera and microphone with a processor and a wireless transmitter. The difficult part was getting it so small. But what I ended up with is a device that acts as a wireless transmitter that I can connect to through Wilhelm's own wireless network. I was afraid that it wouldn't have enough signal strength. And, at first, I wasn't able to get the signal to work. But I went back and hid an amplifier on the outside of his building and now it works fine. The only potential problem is that it has a relatively short operating life because of the limitation of the batteries."

Sheila added sarcastically, "It's good that that's the only potential problem! It wouldn't be an issue at all if Wilhelm were to discover it, *would it?*"

Henry raised his hands in surrender. "Well, yeah, if he notices it the jig is up. But I made it as small as it could possibly be, and I doubt he'll see it."

# Part 4: Resolution

# Chapter 24

For Peter Morgan, February in Hamburg gave new definition to the word *dreary*. It was one of those days when the weather couldn't decide if it wanted to snow or rain and, as a compromise it had decided on the worst of both, *sleet*. The weather had turned overnight and the temperatures were dropping by the hour. As he walked along a back alley of the Reeperbahn struggling against a biting wind, Morgan muttered to himself that this was no weather to be out in. But in his new position, he wasn't going to get any sympathy.

The internal investigation had been concluded with a reprimand for abuse of authority, professional negligence and breach of protocol leading to fatalities. He had been demoted to the lowest appointment of patrol officer, which meant not only the loss of his desk job, it also meant the loss of much of his salary. It had certainly been demeaning to tell his wife of his demotion. And it was truly painful to walk into the very stationhouse each day seeing men he had once commanded, many of whom were now his superiors. But, by far the thing that ate at him the most was that the murders had never been solved. At first, he had dedicated every spare off-duty moment quietly working on his own trying to uncover a lead. But in the past two weeks, he had begun to lose hope.

He had been called out to address a disturbance at a club in the Reeperbahn that turned out to be two men who had consumed considerably more to drink than their limit and were fighting over money lost in some kind of wager. Morgan broke up the altercation and sent the two men on their way, probably to their next appointment with trouble.

It was now approaching seventeen hundred hours, which was his end of shift. With what was now becoming a regularity, he headed to Der Schlupfwinkel, the club where his troubles all began. Somehow it seemed to be the one place where he could wrap his mind around the sequence of events that led to his censure and demotion. Being in the place where the raid had taken place, and where the classified document had been found, had a way of bringing his thoughts into focus.

Morgan entered and was greeted by a waitress serving drinks to a table at the front. It seemed that he was now enough of a regular that most of the staff knew him by name. The owner actually enjoyed having Morgan present, knowing that the overall behavior of the club's clientele improved dramatically when it was known that a police officer was present.

Morgan walked over to the far end of bar and took his usual seat. From this location he could see both the rebuilt booth that had been the focus of attention during the raid, as well as the back room where the classified document had been found. Ordering a beer, he pulled out a small notepad from his coat pocket in which he had written all the details of the case.

Morgan flipped to one of the pages in the notepad where the name Johann Steiner was written and underlined. There was no question that Steiner, the chief financial officer at Hamburg Shipping, was involved in some way. Right from the very moment that he had questioned Steiner, Morgan could tell that he was hiding something. The question was, why would a shipping company in Hamburg be interested in highly technical naval weapons systems design? Whatever the reason, it must be so important that it was worth killing over.

Morgan's attempts to investigate Hamburg Shipping after his duty hours had not turned up anything of value. As far as he could tell, the company was completely above board and didn't have even a trace of questionable dealings. In fact, Hamburg's largest corporation had turned out to be the model of a successful and law-abiding company. Hamburg Shipping included a division that oversaw the procurement of new ships for their fleet and, at first, Morgan had wondered if they were now seeking defense weaponry to ward off the increasing problem of terrorists at sea acting as pirates. But as he investigated it further, he had found that there wasn't any indication that Morgan could find that their new ships were being outfitted with weapons of any kind. In fact, on container ships there was' hardly enough room for the crew, let alone anything else that wasn't directly connected with the cargo.

An hour later, having reviewed his notes for the umpteenth time without seeing that which he knew was hiding right out in plain sight, he left the club and headed home.

***

It had been a busy week at school and Sally, Sheila and Henry found it difficult to find the time to consider a definitive action plan regarding Mr Wilhelm. On top of what seemed like a mountain of homework assignments, they all had to meet with Mr Norris to finalize the plans for their upcoming history competition prize trip to Paris. They each had to get their passports and have a release form signed by a parent that disavowed any and all liabilities of Mr Norris, Billings High School, the Maine Board of Education and anyone else even remotely connected with the trip in any way. In Sally's case, Mrs Witham signed the release form as her temporary guardian.

The trip would be taking place over the week of February vacation from Sunday to the following Sunday. That meant that there were only two weeks to get everything in order. They would be traveling early Sunday morning by car to the Portland jetport, where along with the three boys from Team Q of the competition, who it turned out were from up the coast in Rockland, they would fly to Boston. Upon arriving in Boston, they would be taking an international flight on Air France to Charles de Gaulle Airport just outside Paris, with a quick stopover in London for a change in planes.

Their week's itinerary included landing in Paris early Monday morning. Their hotel was located near the center of the city and each day they would be taking a chartered bus for sightseeing, returning to the hotel by early evening. They were scheduled to spend a day at the Notre Dame cathedral, a day at the Louvre, a day at Versailles, and a day at the Eiffel Tower with time for shopping along the Seine. Friday was scheduled as a free day with the option of spending time on their own in the city doing shopping or whatever the students wished. The return flight back to the US was scheduled for Saturday, arriving back in Boston approximately one hour later than their departure due to the time change.

between Paris and Boston. Their flight back to Portland would get them home in the wee hours of Sunday.

It was Friday after school before the trio could put the finishing touches on their plan. Gathered in his bedroom, Henry began by suggesting his idea.

"I've thought about this all week and I've come up with a plan. I say that we send an email to Wilhelm that will get him to spill the beans on camera. It may not be legal in court, but if we give a copy to the police and tell them all we know, it should be enough to get Sally's dad off the hook."

Sheila thought for a moment and then said, "Well, even if it didn't get Sally's father free, at least it might serve as a strong basis for his appeal. It might work, but what would we say in the email to get Mr Wilhelm to confess to murder?"

Henry turned to his computer and, printing out a page, he replied, "You're right, that's the tough part, but I came up with an idea. Let me read it to you."

*G.W.*

*Have our contact at Billings Shipyard meet you at your apartment on Saturday at two p.m. Find out what he knows about the shooting of the US Naval officer, Peter Ashley, that took place at the BSI annual meeting. It turns out that he has been holding back on us. I will call you at three p.m. to find out what you have learned.*

*J.S.*

Sheila gave Henry a questioning look. "Wait a minute, how do you know that there's an accomplice at BSI?"

Sally, who had remained quiet since arriving, now spoke up.

"Well, it does make sense. My father was working on a classified navy project at BSI, and someone who shouldn't have somehow got ahold of some of the documents from that project. I doubt that Mr Wilhelm could have gotten those documents by himself. He must have had help."

"Come to think of it," said Sheila to Sally, "you remember that your research turned up the fact that it was a recommendation from BSI that got Mr Wilhelm hired as a teacher here. That must mean that there is some connection to someone at BSI."

Henry beamed with pride until Sally spoke again, referring to the email.

"It is an interesting idea, but the email has a number of problems."

Defensively, Henry asked, "Problems... what problems?"

"Well for one thing, you call for the meeting to be at two o'clock and you say that the person will call at three p.m. Europeans refer to time on a twenty-four-hour basis, so two o'clock would be fourteen hundred hours and three o'clock would be fifteen hundred hours."

Henry sulked. "Details. I can fix that."

Sally continued, "And for another thing, you say that Mr Wilhelm should find out what the contact knows about the shooting of Peter Ashley. That might raise suspicions if he knows that the contact already knows all the details of the shooting. Maybe you should just say that he should find out what he knows about Peter Ashley... just leave it at that. That way it implies that the contact might know something that he doesn't. It runs the risk of possibly not having them divulge the details of the shooting, but I like the idea of sowing suspicions among their group. It could lead to confrontation which might get them to say more than they might otherwise."

Sheila, however, still wasn't entirely on board with the idea.

"You refer to the contact as a 'he'. This whole thing could blow up if it turns out to be a 'she'."

Sally responded. "That's true, but the only likely 'she' at BSI would have been Lisa Kerrigan, and we know it's not her. I never heard Dad talk about any other women connected with his project."

Sheila had to agree, but then added, "What if Mr Wilhelm decides to call this J.S., or perhaps email him back?"

"That could be a problem," Henry agreed. "But I say it's a risk we will just have to take. Anyway, even if Wilhelm finds out the email isn't real, there's no way he can trace it back to us."

After several more minutes of discussion, it was decided to have Henry send the revised email. They all agreed to meet back at Henry's tomorrow afternoon to see the results. As Sheila and Sally left, Henry started work on setting up the recording software on this computer.

James Macintyre was speechless. He sat in his office staring at his blank computer screen. As he thought over the phone call that he had just received on his cell phone he became increasing anxious to the point of near panic. What, he wondered, could have possibly gone wrong? Should he make arrangements now for an emergency exit?

It was Friday, six p.m. and he had been working late gathering the final documents of WG-116B project for the next delivery. He had been in a state of euphoria for the past two days as the news had been brought to him on Wednesday that the final design for the guidance system had been finished and the computer model had been satisfactorily tested. It had looked like everything was going to drop into place perfectly and, with this last delivery, he would become a wealthy man.

But now all his hopes seemed to be derailing like a train jumping the track just as it came within sight of the station. He couldn't believe what he had just heard. He replayed the call once again in his mind. The minute he had glanced at his phone's screen he had recognized the caller's ID number, and his nerves immediately were set on edge.

"Hello."

"You have been holding out on us. That is not acceptable."

Macintyre paused in shock trying to comprehend what he had just heard.

"No… no… I mean I don't know what you mean…"

"We had an arrangement and you have been keeping information from us. You will have one chance to explain yourself. If I am not satisfied you will be dealt with."

Macintyre panicked.

"No wait… I haven't kept any information from you. In fact, I have the final delivery right here. I can get it to you…"

"Shut up and listen. Bring the delivery tomorrow to 112 High Street, apartment one-zero-one at fourteen hundred hours. Make certain that you are not followed. You will have only this one chance to talk."

With that, the caller had hung up.

Sweat had arisen on Macintyre's brow. What could this possibly mean? He had no idea what the caller was referring to. This had to be a terrible misunderstanding. Macintyre sat trying to find comfort in the idea that the final delivery would smooth out any difficulties, but the tone of the phone call was anything but comforting.

***

On Saturday at one thirty p.m., James Macintyre grabbed the oversized envelope with the final WG-116B documents and put on his hat and overcoat. The temperature was a chilly twenty-five degrees but as he walked along toward High Street, he hardly noticed the cold. With each step that brought him closer to his destination, his anxiety level rose making it difficult to think about anything but what his contact has told him... *'if I am not satisfied you will be dealt with'*.

Macintyre wracked his brains trying to think of something... *anything*... that he hadn't told his contact that might be critical. But the more he thought, the more he couldn't imagine what that might be. As he approached the apartment house on High Street, he came to the conclusion that whatever it was that had upset his contact, it was a safe bet that it had something to do with Lisa Kerrigan. She was a meddlesome pain that was becoming a real problem. But she had disappeared and that, he had assumed, had taken care of that.

Macintyre walked up the front steps to the entrance and looked for the doorbell to apartment 101. Before he could see which button to push, the front door opened and the man who had collected his delivery packages yanked him inside.

"Were you followed?" the man snarled.

Taken by surprise by the rough handling, Macintyre couldn't collect his thoughts immediately. After a second, he responded, "No... I mean I don't think so."

The man pushed him down the hall and shoved him through a door into the first-floor apartment. Once inside, Macintyre surveyed the nearly bare interior. There were none of the usual signs of home life. Either this man had no personal life, or he didn't consider this apartment home.

Macintyre entered what obviously was intended as a living room and took a seat on a chair at a desk. The man remained standing.

307

Macintyre decided that going on the offense was his best strategy. He extended the package that he had brought for the man to take.

"I've brought the final system plans and a copy of the controls software. I've been assured that it is now fully functional. This should conclude our arrangement. I trust that the final payment will be made upon receipt of the materials."

The man grabbed the package and set it down on a coffee table without opening it.

"Listen, you worthless imbecile, you may have put the entire operation in jeopardy. Tell me what you know about the navy inspector, Peter Ashley. And don't hold anything back. I need to know everything."

Caught off guard, Macintyre had to think for a moment. He then offered, "Commander Ashley? He was shot."

The man moved with the speed of lightning striking Macintyre in the face.

"You idiot! I know he was shot! I arranged to have him shot! Tell what you know about his involvement in the investigation of the project."

Macintyre's mouth was bleeding and he had lost what little control he had upon arriving. Slumped in the chair he pleaded, "Please don't hurt me. I'll tell you everything. But just don't hurt me."

The man stood over Macintyre waiting for him to calm down a bit. Finally, Macintyre spoke again.

"I attended a briefing with navy representatives at the annual meeting last November. That was the first I heard that Commander Ashley was being assigned by the navy to oversee the project. I don't know anything else about him."

The man stood looking at Macintyre as if trying to decide if he was telling the truth. When the man didn't respond immediately, Macintyre spoke again. "*You* arranged to shoot Commander Ashley!"

The man replied with a hateful tone, "I take care of loose ends. That's what I do. I took care of your accountant and I took care of Ashley."

Macintyre looked back in shock. "*You killed Greg Connor?*"

The man replied scornfully, "I shot your accountant because he was making a nuisance of himself. And I hired a professional to shoot the navy officer for the same reason."

Macintyre's mind raced. He had always known that he was entering into a serious relationship in this endeavor, but for the first time he realized just how ruthless these people were. Suddenly, a thought crossed his mind.

"And what about Lisa Kerrigan, did you kill her to?"

The man lit a cigarette and blew smoke in Macintyre's face.

"No, our little nosey bird is not dead yet. She has been put in a cage and sent back home for safe keeping until we successfully conclude this matter. She may yet be useful to our cause. Now, I'm going to ask you again about Peter Ashley and I want to know what you've been holding back from us."

The interrogation lasted for an hour without Macintyre being able to dissuade the man that he knew more. By the end of the hour, Macintyre was badly beaten and had been reduced to a whimpering mass on the floor. At five minutes after three o'clock the man stepped over to the other side of the room and pulled out his cell phone. Macintyre lay on the floor as the man made a call. The man spoke to someone, but Macintyre was unable to understand what was being said since the conversation was being held in German. The man began the conversation pointing to Macintyre on the phone obviously telling the other person that he had gotten nothing from him. Then there was a silence as the man listened. After a moment the man on the other end of the line was screaming something in a voice so loud that Macintyre could hear him through the man's phone all the way across the room.

The man swore violently and threw the phone down. He charged around the room like a mad man pulling the table over, tearing off the shade to a floor lamp, and throwing what few objects there were in the room into a pile in the center of the room. The man then stood in apparent frustration wildly looking around the room. When his eyes fell on the fireplace mantle, he suddenly froze. Macintyre watched as the man rushed over to the mantle and pulled a black box off the mantle and inspected it, all the while with seething rage. Satisfied that the man had apparently found what he had been looking for, he threw the object to the floor and stomped a foot on it, crushing it into pieces.

\*\*\*

"Holy mackerel!" exclaimed Henry. "Did you see that? That was wicked, *awesome!"*

Sally, Sheila and Henry were huddled in Henry's bedroom having just watched the live feed from the Wilhelm apartment on Henry's computer. Henry had started the camera at one minute before two o'clock, not exactly sure if his extremely complicated and delicate instrument would actually work. At first the camera showed an empty living room which seemed to confirm their collective fears that Mr Wilhelm hadn't fallen for the email ruse. But two minutes later, the screen showed Mr Wilhelm following another man into the living room. They watched spellbound as the interrogation unfolded, ending with the phone call, Mr Wilhelm's angry search of the room, and then the loss of the video feed. When Mr Wilhelm had finally discovered the camera and had reached out to grab it, all three instinctively jumped backward as though he was about to grab them through the computer screen.

It took Sally and Sheila a full minute to recover. Sheila turned to Henry and said, "Did you get that? Were you recording what we saw?"

"You betcha," Henry replied with confidence. "But the question is, what do we do with it?"

"Sheila immediately answered. "We take it to the police, that's what we do."

Sally shook her head in disagreement. "I'll bet anything that now that Mr Wilhelm knows that someone is wise to his role, he'll be gone before the police could arrive. In fact, if I don't miss my guess, I'd say that we've probably seen the last of our ignominious chemistry teacher. Unless I'm wrong, he won't even show up at school again."

Henry did a fist pump in the air. "Yes! We should win the school's service award for this one. No more chemistry Nazi!"

Sheila gave Henry a look that clearly said, *grow up.*

Henry responded sheepishly. "I was just saying…"

Sally broke up the tension by returning the conversation to what they had just viewed. "There are several questions in what we saw, and if we can figure out the answers, we just possibly might still have a chance of bringing Mr Wilhelm to justice."

Sheila jumped in. "Right. Like for instance, who was the man being beaten? And for another, who was this man... Greg Connor... that Wilhelm admitted to killing?"

Sally sat for a moment searching her memory, recalling newspaper accounts from the autumn of last year.

"Greg Connor was BSI's chief financial officer. You may remember that he was murdered outside the BSI administration building on the morning of August twenty-second. He was shot twice in the chest. The police were unable to find the perpetrator and eventually issued a statement that the killing was the action of a drug addict. It was reported in the local paper."

"Man, how do you remember these things?" Henry exclaimed in amazement.

Sally just shrugged and continued. "There is little question that the man being questioned by Mr Wilhelm also works for BSI. I have no doubt that if you search the Internet for BSI senior executives you will find our mystery man."

Henry spun around to his computer and began to type commands. In just under a minute, he turned around and said, "Right, again *brainiac*."

On the screen Sheila and Sally could see a picture and brief bio of Mr James Macintyre, Billings Shipyard's chief executive officer.

Sheila pointed to the screen and said, "That's him! That's the guy who Mr Wilhelm was questioning. He's the one who's stealing the top-secret information from your father's project! We need to turn him in!"

Again, Sally shook her head in disagreement. "First of all, we don't even know if he's still alive. After what we heard from the video, it is entirely possible that Mr Wilhelm might have killed him too... how did he put what he does...? *Take care of loose ends*. Remember, our video copy won't be admissible in a court of law. It will be helpful to the police to get to the truth, but if all of the major participants leave the country, there will be no justice. We need to act quickly before it's too late. If we go to the police now, we'll be stuck answering questions so long that Wilhelm and maybe Macintyre will get away."

"So, what do we do?" asked Henry.

Sally frowned and then replied, "We get over to Mr Wilhelm's place right away. Maybe we can see where he will go into hiding, or where he will be delivering the stolen documents. If we can get a line on who he's working for, the police will be able to round up the entire syndicate."

Sheila objected. "But that's going to be dangerous."

"Not really," Sally responded. "Remember, Mr Wilhelm doesn't know who planted the camera. And even if he sees us, he'll likely think that we were coming from the school which is right down the street. Anyway, I doubt that he'll suspect it was high school students who planted the video camera. Henry's electronics looked pretty sophisticated."

Henry got up and motioned to Sheila. "Great! Let's get going. We can get over there in a minute or two if we take your car."

***

It took Wilhelm a minute to regain his composure after destroying the camera. When his anger finally subsided, he was able to think rationally. It had been a mistake to destroy the surveillance device he realized. Left intact, he probably could have had a specialist trace the broadcast to discover who had planted it. But that was probably not possible now. He thought to himself that he must better control his anger from here on out.

Looking over at Macintyre he decided that the best plan of action would be to not create any unnecessary suspicious conditions while he escaped to deliver the final documents. That meant that Macintyre must be reassured and put back in place to resume his normal routine. If Macintyre were to panic and disappear, the police would undoubtedly become involved to a much greater extent, especially given the recent disappearance of another BSI executive, Lisa Kerrigan.

Wilhelm helped Macintyre up, who was still in a state of shock having watched Wilhelm destroy the box from the fireplace mantle.

Macintyre, looked at the crumpled pile on the floor and stammered, "What... what... what was that?"

Wilhelm answered in a calm and collected voice. "That was a digital recording device that I had placed to record your confession. But after talking to my superior, it turns out that we were mistaken about your holding back information from us. I sincerely apologize. I must admit that when I just heard now that there was no reason to suspect you, I lost my composure. I was angry that they made me put you through this."

Macintyre was hurt from the abuse that he had just received, and his mind was not exactly clear. In his state of confusion, he wasn't exactly sure if he was in trouble or not. It sounded like there had indeed just been a misunderstanding. But he was very uneasy about the depth of distrust and cruelty he had just endured.

Seeing the confusion in Macintyre's face, Wilhelm spoke again to defuse the situation.

"You have certainly done all that we have asked of you. You have truly been a worthy partner in our endeavor. And with this final delivery, you will be amply rewarded. As soon as the systems are tested by my people and found to be complete and operational, your final bonus payment will be made."

Confusion still reigned in Macintyre's mind, but the assurance of the final payment seemed to make the difference. Macintyre gave a weak smile and said, "Don't worry. The system software has been tested and retested by our engineers and it is fully functional."

With that, Wilhelm ushered Macintyre out of the apartment and told him to await further instructions on receiving the final payment. It shouldn't take more than a week, he was told, for the money to be released.

As Macintyre stepped out of the apartment onto the front porch, Sally, Sheila and Henry watched from across the street in Sheila's car.

"That's the guy who Wilhelm was beating, and he looks plenty alive to me. So, I guess that answers the question of whether Wilhelm decided to kill him," Henry exclaimed.

"True enough," Sheila replied. "It's James Macintyre, all right."

Turning to Sally, Sheila asked, "What should we do? Should we follow this Macintyre guy or stay watching Mr Wilhelm?"

Sally watched as Macintyre walked down the sidewalk.

"He doesn't seem upset at all, which is a bit surprising after what Mr Wilhelm just did to him," Sally remarked.

"And," Sheila added, "he doesn't seem like he's in any great hurry to get away. I wonder what Mr Wilhelm said to him after he found the camera."

Sally sat deep in thought as Macintyre disappeared from sight and then said, "We should stay and see what Mr Wilhelm does. Maybe he'll lead us to whomever he is receiving the stolen documents from. Or if he has decided to run and hide, maybe we will see where he goes. Anyway, from the look of the way Mr Macintyre left, he didn't look like he was about to flee the country."

The three waited in the car for about fifteen minutes until Mr Wilhelm finally came out of the building. A taxi had just pulled up to the curb and Wilhelm stepped off the front porch carrying a suitcase in one hand and a briefcase in the other. He slid the luggage into the taxi and got in. As the taxi sped off Sheila started her car and followed the taxi.

"Don't get to close," Henry cautioned.

"Listen, sport, I've learned a thing or two from all those lousy action movies you've made me watch. I know how to tail a suspect without being obvious," Sheila said as she slid behind another car for cover. They drove out onto route one and headed south. After several minutes it became clear that they were likely headed to the city of Portland.

As they entered the city, they followed the cab to the local airport and watched as Wilhelm got out and paid the taxi driver. Sheila pulled the car into the parking garage and the trio rushed over to the terminal. Standing at an airline counter, Mr Wilhelm had just put his suitcase on the scale and was paying for a ticket.

The three stood behind a column trying not to attract attention as they watched Mr Wilhelm show his identification to the flight agent.

"It looks like you were right," Sheila said to Sally. "I'd say he's making a quick getaway. What should we do? Can we stop him?"

Sally sat in a chair in despair. "I thought he might go into hiding, but I didn't think he would actually leave Maine. There isn't anything we can do. We don't have anything that would convince the airport security to hold him. I'm afraid he's gone."

Before anyone could see what he was about to do, Henry slid around the column and strode quickly across the terminal waiting area to the airline counter. Sheila said with frustration, "What's he doing now?"

At first, they thought that he was going to approach Mr Wilhelm who was heading off towards his gate. But instead, Henry walked up to the counter and started walking in the opposite direction. The girls watched in dismay as they saw a TSA guard approach Henry from behind as Henry peered over the counter. The guard tapped him on the shoulder and asked, "Can I help you?"

Somewhat startled, Henry replied, "Oh no, sir. I was just watching to see how the bags got into the airplane. They travel along this moving conveyor belt, don't they? I've never been in an airport before."

The guard looked at Henry suspiciously and asked, "Are you ticketed for a departing flight?"

Henry paused for a brief second and then said, "No, I'm just here to meet some arriving friends."

Pointing to Sally and Sheila he exclaimed, "Oh look, there they are! Well, I'll be seeing you." And he rushed over to the girls. Taking their arms, he escorted them out of the terminal.

Once outside, and convinced that they weren't about to be arrested, Sheila fumed, "What was that all about?"

Henry smiled and said, "I had a hunch where our chemistry Nazi was headed, and I just wanted to see if I was right. The tag on his bag said HAM!"

Sheila looked puzzled but Sally gave Henry a high five. "Good work. HAM means our friend is going home... to Hamburg, Germany! He probably has a connecting flight later out of Boston, but he checked his bag through to Hamburg."

# Chapter 25

Each day of the next week brought an increased level of stress to James Macintyre. He had thought that within a day or two he would hear from his contact that his bonus payment had been authorized and that he could collect the funds. He had even typed his letter of resignation and booked a flight to Mexico.

But after three days had passed and he had not heard a word he began to be concerned. He checked his cell phone for missed calls every thirty minutes but each time there was nothing. Twice he even went to the bank to check the transfer account in which the funds were ordinarily deposited but the account balance did not show that the final payment had been made.

Exactly one week after the Saturday that he had last spoken with his contact he could stand the waiting no longer. He decided that it was time to take action. He had been given an emergency phone number that was only to be used under dire circumstances, but this he decided, qualified. If there had been some problem with the final delivery, he wanted to know what it was so that it could be corrected. His flight was due to depart in two days and he didn't want to miss it. Furthermore, he wanted to be around when that pompous prig, Tim Kerrigan, got his letter of resignation to see his reaction. It wouldn't be anywhere near as effective to mail the letter from Mexico.

Macintyre took out his cell phone and dialed the long-distance number. After the connection was made, he heard, "We're sorry. The number that you have just dialed is no longer in service." Furiously, Macintyre hung up. For the first time, a suspicion entered his mind that perhaps he was going to be cheated out of the final payment. Well, he thought with grim determination, that wasn't going to happen.

He picked up his coat and hat and decided that he would go to see his contact. As a result of last week's misunderstanding, he now knew where his contact lived, and he would confront him face to face and demand to know why he hadn't been paid. After all, if they refused to hold up their end of the agreement, he could certainly cause them grief by going to the authorities. It wouldn't look good for him, but he could always say that he was being coerced under threat of his very life. It would be his word against theirs. And if push came to shove, who would the authorities believe, a bunch of crooks or the CEO of Maine's largest corporation?

Arriving at the building, Macintyre boldly went up to the front porch and rang the bell to apartment one-zero-one. After several tries when no one came to answer the door, he went around to the side to look in a window. Peering inside he could see no activity or signs of life. Had the contact, he wondered, picked up and left? That would be just perfect, he thought with irony. He had done all the hard work and when the job was completed, he was just abandoned like some piece of useless trash.

He walked back to his house wondering what to do next. There was no way that he was going to let them get away with this. Just as he arrived back at his house, a car pulled up beside him and the side window rolled down. Inside was what looked like three teenage kids. A boy in the front passenger seat glared at him and said, "Get in, Mr Macintyre."

The rear passenger door opened.

***

After returning from the airport the previous Saturday, Sally, Sheila and Henry had decided that Mr Macintyre was their last link to the crimes. And as such, they had agreed to split up and watch him over the next few days to make sure that he didn't try to escape as well. That meant that one of them would skip school each day keeping an eye on him. If it looked as though he was going to make a run for it, the person doing the surveillance would phone the others and, even though their evidence was thin, they would go to the police and get them to arrest Macintyre before he could get away.

It had been a miserably boring few days for each of them. Sheila had taken the first turn the next day, which was Sunday. She parked her car outside his home and, except for a trip to the grocery store, Macintyre had stayed inside all day.

Henry eagerly agreed to watch Macintyre the next day, which meant skipping out on Monday's classes. He followed Macintyre to the BSI yard and watched him go into the administration building. Henry camped out in the cafe across the street to keep an eye on the building. He positioned himself at a window seat at the serving counter so that he could keep continuous watch on Macintyre's building without taking his eyes off the front door. With his eighth cup of coffee, however, he decided to risk going to the bathroom, knowing that he might miss Macintyre leaving, but it was either that or have a nasty accident at the counter. The day dragged on and on, but one good thing was that he got to know Brenda the waitress very well. At five o'clock, Macintyre left the yard and went home. Henry stayed outside Macintyre's house until seven o'clock when it seemed obvious that Macintyre wasn't going anywhere.

Sally's turn on Tuesday was equally uneventful. It was a day at work for Macintyre, followed by a stop at the corner grocery store, and a return home. At eight o'clock, Sally phoned the others and said that they should all meet tomorrow in the cafeteria during their lunch period to talk things over. It was beginning to be clear that Macintyre wasn't going anywhere soon.

At lunch the next day they agreed that Macintyre might not be going to try to flee from Billings, but they couldn't just sit around and wait. They had to *do* something. After talking over several possibilities, they decided that a direct approach would be best. Time was running out since the following week was February vacation, which meant that the three of them would be off to Paris on the history prize trip. Saturday, they decided, would be when they would approach him and tell him that they knew about his involvement in the theft of the secret documents from BSI and get him to go to the police. With what he knew about the German connection, Sally was sure that he could negotiate a deal with the police for leniency. And, in so doing, Sally was sure that sufficient information would be given to prove her father's innocence.

\*\*\*

Saturday morning arrived and the three met at Henry's to go over the plan. Henry transferred the recording of the video that they had watched from his computer to his cell phone. They agreed that they would show Macintyre the video and tell him that his only option was to confess all to the police. Sheila suggested that they somehow get him to a public place so that they would be covered by the safety of others watching. After considering this for a few minutes, however, the best location they had finally agreed would be Macintyre's house where they would have privacy and wouldn't attract undue attention. With the three of them present, they felt assured that he wouldn't be able to overpower them and make a run for it.

By mid-morning they had worked up enough courage and they piled into Sheila's car. The drive over to Macintyre's house only took a few minutes and they arrived before any of them had had a chance to chicken out. Sheila pulled the car over to the curb in front of the house and turned the car off. The three sat in silence each waiting for one of the others to take the lead. Finally, Sheila said, "Well, if we're going to do this, we'd better get going. I, for one, don't want to wait all day for this to happen."

Henry turned around and said, "Well I wouldn't worry about waiting all day. Here he comes now!"

The three swung their heads in unison to see James Macintyre step out of his front door and walk down the sidewalk towards their car. Without hesitating, Henry rolled down his window and said in a deep voice that sounded as much like a mob boss as he could muster, "Get in, Mr Macintyre."

Macintyre halted and looked in the car. For a moment it looked like he might just continue on. Sally slid over in the back seat and opened the door. A look of curiosity showed on Macintyre's face as if he were trying to figure something out, and then he stepped into the back of the car.

"Who are you? Have you been sent by my contact?"

Sally responded, "Your contact, Gustav Wilhelm, has left the country, Mr Macintyre."

A look of concern showed on Macintyre's face. Clearly, he was uncomfortable, which was exactly what Sally had hoped for.

"Mr Macintyre, we want you to watch a recording that was made last week."

Henry reached over the front seat and passed his cell phone to Macintyre who took it a bit reluctantly. On the cell phone was a video playing of the interrogation from the previous Saturday. Macintyre sat in stunned silence until it finished after which he blurted out, "Who are you? What do you want? Why hasn't the final payment been made?"

Sally waited a moment for Macintyre's concern to take full charge again. She needed to have him understand that not only were they in control of the situation, but he was totally without hope. Over the previous hour she had watched the video over and over again in her nearly perfect memory to get an understanding of what had been happening. She had contemplated each and every word that both Wilhelm and Macintyre had said and had eventually pieced together the gist of what was going on. She still had holes in her understanding, but she knew enough that James Macintyre was definitely the key to getting her father released.

"Mr Macintyre, you have been abandoned. Worse than that, you are even now being set up to take responsibility for this entire sordid affair."

Once again, she waited a moment for the gravity of her words to sink in.

"You have seriously underestimated the people with whom you have joined in partnership. You will not be receiving any final payment. In fact, now that you have delivered the final documents, they have only one use for you... and that is to take the blame for all that has happened."

A look of concern on Macintyre's face changed to one of sheer panic as he considered Sally's words. Finally, he stammered, "How do you know this?"

"Mr Macintyre, we know all the details of this affair. We know that you have betrayed your country and that betrayal is call *treason*. We know that you are involved with the murder of Greg Connor and the shooting of Peter Ashley. And we know that even though you may not have personally orchestrated the disappearance of Lisa Kerrigan, evidence will mysteriously turn up that will lead the authorities to believe that you have murdered her as well."

Sally kept up an appearance of control and authority even though what she was feeling inside was far from anything remotely close to confidence. On the way over she had rehearsed what she would say in

320

her mind but somehow actually saying the words made her stomach churn. She had little doubt that she could say enough of what was actually fact to convince Macintyre, but she still had a nagging apprehension that she was missing some significant detail that would alert him to their charade.

Macintyre sat without saying a word as Sally continued.

"There is no doubt that you will be tried and will be found guilty of high treason and being an accessory to murder. And, if you are lucky, that will mean a life sentence in prison."

Macintyre's voice squeaked a feeble, "No!"

And now it was time for the finishing touch thought Sally... the bait that she hoped he would take.

"You only have one chance for mercy. If you turn yourself in and admit to your crimes, we will show the authorities this video in which you are being beaten. With this video you may be able to convince the police that you had no choice but to do what they told you because your life was being threatened. We will edit out the final part where Wilhelm told you that the beating was a misunderstanding and that you were a *worthy partner* in the endeavor. It will look like you had to cooperate in fear of your life."

The three watched as Macintyre sat quietly. It was clear that he was weighing his options. Before he had a chance to decide, Sally spoke again, hoping against hope that what she was about to say would be accepted.

"For this deal to be made, however, you must admit to the police that Steven Brown had nothing to do with either the theft of classified navy documents or with the shooting of Peter Ashley."

***

This was one hell of a mess, Macintyre thought to himself. Things were way out of control and it looked like his whole world was about to go down the drain.

He had looked with suspicion at the three in the car when the door had opened. His first reaction was, are you kidding? No way am I getting into a car with three suspicious looking people, even if they are just teenagers... perhaps *especially* since they are teenagers! But a thought quickly crossed his mind. He was on his way to an unannounced visit to his contact and immediately he was being told by strangers to get into a car. He didn't believe in coincidence. Perhaps he was being watched, and now these three might be going to take him to see his contact.

Cautiously he got into the back seat of the car. The initial shock he had received was that his contact had left the country. His first reaction was a feeling of relief that whoever these three were they must be connected with his contact since they not only knew his name but also his whereabouts. But then he became concerned that it looked like his worst fears might be true... *he had been abandoned and left holding the proverbial bag.*

The initial shock was quickly replaced by a second, more alarming, shock when he watched the video recording on the cell phone that he had been handed. His contact had said that he had placed the video recorder to make a record of his supposed confession. But he had seen the recorder destroyed when his contact had found out that there would be no confession. How could these three have a copy of that recording, he wondered? And, more importantly, why did they have a copy?

Even though the three looked incredibly young, their having a copy of last Saturday's meeting must somehow mean that they were part of the German connection. Suddenly, a wave of anger overtook him. He had had enough of this game. All he wanted was his money. He had held up his end of the bargain and he damn well expected them to do the same.

"Who are you? What do you want? Why hasn't the final payment been made?"

What he heard in response made his blood run cold. He had been correct. He had been abandoned and was being set up for the fall. He should have known better. The anger in his throat was replaced with panic. They were telling him that he had to turn himself in. They wanted him to seek the mercy of the court, but he knew that that was a mercy that he would never receive. Minutes ago, he was worried about getting his final payment. Now it looked as though he had bigger concerns.

A decision came in a sudden flash. There was no way he was going to be set up for this mess. And *he was going to get his money!* The girl in the back seat was saying something about Steven Brown when he lunged for the door and jumped out, taking the cell phone with him. He ran down the sidewalk and cut into a nearby yard. As he turned to look back at the car, he saw the three just now getting out in pursuit. Good, he thought. The surprise of his leaving had bought him just enough seconds to make a getaway.

Running through the yard, he turned onto a side street where a garbage truck was just pulling away. Quickly he hopped onto the back of the truck and rode away down the street. Several blocks away he hopped off and, seeing none of the three teenagers, he headed off to get his car. If his contacts had abandoned him that didn't mean that he would just lie down and play dead. He wanted his money, and he was determined going to get it... even if that meant flying to Hamburg to confront the boss.

*\*\*\**

The three sat in a state of shock for a full ten seconds before they scrambled out of the car after Macintyre. No one had even considered the possibility that he might just run away. Henry led the way, running down the sidewalk at full speed. He had just seen Macintyre turn into the side yard of a house two blocks ahead and was sure that he could catch up with a man who was old enough to be his father.

When he reached the yard, he could see that there was another house behind with an open yard that connected to a side street beyond. Knowing that Macintyre couldn't be too far ahead, Henry rushed through the snow-covered yards following Macintyre's foot tracks. When he reached the side street, he saw nothing. There was no one to be seen in either direction, and he could see for several blocks each way. Furthermore, Macintyre's tracks showed that he had run into the street and then the tracks just disappeared.

Very much out of breath, Sheila and Sally caught up and Sheila gasped, "Where is he? Did you see which way he went?"

Henry shook his head. "It's like he just vanished. When I got here, I should have been able to see him down the street, one way or the other, but there was no sign of him."

The three spent the next half hour looking around the area trying to see if Macintyre had holed up somewhere, but they found nothing.

Eventually they decided to quit and go back to the car. On the way back, Sally asked the question that she had not wanted to even think about since Macintyre had fled. Turning to Henry she asked, "You *do* have another copy of that video... right?"

Henry winced. "We were in a hurry and I think I just transferred the file rather than copy it."

"Which means," Sheila said with total frustration, "we just lost the only evidence that we had. *Brilliant!*"

***

James Macintyre knew that very likely his proverbial goose was cooked. Having just escaped from the three teenagers, he sat in his car on a back road trying to collect his thoughts. After managing to get away from his pursuers, he had hurried to his house and jumped in his car. He looked down at the cell phone that he had taken with more of a feeling of sadness than anger. How, he wondered, had this turned into such a mess? It seemed that just when one problem was solved another worse situation arose.

One thing was clear, he was now on his own. And it was also equally clear that whatever it took, he was going to get the money that was owed him. He was even more determined now than ever. There was, however, a fundamental question that had to be answered. What was the likelihood that the kids had a second copy of the video file? If that were the case, he would need to leave immediately. If not, he would at least have some time to prepare for what he knew he had to do.

There was only one way to find out for sure. He drove back to town and parked his car in the parking lot of the town's large grocery. He couldn't take any chances of having his car spotted near his house if the police were already after him. From the grocery store he walked to his street and carefully ducked into the shed of his neighbor's house across the street from his house. He knew that Mr and Mrs Crosby spent each winter in Florida escaping the snow and cold temperatures of Maine.

From his position in the shed he could keep an eye on his house. If the kids had another copy of the video and went to the police, it would just be a matter of time before they showed up at his house looking for him. All he had to do was wait and see what happened. If the police arrived, he would have to sneak away and leave the area without delay. If not, he would be able to wait until Monday to get what money he had in his bank. Regardless, he had decided that he would be taking off as soon as possible to confront the people who had not held up their end of the agreement.

After a few minutes, Macintyre saw the three kids cruise by his house in the car that he had seen the video. They slowed down in front of his house obviously looking for him. When they didn't see any sign of him, they sped off. An hour later when the police didn't show up, he felt that it was probably safe to assume that they hadn't turned him in. That could very well mean that the video on the cell phone that he held in his hand was their only copy. With a smile he dropped the phone and stepped on it. The crunch that the phone made gave him an enormous feeling of satisfaction.

# Chapter 26

The three had little time to commiserate over the disappearance of both Macintyre and the video recording. They had driven over to his house but, not surprisingly, no one was home, and his car was gone. The next day, Sunday, was the day that they were to leave on the history prize trip. It was five a.m. and the three stood in front of high school waiting for Mr Norris. They each had a small suitcase and a carry-on bag. Henry's carry-on bag was actually a gym bag with an American flag and the words 'God Bless America' embroidered on the side.

Sheila looked down at Henry's bag and said, "Superb! I'm going to a country that hates Americans and I'm traveling with someone who has a death wish. What does the other side of your bag say, *'The only thing the French ever got right are their fries'*?"

Henry laughed. "Hey, that's pretty good."

Sally, tired from being up all night trying to devise a new plan to help her father, mumbled half asleep in a detached voice, "Actually French fries aren't French at all. Fried potatoes were first noted in 1680 in the Belgian territory of the Spanish Netherlands. The French now call them *pommes frites*."

Neither Henry nor Sally had a response and so they just stood looking at each other. Henry silently mouthed to Sheila, "Wow."

A minute later Mr Norris drove up and they all packed their bags in the car trunk. Once inside the car, Mr Norris asked, "Okay. Are we all set? I trust you have everything, including your passports."

Each of the three nodded in agreement and they were off for the Portland airport. Mercifully, it was a rather quiet ride to Portland and Sheila and Henry took the opportunity to catch up on their sleep. Sally, however, sat staring out the side window, mulling over the plan that she had hatched late last night. It would be very risky, and she had to admit that it certainly had little chance for success. But she also had to admit that at this point there was little else that could be tried. Sally looked over

326

at Sheila who was fast asleep with her head on Henry's shoulder and decided that the plan was too unsafe to ask them to participate. She hoped that they would understand.

The Portland airport was amazingly busy for the early hour of the morning that they arrived. There were several flights scheduled for early departure and the terminal was filled with people checking in and rushing to their gates. There were families flying with their children to vacation spots such as Disney World for the February school vacation. There were businessmen taking flights to arrive a day early for meetings that would take place all over the country. And there was the usual throng of people, typical for this time of year, headed off to ski resorts in the Colorado Rockies seeking deep powder.

They were standing with Mr Norris in a long line waiting to receive their boarding passes and check in their luggage when they heard a commotion behind them as three boys and a stout woman with a stern expression cut through the line towards them.

"Hey, look," Henry said. "It's the geek squad with Nurse Ratched."

Bumbling along in an overly excited way were the three boys from Team Q in the history competition. Standing immediately behind them was their chaperone, a woman of about fifty years of age. Everything about her screamed marine corps drill sergeant, and she looked like this trip was some kind of punishment that she was sure to share with all.

One of the three boys, a skinny fellow with dark curly hair and black-rimmed glasses, reached out an arm to Sheila and exclaimed in an enthusiastic shout, "High five!"

Sheila didn't exactly want to respond, but rather than leave the boy in an embarrassing awkward situation at their very first meeting, she reached up and gave the obligatory hand slap. She then discreetly put her arms behind her back and wiped her hand on her sleeve as if trying to clean away a communicable disease.

The boy never missed a beat. "Hey, all. I'm Jason Kelly. This is going to be awesome!"

Sally wondered, if I was a nerd would I purposefully want to dress and act like one? It immediately triggered a philosophical argument in her mind, *Is one's inward personality driven by their outward persona, or is one's outward persona merely a reflection of their inward personality?* Either way she thought, if I were him, I'd change my look.

Henry, who seemed to be having a great time of it all, spoke up. "Hey, guys! I'm Henry Moore, this is Sheila Warren, and this is Sally Brown. We go to Billings High."

Jason and the other two boys extended hands for a handshake. One of the other two, who looked amazingly like a carbon copy of Jason, said, "Nice to meet you. I'm Mike Walker." He then, pointing to the third boy who even more amazingly could have been a twin of either of the other two, said, "This here's Chad Gifford. We're from Rockland High School."

Henry mumbled, "What's up… did you three have the same father or what?" which was immediately followed by a kick in the shin by Sheila.

Mr Norris approached the woman, extending a hand and said, "Hello, I'm Bill Norris. I'm happy to have you along."

The woman did not take Mr Norris' hand. Instead, she stood rigidly and announced, "My name is *Ms* Hudson. I have instructed my students that I will not tolerate any misbehavior and there will be no funny business on this trip. I expect that you have made it equally clear to your students."

Henry leaned over to Jason and whispered, "Don't worry, there won't be anything funny with her around!"

Jason gave a sad nod of agreement.

The flight to Logan airport in Boston took only about thirty minutes in the air. They hardly reached their flying altitude when the pilot announced their descent. The plane was a small commuter jet with two seats on each side with a center aisle. During the flight, Henry sat with Sheila leaving Sally as the odd person out to sit with Mr Norris. Shortly after take-off Mr Norris turned to Sally and said, "Sally, I've noticed recently that you haven't exactly been yourself in class. You've been distracted, which is certainly understandable given the recent situation with your father."

Sally didn't exactly know what to say and so she sat without responding.

"I hope," Mr Norris continued, "that this trip will provide an enjoyable break for you. You need to relax for a while and take it easy. I know that things have been tough, but if there's anything I can do for you, just let me know."

Sally made an effort to put on at least half a smile and replied, "Thanks. I appreciate it."

Once in Boston, the group checked in for their flight to Paris and headed off to their gate. It meant going through another security check point, this time with one of the new whole-body scanners. As Sally, Sheila and Henry waited in line they heard a commotion up ahead. Suddenly, everyone stepped out of line to see what was going on. Above the din of the crowd a voice was heard to say with considerable stress, "... *No!* Positively, no! There's no way I'm going to have some perv looking at me without my clothes on!"

Henry peered around the group and saw one of the Team Q boys, it was impossible to tell if it was Jason, Mike or Chad, arguing with a TSA security guard. Henry motioned for Sally and Sheila.

"Hey, guys... you gotta see this! One of the geek squad won't go through the scanner. I think he's talking invasion of privacy."

Sheila and Sally stepped around to see one of the boys pleading his case with the guard at the security scanner. Just as it looked like the boy might be taken away, the Rockland chaperone, Ms Hudson, burst onto the scene and physically pushed the young man through the scanner, snarling, "Get through there. You're holding up the line."

The boy tried to object but Ms Hudson cut him off abruptly and, stepping toward him, physically pushed him through the scanner, saying, "I don't want to hear any more. Just get moving."

From behind a TSA guard grabbed her shoulders and yanked her away from the scanner entrance, saying in a commanding voice, "Step away from the scanner, ma'am. Move to the side and stay put."

Ms Hudson shot the guard a look of total contempt but did as she was told.

Immediately, Henry burst out in song in great delight,

"Yeah...! Slap her down again Pa, slap her down again..."

Sheila turned to Henry and in a horrified voice asking, "What are you singing?"

Henry gave Sheila a puzzled look and replied, "It's Arthur Godfrey! Don't tell me you've never heard 'Slap Her Down Again' before. It's a classic! My dad used to sing it all the time."

By now the crowd had lost interest in the scuffle at the scanner but all had grown quiet watching and listening to Henry. As he looked up and saw that all eyes were on him, he stopped singing and with great embarrassment looked down at his shoes.

"I wonder if we need to take our shoes off," he asked sheepishly.

*** 

The flight to Paris wasn't scheduled to depart for an hour after they all reached the waiting area at the gate. On the way they stopped by a donut stand and they each got a cup of coffee. Henry also got a jelly filled donut which he managed to drool much of the filling down the front of his jacket as he took his first bite.

Sheila looked over as Henry was using a totally inadequately sized napkin to wipe off the spill.

"What were you, brought up in a barn?" she asked. "Don't you know how to eat a donut?"

Henry smiled and, pointing to the jelly on his coat he said, "I just wanted to save some for later."

When it finally came time to board the plane, they all grabbed their carry-on bags and headed down the ramp that led to the 747 Air France jet. Once on board they were directed to their seats which were in a middle seating section, about halfway down the plane. Sally had the end seat by the aisle with Sheila seated beside her and Henry next in line. Mr Norris took his seat across the aisle from Sally. The Rockland group was seated in similar seating arrangement in the row immediately in front of them.

As the other passengers boarded the plane each found their seats and stowed their carry-on bags in the luggage compartments above. Henry, Sheila and Sally watched the crowd file through and it became apparent that this would be a full flight. A woman entered with two children, a small girl of about two years of age and a boy who looked to be about five. Henry leaned over to Sheila and said, "What do you bet that they sit right behind Mr Norris?"

True enough, the woman guided the young girl into the row behind Mr Norris, and, with a hand on the boy, they took their seats. After being belted in, the young boy promptly started kicking the seat in front of him where Mr Norris sat. Henry gave a laugh and said, "Told you so!"

A family came on board next with a young mother, her husband, and the obligatory crying baby. As if some kind of payback, they took their seats in the row behind their row, with the mother and wailing baby seated directly behind Henry. Henry overheard an elderly woman who was sitting beside the mother kindly tell her not to worry, that crying babies always sound loudest to the mother. Henry rolled his eyes and whined to Sheila, "Why me, Lord?"

Just when it finally appeared that all had boarded the plane and the flight attendants were going to close the door, an enormously overweight man came onto the plane with a bag that looked the size of a steamer trunk. He checked his boarding pass to locate his seat number which, as fate would have it, turned out to be immediately beside the Rockland chaperone, Ms Hudson.

Henry perked up and said, "This ought to be good. This should be worth the price of admission!"

By this time nearly all the passengers were seated, and many were watching the man to see how he was going to handle his bag. He stood in the aisle and attempted to push his bag into the compartment above Ms Hudson. It was obviously a heavy bag and the effort brought out beads of sweat on the man's face. Try as he might, the bag didn't seem to want to fit in the compartment. All the while, the man's enormous stomach was awkwardly crowding Ms Hudson.

Suddenly, she pushed the man bodily out of the way as she jumped to her feet. She grabbed the bag and, in a move that a Russian Olympic weightlifter would envy, she shoved the bag into the overhead compartment with an audible grunt. Glowering at the man, she pointed to the vacant seat beside her and said, "Sit!" The passengers in the surrounding seats who had been watching broke out into applause.

Henry responded, "Remind me not to mess with mother Schwarzenegger."

During the flight Henry watched the movies being played on the screen mounted to the back of the seat in front of him, while Sheila read from a book that she had picked up at the airport newsstand. Neither paid much attention to Sally who was engrossed in listening with headphones to something on a portable CD player. After an hour or so Sheila looked over and noticed that Sally was changing a CD in her player. The CD label read, *RosettaStone — German Disk Two*.

***

James Macintyre went to work on Monday half expecting the police to be at his office door waiting for him. When he arrived at the office, however, the building was operating as normal and there were no signs of anything suspicious. Entering his office, he immediately sat down at his computer and connected to the Internet to search for airline flights. It only took a few minutes to discover that nearly all of the flights to Europe were entirely booked. Cursing, he remembered that for many students this was their February vacation and no doubt that contributed to the full schedule.

It was quickly evident that there would be no flights with available seats leaving Boston until early evening Tuesday. Grumbling, he secured a reservation on a KLM flight that left Boston at six fifty p.m. and arrived in Hamburg, Germany the next day at eleven a.m., with a stopover in Amsterdam. Adding to his frustration was the fact that the flight cost a small fortune given the short notice of the booking and the fact that he had booked it one way. He wasn't exactly sure when he would be able to leave Germany since that depended on his success in confronting his German contacts.

The first task he told himself was to make arrangements that would allow him to escape without any undue notice. After reviewing his schedule for the week, he called in his secretary.

"Miss Stanley, I will be taking some time off and I would like to reschedule my appointments. I intend to take some vacation and visit relatives. I will be leaving tomorrow evening and I will be gone through next week. I don't believe that there's anything pressing on the calendar."

He figured that if the company wasn't expecting him back before the end of next week, it should give him plenty of time to get his money and be off to his new life. His *new life…* that was a problem. With the threat that the police might get involved because of either those teenagers turning him in, or his so-called partners looking to hang him out to dry, his plans for a life in Mexico was no longer possible. He had to find a new place that met his desires. He wanted a home that would provide warm weather year round, an economic structure that would inflate the worth of his savings beyond its value in the US, a stable government that supported democracy and a population where English would be spoken. More importantly than these desires, however, was the absolute need to find a country that did not have extradition rights with the United States. Should his activities at BSI be uncovered by law enforcement, this would be critical. Hopefully, he thought, it won't come to that.

He spent the next hour on his computer and finally reached a decision. He found the perfect place. He would move to the island of Ebeye in the South Pacific. It was a member island of the Republic of Marshall Islands with a population of about twelve thousand. The Marshall Islands, he learned, had gained their independence from the United States in 1986. Its main island, Majuro, contained the majority of people along with the country's capital. There was a total of twenty-nine atolls and five isolated islands, with Ebeye being the second largest population center. The government was comprised of elected representatives and approximately ten per cent of the population spoke English. The nation's economy was helped annually by foreign aid from the US, which was negotiated through the year 2023, which should make finances relatively stable for at least that long. And best of all… the Republic of Marshall Islands did not have an extradition treaty with the US!

With his work schedule arranged, and his life destination settled, he then picked up the phone and called his bank. After speaking with a bank clerk, he was transferred to the bank manager.

"This is James Macintyre. I would like to close both my checking account and savings account and stop by this afternoon to pick up the funds."

The bank manager took down the account numbers and, after a minute, came back on the line.

"How would you like the funds, Mr Macintyre? Would a bank check be acceptable?"

Macintyre thought for a moment and then said, "That would be fine." When he arrived in the Marshall Islands, he would set up an account with the Bank of the Marshall Islands which had a branch on Ebeye. Sitting back in his chair, he couldn't help but wish that he could get out this afternoon. After considering it for a moment, however, it occurred to him that perhaps the extra time would be beneficial after all. It would allow him to come up with a plan to make certain that he got his money. What he needed, he thought, was leverage. He turned back to his computer and started typing. After typing for an hour, he printed out four pages that detailed everything regarding his involvement with the theft and transfer of the BSI classified documents. He also included everything he could regarding the German connection. The details on that end were a bit sketchy but his mention of Hamburg Shipping and the involvement of the company's chief financial officer would undoubtedly lead the authorities to the right people, should it come to that.

After reading the material through a last time, Macintyre put the pages in an envelope and, sealing it, he wrote the address on the outside:

*Polizeihauptkommissar*
*Davidwache Police District 15*
*Hamburg, Germany 20359*

Macintyre then put the envelope into his pocket and erased the file from his computer. Grabbing his coat and hat, he left his office.

# Chapter 27

The plane touched down at Charles de Gaulle Airport at ten minutes after six in morning, local time, which would have been just after midnight back home. After going through French customs, they took two taxis into the city with the Rockland contingent in one cab and the Billings group in the other. Arriving at the hotel, they were given an hour to get their things settled before gathering downstairs for the complimentary continental breakfast. Sally and Sheila were booked in one room. Jason and Mike were in a second room and Chad and Henry were in a third room. Each of the chaperones had their own rooms, with Ms Hudson's room next to Sheila and Sally's room, and Mr Norris' room across the hall from Chad and Henry.

When they arrived downstairs at the hotel lobby for breakfast, the Rockland boys, along with their new best buddy, Henry, were all enthusiastically ready to get going. Sally and Sheila had changed their clothes and were anxiously looking forward to a cup of coffee to bring them back from a nearly sleepless flight. Mr Norris and Ms Hudson joined them, each looking like death warmed over. The jet lag had been felt by the students, but the excitement of the trip counteracted its effects to a large degree. The adults, however, had felt its full force and their faces showed the effects of every lost hour between Boston and Paris.

It turned out that the complimentary breakfast wasn't exactly what they had expected. The coffee was hardly what any American would call coffee. Sally decided that it was probably more like espresso than traditional coffee but, regardless, it was downright horrible. And the breakfast consisted of a sweet roll with a small container of lukewarm juice.

The boys didn't seem to mind much as they were each on their fifth roll when the adults called for the group to head out into the hotel lobby. When they all got seated in the lobby, Ms Hudson stood and gave the day's instructions.

"The bus will arrive here in approximately ten minutes. I want to take this time to go over the rules for today."

Henry leaned over to Jason and whispered in a voice that was not quite low enough, *"Und you vill obey, or you vill suffer sie consequences!"*

Sheila gave a low groan as Ms Hudson stopped speaking and walked over to stand immediately in front of Henry. Looking straight down at him with an expression that made everyone's hearts stop beating, she said, "I can see that we will be having a problem with you, young man. I will not repeat myself, so you had better listen. One more display of insubordination and you will be left in your room for the rest of the week... with me as your personal chaperone."

Henry gave a remorseful nod which Sheila thought was less an expression of sorrow and more an acknowledgement that spending one-on-one time with Ms Hudson would be a fate worse than death.

With that, Ms Hudson continued.

"When the bus arrives, we will be heading off to the Notre Dame cathedral for the day. When we get to the cathedral, we will have time to walk around and take pictures. At ten o'clock we will be taking a guided tour of the cathedral. At noon the bus will return, and we will head off to lunch at a nearby cafe. We will be eating at the LeLutetia Cafe which is on Quai De Bourbon opposite the Pont Louis Phillipe."

She spoke the French names with what was obviously a practiced accent, no doubt to impress her students, but the names came out with such a mangled American accent that the effect was actually comical. No one even smiled, however.

Taking a breath, Ms Hudson went on.

"Following lunch, we will walk to the Berthillon ice cream shop, which is near the cafe, for dessert. The bus will then pick us up and return us to the cathedral. We have arranged for the staff to conduct a class in the afternoon explaining the history and architecture of the cathedral and to take us to places in the cathedral that are not normally open to the public."

At the mention of the word *class*, all four boys gave a painful look, but no one said a word.

"After our private tour, the bus will pick us up to return to the hotel. We will be eating our evening meal at the hotel. It will be an early evening tonight as I'm sure that we all could do with a bit of rest from the long flight. When we return to the hotel, I will give further instructions for the evening. Are there any questions?"

No one uttered a sound and, just as the silence was becoming a bit awkward, the bus driver entered the lobby and announced, "The American bus to Notre Dame is ready."

Notre Dame was even more impressive, thought Sally, than she had imagined it might be. The recent fire had necessitated construction staging be erected along the inside walls of the nave. Laborers could be seen high up at the roof working on repairs that would likely take years to complete. But even with the staging still in place, the interior was breathtaking and the detailing of stained glass and sculpted figures were incredible to behold. Sheila and Sally had headed off to view the grounds outside together while the four boys immediately went inside. They had all been informed when they had arrived that Notre Dame was Paris' most popular landmark with more than thirteen million visitors each year before the fire. The grounds were filled with hundreds of tourists from many countries, each speaking their different languages, with a commonality being the unmistakable awe heard in all the voices.

After taking pictures around the outside, Sheila and Sally entered the cathedral through the main doors in the Portal of Judgment on the west facade. When they got inside it took a moment for their eyes to adjust to the lower light level. As their eyesight adjusted, they were overtaken by the immense scale of the nave as it stretched out before them. In the distance stood the side transepts with an altar decorated with lighted candles at the intersection of the transepts.

Looking around, Sally spotted the boys not far away huddled in a circle. Turning to Sheila, Sally pointed to the boys and asked, "What do you think they are up to now?"

Sheila looked over and saw that the boys were working intently on something that she couldn't quite make out.

"We'd better go find out what's so fascinating," Sheila responded.

When they reached the boys, Henry saw them and said excitedly, "Hey check this out! This is going to be fantastic!"

Immediately, Sheila became worried.

The boys each held large paper airplanes that they had apparently been working on. Mike, or maybe it was Chad, Sally couldn't be sure, spoke up.

"The cathedral nave is 68.58 meters long and 11.89 meters wide, not counting the side aisles. The height of the ceiling vault is 31.09 meters. Given an inside ambient temperature of approximately 21.11 degrees Celsius at the floor level, and an outside ambient temperature of approximately 16.66 degrees Celsius, we have calculated that the dimensions of this space will result in three distinct thermal levels of air between the floor and ceiling. These thermal variations will create a convection current of air that will carry a paper airplane whose mass is no more than 21.26 grams for at least a distance equal to the nave."

Sally looked at the boys with an obvious degree of skepticism.

Chad (or, was it Mike?) responded to her questioning look.

"Well, admittedly our calculations are based on only an estimated thickness of the perimeter masonry walls and a corresponding overall thermal resistive value to figure heat loss. But I think that our figures are acceptably accurate."

Henry showed his airplane with pride.

"The guys brought along an extra sheet of paper for me. We each have made what we think is the best plane design. We're going to test their theory to see if we can reach the end of the nave!"

Sheila interrupted. "Wait just a minute, guys. I don't think it's such a good idea to be floating paper airplanes in Paris' most sacred church. What if Ms Hudson catches you? I wouldn't want to be you then."

Jason responded, "Don't worry. I saw her heading off to the gift shop. She won't see anything."

Before Sheila could object, the four boys lined up facing the far end of the nave and let their airplanes fly. Amazingly, all four planes soared high into the nave and drifted down its length. Luckily, they were high enough that most of the throng of people walking through the space didn't take notice.

The planes drifted down the nave crisscrossing each other's flight paths, looking much like four white doves sailing overhead. About three-quarters of the way down the length of the nave the first plane came back to earth. Mike let out a disappointed groan. Shortly afterward, the second and third plane fell as they collided with each other. Chad cried out accusing Jason, "Hey, that's not fair; your plane took mine down before it could reach the end!"

With three of the planes now on the floor, only Henry's plane continued its flight. Sheila and Sally watched in dismay as it reached the location of transept and fell towards the altar. The plane glided toward the altar and sailed right through the flame of one of the altar candles, immediately becoming a flying torch.

Seeing that his plane had reached the transept, Henry shouted, "Yes!" which was immediately followed by an exclamation of, "Oh-no!"

The flaming projectile came to rest on the floor just behind the altar, with a column of smoke rising toward the ceiling as the altar cloth caught on fire. Before they could react, a piercing audible smoke alarm sounded. Henry glanced over to the gift store just in time to see Ms Hudson exiting to investigate the commotion. He spoke only a single word, "Run!"

\*\*\*

Officer Peter Morgan looked at his watch and saw that it was now seventeen thirty and the darkness of the night had already largely claimed its place in the Hamburg sky overhead. It had been a routine Monday patrol day. Now officially off duty, he was walking along Herbertstrasse toward the club Der Schlupfwinkel. He had decided that he would stop in for just one beer on his way home, hoping deep in his subconscious that this might be the time when he would be able to see what had eluded him for so long regarding the unsolved murder. As he approached the club across the street, he abruptly stopped in a complete state of shock. Quickly returning to rational thought, he hustled behind a bus stand shelter out of view from the club entrance. To his utter amazement, Johann Steiner and another man had just exited through the front door and were standing talking on the sidewalk.

Morgan was too far away to hear what was being said and he didn't dare to peer around the bus stand to get a good look at the pair for fear of being seen. Looking through the glass panel of the bus stand, Morgan could just make out that the other man with Steiner was an Asian who was approximately in his mid to late thirties. The two men concluded their talks and then separated. Steiner got into his Mercedes that was parked half a block down the street. The Asian man continued walking in the opposite direction toward the center of the city.

Years of police detective experience had taught Morgan not to believe in coincidence. While this could have been just a chance meeting, it seemed highly suspicious that the chief financial officer of Hamburg's largest company would spend recreational time in a somewhat sleazy club in the Reeperbahn. And the fact that this was the very club where the classified US military document had been retrieved seemed to make this even more unlikely as a coincidental encounter.

Morgan walked along the street as inconspicuously as possible following the Asian man. After about a block the man reached a stand of taxis. He spoke briefly to the driver and then they headed off. Morgan quickly rushed across the street and jumped into a waiting cab.

He recognized how corny his instructions were, but he had no choice.

"Follow that cab," he ordered.

The cab driver, seeing that Morgan was a police officer, immediately put the car in gear and headed off without a word.

After a short drive, the taxi they were following turned onto Bugenhagenstrasse and pulled up to the Park Hyatt Hotel. Morgan instructed his driver to stop a block short of the hotel. He paid the driver and stepped out of the taxi just in time to see the man enter the hotel.

Morgan was familiar with the hotel but had never actually been inside. It was one of Hamburg's most exclusive accommodations that catered to those who are rather well off financially, which he most certainly was not. Rooms went for as much as two hundred and fifty Euros a night, which was a bit out of his price range.

Feeling a bit self-conscious, Morgan entered the hotel's main lobby. It was stunning in its sense of luxuriousness. Well-dressed people were hurrying through the lobby, likely on their way to an evening meal and entertainment that would probably cost more than he now made in a week. Looking around the lobby, Morgan finally spotted the Asian man at the front desk who was speaking to a clerk. The man was given an envelope and then he headed off toward the elevators. As soon as the man entered an elevator, Morgan walked over to the clerk who had just been speaking with the man.

"Excuse me, I'm Officer Morgan. Who was that man that you were just talking to? Is he a guest at the hotel?"

The clerk looked at Morgan's uniform and, for a moment, didn't appear to know what to do. He finally spoke. "I'm sorry, but it is the hotel's policy not to give out information pertaining to the guests."

Morgan frowned but he was not going to be turned away. Mustering up a voice of authority, he looked down at the young clerk and said, "Listen, I'm working on a homicide case, and it's essential that I find out about this man. I need to see his hotel registration. This is official police business. If you won't let me see the register, I'll have to speak with the hotel manager. And if I have to waste time doing that, I'll be sure to let him know how uncooperative you have been in my investigation."

Morgan knew that he did not have any authority to see the man's registration information. He also knew that his only chance to do so would be to convince this young clerk to break the hotel's policy on guest privacy. Furthermore, if word got back to the department that he was making illegal requests outside the department's district jurisdiction, he would be in big trouble. It was a significant risk, but his little voice deep inside said that it was a risk worth taking.

The young clerk stood frozen for a moment considering the consequences. Finally, the weight of the police uniform and Morgan's commanding tone seemed to make up his mind. He stammered, "Well if this is an official police matter, I guess it would be okay. We are talking murder here, right?"

Morgan nodded gravely and waited for the clerk to bring up the record on his computer. In a minute the clerk looked up and asked, "What would you like to know?"

Clearly, the clerk was not going to let Morgan directly see the record. But it didn't matter as long as he could find out what he wanted to know.

"Let's start with the man's name and address," Morgan replied as he took out his notepad and a pen.

The clerk scanned the record and then said, "His name is Mr Takeshi Fumiko. He listed his business address only. It is entered as Tokushima Industries, Osaka, Japan. There is no phone number."

"What's his room number and how long is he staying at the hotel?"

The clerk glanced back at his computer screen and then answered. "He checked in this morning. He is staying in room six-seven-five. He has a reservation through Saturday."

Morgan thought for a moment. Whatever this man's business was with Steiner, it was a sure bet that it wasn't official Hamburg Shipping business. And whatever it was, it looked like it wouldn't be completed until sometime Friday or Saturday. This was Monday, which meant that the man would be here for another five days.

Morgan looked back at the clerk and asked, "Is there anything else on the record, or has he left or received any messages?"

The clerk shook his head. "No, sir. There's nothing else here and as far as I know, he hasn't gotten or left any messages."

Morgan was about to go, thinking that there would be no more information to be had, when the clerk spoke again.

"There is one more thing. When Mr Fumiko checked in, he reserved two more rooms for Thursday evening, also checking out on Saturday."

So, thought Morgan, our mystery man will be meeting others. Perhaps he is here in advance of the others to see that whatever they are doing is all set before they arrive. Unfortunately, unless he learned more, he would have no idea what it was that they were planning with Steiner. His best bet, he thought, would be to check into Tokushima Industries in Osaka, Japan to see what he might learn.

\*\*\*

The evening meal back at the hotel was eaten in total silence. It had taken Ms Hudson and Mr Norris an hour to explain to the Notre Dame authorities who they were, and that they were not, in fact, ringleaders of an international terrorist group bent on destroying one of Paris' most famous landmarks. That afternoon on the bus ride back to the hotel, Ms Hudson began by telling the three Rockland boys that their parents would be informed of their misbehavior and that she would see to it personally

342

that they spent the rest of the year in detention. When she had finally finished her litany of threats, she turned her attention to Henry.

"I know that our boys do not represent the model of decorum that is expected, but I have no doubt that you, young man, are behind this most recent breach of conduct."

Henry started to object but Sheila kicked his leg as a warning, and he sat in defiant silence.

"I warned you that if you couldn't control yourself that I would become your personal chaperone. Tomorrow when we visit the Louvre, I want you to be by my side at all times. And I don't want you anywhere near any of my boys."

When they got back to the hotel it was decided that everyone would have a half hour in their rooms to get ready for the evening meal. When everyone had gone into their rooms, Henry slipped across the hall to Sally and Sheila's room.

"It's not fair!" Henry exclaimed. "I have to be chained to that battleax all day just because my plane took a nosedive into a candle. It wasn't my fault. It wasn't even my idea to fly the planes in the first place!"

Sheila looked sympathetically at Henry but said nothing. It was Sally who spoke up in response.

"Look, one day won't be so bad. We're just going to a museum anyway. There won't be anything to do other than look at famous paintings. Just tag along behind Ms Hudson and make the best of it. We'll be right there with you."

***

Tuesday began with bright sunshine which was a hopeful sign. After eating breakfast at the hotel, the group loaded onto the bus again for their day at the Louvre. Henry seemed to be in somewhat better spirits and, as they all entered the museum, it was almost as if the events of yesterday had been forgotten by all. All, that is, except Ms Hudson, who walked behind Henry never letting him out of her sight.

Immediately upon entering the Louvre they grasped the fact that the immense size of the museum meant that even by spending their entire day there they wouldn't begin to see everything. They wandered from gallery to gallery seeing wall-sized paintings that were fronted by large crowds of admiring people. By noon they were beginning to be desensitized to the overwhelming impact of the vast collection.

Standing in front of the *Mona Lisa*, Sally found herself alone as Henry and Sheila had moved on to the next wing. Being tired from standing and walking all morning she took a seat at a bench in the middle of the hall. Seated at the other end of the bench was a girl who appeared to be a little older than Sally. The girl had shoulder length blonde hair and was reading a book. Sally could see that the book appeared to be a book of poetry. Glancing at the book, Sally could just make out the author's name, Rainer Maria Rilke.

After a moment, the girl looked up and smiled at Sally. Sally smiled back and said, "You come to an art museum to read poetry?"

The girl shook her head and responded in broken English. "Sorry, I not speak English."

Sally took a breath and repeated her question in German, hoping that the audio course she had worked on so diligently during the flight over would have given her sufficient fluency.

Upon hearing Sally speak her native language the girl brightened.

"You speak German! That's terrific. And to answer your question, no I don't usually spend time in museums reading, but this place is so large that I felt like I needed a break."

Sally found it a bit difficult to keep up in German, but her memory skills had allowed her to retain a fairly large vocabulary.

"Good day," she said. "My name is Sally Brown. I'm an American high school student here on a tour of the museum."

The girl put her book down and replied, "Nice to meet you, Sally. My name is Jane Morgan. I'm taking some time to travel a bit before returning to my university classes."

Sally waited until a crowd of students being lectured to by one of the museum's staff moved on from standing in front of Da Vinci's masterpiece. When it was reasonably quiet again, she continued. "Where do you go to school?" she asked.

Jane answered. "I am in my last year at the Universität Hamburg. My major is European History."

Sally gave Jane an excited look. "Hamburg, did you say? Wow! This is really a coincidence. I need to get to Hamburg, and I know nothing about the city. Maybe you could help me."

Jane slid closer on the bench and asked, "Are you here with your class? I'm sure your chaperones know the city if they are taking you there."

Sally hesitated. "Well... the truth is... I'm not going with our chaperones. Actually, I'm going on my own."

Jane gave Sally a quizzical look.

"Do you mean that you're going without their knowing?"

Sally nodded sheepishly and then continued. "It's a long story."

When Jane didn't move, Sally decided to tell her everything about what had happened to her father and why she felt that his only hope would be to uncover the truth in Hamburg. They sat discussing the situation for several minutes.

Just as they were finishing, Henry and Sheila arrived and stood behind the bench where Sally and Jane were seated. Henry and Sheila looked on in utter amazement as they heard Sally speaking German without a hitch. When the conversation stopped momentarily, Henry spoke up, surprising Sally.

"Okay, Heidi, since when did you learn German?"

After recovering from the surprise of seeing Henry and Sheila, Sally nodded a hello to Sheila and then said to Henry, "I think you'll find that Heidi was Austrian, not German."

"Whatever," Henry exclaimed. "You know German! That's amazing!"

Looking over at Jane, Sheila asked, "Who's your friend?"

Sally introduced Jane, mentioning that she did not speak English.

Sally gave Henry and Sheila a long look, trying to make a decision, and then, finally making up her mind, she said, "Listen, guys. I just met Jane. She's from Hamburg. I've decided to go to Hamburg and Jane's agreed to help, out—"

Immediately, Henry interrupted. "All right! We're going to Hamburg!"

Jane couldn't stay silent any longer. Turning to Sally she asked, "What did he say?"

Quickly, Sally filled Jane in and then turned to Henry and Sheila.

"Look, *I* have to do this. But I don't want you guys to risk getting in trouble."

This time it was Sheila who spoke.

"If you go, we all go. That's final. How are we going to get there and what's the plan when we arrive? I assume that we're going to be looking for Mr Wilhelm."

Sally looked at her two friends and saw determination that she knew would not be denied. With resignation she turned back to Jane to explain the fact that they all would be going to Germany.

Jane suggested that they head down to the museum cafe where they all could talk without interrupting the museum patrons. After Sally interpreted Jane's suggestion, Henry responded. "Good idea. I've given my parole officer the slip but I don't want to stay in plain sight for too long."

# Chapter 28

Tuesday had been a patrol day for Officer Peter Morgan. All day he struggled trying to decide what action to take. By the end of the day his mind was made up. He would go back to the hotel and, when the man appeared again, he would try to follow the mysterious Mr Fumiko to see what he might discover about the relationship between Fumiko and Steiner. He also had decided that he would need to find out whatever he could about Fumiko's company, Tokushima Industries.

Ordinarily, Wednesday was the low point of the week for Morgan as it was the day that he was assigned to the stationhouse to complete paperwork. But today, he thought, would be different. Sitting at his desk, he faced a mountain of forms that needed completing and so he knew that he wouldn't be able to get out to tail Fumiko until the paperwork was completed. Furiously he worked, typing the numerous reports on his desk. As he finished submitting the final form, the station clock indicated that it was noon. Looking around he saw other patrol officers busily working at their desks paying no attention to him.

Seeing that he could work without notice, he logged onto the police investigation network and typed in the name *Tokushima Industries, Osaka, Japan*. Nothing was returned in the German database, which didn't exactly surprise him. He had never heard of the company and doubted that it had any significant German presence. Switching over to the international database administered by Interpol, he again entered the company's name.

This time the search produced a brief description for the company.

*Company: Tokushima Industries*
*Address: 1-3-27 Sakaisuji*
*Osaka, Japan*
*Contact: 06-6208-000 telephone*
*No. of Employees: Unknown*

*Ownership: Unknown*

*Financial:141,00,000 — 176,000,00 JPY (as reported in previous five years).*

*Privately held company specializing in the sale of technology systems.*

*Current ownership held through an independent holding company.*

*No known connections with European or North American corporations.*

The report was surprisingly lacking in detail for what must be the size of the company, Morgan thought. The estimated annual income translated into over one and a half million Euros. Whatever Tokushima Industries did, it appeared to be a very lucrative business. The description 'technology systems' didn't provide much information regarding the nature of the company's dealings.

After another thirty minutes of searching and finding little or nothing of use about the company, Morgan decided to see what Interpol might have on file for Mr Fumiko. After entering the name, he was distressed to see the number of entries that were returned. Apparently, Takeshi Fumiko was a relatively common name in Japan.

Narrowing his search a bit, by limiting the entry to those with a residence in Osaka, Morgan was able to reduce the list to three names. The first name that came up was an eighty-seven-year-old man with no criminal record. The second name held more promise. It was a record for a thirty-one-year-old who was listed as an engineer. The record did not include a photo, but Morgan's interest was piqued by the fact that the man had technology background as an engineer. It wasn't until he read further to discover that the man was a civil engineer working in the municipal streets department that he decided that perhaps this wasn't his man after all.

With diminishing expectations Morgan retrieved the record of the third man listed as Takeshi Fumiko of Osaka, Japan. Immediately upon seeing the photo that came up Morgan knew that he had gotten lucky. The photo showed the man crossing a street at some distance away, but there was no doubt that this was the man staying at the Park Hyatt Hotel.

The file stated that the man was twenty-eight years of age with an unknown current address. His last known address was listed in Osaka. He was identified as a person of interest in a recently unsolved murder of a businessman that had taken place in Tokyo two years ago, but insufficient evidence had been uncovered to make formal charges. The file referred to a Tokyo municipal police case number.

Interestingly enough, the file did not list Mr Fumiko's current employment status, but it did mention that his previous employment had been with a computer systems software design company that had been indicted on charges of industrial espionage. The file stated that Fumiko had left the company last year, shortly after the charges were filed against his employer, and had taken up residence in Osaka. He apparently escaped prosecution himself after moving to an unknown address and dropping out of sight.

Morgan had worked straight through lunch, but his diligence had paid off. He could now knock off early and, just perhaps, he might get lucky and catch Mr Fumiko at the hotel. He wasn't exactly certain what he would do, but he decided that if he was going to find out anything useful, he would have to try to find out what the man was up to here in Hamburg.

After shutting down his computer Morgan hurried down to the station locker room to change. Morgan had driven his auto to work that morning to facilitate his surveillance efforts that afternoon. Traffic was heavier than usual, and it was already after sixteen hundred hours by the time he reached the hotel and found a parking spot across the street from the main entrance. Entering the hotel, he grabbed a newspaper from a stand beside the front desk and took a seat in the lobby where he could see both the front entry doors as well as the main elevators.

It was nearly an hour before he caught sight of Fumiko exiting one of the elevators. As Fumiko left the lobby, Morgan casually folded his newspaper and walked out onto the street in time to see him get into a taxi. He crossed the street and got into his car, allowing for enough time before pulling out so that it wouldn't be obvious that he was following the taxi. As he followed the taxi back towards his stationhouse it occurred to him that it was likely that Fumiko was going back to Der

Schlupfwinkel where the meeting with Steiner had taken place yesterday. If he was lucky, Fumiko was on his way back to meet Steiner again.

Taking a chance, Morgan left off following the taxi that was undoubtedly taking the long way for an increased fare. Morgan cut through the back streets and parked a block away from the club. As he waited for the taxi to arrive, he began to think that he had perhaps made a gross error in anticipating the destination. However, just as he had decided to quit, suddenly the taxi pulled up and Fumiko got out.

Morgan waited for a few minutes and then entered the club. As his eyes adjusted to the darkness inside, he could see that Fumiko was not seated at any of the tables in the front. Morgan walked to the back room where he saw Fumiko sitting alone at a booth in the far corner. Morgan walked over and took a seat in the adjacent booth with his back to the half-height partition that separated him from Fumiko sitting on the other side.

When the waitress came over, she took a drink order from Fumiko. Recognizing Morgan as the police officer who normally sat at the front bar, she come around to Morgan's booth and slid into the seat opposite him.

"You're not in your usual seat tonight. What's up?"

Morgan shrugged and said, "I need a little quiet time tonight, so I thought I'd come out back."

He put his finger to his lips and motioned for her to be quiet. Taking out a pen and a piece of paper he wrote a quick note and slid it over to her. The note read:

*I'm working a case here…… official business.*
*Please don't have any of the girls say that they know that I'm police.*

Morgan let the waitress read the note and then said, "I'll have a beer."

The girl looked up from reading the note and was obviously impressed and thoroughly excited to be let in as a partner in 'official police business'. She responded with devoted seriousness. "Yes sir. You can count on me!"

Ten minutes after Morgan had been served his beer, a man he did not recognize entered the back room and took a seat in Fumiko's booth. Morgan was disappointed that it wasn't Steiner but nevertheless, he thought, this man might shed light on what's going on.

Both men spoke German, the new arrival speaking in what was obviously his native language, and Fumiko, surprisingly enough, speaking adequate German, albeit with a strong accent.

After the man who had just arrived was served a beer, their conversation continued.

The man spoke to Fumiko.

"We want to know that you'll have the final payment ready."

Fumiko responded politely, but with a tone of irritation in his voice.

"Herr Wilhelm, I informed your boss that we will be ready on our end. My associates will arrive on Friday to test your final product. If it tests successfully the funds will be electronically deposited into your account."

The man whose name was Wilhelm seemed to accept the answer.

"We will have the software simulation for the test at this address."

He passed a piece of paper across the table to Fumiko and asked, "I anticipate that the test should take about an hour to complete. When will you people be ready to start?"

Fumiko looked at the address and said, "We will be at this address at noon."

Fumiko then rose without a word, leaving Morgan to decide what to do next. He could follow Fumiko, but it was likely that he would just be heading back to the hotel. On the other hand, he could follow the man who remained in the booth to try to find out more about him. He had no idea who this man Wilhelm was, but he decided that he must be connected with Steiner. And that suspicion was confirmed in the next minute.

As Morgan waited for the man to leave, he heard the man speak quietly into a cell phone.

"Connect me with Herr Steiner."

Morgan slid over to the end of the booth to be able to hear. After a brief pause the man spoke again.

"It's me. Our Asian friend says that they want to test the system software before they transfer the funds. Their engineers will be arriving Friday and want to meet at noon."

There was another brief pause as the man apparently listened to instructions from Steiner.

"I'll take care of it. Now I'm going to check on our little bird in the cage. What are we going to do with her when the deal is completed?"

Morgan waited as the man listened further. Finally, the man concluded the conversation and got up to leave. Morgan quickly decided that he should follow the man to learn what he could. Paying for his drink at the bar, he followed the man out into Hamburg's darkening early evening sky.

When he reached the sidewalk, he casually looked in either direction but, to his amazement, he couldn't see the man anywhere. It didn't seem possible that the man could have gotten a cab and left in the short time that Morgan had paid his check and left. He buttoned his coat against the biting February wind and hurried along the walk in the direction toward the center of the city. If the man had indeed gotten into a taxi, there would be no finding him now. But if he had walked away, perhaps, Morgan thought, he might have turned up the next street, a block away. When he reached the end of the block, he saw the man getting into a black sedan.

Morgan turned and rushed back to his car. As he got in, he saw the black sedan pass by heading toward the waterfront. Morgan pulled out into traffic and followed, being careful to maintain at least two cars between them to keep out of sight. After thirty minutes of driving the sedan pulled into the dock and warehouse area along the waterfront. Morgan pulled over knowing that there wouldn't be the usual traffic to hide behind with his headlights on. Keeping his eye on the sedan he saw that it turned between two somewhat dilapidated warehouses.

Morgan got out of his car and walked up to the closest warehouse, being careful to stay in the shadows. Neither warehouse building had any identifying signage that might give a clue as to the owner. In fact, it looked like neither had been used in a very long time. Morgan heard the car door around the corner and he slowly peered around to see what the man might be going.

There were no lights between the buildings, but the sedan's headlights shone on the side of the building where Morgan could see a door. The man retrieved keys from his coat pocket and opened the door. When several minutes had passed and Morgan was reasonably sure that the man wasn't going to be coming right back out, he hurried over to the end of the building, where there was a small window.

As he raised his head to window height a light came on inside. At first, he couldn't see anything of interest. It looked exactly like what it apparently was, an abandoned warehouse. But after several seconds he heard a noise that attracted his attention. Looking over in the far corner Morgan could just make out a form sitting on the floor. As his eyes adjusted to the dim light in that area, he could make out that the form was a person.

Suddenly the man he had been following entered the space and walked over to the person on the floor. The man carried a flashlight which he directed into the face of the person. Instantly, Morgan caught his breath. The person was a woman who looked to be in terrible condition. As he looked closer, he could see that the woman was handcuffed to a length of steel chain which was, in turn, handcuffed to a nearby steel pipe column. She had obviously been mistreated and it appeared as if she had been held in this place for several days, if not weeks. There were the remains of food containers scattered around the floor and within the reach of her chain was a cot and a filthy toilet.

The woman, when she saw the man, began to cry. She was pleaded something that Morgan couldn't hear but whatever she was saying the man wasn't having have part of it. He walked over to her and dropped a bag and a water bottle which the woman quickly grabbed. The man turned from the woman and Morgan's heart froze as he saw the man look directly at his window. Morgan ducked out of sight and tried not to make a sound.

Clearly this was an abduction that might very well end up as a murder. Morgan couldn't help but think that this might be just what he needed to get his position as inspector back. If he could bring this man in, the chief inspector would have to realize that there was more to the case of the death of Manfred Spear and Richard Gross than the department has assumed. And Morgan had no doubt that this man could be pressured into giving up Steiner as a collaborator, which might mean implicating Hamburg Shipping in the process!

Morgan reached for his cell phone to call in for backup. Unfortunately, he never got past dialing the first two numbers before he saw the man come around the corner pointing a gun directly at him. Morgan spun around just as he saw the flash of the gun as it was fired.

\*\*\*

For James Macintyre, time had seemed to drag by in slow motion. He had thought that the time to depart on his Tuesday evening flight would never come. But here it was, and he was arriving in Hamburg. The clock in the airport terminal read eleven o'clock in the morning. Macintyre hadn't been able to sleep during the flight and, with the time change, his body couldn't tell whether it was night or day.

After he retrieved his bags, Macintyre headed out to catch a cab. He had reserved a room in a downtown hotel in the historic district and he thought that perhaps he might take a short nap to catch up on some of the lost sleep. He didn't come here to sleep, however, he thought to himself. He had something that needed to get done, but maybe an hour or two of rest wouldn't hurt.

When he arrived at the Park Hyatt Hotel he checked in and headed to his room. He unpacked his bags and stretched out on the bed for what he thought would be just a short respite from his travels. When he awoke, however, the travel clock he had brought showed that it was nearly five o'clock. Cursing, he jumped up and started for the door. But as his mind cleared, he realized that it was probably too late to accomplish what he needed to do. Crossing back over the room he grabbed his jacket and took out an envelope from the inside pocket.

Macintyre headed out of his room with the envelope in his hand. In the hall as he waited for the elevator an Asian man approached and stepped into the elevator car with him when it arrived. The Asian man looked at Macintyre as if he recognized him and it looked like the man was going to say something, but he did not. Macintyre searched his memory but couldn't recall ever seeing the man before.

When Macintyre reached the main floor lobby, he watched the Asian man depart through the front doors. Macintyre also noticed another man who had been sitting in the lobby who appeared to be watching the Asian man leave as well. As soon as the Asian man left, the seated man arose and followed him out. Macintyre shook his head and chided himself for imagining things. He was obviously still very tired.

Approaching the main desk Macintyre asked for the hotel concierge. A smartly dressed man in a hotel jacket came out from a back room.

"May I help you?" the man asked.

Macintyre handed his envelope to the concierge. The concierge glanced at the envelope and saw that it was addressed to the Davidwache Police District.

Macintyre explained. "I will be attending to several errands over the next two days and will be out of the hotel for much of that time. If I am not back to retrieve this letter by Friday evening, say seventeen hundred hours, I would like you to see that this gets posted in the mail. I would appreciate your keeping it in the hotel safe until then."

The concierge knew better than to ask any questions. He simply took the envelope and said, "I'll see personally that it is taken care of."

***

The students had arrived back at the hotel late Wednesday afternoon after having spent the day at Versailles. It had been a day of much walking and the students, as well as the chaperones, were tired and ready to call it a day. After an evening meal at the hotel everyone retired to their rooms.

When he felt it was safe to venture forth, Henry slipped quietly across the hall to Sheila and Sally's room. On the previous day they had made arrangements with their new friend, Jane, to meet at the girl's room at six o'clock to discuss plans for a trip to Hamburg. Precisely at six o'clock they heard a knock on the door and Sally let Jane in.

"Thanks for coming," Sally said in German.

Jane smiled and replied, "I wouldn't miss this for anything. My vacation was becoming a bit boring and this will certainly add some excitement."

Then taking a moment to gather her thoughts, Jane said in halting English, "I have spent the day working on my English vocabulary. I took English all my years at gymnasium… I believe you Americans call it… high school. But I wasn't very good at it. I barely passed my *Abitur*… how do you say… final exams, I believe. You must help me."

Sheila laughed and said, "Don't worry if your English isn't very good. Henry, here, can hardly speak English either, although it's his only language!"

Henry gave a feigned look of hurt. "I can't help it if I don't speak good English. I'm a product of the failing public school system in America!"

Jane took a seat on the end of one of the beds and said to Sally, "I want to know more about what is going on with your father. You said that he was involved in a crime that is connected to people in Hamburg. Tell me exactly what happened so that I can know how to help."

The girls all sat on the two beds and Henry grabbed the one chair in the room. Sally thought for a moment and then began.

"It all started last June when my father was hired by Billings Shipyard to become the lead engineer on a high-tech systems contract. I don't exactly know what he was working on but it had something to do with a top-secret design for a series of US Navy ships being planned for construction at the shipyard."

Seeing that Jane was apparently able to follow as she spoke English, Sally continued.

"This past November, Billings Shipyard held their annual corporate meeting in Connecticut at a casino and conference center. My father went along, I guess, to explain his project. Anyway, we found out later that during the meeting, a US Navy officer, Peter Ashley, was shot. It happened that the shooting took place in the men's room and the only other person in there, other than the shooter that is, was my father. The person who shot Commander Ashley got away without anyone noticing and my father was left being accused of the crime."

Seeing that Sally was having a hard time holding back tears, Sheila jumped in to continue the story.

"The thing is, we learned that Commander Ashley had just been assigned by the navy to investigate a security breach at the shipyard.

There could be no doubt that the breach involved Sally's father's work. The shooter must have known that Commander Ashley was about to investigate the security leak and shot him to keep him from finding anything out."

Jane interrupted and asked, "How did you find out about all this?"

Henry had been quietly listening up to this point but now couldn't help jumping in.

"That's the coolest part. We were at the conference center when all this happened! We had decided to take a road trip to do research on a debate topic and, amazingly enough, we were at the very place when the shooting went down! It was wicked, awesome!"

It was obvious that Jane was having difficulty understanding what Henry had said. Sally, having recovered a bit, offered a quick interpretation in German, leaving out Henry's American colloquialisms. She then went on in English for the benefit of the others.

"We did some investigating of our own when we returned. One item of curiosity was that while we had been there, we saw our high school chemistry teacher, Mr Wilhelm. It could have been just coincidence, but he was definitely acting suspiciously. And then we found out that he had left a message at the front desk for Commander Ashley, which seemed to tie him somehow to the crime."

Henry excitedly interrupted again.

"And don't forget to tell how he's a German Nazi!"

With that, an awkward silence descended over the room. Henry looked back and forth between Sally and Sheila with an expression that pleaded, *What did I say?* He then he saw that they were looking with embarrassment at Jane and he caught on. Speaking to Jane he mumbled, "Er... sorry about the Nazi crack. What I meant to say was..."

Sheila spoke up giving Henry a look of disapproval. "Please excuse my friend. His mouth operates sometimes before his brain is engaged. He didn't mean any disrespect."

Jane smiled and, suppressing a laugh in Henry's direction, she responded, "No, that is fine. Tell me though, your teacher is German?"

"He began teaching this year," Sally said, "having just come directly from Germany. We found out that although he doesn't have any real teaching credentials, he got the position based on a letter of recommendation written by a man named Timothy Kerrigan who is the head of the Billings Shipyard corporate board of directors. That was another clue that he might be connected in some way to the crime."

Sheila added, "And don't forget the fact that one of the so-called pieces of evidence that was used against Sally's father was that an envelope with money was left at the conference center's coat check room. The tag that would be used to retrieve the envelope was found in her father's room. But we found out that the person who left the envelope had a strong German accent. It had to be a set-up staged by Mr Wilhelm."

Jane was obviously impressed with what she was hearing. "You have all done a great amount of work trying to figure this out."

Henry replied, "You ain't heard nothin' yet!"

Before Henry could start on another mangling of English, Sheila took over again.

"When we returned to Maine, we decided to concentrate on looking into Mr Wilhelm more closely. Just after we returned, we heard about a vice president at the shipyard who mysteriously disappeared. Lisa Kerrigan, the wife of Tim Kerrigan, just didn't show up for work one day. What made us suspicious was that her primary account at the shipyard was a project for Hamburg Shipping in Germany."

Jane quickly interjected. "I know Hamburg Shipping! They are the largest shipping company in Hamburg."

Sally nodded and took up telling the story.

"We went over to Mr Wilhelm's apartment when he wasn't home and took a look around. Henry found a woman's sweater in the closet with blood on it. Henry then was able to copy files off a laptop computer that was in the apartment living room and, when we got back to his house, he was able to read an email that was sent from Hamburg. The email suggested that Lisa Kerrigan might have been kidnapped and sent back to Hamburg as a prisoner."

Jane sat staring in amazement. "You three are incredible! I know that my father would like to meet you. He's an inspector with the Hamburg police."

Sally's eyes widened. "Really? Do you think he can help us?"

Jane thought for a moment and then offered, "Maybe. The problem is, however, you don't really have any hard evidence. It might be difficult for you to convince the police to accept your story. After all, you don't even really know if this man, Wilhelm, has actually done anything you suspect him of."

Sally, Sheila and Henry all started to object at once before Sally took over again.

"Actually, we *do* know that Mr Wilhelm is guilty. When we were in his apartment Henry left a wireless camera with a microphone. We sent an email to Mr Wilhelm hoping to trick him into getting his contact at the shipyard, the man who had to be responsible for smuggling the secret documents out of the shipyard, to come over to his apartment so that we could get some incriminating evidence on a recording."

Henry spoke up. "And we hit pay dirt!"

Jane gave a confused look and Sally said, "We were successful."

Henry responded. "Yeah, we were successful, like I said. Anyway, we saw the company's chief executive officer, a Mr James Macintyre, being interrogated by Wilhelm and Wilhelm admitted to murdering a financial officer at the shipyard and arranging for the shooting that Sally's dad is accused of. And he also admitted sending Lisa Kerrigan to Hamburg."

"And don't forget," Sheila added, "we also saw Mr Macintyre deliver a package that presumably had stolen documents from the shipyard."

Jane stood up in excitement. "Then you have the proof that you need!" But immediately after her exclamation she sat down again and asked, "So why didn't you go to the police and have these men arrested and free Sally's father?"

All three Americans looked at each other guiltily, and after a moment, Sheila explained.

"In America, a recording taken without proper legal authority wouldn't be admissible in a trial as evidence. So, we decided to see if we could convince the shipyard CEO to give himself up and identify the others who were involved. We thought that if we showed him the recording and threatened to go to the police that he would realize that he would have to cooperate. We thought he might choose to bargain for a lesser sentence by turning the others into the authorities."

"Yeah, well, that's what we thought," Henry added glumly. "But that slime bag Macintyre had other thoughts."

Sally continued without interpreting Henry's slang.

"We met with Mr Macintyre to try to convince him to turn himself in, but he stole the only copy of the recording that we had and ran away. So, this is our only chance to set things right. We know that whoever is running the espionage ring that is stealing documents from my father's project is most likely operating out of Hamburg. Mr Wilhelm's email originated from there and it looks like Lisa Kerrigan is being held there against her will. We don't know for sure, but it's my guess that both Mr. Wilhelm and Mr Macintyre are in Hamburg right now. We believe that Hamburg Shipping is the key. We have to find the man with the initials *J.S.* who sent emails from Hamburg to Mr Wilhelm, and the best place to look is Hamburg Shipping."

Turning to Jane, Sheila added, "We have to get to Hamburg early Friday and return that same evening. It's the only free day that we have when we can slip away and not be noticed. Can you help us?"

Jane pulled out a worn booklet from her purse and flipped through several pages. After studying the booklet for several moments, she looked up.

"My aunt works for Lufthansa Airlines and I'm sure she can work a deal for us. We can leave on Friday at six twenty-five and arrive at nine thirty. There is a return flight Friday evening at eighteen hundred fifty-five, arriving back in Paris at nineteen hundred thirty-five. Let me give Aunt Helga a call."

Jane got her cell phone out and, after what seemed like a very long ten minutes of conversation in German, she hung up.

"We are in luck. Aunt Helga has reserved four seats for us and, as a special favor, there will be no cost!"

Henry did a fist pump in the air and said enthusiastically to Jane, "You're awesome!" Rushing over to her, he gave Jane a hug and exclaimed, "You're the best thing that's happened on this trip!" Sally sat smiling as Sheila gave Henry a look that could kill. After a second or two, Henry returned to the moment and awkwardly let go of Jane. Turning around and seeing Sheila he asked, "What...?"

# Chapter 29

Thursday morning was ushered in with bright sunshine and the Hamburg air was delightfully cool and crisp. James Macintyre couldn't help but remark to himself that this was a pleasant change from the last time that he had been in this city nearly a year ago. This was going to be the day when he would see that he got what was due him from his contact at Hamburg Shipping, regardless of what it would take to make this happen. He had held up his end of the deal over these past ten months, at great risk he might add, and it was time for his German partners to come through on their end. All he wanted was his final payment and he would be off to spend the rest of his life without a care in the world.

The hotel restaurant was nearly empty, which Macintyre thought a bit strange since at seven thirty in the morning he would have guessed that there would be a fair number of business travelers getting a start on the day. He was ushered to a table in the back corner next to two Asian men at an adjacent table. The waiter gave him a menu which, to his dismay, was entirely written in German. Putting the menu down, he ordered in English, asking for a cup of coffee and eggs with sausage and toast. The waiter nodded, apparently understanding the request, and left.

Macintyre sat looking across the room as he waited for his coffee. When it arrived, he took a sip and memories of just how bad European coffee was immediately returned. When his breakfast was delivered, he ate, thinking about his plan for the day. When he had finished his meal, the waiter came over and delivered his check. Macintyre looked at the amount but didn't have a clear idea of the price as he had neglected to check the exchange rate between Euros and US Dollars before he had left. Nevertheless, he handed over his credit card and the waiter disappeared.

When the waiter returned with his credit card and receipt to be signed Macintyre was studying a city map that he had picked up in the lobby. As he put down the map to sign the receipt, he noticed that the two Asian men who were seated at the next table were excitedly discussing something in what sounded like Japanese, and it looked like one of them was pointing at him. After a moment the waiter arrived, and the men said something that Macintyre couldn't quite make out. Immediately, the waiter began speaking in German in what sounded like an apology and he grabbed the credit card and receipt from their table. Before Macintyre could figure out what was going on the waiter rushed over to his table and laid the card and receipt from the Asians' table down on his own table.

Speaking in barely understandable English, the waiter said, "I am not correct, mister. I do a mistake. This is your credit card and bill."

The waiter grabbed the card and receipt that he had originally laid on Macintyre's table and hurried back to the Asians. With the switch successfully made, the waiter hurriedly disappeared, hoping no doubt, to avoid any further embarrassment.

Macintyre picked up his card and noted that it was indeed his. He looked across at the Asian men and nodded. He signed the receipt and started to leave when the two Asian men came over and stood at his table. Macintyre stood awkwardly for a moment as the men looked at him expectantly. When Macintyre didn't speak one of the two men bowed and said in very clear English, "Mr Macintyre. My name is Takeshi Fumiko."

Motioning to the other man, he continued. "This is my associate, Naoki Oshiro. Forgive our intrusion, please. We recognized your name from the credit card. We assume that you have come from the Billings Shipyard in America to supervise the test. That is most unexpected, but we very much appreciate your dedication to stand by your design."

Macintyre stood in silence in a state of absolute shock. He had no idea who these men were nor how they would know that he was from Billings. Before he could ask any questions, the man who had identified himself as Takeshi Fumiko spoke again.

"Perhaps we could return to our suite and discuss the test. We have a few questions that perhaps you would be willing to answer. Our engineers will be arriving tomorrow, and I know that they will be anxious to thoroughly test the guidance system software."

Not knowing what to say, Macintyre simply nodded and followed the two men out of the restaurant. Somehow these men knew about the WG-116B guidance system and he quickly figured that it would be prudent to find out how this could be. Up until now, he had thought that his only partners were the Germans with whom he had had contact. Obviously, there was more to the German connection than he had assumed.

When they reached the room of the two Asian men Macintyre could contain himself no longer.

"Listen, I thought that this…" he hesitated trying to find the right words, "…this *operation* was being run by Johann Steiner of Hamburg Shipping. He never mentioned any other partners."

Mr Fumiko responded. "We understand that you have been working directly with Mr Steiner and his people. We represent Tokushima Industries, of Osaka, Japan. We will be purchasing the system from Mr Steiner, pending, of course, a satisfactory trial of the demonstration software tomorrow. We have been made aware that you are the primary contact at the American facility where the design was developed."

Macintyre sat down in a state of shock. Never had he considered that there might be more to the relationship with Hamburg Shipping than appeared on the surface. But now that he thought of it, it made perfect sense. What would a container shipping company want with a sophisticated military weapons guidance system? It was now clear that Billings' design was going to be sold to what had probably been the highest bidder on the black market.

Over the next hour Macintyre explained how he had been able to get the classified documents out of the shipyard and his relationship with the Germans. He ended by telling the Asians that the scheme had gotten messy in America which had forced him to leave. He also told them that he was here to obtain the final payment which, so far, he had been refused.

Mr Fumiko responded. "I am sure that your partners are waiting until a successful test is conducted tomorrow and they have received the payment from us. Our engineers will be here tomorrow and will be putting the demonstration model through a complete test. We have made arrangements to transfer the funds when we are satisfied that the software is fully functional."

Macintyre thought for a moment and then decided what would be best. Turning to Mr Fumiko he said, "I think it would be best in all our interests if I were to attend the test tomorrow. If anything were to happen... that is if there were any questions... perhaps I should be there to help out."

Although Macintyre understood the ridiculousness of his statement, that is, there would be no way that he could answer any technical questions about the software, he hoped that his new acquaintances might buy into his proposal. The real reason he needed to be at the meeting was to increase the chances of getting paid. Rather than having to confront Steiner by himself, trusting on convincing Steiner to do the right thing by his words alone, fate had created an opportunity to assure that Steiner would do right by him. With the buyers present, he doubted that Steiner would refuse to cooperate.

"That would be very good of you," Mr Fumiko replied as he wrote an address on a piece of paper. "Here is where the test will take place. It is a warehouse in the dock area. Be certain that you are not followed when you leave the hotel. We intend to start the test at noon."

Macintyre took the paper with the address and stood to leave.

"It has been a pleasure meeting you both. I look forward to seeing you and our German partners tomorrow in what I know will be a very profitable occasion for us all."

\*\*\*

Officer Peter Morgan awoke with a severe pain in his right shoulder. He was in total darkness and, for a moment, panic set in as he thought that perhaps he was dead. Slowly his eyes adjusted to the darkness and the pain in his shoulder clearly testified to the fact that he was very much alive. He gave a weak groan and started to stand. Before he could do so, however, he immediately fell back to the floor as he realized that his left hand was handcuffed to a column.

A voice speaking in English came from the darkness, which startled him as he sat trying to catch his breath on the bare cement floor.

"You'd better take it easy. You've been shot and I don't know how bad it is."

The voice was that of a woman and suddenly memories flooded into his mind of the woman he had seen in the warehouse and the man coming around the corner with a gun.

"What happened?" was all that Morgan could manage to say.

The woman, who was handcuffed to an adjacent column, replied, "I assume that you were outside and Wilhelm… that is Gustav Wilhelm… caught you and you were shot. I don't think it's too bad. After dragging you in here and securing you to the column he left. When he came back in an hour, he had bandages and he took care of your wound. He said that the bullet had just grazed your shoulder and that the wound was clean. He gave you some kind of drug and you have been out ever since."

Morgan fought to clear his mind. He saw the window he had been looking through but it was covered with dirt and it was impossible to tell what time of day it was with the tiny amount of light that filtered through.

"What time is it?"

The woman answered. "I think it's Thursday. It must be about midmorning. Are you a policeman?"

"Yes, I'm with the Hamburg Davidwache police division. I've been investigating a case and I followed one of the suspects to this warehouse. You know who this man is?"

Lisa Kerrigan sat in silence for a moment and then began. "It's a rather long story, but it looks like we have some time on our hands, so let me tell you all that I know."

She explained that she was a vice president at Billings Shipyard in America and that her company had been working on a top-secret project for the United States Navy. She became aware that there was a security leak at the shipyard and details of the project were being stolen. Much to her surprise, she had discovered that the company's CEO, James Macintyre, was responsible for stealing the documents. She had followed his contact but had been caught by the man before she could do anything about it. Later she had learned that the man's name was Gustav Wilhelm. He had tortured her to find out what she knew and then she had been drugged. The next thing she knew she had awoken here in this abandoned warehouse. That was at least seven or eight weeks ago.

365

"I assume," she said, "that this is Hamburg, Germany. The irony is that the principal project that I was responsible for at the shipyard was a contract with Hamburg Shipping. I never put two and two together until, when Wilhelm was beating me to find out what I knew, he asked about what I knew about Hamburg Shipping and its tie to our navy contract. Somehow they must be connected."

Peter Morgan sat listening to the story in amazement. It all made sense now. After Lisa paused, he filled her in on his investigation. He told her of how his men had found the classified document in the Reeperbahn bar and how it had been stolen from the police station. He went on to tell of the murders of Manfred Spear and duty officer Gerhardt Frank at the stationhouse as part of the theft. He had figured out that whoever had stolen the document must have had an inside man and he had determined that this had to be one of his inspectors, Leo Krauss. He had assigned inspector Richard Gross to twenty-four-hour surveillance of Krauss and apparently, Inspector Gross had stumbled onto something just before he was murdered. The night of Gross' murder, Morgan had received a phone call from Gross saying that he was at an office at 157 Braunstrasse. But by the time Morgan had arrived there was nothing to be seen. Gross had disappeared and turned up dead several days later.

Morgan paused in telling his story as his emotions kept him from speaking. This whole sordid affair, he thought to himself, had cost the lives of three good men... and in the case of Richard Gross... a good friend. Lisa waited patiently for Morgan to continue.

"That's when an internal investigation was held, and I was demoted to patrol officer for breach of department protocol and placing an illegal wiretap. I had gone out of my way to conduct an investigation without informing the captain and it eventually cost the life of one of my senior officers. But what really caused the department to... how do you Americans say... throw me under the bus... was my visit to Hamburg Shipping."

Lisa interjected, "You suspected Hamburg Shipping was behind the theft? How did you know?"

Morgan answered. "I checked into the office on Braunstrasse that Inspector Gross had called from. It was under a short-term lease and the owner didn't know who had leased it. It was paid for in cash and the man did not identify himself. But the owner said that he had noticed the man had driven away in a white van that belonged to Hamburg Shipping. I visited Hamburg Shipping to ask about the leased office, but no one knew anything about it. I eventually was directed to Johann Steiner, the company's chief financial officer. He didn't say much but I knew that he was hiding something. I had his phone tapped and I discovered that he was communicating with someone in the States. I would guess that it was with our man Wilhelm."

Lisa spoke up. "I met Johann Steiner at Billings Shipyard's annual meeting when I had to bring Hamburg Shipping up to date on the project status. I questioned him about a mysterious bank account, and he was equally uncooperative. I too felt that he knew more than he was letting on but there wasn't anything I could do."

"Anyway," Morgan continued, "Hamburg Shipping is a powerful, politically connected company in Hamburg. Word got back to the department commander that I had been pressuring Herr Steiner and that wasn't to be tolerated. The result was that I was demoted and told to have nothing more to do with the case and especially Hamburg Shipping."

Morgan shifted his position as he leaned against the column to ease the pain in his shoulder, and then he went on.

"Even though I was reduced to patrol officer in rank I didn't give up trying in my off-duty time to investigate what Steiner was up to. By chance I saw Steiner one evening outside the same bar where the classified document had been found. He was speaking with an Asian man. When they separated, I decided to follow the Asian man to see if I could learn more. I tailed him to the Park Hyatt Hotel where I learned he was staying. I found out that the man's name was Takeshi Fumiko and that he worked for a company that specializes in technology systems in Osaka, Japan called Tokushima Industries."

Lisa spoke up excitedly. "Tokushima Industries! That's the company that set up the special account on the Billings navy project that I was checking into! It was an account that didn't seem to have any purpose and it wasn't properly entered in the project finances. Our company's chief accountant discovered it and, before he could get to the bottom of it, he was murdered. If Steiner is connected to this Tokushima

Industries, it's no wonder that he wouldn't talk about the account when I asked him."

Morgan sat thinking for a few moments and then continued.

"I couldn't find out much about the Asian man or his company, but I did see enough to suggest that there likely was something illegal going on. With what I now know it is obvious. Herr Steiner made arrangements through Gustav Wilhelm to receive the stolen classified documents from the Billings Shipyard CEO, Macintyre. It must be that he intends to sell the design to Tokushima Industries who will undoubtedly see that it gets into the wrong hands... my guess would be China. Who else would have the financial wherewithal to back such a program? And the best of it is, there is nothing to trace the whole sordid affair back to the government of China if anything goes wrong. The operation appears on the surface to be a German-Japanese endeavor."

Lisa nodded in agreement. Then she couldn't help but ask the question that had been on her mind since she had been taken prisoner.

"Why do you think we're being held here? I mean... why are we still alive? I've seen how Wilhelm works and he wouldn't think twice about killing either of us."

"My guess is," Morgan responded, "that Herr Steiner is waiting until a meeting that is scheduled for tomorrow is concluded. When I questioned the hotel clerk about the Asian man, the clerk said that two more men were scheduled to arrive Thursday evening and they all had reservations through Saturday. It might mean that Herr Steiner thinks that we might be of some use to him until the deal is finalized, although what that might be, I can't imagine."

"Maybe so," Lisa responded. "I'm sure that my husband is looking for me and hasn't given up hope yet. Each day I pray that this will be the day when he rescues me. He is the president of the Billings Shipyard board of directors and he has considerable influence with the authorities. I just know that he will show up soon."

Morgan closed his eyes and thought to himself, *let's hope that it's soon enough.* Tomorrow is Friday!

*\*\*\**

368

The noonday sun in Paris was warm and felt good as it shone down from the clear blue sky. Thursday was the day when the students were to visit the Eiffel Tower and later in the afternoon visit shops along the Seine. The group had assembled for lunch at a cafe just down the street from the tower that was packed with tourists of every nationality. Henry, Sally, Sheila and Mr Norris were seated at an outside table while the Rockland contingent was seated together at an adjacent table. The tower had two restaurants, one at the first level and the other at the second level, but both had been identified by the chaperones as too expensive.

The climb up the tower had gone without incident, that is unless Henry's altercation with the ticket seller was considered. The ticket salesperson was an attractive young girl who Henry decided to impress with his command of French. Unfortunately, Henry had never been a dedicated language student at Billings High and more often than not he had spent time in French class studying computer magazines rather than his French textbook.

He stepped to the window and, speaking in French, he boldly called the young lady the prettiest attendant he had ever seen. Unfortunately, he had forgotten the word for attendant and had decided to substitute the word 'proletaire', translated as worker, which he had quickly looked up in his pocket French dictionary and thought was close enough. When he got the sentence started, however, as he got to the word for worker, he glanced down at the dictionary page just to make sure that he got it right. By unfortunate circumstance, his eye slipped several words down the page and he spoke the word, 'prostituée', which has a decidedly different meaning.

Instantly the female clerk slapped Henry across the face and called for security. It had all the potential of becoming a typical Henry botch-up but, at the last minute, Sally stepped forward and explained in perfect French that Henry was mentally handicapped, and they were here on an outing from the asylum. She apologized profusely and said that Henry had no idea what he was saying most of the time, and therefore not to take offense.

Luckily neither Mr Norris nor Ms Hudson saw the encounter and Sally and Sheila hustled Henry back to the group before any notice of the commotion could be made by their chaperones. After they all headed toward the tower Henry asked, "What was that all about?"

Sally smiled and said, "Nothing really, other than you just called that girl a prostitute!"

"I did? Henry mumbled. "I forgot which word to use."

Laughing, Sheila warned, "From now on you stick to mangling English, mister."

Henry turned to Sally and asked, "What did you say to her to get her to calm down?"

Laughing once again, Sheila replied, "Sally just told them that you were out on a field trip and were a bit confused in the head."

After lunch the students were allowed to stroll by themselves through the shopping district to look for souvenirs. Sally had arranged for them to meet Jane at one of the tourist trap shops along the way and when they arrived Jane was standing outside looking anxious.

Sally asked, "What's wrong? You look troubled. Are there problems with our flight?"

Jane greeted each of them warmly and then said, "I tried to call my father after we spoke last night to tell him about what we discussed. But when I called his cell phone he didn't answer. I thought that perhaps he had just turned it off. But when I called this morning again and didn't get an answer, I called my mother. She said that he didn't return home last night from work and that she is very worried. This isn't like him at all. Apparently, he didn't report to work this morning either."

Sheila put an arm around Jane, trying to comfort her by saying, "You said, your father was a police officer. He probably is involved in some complicated case and just wasn't able to contact you mom."

Jane smiled at her new friends and said, "Thanks. You're probably right. Anyway, I'll be home tomorrow and I can find out more. The flight out is scheduled to leave at six twenty-five. Are you sure that you can make it?"

Henry replied, "We'll be there, don't worry. Last night I called down to the hotel front desk and arranged for a taxi to pick us up at five a.m. The only problem may be being awake enough at that hour to remember to put on my pants. I'm never totally awake that early."

After agreeing to meet at the Lufthansa check-in counter at the airport, Jane said goodbye and left the three Americans to hunt for miniature replicas of the Eiffel Tower for friends at home.

# Chapter 30

Five a.m. came sooner than Henry could have imagined. It felt like he had just gotten into bed and closed his eyes when the alarm clock sounded. Henry had told his Rockland roommate, Chad Gifford, that he intended to get up early and go for a run before the traffic got too heavy. He had been a bit concerned that Chad would see him dressing in street clothes rather than running clothes, but as it turned out, his concern was for not. As Henry dressed, Chad snored away in his bed.

The students were being allowed to spend Friday as a free day doing whatever they wanted as long as they went forth in groups of at least three. Sally, Sheila and Henry had told the others that they intended to spend the day back at the Louvre to see the thousands of things that they had missed on their visit on Tuesday, and then eat supper together at a restaurant just down from the museum that specialized in French vegetarian cuisine.

The students had agreed to be back at the hotel no later than eight o'clock. They were required to check in by phone at noon and then again at four o'clock in the afternoon. Henry, Sheila and Sally knew that their return flight was scheduled to land in Paris at seven thirty, which would make arriving at the hotel by eight o'clock a bit close but, if all went well, they felt that they could make it.

Henry dressed quickly and silently slid out of his room, carefully looking both ways up and down the hall to see that no one was about. When he arrived in the lobby, he saw Sheila and Sally waiting at the front door.

Sheila motioned to Henry. "Hurry up the taxi is waiting outside."

Sally held open the door to the street and as Henry approached, she asked, "You've got your passport, right?"

Henry felt his coat pocket and then answered, "Yes mom, and I have my lunch money here too."

When they reached the airport, they were amazed at the number of people at such an early hour waiting to catch flights. Sally led them over to the Lufthansa ticket counter and, just as she was about to explain that tickets were being held for them, Jane arrived.

'Good morning!" she greeted them. "Are you three still sure you want to go through with this? You could get into much trouble with your school, you know."

Sheila answered for the three of them. "We have to do this. Don't worry, we know what we are doing."

They all got in line for their tickets and Sally asked Jane, "Have you heard any more about your father?"

"Unfortunately, he still has not been heard from as of last night. My mother told me that the police are now looking for him. I need to get home to be with her." They all gave Jane a hug.

At the ticket counter they were checked in for the flight and were told that it was scheduled to leave on time. Since only Jane had a bag to be checked, the check-in process took very little time. Once they passed though the security gate, the reality of what they were doing began to finally sink in to the three Americans.

"If we get caught," Henry told Sheila on the way to their gate, "I'm going to say that you made me do this. I'll say that unless I came along, you threatened to tell the guys from Rockland that I had developed a thing for their battleax chaperone and that I wanted them to see if they could get her to give me her phone number so that she might be my private tutor."

"Oh, what I great idea," Sheila said. "I might just do that anyway!"

Once on the plane, Jane asked Sally what their plan was. She explained that they would take a taxi to the offices of Hamburg Shipping. The idea was to first find the man with the initials J.S., and then confront him about what they knew.

"Won't that be dangerous?" asked Jane.

Sheila spoke up. "With people around, I doubt that the man will do anything stupid. What we want him to do is either admit to what his role is, or if not, maybe he will lead us to the others who are involved. Surely he can't be acting alone."

Sally continued. "Henry has a recorder in his pocket so if the man says anything incriminating, we'll have a record of it. If he does, we'll call the police."

With a look of concern, Jane replied, "I don't know... it sounds dangerous to me." Taking out a piece of paper and a pen, she wrote down a number.

"Here is a number for the station's private cell phone where my father works. The station duty officer for the day keeps the phone in cases of emergency when officers might not have access to their radios. My father gave it to me. If you get into any trouble, be sure to give them a call. When I get home, I'll call the station and tell them what you're up to."

The plane touched down in Hamburg precisely on time at nine thirty. As they entered the terminal customs area, they saw a sign over head that read, *Willkommen — Flughafen Hamburg-Fuhlsbüttel*.

Sally said to Jane, "You need to get your bag and head home as soon as possible. We're going straight to the office of Hamburg Shipping to see what we can find out about our mystery man. Let me give you my cell phone number. Call me when you hear anything about your father."

Sheila gave Jane a hug and said, "Thank you so much for all you have done for us. I don't know how we could ever pay you back."

Henry stepped forward to give Jane a hug, but Sheila gave him a sharp look and he awkwardly stepped back. "Yah, thanks. I hope things work out for you and your dad. If you're ever in Maine, come see us."

Jane smiled and said, "Good luck you guys." She then headed off towards the baggage area, waving as she went.

It took them half an hour to get through customs. The officer let Sheila and Sally pass without incident but as they stood on the Hamburg side of the security line, they saw Henry being questioned by the officer, and, after a moment, a second officer came over to apparently ask him further questions. Just when it looked like he would be detained, he was finally released to pass through.

Sheila fumed. "What was that all about? Why is it that every time we try something you always get in trouble?"

Henry replied, "Hey, it's not me. I didn't say anything wrong... well maybe I shouldn't have made that crack about being here for the day to see the fatherland... hey, it was just a joke."

Sheila shook her head in disbelief.

Sally broke the tension by saying, "We can get a taxi into town. I checked and it's about five miles. Perhaps when we get into the city, we should find a place to eat before heading out to Hamburg Shipping. I'm famished!"

***

James Macintyre awoke on Friday morning a bit later than he had planned. All through the night he had been awakened from a semi-sleep as he couldn't get the thoughts of meeting Steiner and what he would say to him out of his mind. He had made arrangements to meet Mr Fumiko and his associates in the hotel restaurant for breakfast. After taking a shower and getting dressed he decided to go down to the hotel lobby to see if he could get a newspaper in English. When he reached the lobby, he was surprised to see several police officers at the front desk questioning the desk clerk. When they finally finished, the policemen stepped over to the lobby lounge and, huddled in a group, they stood talking with each other.

Macintyre walked up to the desk clerk to ask for a newspaper. He saw a *USA Today* on the counter and picked one up. Pointing to the policemen who were now leaving, he asked the clerk, "What was that all about?"

The clerk, who looked a bit shaken, replied, "They were looking for one of their missing officers. Apparently, they are checking all the hotels to see if he had taken a room. They showed me a picture of the man and I recognized him. He had been in here a few days ago asking about one of our guests, but he didn't get a room. He just left and I didn't see him again."

Just then Mr Fumiko and three others came out of the lobby elevator. Seeing Macintyre, they motioned to him.

Macintyre told the clerk to have a good day and then joined Fumiko and the others.

Takeshi Fumiko bowed and said, "Mr Macintyre, you met my associate, Naoki Oshiro, yesterday. I would like to introduce you to our engineers from Tokushima Industries who will be conducting today's test, Hideo Nakamura and Minoru Ito."

Both men bowed, and Macintyre, somewhat awkwardly, returned the gesture. They all entered the restaurant and took seats at a table in the far corner. The waiter came over to take their order and Macintyre ordered toast and coffee with a single fried egg. He expected the Japanese men to place their order, but the waiter seemed to already know what they wanted. When the food was served, each of the Japanese men was served a bowl of steamed rice, a bowl of soup, and a plate with some kind of omelet.

Macintyre looked at their breakfast for a moment and Mr Fumiko explained.

"We have pre-ordered our meals to have more traditional food than that which the Europeans seem to prefer. The hotel has graciously accommodated us."

With that said, all four Asians simultaneously swapped the bowl of rice and the bowl of soup at their place settings.

Fumiko continued. "Our hosts do their best, but it is proper etiquette to serve the rice on the left and the soup on the right."

One of the engineers took a bite and commented, in Japanese.

"Please excuse my associates," Fumiko said. "They do not speak English. Mr Ito said that the tamagoyaki is quite good for being prepared by Westerners. I must compliment the chef when we leave."

When the breakfast was finished the Japanese men stood and Fumiko said, "We are now leaving to make certain that the test equipment has arrived and is being set up correctly. I gave you the address yesterday where the test will be performed. If you arrive at noon, we will be ready to begin. I anticipate that the test will take no more than two hours. I will tell Mr Steiner that you will be joining us."

That should just make his day, thought Macintyre.

***

Henry, Sheila, and Sally found a cafe in the middle of the business district where they had been left off by the taxi. After having Sally translate the menu that was handwritten on a chalk board on the wall, they each ordered breakfast consisting of bagels and coffee. While they were eating, they discussed what they would say when they arrived at Hamburg Shipping's corporate offices.

"It's likely that the offices should be open by now," Sheila said.

Sally took out a map from her purse and unfolded it on the table. Pointing to the map she said, "We are here. The Hamburg Shipping office is over here. I estimate that by taxi it will take us about twenty minutes to get there. I suggest we leave shortly. We will want to check the place out to see what we can learn, if anything, before going in."

Henry pulled out a miniature digital recorder from his pocket. "I checked this out last night. It works like a charm. I have it clipped to the inside of my underwear. I wear oversized baggy shorts so it fits snug as a bug in a rug and I can't even feel it."

Sheila responded. "Okay, that's more than I wanted to know."

Unfazed, Henry continued. "I tried it out and I could hear the recording of voices ten feet away. If we're much further away than that, however, the sound quality degrades to the point that voices can't be understood."

"Then we'll have to make sure that Henry stands closest to our man 'J.S.' when he talks," Sally said.

"That's *if* we can find out who he is," Sheila added.

When they had all finished their breakfast, Sally stepped up to the cafe counter and paid their bill. Speaking in German, she asked if she could use the phone to call a taxi. The young man behind the counter said that he would place the call for her. Ten minutes later, the taxi arrived and the three got in with Sally giving the address.

It took about thirty minutes to reach their destination, due in large part, Sally thought, because the taxi driver took a 'scenic route' on their way. They paid the driver and stepped out onto the sidewalk. They were immediately greeted by heavy traffic and businessmen and women rushing along the sidewalk headed to work.

The three stood looking across the street at a seven-story office building. The building looked relatively new and was constructed largely of glass and steel. Across the entry doorway was a lettered sign that simply read, **Hamburg Shipping.**

Sally looked at the other two and said, "Well, here goes nothing."

They crossed the street and entered the lobby. There was a throng of people in the lobby heading to the bank of elevators at the rear of the lobby.

Glancing at desk at the center of the enormous lobby, Henry was the first to speak what they were all thinking. "Oh-oh… this isn't good."

All three stood looking at a security desk and a metal detector doorway that was flanked by two uniformed security officers. Everyone who was heading to the elevators showed a security badge of some kind before stepping through the metal detector doorway.

Sheila asked, "What are we going to do? We don't even know the name of the person we're here to see."

Henry stepped over to the side of the lobby and called back to the others. "Hey, check this out!"

Sally and Sheila walked over to see what Henry had found and when they got there, they saw a wall directory of company names. Henry turned to Sheila and said, "And you didn't think we'd find our Mr J.S."

Looking where he was pointing on the directory, they saw the name Johann Steiner, Hauptfinanzoffizier, Zimmer seven-zero-four.

"I'd say that's our mystery man 'J.S.'," Henry said. "What's that German gobbledygook mean after his name?"

Sally replied, "He's the chief financial officer for the company. His office is on the top floor, so I'd guess that he's pretty important."

But just when Sally thought that they had found their man, Sheila pointed to the directory and said, "Wait just a minute. What about Jan Shröder, Postbüroangestellter, Zimmer four-three-three. Judging by the length of his title he must be somebody important also."

Sally thought for a moment and said, "Actually I think that's the office mail clerk. He might be our man, but I wouldn't bet on it. I'd place my money on Johann Steiner. As the head of finance, he'd be in a position to be able to oversee the money transactions for buying the stolen documents and no one would likely find out."

"The question is," asked Henry, "how do we get to see him?"

Sally headed back toward the security desk. "The direct way is always the best."

Stepping up to the desk, Sally asked in German with as confident a voice as she could muster, "Good day. My friends and I are here to see Herr Steiner. Could you see if he's available please?"

The security officer looked at the three suspiciously and then responded, "You've just missed him." Then pointing to the entrance door, he said, "In fact, there goes Herr Steiner now. I believe he said that he will be gone for the day."

Sally quickly turned to see a late middle-aged man in a dark blue suit exiting through the front doors. She thanked the security officer and grabbed Sheila and Henry.

"There he is now! He's leaving for the day. We need to catch him if we can!"

The three hurried out of the building just in time to see Steiner get into the back of a white car that was marked with the Hamburg Shipping insignia on the door. As a mixture of panic and disappointment grabbed Sally, a taxi pulled up at the curb and let a man out. Sally pushed Sheila and Henry toward it.

"Quick," she said, "let's follow him and see if we can talk to him when he gets to wherever he's going."

The three piled into the taxi and Henry blurted out, "Follow that car!"

Unfortunately, the driver didn't speak English and so Sally had to ask him, in a bit more restrained tone, to follow the Hamburg Shipping car that had just pulled away."

Disappointed that Sally had to translate his command, Henry said, "I've always wanted to say that. Too bad it had to be in a cab with a driver who had to ruin it by not understanding English."

The taxi followed the white Hamburg Shipping car as it wound its way toward the shipping docks. They had expected that it would pull over when they reached a section of the docks that had a large sign with a warning in large red letters, **Hamburg Shipping** — *Autorisiertes Personal Nur!*

But instead of turning into the Hamburg Shipping dock area, the white car continued past more of the dockyards. As they went further, the condition of the docks and the warehouses could be seen to be more and more dilapidated. When the car finally stopped it had pulled up to a warehouse that looked in poor condition and had obviously been abandoned for a considerable time.

Sally told the cab driver to pull up next to the white car. She paid the driver and told him to please wait for them. As the three got out of the taxi no one exited the white car. After waiting for a several minutes wondering what to do, Sally decided to approach the car and see if she could speak with Johann Steiner. Just as she reached the car, the driver opened his door and stepped out. He was a thin man who wore black pants and a black sweater. The color of his clothes stood in stark contrast to his pure white hair.

The man spoke to Sally in German in a menacing tone.

"What are you doing here? This is private property. You must leave immediately."

Sally spoke as calmly as she could. "We would like to speak with Herr Steiner."

When the man didn't respond Sally decided to go for broke.

"We have something important to tell him about the Billings Shipyard technology system that he is stealing."

The man looked surprised but said nothing. After appearing to consider what Sally had said he turned around and got back into the car. He could be seen speaking with Steiner who was in the back seat. Sally looked back at Sheila and Henry and motioned to have them join her.

Henry asked, "What did you say?"

"I told him that we wanted to speak with Steiner. And I took a chance and told him that we know that he is involved with the theft of Billings Shipyard secret technology."

"Whoa," Henry breathed. "Was that wise?"

Sheila interjected. "Look, Sally had to do something. We can't just wait around hoping. We don't have the time."

Henry took out his cell phone and entered a number and then put it away back in his pocket. He was about to say something when the man with the white hair stepped out of the Hamburg Shipping car again. He walked past the trio and went over to the taxi that sat waiting. The taxi driver wound down his window and, after the man in black said

380

something that couldn't be overheard, he handed the driver what looked like a roll of money.

Much to their surprise the three watched as their taxi drove away. The man then turned to face them. Pulling out a gun from under his sweater he growled in German, "You three move into the warehouse and no one will get hurt."

The three stood frozen, afraid to move.

Steiner got out of the car and headed into the warehouse without speaking. The man with the gun walked over to where the three stood and simply said, *"Move!"*

Sally said, "He wants us to go into the warehouse. I think we'd better not argue."

They hurried toward the door that Steiner had just entered with the armed man following close behind. When they reached the door, the man shoved them inside to what was a dark interior. It took a while for their eyes to adjust.

It was obvious that this building hadn't been used in a long time. The main space was empty and there was only a single light on at the far end of the floor. Sally could see that the light illuminated a stair that led to a mezzanine above. The mezzanine had a single window that overlooked the main floor below and through this window came the light from what appeared to be an office of some kind within. Steiner was already mounting the stairs when the three entered. Steiner called to the gunman, "Bring them up to the office."

The man used the gun to point the way and motioned for them to move to the stairs. At the base of the stairs the man yanked Henry to a stop and ordered, "Everyone, empty your pockets."

Sally and Sheila stopped by Henry's side and Sally translated for the others. They emptied their pockets of change and cell phones, which the man took and put on a small table that stood by the wall. He then searched them, presumably Sally thought, for concealed weapons. When the man got to Henry, both Sally and Sheila held their breath, afraid that his recorder would be discovered.

When the man seemed satisfied, Sheila whispered to Sally. "I never thought I'd ever say it but thank God for Henry's baggy underwear!"

The man turned to the girls and barked, *"Halt's maul, doof kuh!"*

Sheila wasn't exactly sure of its meaning, but she knew it wasn't good. The man pushed Henry up the stairs and signaled the girls to follow. When they reached the top, they entered the door that led to a brightly lit interior. Coming in from the relative darkness of the warehouse, they all squinted at the bare fluorescent light bulbs that hung from the ceiling.

Looking around they could see that this had probably been an office at one time long ago. There were dusty office desks and filing cabinets around the perimeter of what looked to be about a fourteen-foot-deep room that stretched the width of the building. In the center of the room was a long table with computer equipment sitting on it from one end to the other. Seated at chairs around the table were four Asian men who were busily talking in what Sally recognized as Japanese. They seemed to be in the process of starting up the computer system and were arguing about some detail, although Sally didn't know enough of the language and so she couldn't understand exactly what the issue was that was being heatedly discussed. They took no notice of the three Americans.

The man with the gun motioned for them to head to the end of the room where Johann Steiner sat smoking a cigar. He leaned back in a large, antique wooden office chair, and speaking in English he said, "Well now, what do we have here? I understand that you three have something to share about our little business venture."

Sally straightened and began trying to sound as though she was in control. She spoke in English for the benefit of Sheila and Henry.

"Herr Steiner, we know all about your 'business venture' as you call it. We know that you have been working with a man named Gustav Wilhelm, whom you set up as a chemistry teacher in the local high school in Billings, Maine. Herr Wilhelm served as your local henchman to receive and transmit stolen technology on a US Navy design contract at Billings Shipyard. Your inside man at Billings Shipyard was James Macintyre, the company's CEO. You paid him off to secretly steal the details of a classified missile guidance system."

Steiner smiled and then replied, "You have me at a distinct disadvantage. Although you obviously know me, I haven't had the pleasure of meeting you or your associates."

Before Sally could answer Sheila interjected, "Listen, we know all about your espionage activities. Are you going to deny what Sally has said?"

Steiner turned to Sheila and said, "No, you are quite right. With a little help I have indeed managed to obtain the American missile guidance system design and, in fact, the purchaser of this design is getting ready to test its operation right at this very moment. Your timing is impeccable." Steiner pointed back to the center table where the four Japanese men were busy with the computer equipment.

Steiner took a long pull on his cigar and blew smoke rings toward the ceiling.

"As for the Herr Wilhelm... how did you call him... my henchman... he is downstairs attending to two uninvited visitors. And Herr Macintyre, I have been informed, will be joining us shortly."

As if operating on cue, the office door opened and James Macintyre entered. He looked around the room and, seeing Steiner, he marched to the back of the office. Just as he passed the center table, he saw Sally, Sheila and Henry and abruptly stopped short in shock. After recovering his composure a bit, he demanded, "What are these three delinquents doing here?"

Steiner laughed and replied, "Good morning... or should I say good afternoon now that it is just past noon, Mr Macintyre. It's so good to see you again, although I must say that this is a bit of a surprise. Apparently, you know our three young guests. I assume that they have traveled from your home city."

*"Know them,"* Macintyre sputtered. "They threatened to go to the police and turn us all in!"

Sally could contain herself no longer. "This is superb. The entire cast of characters is here."

Turning to Macintyre she continued. "You're a traitor! You won't get away with this."

"Traitor is such a harsh word," Steiner spoke with a relaxed voice that served to further infuriate Sally.

"Traitor is just the beginning. You are all murderers as well. Your man, Wilhelm, shot and killed Greg Connor, the financial officer at Billings Shipyard. And he likely killed the company's vice president,

Lisa Kerrigan, and he shot the naval officer, Peter Ashley… all per your instructions no doubt!"

Steiner raised a hand in protest. "Yes, it is true that Gustav shot your Greg Connor. That was an unfortunate necessity. He was getting a bit close to finding out our plan and we couldn't have that. But he didn't kill Frau Kerrigan. She is safe and sound, at least for the moment, downstairs. And you certainly can't blame the shooting of the naval commander on Gustav. That was the fine handy work of Siegfried, here, my assistant." He pointed to the man dressed in black with the pure white hair who was still holding the gun menacingly in his hand. Siegfried smiled back appreciatively.

"You bastard!" shouted Sheila. "You shot Commander Ashley and then made it look like Sally's father did the shooting!"

Steiner gave a knowing look. "Ah, so… this explains who you are. You are teenaged vigilantes just like from the American West seeking justice for wrong done to this young lady's father! You are like cowboys! I love it!"

Macintyre gave Steiner a sour look. "Look, I'm here to get what you promised. I don't care a whit about these teenagers. I want my money. I've done everything you've asked. I got the classified documents out of Billings Shipyard and you now have the finished product. I want my final payment then then I'm off, never to be heard from again."

Steiner laughed and, through an exhaled cloud of smoke he said to Macintyre, "Well you've got that last part right. You'll never be heard from again."

Steiner motioned to the white-haired man who still had his gun raised.

"Siegfried, please take our unwanted guests below and see that they are secured. Have Gustav look after them."

Macintyre began to protest but the man viciously swung the gun and hit Macintyre in the face. Blood immediately erupted from his nose as he fell to the floor. Henry, Sheila and Sally decided to move to the office door without objection. The man with the gun grabbed Macintyre by the shirt collar and dragged him to his feet. Steiner called out from his seat. "Why don't you leave Herr Macintyre here with us. I don't think he'll be giving us any trouble." Whimpering, Macintyre fell back to the floor trying to stop his nose from bleeding.

The comparative darkness of the warehouse main level made it difficult to see once again. Henry reached the bottom of the stairs first and saw a door at the foot of the stairs that he had missed when going up to the office earlier. He opened the door to more darkness beyond, and everyone passed through. Once through the door it could be understood that the office mezzanine was situated approximately halfway down the length of the warehouse and they had just entered the second half of the warehouse. It was vacant like the side that they had just left. Hanging from the ceiling several bays ahead was a single bare incandescent light bulb that gave a yellow pool of light. Squinting, Sally could just make out several figures in the dim light.

When they arrived at the lighted area Sheila gave a gasp. Chained to separate columns were a man and a woman. It was hard to make out details, but there was no question that the woman was Lisa Kerrigan. Before anyone could speak, however, Gustav Wilhelm came out of the shadows.

Wilhelm stood in surprise looking at Henry then at Sheila and finally at Sally. He then looked over at Siegfried who announced in German, "The boss wants you to secure these intruders. We'll take care of them for good once the client has confirmed the test and transferred the funds. Keep a close eye on them."

# Chapter 31

Each of the captives was handcuffed to a pipe column, which placed them about twenty feet apart. Lisa Kerrigan was on Sally's left and the as of yet unidentified man was on her right. When Wilhelm went back to his chair up against the wall and put headphones on that were connected to an MP3 player, Lisa asked, "Who are you?"

Sally answered, "I'm Sally Brown. My father is Steven Brown. He works at BSI with you. Over there are my friends, Sheila Warren and Henry Moore. We go to Billings High School."

Lisa stared at Sally with incredulity. "What on earth are you three doing here?"

Sally hung her head and replied, "We're here to try to prove my father's innocence. But I guess that won't happen now."

The man spoke up and announced, "I'm Peter Morgan. I'm an officer with the Hamburg Police."

Listening to their conversation, Sheila looked at Sally who looked back at the man with a questioning expression. Sally asked, "You wouldn't happen to be Jane Morgan's father, would you?"

Officer Morgan looked back in surprise and said, "Why yes, Jane is my daughter. Do you know her?"

Henry called over. "Do we know her!? Yeah, we know her. She helped us get to Hamburg!"

Before Morgan could find out more, Lisa jumped in with a stream of questions. "How do you know that your father is innocent? And how do you know that I work at BSI? And most of all, what led you here to this snake pit?"

"We became suspicious of our chemistry teacher, who just happens to be sitting over there against the wall, by the way. We knew he was involved in this mess somehow when we saw him at Foxwoods at the BSI annual meeting."

"*You* were at the annual meeting?" Lisa asked in surprise.

"Yeah, well it's a long story but we were there, and after Commander Ashley was shot, we saw Mr Wilhelm speed away. We also found out that a man with a German accent left money at the coat check closet which the police think was the pay-off to my father for the shooting. We're pretty sure that that was Mr Wilhelm."

Sally took a breath before continuing.

"When we returned home, we spun our wheels for a long time trying to figure out what to do. Finally, we decided to break into Mr Wilhelm's apartment to see if we could find anything that might serve as physical evidence of our suspicions. That's when we found your sweater with blood on it and we guessed that Wilhelm had either kidnapped or killed you. Your disappearance was big news in Billings."

"I'll bet it was," Lisa said.

"We... actually Henry... got a file off Mr Wilhelm's computer that contained an email from a man with the initials J.S. Henry traced it and found out that it had been sent from Hamburg which made a connection to you and your work on the Hamburg Shipping project at BSI. Also, the email suggested that you might still be alive and had been taken to Hamburg."

Lisa exclaimed, "You know about my project at BSI?"

Sally continued. "Henry rigged up a video and audio recorder in Mr Wilhelm's apartment. We then sent an email to Mr Wilhelm routing it as if it had been sent by J.S. from Hamburg. The email told Wilhelm to meet with his local contact. We hoped to get everything on a recording as evidence. Everything went well and it was Mr Macintyre who showed up. We got their confessions recorded but before we could do anything with it Mr Wilhelm flew out of the country back here. That left us Mr Macintyre as our last hope. We tried to get him to go to the authorities and confess. Unfortunately, that didn't go so well and, in fact, we lost our only copy of the recording."

Lisa interrupted, "I can't believe how much you three were able to discover when the police couldn't turn up a thing."

Suddenly, there was a screeching of tires from an automobile outside. Wilhelm jumped up and ran to the door that led to the other side. Siegfried could be heard through the open doorway yelling, "It's the police! It looks like only one car with two officers. You go around the back and I'll meet them at the front. If there's any trouble, we'll have to take care of them."

With that both men disappeared into the darkness.

Henry did a fist pump in the air and said, "Hey, you all can thank me for notifying the police! Before we met Siegfried and Roy here, I texted the police station cell number that Jane gave us asking for help. Call me a chicken, but I had a bad feeling about this the minute I saw our man Siegfried."

Sally and Sheila gave a shout for joy and then all of them began shouting. "Hey, we're in here! Help us!"

Gunshots were heard outside and after a while there was only silence. All the captives stood in nervous anticipation for what seemed an eternity until finally a uniformed police officer came through the door with his gun drawn. Immediately Peter Morgan shouted, "We're prisoners. Don't Shoot!"

The police officer came closer and, looking at Morgan, he recognized his fellow officer.

"Peter, is that you?"

Morgan responded without acknowledging the greeting. "Quick, get up to the mezzanine. There are at least four or five more, possibly armed." The officer spun around and headed back through the door. As he left, he spoke into a radio calling his partner.

It was a full five minutes before the officer returned. He quickly unlocked all the handcuffs with a key that he had apparently gotten from one of the Germans. Everyone followed the officer up to the mezzanine as Peter Morgan spoke with the officer, letting him in on the details of his capture. When they reached the office, they saw the other officer holding a gun on the men who were lined up against a wall. The men were all seated with their hands handcuffed behind their backs. The group included the Japanese contingent as well as Steiner, Wilhelm and Macintyre.

As if to answer the unasked question, the officer who was standing with Peter Morgan explained. "The other man was shot fatally and is downstairs awaiting the crime scene squad."

Macintyre, seeing Lisa Kerrigan, whined, "Lisa... finally... it's so good to see you. Tell these policemen that I work with you. I have nothing to do with this!"

Lisa walked over and gave him a kick in the shins. "You disgust me, James. It's good to see you too. Now I'll get the pleasure of seeing you returned home and thrown in jail for the rest of your miserable life."

She then walked over to Wilhelm and said, "You, I hope, try to escape. I would like nothing better than to see you shot in the most inconvenient place."

Henry stood behind her and added, "And for your information, I doubt that you will make the yearbook at Billings High as teacher of the year. In fact, let me say that as a chemistry teacher, you stink!"

Sally stood in front of Steiner and said in German, "I really don't care about your attempt to steal technology from America. But because you tried to hang this on my father, I hope that your country puts you away in the worst jail there is for a very, very long time. And if I ever hear that you petition for early release, know this, I'll gladly come back to testify against you."

Peter Morgan spoke up. "Don't worry, he'll be incarcerated for life for certain."

"I wouldn't be so sure of that."

Everyone in the room turned to see who had just spoken. Standing in the doorway with a pistol aimed directly at Sheila who stood just three feet away was Tim Kerrigan.

Speaking to the two police officers, Kerrigan said, "Slowly put your guns down and kick them over to me."

The officer with the drawn gun looked at his partner who nodded and they did as they were told.

As if awakening from a dream, Lisa spoke up. "Tim, what are you doing?"

Kerrigan looked at his wife and replied, "Why Lisa, dear, what does it look like I'm doing? I'm closing a deal. When our Japanese friends here are satisfied, I'm going to be one hundred and seventy-five million dollars richer."

Lisa replied in amazement, "You're behind all this? You are responsible for the theft of the guidance system design at BSI?"

Kerrigan replied with unmistakable arrogance, "Yes, it was I who masterminded this whole endeavor. I worked out the details with Herr Steiner when I visited over a year ago. Oh, I admit that it hasn't exactly gone flawlessly."

Turning to Steiner he said, "Misplacing that paperwork in the Hamburg bar was a bit of a problem. It launched an investigation by the navy, but I was able to take care of that, thanks to dearly departed Siegfried."

Sally turned to look at the four Japanese men who were still handcuffed on the floor and said, "I can't believe that the Japanese would use top secret military technology stolen from the US."

Kerrigan chuckled. "No, my naive young lady. These men are just auctioneers. The guidance system will be bought by the Chinese, or by the North Koreans, or by whomever... does it really matter?"

Turning back to his wife, Kerrigan explained, "You see, this was the perfect plan. There was no way I could be caught. All the arrangements for stealing the design were handled by our German partners. And our ambitious CEO here, Mr Macintyre, served as both the thief and fall guy. When this is over, the navy will investigate and it will be clear that you and James were in this together. And they already suspect the lead engineer, Stephen Brown."

"That's crap!" shouted Sally.

Kerrigan smiled and said, "Yes, you know that, but no one else will know. And no one will know, period, as soon as we silence you all."

Lisa fumed. "When they discover that you are missing, you'll be suspected as well."

Kerrigan laughed. "Oh, that's right, you've been away for a while. You see, sadly enough, I announced that the grief I was feeling over losing my dear wife was too much to handle and I felt that I needed some time away from the BSI board of directors to get myself together. The board understood and said for me to take as much time as I needed. When today's test is completed, I'll just stop back by good old BSI and turn in my resignation. The issue of your association with James and the heinous deed you both committed will just be too much for me to take. I'm sure that the board will welcome leadership in their effort to try to get back on the good side of the navy."

Turning to one of the police officers, Kerrigan snapped, "Uncuff these men."

When Wilhelm was released, Kerrigan instructed him. "Get these people below and take care of them. Make sure there are no survivors. And be quick about it. No doubt other police are already on the way. We need to move this test to a secure site."

Macintyre pleaded, "Tim... Tim... I helped you make this happen. I'm on your side! I can disappear too. In fact, I already have a place set up in the South Pacific..."

Kerrigan sneered, "Your work is done. Now it is time for you to go away, but it won't be to the South Pacific."

***

Wilhelm herded the group at gunpoint out of the office. As they descended the stairs to the main level Henry whispered to Sally, "Any brilliant ideas?" Sally just looked back and shrugged her shoulders.

They all passed through the door that led to the back side of the warehouse where the prisoners had been kept. Just as their sight was improving to the point where they could see a bit more clearly, they heard a soft crashing sound behind them. Everyone whirled around to see what the noise was but initially there was nothing to be seen.

Sally looked around and asked, "Where's Wilhelm?"

The answer came through the doorway in halting English. "He's taking a brief nap."

In through the door stepped Jane Morgan holding a broken bottle in one hand and Wilhelm's gun in the other.

Sally, Sheila and Henry all rushed over and hugged Jane. Each started talking at once.

"Hold on just a minute, one at a time!" Jane said. But before any of them could say a word, Jane saw her father.

"Dad! What are you doing here?"

Her father and the two police officers quickly rushed over.

"No time to talk now, honey. Good to see you though. You all stay here." He grabbed the gun, and the three men ran up the mezzanine stairs. Those remaining stood in shocked amazement, watching.

Sally drew Jane's attention away from watching her father climb the mezzanine stairs and asked, "How did you know to come here?"

Jane replied, "I was at my house with my mother when the police station called. They told me that the station private cell phone received a cryptic text that had my name and they were checking up on it. They said it read, *'help. come quick. hamburg shipping. dock warehouse. jane morgan.'*

Henry laughed. "That was me. Sorry, but I was in a hurry and I knew that if I used your name they'd come for sure."

Jane turned to Henry and said, "That was brilliant. They instantly gave my mother a call. They thought it might have something to do with my father's disappearance. Little did they know how right they were!"

Lisa Kerrigan, who had been standing by listening to Jane's story, could hold herself back no longer. In frustration she exclaimed, "Listen, I've got to go up there and talk with my husband."

With that she quickly mounted the stairs and headed up toward the office. The others looked at each other trying to decide what to do when Henry spoke up. "If it's okay for her to see what's going on, I'm going too. I wouldn't want to miss out seeing the expression on our beloved chemistry teacher's face when he finally realized that the jig is up for him."

They all headed up to the office and when they entered, they saw that Tim Kerrigan, Steiner, Wilhelm and the Japanese men were all in handcuffs again with one of the officers standing watch over them. Peter Morgan was speaking to the other patrol officer.

"This time I want you to patrol the perimeter and keep a watch out for any other visitors. Backup should be here momentarily."

Jane ran over and hugged her father.

"Dad, when I heard you were missing, I came home immediately."

Her father released his daughter and said, "And it looks like you brought home some friends."

Jane motioned for Sally, Sheila and Henry to come over.

Switching to English she said, "Dad, you won't believe how these three cracked this case. Wait 'til I tell you what happened. They're amazing!"

Lisa walked over to her husband who was seated with his hands cuffed behind him.

"I knew you were up to something when I discovered that account on the Hamburg Shipping that couldn't be explained. Poor Greg Connor knew it was bogus as well and it cost him his life."

"Yes, that account was necessary to transfer the funds to get Tokushima on board. I knew it was a mistake keeping that account active. You understand I'm sure that I had to have our nosey accountant, Mr Connor, taken care of. I had no idea, however, that he had written you a letter. That was most inconvenient, indeed."

Lisa started crying and, amongst the tears she sobbed, "How could you? You did this just for money? I hope you rot in jail."

Kerrigan smiled and responded. "I doubt seriously that that will happen. There's no real evidence against me. After all there's nothing really to connect me to the theft. It was Macintyre who actually did the stealing. And you can't connect me to either Greg Connor's nor Peter Ashley's shooting. I'm just going to deny everything. It'll be my word against all of you. And without any tangible proof of my involvement in any way, I'll never even be charged."

Lisa fumed but said nothing.

By now everyone in the room was listening to Kerrigan as he explained his plan. Henry reached inside the front of his pants and pulled out the digital recorder. He wiped it off on his sleeve and offered it to Officer Morgan.

"You might find what's on this interesting."

Peter Morgan reached out with two fingers and took the recorder.

Looking down at Tim Kerrigan, he said with a smile in correct, but somewhat accented, English, "I'll just save this for the crime scene boys when they arrive."

Everyone heard the sound of approaching police sirens. Suddenly, Sally shouted, "Hey, where's Mr Macintyre?"

Henry shook his head in disbelief. "I don't believe we let that rat get away. He must have slipped out in the darkness in all the excitement."

The sound of sirens ceased as patrol cars pulled up outside with screeching tires. Sally, Sheila and Henry rushed down to let the policemen know that Macintyre has escaped. When they got outside, they were greeted with policemen with guns drawn.

Henry shouted, "Wait, don't shoot!"

Sally then spoke in German. "We're not the criminals! Officer Morgan is upstairs with the criminals secured in handcuffs. Have you seen a man running from here? One of the hostiles escaped. He's a white male, in his late forties, with brown hair, approximately six foot in height and about one-hundred kilograms. He's an American and his name is James Macintyre."

One of the officers who was standing beside a patrol car looked up and said, "You mean this suspicious looking character?" He pointed to a man seated in the back of the car."

Sally walked over and saw James Macintyre seated with restraints on his hands and feet looking like the world had just come to an end.

Sally turned to the officer and said, "That's him, all right. How did you get him?'

"We saw him walking down the road and when we stopped to ask who he was he started running away. Unfortunately for him he ran down a pier and there was no way to escape. We thought we'd hold him for questioning."

Sally replied, "He's one of the criminals that need to be arrested. Officer Morgan, inside, will explain."

Henry and Sheila joined Sally and she told them of Macintyre's capture. They stood together on the apron of the warehouse dock watching the many policemen coming and going from the warehouse as the crime scene was being established for forensics. For the first time in many weeks Sally felt a feeling of relief that washed over her entire body. It was finally over. Turning to Sheila and Henry, she gave them each a hug and said, "Thank you guys for all that you've done. You stuck with me right from the very beginning. You're the best friends that anyone could ever have."

The sun shone brightly overhead in a perfectly clear blue sky. Sheila looked up and said, "What a wonderful day. God is surely blessing this place."

# Epilogue

It was nearly sunset on the first day of April vacation from Billings High and there was a party going on at the Brown's' house. People were jammed into the living and dining rooms celebrating the return of Steven Brown. Sally stood on the third step of the stair that led from the living room up to the second floor. Facing the crowd, Sally tried to get everyone's attention. Seeing that Sally was having little success, Sheila clanged a glass with a spoon and the din of the conversations quickly ceased.

Sally held up a hand and announced, "There's still plenty of pizza left in the kitchen, so eat up. If you're willing to suffer with me for a few minutes, I thought I would just say a few words. First, thanks to everyone for coming to help celebrate my father's return. I realize that he's been back now for some time, but I'm sure you'll understand that I wanted him to myself for a few weeks. Welcome home, Dad."

The crowd turned and applauded Steven Brown who stood in the doorway to the kitchen.

When the applause died down, Sally continued. "I understand that someone else in the room also has reason to celebrate. For those of you who haven't yet heard, Lisa Kerrigan was named Billings Shipyard chief executive officer this week!"

Lisa, sitting on the living room couch, waved a hand. Again, the crowd burst into applause.

"And I would like to extend a very special welcome to Commander Ashley who came all the way from Washington to be with us this evening. It's so good to see you up and about again."

Commander Ashley, recently released from a lengthy rehabilitation facility in Washington, stood with the aid of a cane. When the applause drew to a close, he said, "Let me tell you how good it is to be here. I came because I wanted to express the appreciation of the United States Navy, and to say my personal thanks to Sally Brown, Sheila Warren and

Henry Moore for their diligent efforts in thwarting the theft of classified materials. I have here a letter signed by the secretary of the navy and the president of the United States for each of you as a gesture of appreciation."

Once again, applause broke out in the room. Henry and Sheila joined Sally on the stairs and took bows. Each of them took their letters and then retreated to the kitchen where the noise was considerably less.

Henry grabbed another piece of pizza and, with a full mouth said, "Did you hear about the trial? I heard on the news that Germany has finally agreed to expedite our favorite chemistry professor to stand trial for the murder of the BSI accountant."

Sheila laughed. "I think you mean he's being *extradited*, not expedited, and don't talk with your mouth full."

Sally poured a cup of soda and said, "Well that would be fantastic. With both Tim Kerrigan and James Macintyre convicted of treason without parole, it would make a complete set to get Wilhelm behind bars with them. I thought for a while that Kerrigan and Macintyre might be acquitted. But when that letter written by Macintyre in which he admitted everything was forwarded from Jane's father in Germany, that cinched it. The letter apparently mysteriously showed up in the mail at the police station the very next week after we left."

Sheila nodded in agreement. "Unfortunately, it doesn't look like Steiner will be extradited but I understand that he is facing a long list of charges in the German court system."

Changing the subject, Sally asked, "Sheila, I understand that you have some news for this summer!"

Sheila proudly pulled out a folded letter from her pocket. "This is from the editor of the *Boston Globe*. Let me read a couple lines:

*"...we are looking forward to your summer internship at the Globe. You will be assigned to work with our special features editor, Marion Gladstone, to develop the story of your involvement with the Billings Shipyard espionage case. "*

Henry interrupted, "Hey, what about my involvement? If they're going to make a movie, I want Tom Cruise to play my part!"

Sally laughed and said, "Well, Henry, if you're going to be away this summer lounging around at Foxwoods it's only fair that Sheila should get a chance to do something exciting while you're away."

"Hey," Henry objected. "I'm not going to be lounging around. When the security chief, Molly Burgess, heard about how I broke the case she gave me a call. She said that there was a student position open for the summer in the security office. When I happened to mention my extreme expertise in computer systems, she made me an offer that I couldn't refuse."

Sheila gave Henry a shove. "How *you* broke the case? And tell us, mister extreme computer geek, exactly how did the security chief hear about our role?"

Henry hung his head a bit. "Okay, well just maybe I might have hacked into their system and left a piece on how I... that is... how *we* were able to work the case. Molly was interested in finding out how we got past the security guards. We talked computers a bit and the next thing you know, she offered me a position for the summer working with the security IT group."

"Well, I'm sure it's going to be a great opportunity," said Sally.

Sheila turned to Sally and asked, "So what are you going to do this summer?"

Sally smiled and answered, "I've been texting with Jane and she invited me to come over for the summer. She said that her father has been reinstated as the chief inspector of his division. She's taking courses at the university and has managed to get me enrolled to audit one of her psychology classes."

Henry groaned. "Wow! What an ideal break from school. Why didn't I think of taking classes as a break?"

Sheila replied, "The way you're going, brainiac, you may have to take summer classes if you don't get your act together in English. Better yet, maybe I could get Ms Hudson as your tutor. It's only forty minutes to Rockland."

"Very funny," Henry responded. "But speaking of mother Schwarzenegger, I heard from Mike Walker that she almost dropped dead with apoplexy when she heard that we were in Germany that last day of the trip. She ranted and raved and accused Mr Norris of sabotaging the trip. She even threatened to have Billings High expel us and have Mr Norris fired."

They all laughed, and Sally said, "Well, when the State Department called and told Ms Hudson and Mr Norris that we were going home directly from Hamburg in a private State Department jet, I'll bet that really pushed her over the top."

Henry grabbed another slice of pizza and said, "I would have given anything to see her face when that call came in!"

Sally raised her cup and said, "Here's to the best friends possible. May our summer be a bit less eventful, but no less exciting!"

Henry and Sheila raised their cups and Sheila said, "To Sally Brown, the most gifted and talented person I know!"

Sally groaned.


# The End